Labyrinths, *Selected Stories & Other Writings, by Jorge Luis Borges, has been translated and published by agreement with Emecé Editores, S. A., Bolívar 177, Buenos Aires, Argentina. All selections here included and translated into English have been taken from the following volumes originally published in Spanish by Emecé:* Ficciones *(1956),* El Aleph *(1957),* Discusión *(1957),* Otras inquisiciones *(1960) and* El Hacedor *(1960).*

We also acknowledge permission to reprint those translations into English here included which have previously appeared in magazines and books, as follows: translated by Donald A. Yates: 'The Garden of Forking Paths', Michigan Alumnus Quarterly Review, *Spring 1958; translated by James E. Irby:* 'Tlön, Uqbar, Orbis Tertius', New World Writing No. 18, *April 1961, and* 'The Waiting', Américas, *June 1959; translated by John M. Fein:* 'The Lottery in Babylon', Prairie Schooner, *Fall 1959; translated by Harriet de Onís:* 'The Secret Miracle', Spanish Stories and Tales, Pocket Books *(PL 40) 1956; translated by Julian Palley:* 'Deutsches Requiem', New World Writing No. 14, *1958 (Property of The Rutgers Translators); translated by Dudley Fitts:* 'The Zahir', Partisan Review, *February 1950; translated by Anthony Kerrigan:* 'The Fearful Sphere of Pascal', Noonday No. 3, *1959.*

LABYRINTHS

Jorge Luis Borges was born in Buenos Aires in 1899 and was educated in Europe. One of the major writers of our time, he published many collections of poems, essays and short stories. In 1961, Borges shared the International Publishers' Prize with Samuel Beckett. The Ingram Merrill Foundation granted him its Annual Literary Award in 1966 for his 'outstanding contribution to literature'. In 1970 he was awarded the degree of Doctor of Letters, *honoris causa*, from both Columbia and Oxford, the following year won the fifth biennial Jerusalem Prize, and in 1973 was awarded the Alfonso Reyes Prize. He was Director of the National Library of Buenos Aires from 1955 until 1973. On his death in June 1986, *The Times* obituary described him as 'an acknowledged master of style; his verbal rigour, his refusal of ostentation, his skilful anglicizing of his mother tongue, indeed his intense consciousness of language itself . . . have indebted later writers'. Mario Vargas Llosa, in a tribute to Borges, wrote: 'I do not consider it rash to acclaim Borges as the most important thing to happen to imaginative writing in the Spanish language in modern times, and as one of the most memorable artists of our age . . . His is a world of clear, pure and, at the same time, unusual ideas . . . a superb storyteller.'

Penguin also publish *The Book of Imaginary Beings*, *The Book of Sand*, *Doctor Brodie's Report*, *Selected Poems 1923–1967* and *A Universal History of Infamy*.

LABYRINTHS

SELECTED STORIES AND OTHER WRITINGS

━━━

JORGE LUIS BORGES

Edited by
Donald A. Yates and James E. Irby

Preface by André Maurois

PENGUIN BOOKS

PENGUIN BOOKS

Published by the Penguin Group
Penguin Books Ltd, 27 Wrights Lane, London W8 5TZ, England
Penguin Books USA Inc., 375 Hudson Street, New York, New York 10014, USA
Penguin Books Australia Ltd, Ringwood, Victoria, Australia
Penguin Books Canada Ltd, 10 Alcorn Avenue, Toronto, Ontario, Canada M4V 3B2
Penguin Books (NZ) Ltd, 182–190 Wairau Road, Auckland 10, New Zealand

Penguin Books Ltd, Registered Offices: Harmondsworth, Middlesex, England

First published in the USA by New Directions 1964
Published in Penguin Books 1970
23 25 27 29 30 28 26 24 22

Printed in England by Clays Ltd, St Ives plc
Set in Linotype Pilgrim

Contents

Contents

Preface

JORGE LUIS BORGES is a great writer who has composed only little essays or short narratives. Yet they suffice for us to call him great because of their wonderful intelligence, their wealth of invention and their tight, almost mathematical, style. Argentine by birth and temperament, but nurtured on universal literature, Borges has no spiritual homeland. He creates, outside time and space, imaginary and symbolic worlds. It is a sign of his importance that, in placing him, only strange and perfect works can be called to mind. He is akin to Kafka, Poe, sometimes to Henry James and Wells, always to Valéry by the abrupt projection of his paradoxes in what has been called 'his private metaphysics'.

I

His sources are innumerable and unexpected. Borges has read everything, and especially what nobody reads any more: the Cabalists, the Alexandrine Greeks, medieval philosophers. His erudition is not profound – he asks of it only flashes of lightning and ideas – but it is vast. For example, Pascal wrote: 'Nature is an infinite sphere whose centre is everywhere, whose circumference is nowhere.' Borges sets out to hunt down this metaphor through the centuries. He finds in Giordano Bruno (1584): 'We can assert with certainty that the universe is all centre, or that the centre of the universe is everywhere and its circumference nowhere.' But Giordano Bruno had been able to read in a twelfth-century French theologian, Alain de Lille, a formulation borrowed from the *Corpus Hermeticum* (third century): 'God is an intelligible sphere whose centre is everywhere and whose circumference is nowhere.' Such researches, carried out among the Chinese as among the Arabs or the Egyptians, delight Borges, and lead him to the subjects of his stories.

Many of his masters are English. He has an infinite admiration for Wells and is indignant that Oscar Wilde could define him as 'a scientific Jules Verne'. Borges makes the observation that the fiction of Jules Verne speculates on future *probability* (the submarine, the trip to the moon), that of Wells on pure *possibility* (an invisible man, a flower that devours a man, a machine to explore time), or even on *impossibility* (a man returning from the hereafter with a future flower). Beyond that, a Wells novel symbolically represents features inherent in all human destinies. Any great and lasting book must be ambiguous, Borges says; it is a mirror that makes the reader's features known, but the author must seem to be unaware of the significance of his work – which is an excellent description of Borges's own art. 'God must not engage in theology; the writer must not destroy by human reasonings the faith that art requires of us.'

He admires Poe and Chesterton as much as he does Wells. Poe wrote perfect tales of fantastic horror and invented the detective story, but he never combined the two types of writing. Chesterton *did* attempt and felicitously brought off this *tour de force*. Each of Father Brown's adventures proposes to explain, in reason's name, an unexplainable fact. 'Though Chesterton disclaimed being a Poe or Kafka, there was, in the material out of which his ego was moulded, something that tended to nightmare.' Kafka *was* a direct precursor of Borges. *The Castle* might be by Borges, but he would have made it into a ten-page story, both out of lofty laziness and out of concern for perfection. As for Kafka's precursors, Borges's erudition takes pleasure in finding them in Zeno of Elea, Kierkegaard and Robert Browning. In each of these authors there is some Kafka, but if Kafka had not written, nobody would have been able to notice it – whence this very Borgesian paradox: 'Every writer creates his own precursors.'

Another man who inspires him is the English writer John William Dunne, author of such curious books about time, in which he claims that the past, present and future exist simultaneously, as is proved by our dreams. (Schopenhauer, Borges remarks, had already written that life and dreams are leaves of the same book: reading them in order is living; skimming through them is dreaming.) In death we shall rediscover all the instants of our life and we shall freely combine them as in dreams. 'God, our friends, and Shakespeare will collaborate with us.' Nothing pleases Borges better than to play in this way with mind, dreams, space and time. The more complicated the game becomes, the happier he is. The dreamer can be dreamed in his turn. 'The Mind was dreaming; the world was its dream.' In all philosophers, from Democritus to Spinoza, from Schopenhauer to Kierkegaard, he is on the watch for paradoxical intellectual possibilities.

2

There are to be found in Valéry's notebooks many notes such as this: 'Idea for a frightening story: it is discovered that the only remedy for cancer is living human flesh. Consequences.' I can well imagine a piece of Borges 'fiction' written on such a theme. Reading ancient and modern philosophers, he stops at an idea or a hypothesis. The spark flashes. 'If this absurd postulate were developed to its extreme logical consequences,' he wonders, 'what world would be created?'

For example, an author, Pierre Menard, undertakes to compose *Don Quixote* – not another Quixote, but *the* Quixote. His method? To know Spanish well, to rediscover the Catholic faith, to war against the Moors, to forget the history of Europe – in short, to *be* Miguel de Cervantes. The coincidence then becomes so total that the twentieth-century author rewrites Cervantes's novel literally, *word for word*, and without referring to the original. And here Borges has this astonishing sentence: 'The text of Cervantes and that of Menard are verbally identical, but the second is almost infinitely richer.' This he triumphantly demonstrates, for this subject, apparently absurd, in fact expresses a real idea : the *Quixote* that we read is not that of Cervantes, any more than our *Madame Bovary* is that of Flaubert. Each twentieth-century reader involuntarily rewrites in his own way the masterpieces of past centuries. It was enough to make an extrapolation in order to draw Borges's story out of it.

Often a paradox that ought to bowl us over does not strike us in the abstract form given it by philosophers. Borges makes a concrete reality out of it. The 'Library of Babel' is the image of the universe, infinite and always started over again. Most of the books in this library are unintelligible, letters thrown together by chance or perversely repeated, but sometimes, in this labyrinth of letters, a reasonable line or sentence is found. Such are the laws of nature, tiny cases of regularity in a chaotic world. The 'Lottery in Babylon' is another ingenious and penetrating staging of the role of chance in life. The mysterious Company that distributes good and bad luck reminds us of the 'musical banks' in Samuel Butler's *Erewhon*.

Attracted by metaphysics, but accepting no system as true, Borges makes out of all of them a game for the mind. He discovers two tendencies in himself : 'one to esteem religious and philosophical ideas for their aesthetic value, and even for what is magical or marvellous in their content. That is perhaps the indication of an essential scepticism. The other is to suppose in advance that the quantity of fables or metaphors of which man's imagination is capable is limited, but that this small number of inventions can be everything to everyone.'

Among these fables or ideas, certain ones particularly fascinate him : that of Endless Recurrence, or the circular repetition of all the history of the world, a theme dear to Nietzsche; that of the dream within a dream; that of centuries that seem minutes and seconds that seem years ('The Secret Miracle'); that of the hallucinatory nature of the world. He likes to quote Novalis : 'The greatest of sorcerers would be the one who would cast a spell on himself to the degree of taking his own phantasmagoria for autonomous apparitions. Might that not be our case?' Borges answers that indeed it *is* our case: it is we who have dreamed the universe. We can see in what it consists, the deliberately constructed interplay of the mirrors and mazes of this thought, difficult but always acute and laden with secrets. In all these stories we find roads that fork, corridors that lead nowhere, except to other corridors, and so on as far as the eye can see. For Borges this is an image of human thought, which endlessly makes its way through concatenations of causes and effects without ever exhausting infinity, and marvels over what is perhaps only inhuman chance. And why wander in these labyrinths? Once more, for aesthetic reasons; because this present infinity, these 'vertiginous symmetries', have their tragic beauty. The form is more important than the content.

3

Borges's form often recalls Swift's: the same gravity amid the absurd, the same precision of detail. To demonstrate an impossible discovery, he will adopt the tone of the most scrupulous scholar, mix imaginary writings in with real and erudite sources. Rather than write a whole book, which would bore him, he analyses a book which had never existed. 'Why take five hundred pages', he asks, 'to develop an idea whose oral demonstration fits into a few minutes?'

Such is, for example, the narrative that bears this bizarre title: 'Tlön, Uqbar, Orbis Tertius'. This concerns the history of an unknown planet, complete 'with its architectures and quarrels, with the terror of its mythologies and the uproar of its languages, its emperors and seas, its minerals and birds and fish, its algebra and fire, its theological and metaphysical controversies.' This invention of a new world appears to be the work of a secret society of astronomers, engineers, biologists, metaphysicians and geometricians. This world that they have created, Tlön, is a Berkeleyan and Kierkegaardian world where only inner life exists. On Tlön everyone has his own truth; external objects are whatever each one wants. The international press broadcasts this discovery, and very soon the world of Tlön obliterates our world. An imaginary past takes the place of our own. A group of solitary scientists has transformed the universe. All this is mad, subtle and gives food for endless thought.

Other stories by Borges are parables, mysterious and never explicit; still others are detective narratives in the manner of Chesterton. Their plots remain entirely intellectual. The criminal exploits his familiarity with the methods of the detective. It is Dupin against Dupin or Maigret against Maigret. One of these pieces of 'fiction' is the insatiable search for a person through the scarcely perceptible reflections that he has left on other souls. In another, because a condemned man has noticed that expectations never coincide with reality, he imagines the circumstances of his own death. Since they have thus become expectations, they can no longer become realities.

These inventions are described in a pure and scholarly style which must be linked up with Poe, 'who begat Baudelaire, who begat Mallarmé, who begat Valéry,' who begat Borges. It is especially by his rigour that he reminds us of Valéry. 'To be in love is to create a religion whose god is fallible.' By his piled-up imperfects he sometimes recalls Flaubert; by the rarity of his adjectives, St John Perse. 'The inconsolable cry of a bird.' But, once these relationships are pointed out, it must be said that Borges's style is, like his thought, highly original. Of the metaphysicians of Tlön he writes: 'They seek neither truth nor likelihood; they seek astonishment. They think metaphysics is a branch of the literature of fantasy.' That rather well defines the greatness and the art of Borges.

ANDRÉ MAUROIS
Translated by Sherry Mangan   *of the French Academy*

Introduction

JORGE LUIS BORGES was born on 24 August 1899 in Buenos Aires, of Spanish, English and (very remotely) Portuguese Jewish origin. His parents were of the intellectual middle class and descended from military and political figures prominent in the struggles for Argentine national independence and unity that occupied most of the nineteenth century. After completing his secondary education in Geneva and then spending some three years in Spain associated with the *avant-garde ultraísta* group of poets, Borges returned to Buenos Aires in 1921. There he immediately became the leading exponent and theorist of Argentine *ultraísmo*, distinguished from its Spanish counterpart by a peculiar fusion of modern expressionist form and anachronistic nostalgia for certain national values – values most palpably embodied for those writers in the old *criollo* quarters of Buenos Aires – which were by then disappearing amid the post-war boom and rush of foreign immigration. Borges's and his companions' situation was not unlike that of some North American writers of the same generation who suffered the impact of war, industrialism and modern European art on a tranquil Midwestern or Southern heritage.

But out of these general conditions, shared by many in our time, Borges has created a work like no other. Perhaps the most striking characteristics of his writings is their extreme intellectual reaction against all the disorder and contingency of immediate reality, their radical insistence on breaking with the given world and postulating another. Born into the dizzying flux and inconstancy of a far-flung border area of Western culture, keen witness of the general crisis of that culture, Borges has used his strangely gifted mind – the mind of a

15

Cabalist, of a seventeenth-century 'metaphysical', or a theorist of pure literature much like Poe or Valéry – to erect an order with what Yeats called 'monuments of unageing intellect'. Borges is sceptical as few have ever been about the ultimate value of mere ideas and mere literature. But he has striven to turn this scepticism into an ironic method, to make of disbelief an aesthetic system, in which what matters most is not ideas as such but their resonances and suggestions, the drama of their possibilities and impossibilities, the immobile and lasting quintessence of ideas as it is distilled at the dead centre of their warring contradictions.

Until about 1930 Borges's main creative medium was poetry: laconic free-verse poems which evoked scenes and atmospheres of old Buenos Aires or treated timeless themes of love, death and the self. He also wrote many essays on subjects of literary criticism, metaphysics and language, essays reminiscent of Chesterton's in their compactness and unexpected paradoxes. The lucidity and verbal precision of these writings belie the agitated conditions of *avant-garde* polemic and playfulness under which most of them were composed. During these years Borges was content to seek expression in serene lyric images perhaps too conveniently abstracted from the surrounding world and have all his speculations and creations respond primarily to the need for a new national literature as he saw it. The years from 1930 to 1940, however, brought a deep change in Borges's work. He virtually abandoned poetry and turned to the short narrative genre. Though he never lost his genuine emotion for the unique features of his native ground, he ceased to exalt them nationalistically as sole bulwarks against threatening disorder and began to rank them more humbly within a context of vast universal processes: the nightmarish city of 'Death and the Compass' is an obvious stylization of Buenos Aires, no longer idealized as in the poems, but instead used as the dark setting for a tragedy of the human intellect. The witty and already very learned young poet who had been so active in editing such little reviews as *Martín Fierro*, *Prisma* and *Proa*, became a sedentary writer-scholar who spent many solitary

hours in reading the most varied and unusual works of literature and philosophy and in meticulously correcting his own
manuscripts, passionately but also somewhat monstrously devoted to the written word as his most vital experience, as
failing eyesight and other crippling afflictions made him more
and more a semi-invalid, more and more an incredible mind in
an ailing and almost useless body, much like his character
Ireneo Funes. Oppressed by physical reality and also by the
turmoil of Europe, which had all-too-direct repercussions in
Argentina, Borges sought to create a coherent fictional world of
the intelligence. This world is essentially adumbrated in 'Tlön,
Uqbar, Orbis Tertius'. As Borges slyly observes there, Tlön is no
'irresponsible figment of the imagination'; the stimulus which
prompted its formulation is stated with clarity (though not
without irony) towards the end of that story's final section,
projected as a kind of tentative utopia into the future beyond
the grim year 1940 when it was written:

Ten years ago any symmetry with a semblance of order – dialectical materialism, anti-Semitism, Nazism – was sufficient to charm
the minds of men. How could one do other than submit to Tlön,
to the minute and vast evidence of an orderly planet? It is useless
to answer that reality is also orderly. Perhaps it is, but in accordance with divine laws – I translate: inhuman laws – which we
never quite grasp. Tlön is surely a labyrinth, but it is a labyrinth
devised by men, a labyrinth destined to be deciphered by men.

Borges's metaphysical fictions, his finest creations, which are
collected in the volumes *Ficciones* (1945) and *El Aleph* (1949),
all elaborate upon the varied idealist possibilities outlined in
the 'article' on Tlön. In these narratives the analytical and
imaginative functions previously kept separate in his essays
and poems curiously fuse, producing a form expressive of all
the tension and complexity of Borges's mature thought.

His fictions are always concerned with processes of striving
which lead to discovery and insight; these are achieved at
times gradually, at other times suddenly, but always with dis-
concerting and even devastating effect. They are tales of the

fantastic, of the hyperbolic, but they are never content with fantasy in the simple sense of facile wish-fulfilment. The insight they provide is ironic, pathetic: a painful sense of inevitable limits that block total aspirations. Some of these narratives ('Tlön, Uqbar, Orbis, Tertius', 'Pierre Menard, Author of the *Quixote*', 'Three Versions of Judas', 'The Sect of the Phoenix') might be called 'pseudo essays' – mock scrutinies of authors or books or learned subjects actually of Borges's own invention – that in turning in upon themselves make the 'plot' (if it can be called that) an intricate interplay of creation and critique. But all his stories, whatever their outward form, have the same self-critical dimension; in some it is revealed only in minimal aspects of tone and style (as, for example, in 'The Circular Ruins'). Along with these 'vertical' superpositions of different and mutually qualifying levels, there are also 'horizontal' progressions of qualitative leaps, after the manner of tales of adventure or of crime detection (Borges's favourite types of fiction). Unexpected turns elude the predictable; hidden realities are revealed through their diverse effects and derivations. Like his beloved Chesterton, who made the Father Brown stories a vehicle for his Catholic theology, Borges uses mystery and the surprise effect in literature to achieve that sacred astonishment at the universe which is the origin of all true religion and metaphysics. However, Borges as theologian is a complete heretic, as the casuistical 'Three Versions of Judas' more than suffices to show.

Borges once claimed that the basic devices of all fantastic literature are only four in number: the work within the work, the contamination of reality by dream, the voyage in time and the double. These are both his essential themes – the problematical nature of the world, of knowledge, of time, of the self – and his essential techniques of construction. Indeed, in Borges's narratives the usual distinction between form and content virtually disappears, as does that between the world of literature and the world of the reader. We almost unconsciously come to accept the world of Tlön because it has been so subtly inserted into our own. In Theme of the Traitor and the

Hero', Borges's discovery of his own story (which is worked up before our very eyes and has areas 'not yet revealed' to him), Nolan's of Kilpatrick's treason, Ryan's of the curious martyrdom and ours of the whole affair, are but one awareness of dark betrayal and creative deception. We are transported into a realm where fact and fiction, the real and the unreal, the whole and the part, the highest and the lowest, are complementary aspects of the same continuous being : a realm where 'any man is all men', where 'all men who repeat a line of Shakespeare *are* William Shakespeare'. The world is a book and the book is a world, and both are labyrinthine and enclose enigmas designed to be understood and participated in by man. We should note that this all-compromising intellectual unity is achieved precisely by the sharpest and most scandalous confrontation of opposites. In 'Avatars of the Tortoise', the paradox of Zeno triumphantly demonstrates the unreality of the visible world, while in 'The Library of Babel' it shows the anguishing impossibility of the narrator's ever reaching the Book of Books. And in 'The Immortal', possibly Borges's most complete narrative, the movements towards and from immortality become one single approximation of universal impersonality.

Borges is always quick to confess his sources and borrowings, because for him no one has claim to originality in literature; all writers are more or less faithful amanuenses of the spirit, translators and annotators of pre-existing archetypes. (Hence Tlön, the impersonal and hereditary product of the 'secret society'; hence Pierre Menard, the writer as perfect reader.) By critics he has often been compared with Kafka, whom he was one of the first to translate into Spanish. Certainly, we can see the imprint of his favourite Kafka story, 'The Great Wall of China', on 'The Lottery in Babylon' and 'The Library of Babel'; the similarity lies mainly in the narrators' pathetically inadequate examination of an impossible subject, and also in the idea of an infinite, hierarchical universe, with its corollary of infinite regression. But the differences between the two writers are perhaps more significant than their likenesses. Kafka's minutely and extensively established portrayals of degradation, his irreducible and enigmatic situations, contrast strongly with Borges's compact but vastly significant theorems, his all-dissolving ratiocination. Kafka wrote novels, but Borges has openly confessed he cannot; his miniature forms are intense realizations of Poe's famous tenets of unity of effect and brevity to the exclusion of 'worldly interests'. And no matter how mysterious they seem at first glance, all Borges's works contain the keys to their own elucidation in the form of clear parallelisms with other of his writings and explicit allusions to a definite literary and philosophical context within which he has chosen to situate himself. The list of Pierre Menard's writings, as Borges has observed, is not 'arbitrary', but provides a 'diagram of his mental history' and already implies the nature of his 'subterranean' undertaking. All the footnotes in Borges's fictions, even those marked 'Editor's Note', are the author's own and form an integral part of the works as he has conceived them. Familiarity with Neo-Platonism and related doctrines will clarify Borges's preferences and intentions, just as it will, say, Yeats's or Joyce's. But, as Borges himself has remarked of the theological explications of Kafka's work, the full enjoyment of his writings precedes and in no way depends upon such interpretations. Greater and more important than his intellectual ingenuity is Borges's consummate skill as a narrator, his magic in obtaining the most powerful effects with a strict economy of means.

Borges's stories may seem mere formalist games, mathematical experiments devoid of any sense of human responsibility and unrelated even to the author's own life, but quite the opposite is true. His idealist insistence on knowledge and insight, which means finding order and becoming part of it, has a definite moral significance, though that significance is for him inextricably dual : his traitors are always somehow heroes as well. And all his fictional situations, all his characters, are at bottom autobiographical, essential projections of his experiences as writer, reader and human being (also divided, as 'Borges and I' tells us). He is the dreamer who learns he is the dreamed one, the detective deceived by the hidden pattern of crimes, the perplexed Averroes whose ignorance mirrors the author's own in portraying him. And yet, each of these intimate failures is turned into an artistic triumph. It could be asked what such concerns of a total man of letters have to do with our plight as ordinary, bedevilled men of our bedevilled time. Here it seems inevitable to draw a comparison with Cervantes, so apparently unlike Borges, but whose name is not invoked in vain in his stories, essays and parables. Borges's fictions, like the enormous fiction of *Don Quixote*, grow out of the deep confrontation of literature and life which is not only the central problem of all literature but also that of all human experience: the problem of illusion and reality. We are all at once writers, readers and protagonists of some eternal story; we fabricate our illusions, seek to decipher the symbols around us and see our efforts overtopped and cut short by a supreme Author: but in our defeat, as in the Mournful Knight's, there can come the glimpse of a higher understanding that prevails, at our expense. Borges's 'dehumanized' exercises in *ars combinatoria* are no less human than that.

Narrative prose is usually easier to translate than verse, but Borges's prose raises difficulties not unlike those of poetry, because of its constant creative deformations and cunning artifices. Writers as diverse as George Moore and Vladimir Nabokov have argued that translations should sound like translations. Certainly, since Borges's language does not read 'smoothly' in Spanish, there is no reason it should in English. Besides, as was indicated above, he considers his own style at best only a translation of others': at the end of 'Tlön, Uqbar, Orbis Tertius' he speaks of making an 'uncertain' version of Sir Thomas Browne's *Urn Burial* after the manner of the great Spanish Baroque writer Francisco de Quevedo. Borges's prose is in fact a modern adaptation of the Latinized Baroque *stil coupé*. He has a penchant for what seventeenth- and eighteenth-century rhetoricians called 'hard' or 'philosophic' words, and will often use them in their strict etymological sense, restoring radical meanings with an effect of metaphorical novelty. In the opening sentence of 'The Circular Ruins', 'unanimous' means quite literally 'of one mind' (*unus animus*) and thus fore-shadows the magician's final discovery. Elevated terms are played off against more humble and direct ones; the image joining unlike terms is frequent; heterogeneous contacts are also created by Borges's use of colons and semicolons in place of casual connectives to give static, elliptical, overlapping effects. Somewhat like Eliot in *The Waste Land*, Borges will deliberately work quotations into the texture of his writing. The most striking example is 'The Immortal', which contains many more such 'intrusions or thefts' than its epilogue admits. All his other stories do the same to some degree : there are echoes of Gibbon in 'The Lottery in Babylon', of Spengler in 'Deutsches Requiem', of *Borges himself* in 'The Library of Babel' and 'Funes the Memorious'. Borges has observed that 'the Baroque is that style which deliberately exhausts (or tries to exhaust) its possibilities and borders on its own caricature'. A self-parodying tone is particularly evident in 'Pierre Menard, Author of the *Quixote*', 'The Zahir', 'The Sect of the Phoenix'. In that sense, Borges also ironically translates himself.

Most of the present volume is given over to a sizeable selection of Borges's fictions. The essays here represent only a very small portion of his production in that form; they have been chosen for the importance of their themes in Borges's work as a whole and for their relevance to the stories, which were written during the same years. All are taken from his best essay collection, *Otras inquisiciones* (1952), with the exception of 'The Argentine Writer and Tradition' (originally a lecture), which is contained in the revised edition of another collection entitled *Discusión* (1957). Because of his near-blindness, Borges ceased to write stories after 1953 (though 'Borges and I' suggests other reasons for the abandonment of that genre), and since then he has concentrated on even shorter forms which can be dictated more easily. The parables concluding this collection are examples of that later work. They are all found in the volume *El hacedor* (1960).

Borges's somewhat belated recognition as a major writer of our time has come more from Europe than from his native

America. The 1961 Formentor Prize, which he shared with Samuel Beckett, is the most recent token of that recognition. In Argentina, save for the admiration of a relatively small group, he has often been criticized as non-Argentine, as an abstruse dweller in an ivory tower, though his whole work and personality could have emerged only from that peculiar cross-roads of the River Plate region, and his non-political opposition to Perón earned him persecutions during the years of the dictatorship. Apparently, many of his countrymen cannot pardon in him what is precisely his greatest virtue – his almost superhuman effort to transmute his circumstances into an art as universal as the finest of Europe – and expect their writers to be uncomplicated reporters of the national scene. A kind of curious inverse snobbism is evident here. As the Argentine novelist Ernesto Sábato remarked in 1945, 'if Borges were French or Czech, we would all be reading him enthusiastically in bad translations'. Not being French has undoubtedly also relegated Borges to comparative obscurity in the English-speaking countries, where it is rare that a Hispanic writer is ever accorded any major importance at all. Perhaps this selection of his writings will help correct that oversight and justify the critical judgements of René Etiemble and Marcel Brion, who have found in Borges the very perfection of the cosmopolitan spirit, and in his work one of the most extraordinary expressions in all Western literature of modern man's anguish of time, of space, of the infinite.

J.E.I.

Fictions

Tlön, Uqbar, Orbis Tertius

I

I OWE the discovery of Uqbar to the conjunction of a mirror and an encyclopedia. The mirror troubled the depths of a corridor in a country house on Gaona Street in Ramos Mejía; the encyclopedia is fallaciously called *The Anglo-American Cyclopaedia* (New York, 1917) and is a literal but delinquent reprint of the *Encyclopaedia Britannica* of 1902. The event took place some five years ago. Bioy Casares had had dinner with me that evening and we became lengthily engaged in a vast polemic concerning the composition of a novel in the first person, whose narrator would omit or disfigure the facts and indulge in various contradictions which would permit a few readers – very few readers – to perceive an atrocious or banal reality. From the remote depths of the corridor, the mirror spied upon us. We discovered (such a discovery is inevitable in the late hours of the night) that mirrors have something mon- strous about them. Then Bioy Casares recalled that one of the heresiarchs of Uqbar had declared that mirrors and copulation are abominable, because they increase the number of men. I asked him the origin of this memorable observation and he answered that it was reproduced in *The Anglo-American Cyclopaedia*, in its article on Uqbar. The house (which we had rented furnished) had a set of this work. On the last pages of Volume XLVI we found an article on Upsala; on the first pages of Volume XLVII, one on Ural-Altaic Languages, but not a word about Uqbar. Bioy, a bit taken aback, consulted the volumes of the index. In vain he exhausted all of the imagin- able spellings: Ukbar, Ucbar, Ooqbar, Ookbar, Oukbahr....

27

Before leaving, he told me that it was a region of Iraq or of Asia Minor. I must confess that I agreed with some discomfort. I conjectured that this undocumented country and its anonymous heresiarch were a fiction devised by Bioy's modesty in order to justify a statement. The fruitless examination of one of Justus Perthes's atlases fortified my doubt.

The following day, Bioy called me from Buenos Aires. He told me he had before him the article on Uqbar, in Volume XLVI of the encyclopedia. The heresiarch's name was not forthcoming, but there was a note on his doctrine, formulated in words almost identical to those he had repeated, though perhaps literarily inferior. He had recalled: *Copulation and mirrors are abominable*. The text of the encyclopedia said: *For one of those gnostics, the visible universe was an illusion or (more precisely) a sophism. Mirrors and fatherhood are abominable because they multiply and disseminate that universe*. I told him, in all truthfulness, that I should like to see that article. A few days later he brought it. This surprised me, since the scrupulous cartographical indices of Ritter's *Erdkunde* were plentifully ignorant of the name Uqbar.

The tome Bioy brought was, in fact, Volume XLVI of the *Anglo-American Cyclopaedia*. On the half-title page and the spine, the alphabetical marking (Tor–Ups) was that of our copy, but, instead of 917, it contained 921 pages. These four additional pages made up the article on Uqbar, which (as the reader will have noticed) was not indicated by the alphabetical marking. We later determined that there was no other difference between the volumes. Both of them (as I believe I have indicated) are reprints of the tenth *Encyclopaedia Britannica*. Bioy had acquired his copy at some sale or other.

We read the article with some care. The passage recalled by Bioy was perhaps the only surprising one. The rest of it seemed very plausible, quite in keeping with the general tone of the work and (as is natural) a bit boring. Reading it over again, we discovered beneath its rigorous prose a fundamental vagueness. Of the fourteen names which figured in the geographical part, we only recognized three – Khorasan, Armenia, Erzerum –

interpolated in the text in an ambiguous way. Of the historical names, only one: the impostor magician Smerdis, invoked more as a metaphor. The note seemed to fix the boundaries of Uqbar, but its nebulous reference points were rivers and craters and mountain ranges of that same region. We read, for example, that the lowlands of Tsai Khaldun and the Axa Delta marked the southern frontier and that on the islands of the delta wild horses procreate. All this, on the first part of page 918. In his historical section (page 920) we learned that as a result of the religious persecutions of the thirteenth century, the orthodox believers sought refuge on these islands, where to this day their obelisks remain and where it is not uncommon to unearth their stone mirrors. The section on Language and Literature was brief. Only one trait is worthy of recollection: it noted that the literature of Uqbar was one of fantasy and that its epics and legends never referred to reality, but to the two imaginary regions of Mlejnas and Tlön. . . . The bibliography enumerated four volumes which we have not yet found, though the third – Silas Haslam: *History of the Land Called Uqbar*, 1874 – figures in the catalogues of Bernard Quaritch's book shop.* The first, *Lesbare und lesenswerthe Bemerkungen über das Land Ukkbar in Klein-Asien*, dates from 1641 and is the work of Johannes Valentinus Andreä. This fact is significant; a few years later, I came upon that name in the unsuspected pages of De Quincey (*Writings*, Volume XIII) and learned that it belonged to a German theologian who, in the early seventeenth century, described the imaginary community of Rosae Crucis – a community that others founded later, in imitation of what he had prefigured.

That night we visited the National Library. In vain we exhausted atlases, catalogues, annuals of geographical societies, travellers' and historians' memoirs: no one had ever been in Uqbar. Neither did the general index of Bioy's encyclopedia register that name. The following day, Carlos Mastronardi (to whom I had related the matter) noticed the black and gold covers of the *Anglo-American Cyclopaedia* in a bookshop on

*Haslam has also published *A General History of Labyrinths*.

Corrientes and Talcahuano.... He entered and examined Volume XLVI. Of course, he did not find the slightest indication of Uqbar.

2

Some limited and waning memory of Herbert Ashe, an engineer of the southern railways, persists in the hotel at Adrogué, among the effusive honeysuckles and in the illusory depths of the mirrors. In his lifetime he suffered from unreality, as do so many Englishmen; once dead, he is not even the ghost he was then. He was tall and listless, and his tired rectangular beard had once been red. I understand he was a widower, without children. Every few years he would go to England, to visit (I judge from some photographs he showed us) a sundial and a few oaks. He and my father had entered into one of those close (the adjective is excessive) English friendships that begin by excluding confidences and very soon dispense with dialogue. They used to carry out an exchange of books and newspapers and engage in taciturn chess games.... I remember him in the hotel corridor, with a mathematics book in his hand, sometimes looking at the irrecoverable colours of the sky. One afternoon we spoke of the duodecimal system of numbering (in which twelve is written as 10). Ashe said that he was converting some kind of tables from the duodecimal to the sexagesimal system (in which sixty is written as 10). He added that the task had been entrusted to him by a Norwegian, in Rio Grande do Sul. We had known him for eight years and he had never mentioned his sojourn in that region.... We talked of country life, of the *capangas*, of the Brazilian etymology of the word *gaucho* (which some old Uruguayans still pronounce *gaúcho*) and nothing more was said – may God forgive me – of duodecimal functions. In September of 1937 (we were not at the hotel), Herbert Ashe died of a ruptured aneurysm. A few days before, he had received a sealed and certified package from Brazil. It was a book in large octavo. Ashe left it at the bar, where – months later – I found it. I began to leaf through it and experienced an astonished and airy feeling of vertigo which I shall not describe, for this is not the story of my emotions but of Uqbar and Tlön and Orbis Tertius. On one of the nights of Islam called the Night of Nights the secret doors of heaven open wide and the water in the jars becomes sweeter; if those doors opened, I would not feel what I felt that afternoon. The book was written in English and contained 1,001 pages. On the yellow leather back I read these curious words which were repeated on the title page: *A First Encyclopaedia of Tlön. Vol. XI. Hlaer to Jangr.* There was no indication of date or place. On the first page and on a leaf of silk paper that covered one of the colour plates there was stamped a blue oval with this inscription: *Orbis Tertius.* Two years before I had discovered, in a volume of a certain pirated encyclopaedia, a superficial description of a non-existent country; now chance afforded me something more precious and arduous. Now I held in my hands a vast methodical fragment of an unknown planet's entire history, with its architecture and its playing cards, with the dread of its mythologies and the murmur of its languages, with its emperors and its seas, with its minerals and its birds and its fish, with its algebra and its fire, with its theological and metaphysical controversy. And all of it articulated, coherent, with no visible doctrinal intent or tone of parody.

In the 'Eleventh Volume' which I have mentioned there are allusions to preceding and succeeding volumes. In an article in the *N.R.F.* which is now classic, Néstor Ibarra has denied the existence of those companion volumes; Ezequiel Martínez Estrada and Drieu La Rochelle have refuted that doubt, perhaps victoriously. The fact is that up to now the most diligent inquiries have been fruitless. In vain we have upended the libraries of the two Americas and of Europe. Alfonso Reyes, tired of these subordinate sleuthing procedures, proposes that we should all undertake the task of reconstructing the many and weighty tomes that are lacking: *ex ungue leonem.* He calculates, half in earnest and half jokingly, that a generation of *tlönistas* should be sufficient. This venturesome computation brings us back to the fundamental problem: Who are the inventors of Tlön? The plural is inevitable, because the hypothesis of a lone inventor – an infinite Leibniz labouring away darkly and modestly - has been unanimously discounted. It is conjectured that this brave new world is the work of a secret society of astronomers, biologists, engineers, metaphysicians, poets, chemists, algebraists, moralists, painters, geometers … directed by an obscure man of genius. Individuals mastering these diverse disciplines are abundant, but not so those capable of inventiveness and less so those capable of subordinating that inventiveness to a rigorous and systematic plan. This plan is so vast that each writer's contribution is infinitesimal. At first it was believed that Tlön was a mere chaos, an irresponsible licence of the imagination; now it is known that it is a cosmos and that the intimate laws which govern it have been formulated, at least provisionally. Let it suffice for me to recall that the apparent contradictions of the Eleventh Volume are the fundamental basis for the proof that the other volumes exist, so lucid and exact is the order observed in it. The popular magazines, with pardonable excess, have spread news of the zoology and topography of Tlön; I think its transparent tigers and towers of blood perhaps do not merit the continued attention of *all* men. I shall venture to request a few minutes to expound its concept of the universe.

Hume noted for all time that Berkeley's arguments did not admit the slightest refutation nor did they cause the slightest conviction. This dictum is entirely correct in its application to the earth, but entirely false in Tlön. The nations of this planet are congenitally idealist. Their language and the derivations of their language – religion, letters, metaphysics – all presuppose idealism. The world for them is not a concourse of objects in space; it is a heterogeneous series of independent acts. It is successive and temporal, not spatial. There are no nouns in Tlön's conjectural *Ursprache*, from which the 'present' languages and the dialects are derived: there are impersonal verbs, modified by monosyllabic suffixes (or prefixes) with an adverbial value. For example: there is no word corresponding to the word 'moon', but there is a verb which in English would be 'to moon' or 'to moonate'. 'The moon rose above the river' is *hlör u fang axaxaxas mlö*, or literally: 'upward behind the onstreaming it mooned'.

The preceding applies to the languages of the southern hemisphere. In those of the northern hemisphere (on whose *Ursprache* there is very little data in the Eleventh Volume) the prime unit is not the verb, but the monosyllabic adjective. The noun is formed by an accumulation of adjectives. They do not say 'moon' but rather 'round airy-light on dark' or 'pale-orange-of-the-sky' or any other such combination. In the example selected the mass of adjectives refers to a real object, but this is purely fortuitous. The literature of this hemisphere (like Meinong's subsistent world) abounds in ideal objects, which are convoked and dissolved in a moment, according to poetic needs. At times they are determined by mere simultaneity. There are objects composed of two terms, one of visual and another of auditory character: the colour of the rising sun and the far-away cry of a bird. There are objects of many terms: the sun and the water on a swimmer's chest, the vague tremulous rose colour we see with our eyes closed, the sensation of being carried along by a river and also by sleep. These second-degree objects can be combined with others; through the use of certain abbreviations, the process is practically infinite. There are famous poems made up of one enormous word. This word forms a *poetic object* created by the author. The fact that no one believes in the reality of nouns paradoxically causes their number to be unending. The languages of Tlön's northern hemisphere contain all the nouns of the Indo-European languages – and many others as well.

It is no exaggeration to state that the classic culture of Tlön comprises only one discipline: psychology. All others are subordinated to it. I have said that the men of this planet conceive the universe as a series of mental processes which do not develop in space but successively in time. Spinoza ascribes to his inexhaustible divinity the attributes of extension and thought; no one in Tlön would understand the juxtaposition of the first (which is typical only of certain states) and the second – which is a perfect synonym of the cosmos. In other words, they do not conceive that the spatial persists in time. The perception of a cloud of smoke on the horizon and then of the burning field and then of the half-extinguished cigarette that produced the blaze is considered an example of association of ideas.

This monism or complete idealism invalidates all science. If we explain (or judge) a fact, we connect it with another; such linking, in Tlön, is a later state of the subject which cannot affect or illuminate the previous state. Every mental state is irreducible : the mere fact of naming it – i.e., of classifying it – implies a falsification. From which it can be deduced that there are no sciences on Tlön, not even reasoning. The paradoxical truth is that they do exist, and in almost uncountable number. The same thing happens with philosophies as happens with nouns in the northern hemisphere. The fact that every philosophy is by definition a dialectical game, a *Philosophie des Als Ob*, has caused them to multiply. There is an abundance of incredible systems of pleasing design or sensational type. The metaphysicians of Tlön do not seek for the truth or even for verisimilitude, but rather for the astounding. They judge that metaphysics is a branch of fantastic literature. They know that a system is nothing more than the subordination of all aspects of the universe to any one such aspect. Even the phrase 'all aspects' is rejectable, for it supposes the impossible addition of the present and of all past moments. Neither is it licit to use the plural 'past moments', since it supposes another impossible operation.... One of the schools of Tlön goes so far as to negate time : it reasons that the present is indefinite, that the future has no reality other than as a present hope, that the past has no reality other than as a present memory.* Another school declares that *all time* has already transpired and that our life is only the crepuscular and no doubt falsified and mutilated

* Russell (*The Analysis of Mind*, 1921, page 159) supposes that the planet has been created a few minutes ago, furnished with a humanity that 'remembers' an illusory past.

memory or reflection of an irrecoverable process. Another, that the history of the universe – and in it our lives and the most tenuous detail of our lives – is the scripture produced by a subordinate god in order to communicate with a demon. Another, that the universe is comparable to those cryptographs in which not all the symbols are valid and that only what happens every three hundred nights is true. Another, that while we sleep here, we are awake elsewhere and that in this way every man is two men.

Among the doctrines of Tlön, none has merited the scandalous reception accorded to materialism. Some thinkers have formulated it with less clarity than fervour, as one might put forth a paradox. In order to facilitate the comprehension of this inconceivable thesis, a heresiarch of the eleventh century* devised the sophism of the nine copper coins, whose scandalous renown is in Tlön equivalent to that of the Eleatic paradoxes. There are many versions of this 'specious reasoning', which vary the number of coins and the number of discoveries; the following is the most common:

On Tuesday, X crosses a deserted road and loses nine copper coins. On Thursday, Y finds in the road four coins, somewhat rusted by Wednesday's rain. On Friday, Z discovers three coins in the road. On Friday morning, X finds two coins in the corridor of his house. The heresiarch would deduce from this story the reality – i.e. the continuity – of the nine coins which were recovered. *It is absurd* (he affirmed) *to imagine that four of the coins have not existed between Tuesday and Thursday, three between Tuesday and Friday afternoon, two between Tuesday and Friday morning. It is logical to think that they have existed – at least in some secret way, hidden from the comprehension of men – at every moment of those three periods.*

The language of Tlön resists the formulation of this paradox; most people did not even understand it. The defenders of common sense at first did no more than negate the veracity of the anecdote. They repeated that it was a verbal fallacy, based

---

* A century, according to the duodecimal system, signifies a period of a hundred and forty-four years.

on the rash application of two neologisms not authorized by usage and alien to all rigorous thought: the verbs 'find' and 'lose', which beg the question, because they presuppose the identity of the first and of the last nine coins. They recalled that all nouns (man, coin, Thursday, Wednesday, rain) have only a metaphorical value. They denounced the treacherous circumstance 'somewhat rusted by Wednesday's rain', which presupposes what is trying to be demonstrated: the persistence of the four coins from Tuesday to Thursday. They explained that *equality* is one thing and *identity* another, and formulated a kind of *reductio ad absurdum*: the hypothetical case of nine men who on nine successive nights suffer a severe pain. Would it not be ridiculous – they questioned – to pretend that this pain is one and the same?* They said that the heresiarch was prompted only by the blasphemous intention of attributing the divine category of *being* to some simple coins and that at times he negated plurality and at other times did not. They argued: if equality implies identity, one would also have to admit that the nine coins are one.

Unbelievably, these refutations were not definitive. A hundred years after the problem was stated, a thinker no less brilliant than the heresiarch but of orthodox tradition formulated a very daring hypothesis. This happy conjecture affirmed that there is only one subject, that this indivisible subject is every being in the universe and that these beings are the organs and masks of the divinity. X is Y and is Z. Z discovers three coins because he remembers that X lost them; X finds two in the corridor because he remembers that the others have been found.... The Eleventh Volume suggests that three prime reasons determined the complete victory of this idealist pantheism. The first, its repudiation of solipsism; the second, the possibility of preserving the psychological basis of the

---

*Today, one of the churches of Tlön Platonically maintains that a certain pain, a certain greenish tint of yellow, a certain temperature, a certain sound, are the only reality. All men, in the vertiginous moment of coitus, are the same man. All men who repeat a line from Shakespeare *are* William Shakespeare.

sciences; the third, the possibility of preserving the cult of the gods. Schopenhauer (the passionate and lucid Schopenhauer) formulates a very similar doctrine in the first volume of *Parerga und Paralipomena*.

The geometry of Tlön comprises two somewhat different disciplines: the visual and the tactile. The latter corresponds to our own geometry and is subordinated to the first. The basis of visual geometry is the surface, not the point. This geometry disregards parallel lines and declares that man in his movement modifies the forms which surround him. The basis of its arithmetic is the notion of indefinite numbers. They emphasize the importance of the concepts of greater and lesser, which our mathematicians symbolize as $>$ and $<$. They maintain that the operation of counting modifies quantities and converts them from indefinite into definite sums. The fact that several individuals who count the same quantity should obtain the same result is, for the psychologists, an example of association of ideas or of a good exercise of memory. We already know that in Tlön the subject of knowledge is one and eternal.

In literary practices the idea of a single subject is also all-powerful. It is uncommon for books to be signed. The concept of plagiarism does not exist: it has been established that all works are the creation of one author, who is atemporal and anonymous. The critics often invent authors: they select two dissimilar works – the *Tao Te Ching* and the *1001 Nights*, say – attribute them to the same writer and then determine most scrupulously the psychology of this interesting *homme de lettres* . . .

Their books are also different. Works of fiction contain a single plot, with all its imaginable permutations. Those of a philosophical nature invariably include both the thesis and the antithesis, the rigorous pro and con of a doctrine. A book which does not contain its counterbook is considered incomplete.

Centuries and centuries of idealism have not failed to influence reality. In the most ancient regions of Tlön, the duplication of lost objects is not infrequent. Two persons look for a pencil; the first finds it and says nothing; the second finds a second pencil, no less real, but closer to his expectations. These secondary objects are called *hrönir* and are, though awkward in form, somewhat longer. Until recently, the *hrönir* were the accidental products of distraction and forgetfulness. It seems unbelievable that their methodical production dates back scarcely a hundred years, but this is what the Eleventh Volume tells us. The first efforts were unsuccessful. However, the *modus operandi* merits description. The director of one of the state prisons told his inmates that there were certain tombs in an ancient river bed and promised freedom to whoever might make an important discovery. During the months preceding the excavation the inmates were shown photographs of what they were to find. This first effort proved that expectation and anxiety can be inhibitory; a week's work with pick and shovel did not manage to unearth anything in the way of a *hrön* except a rusty wheel of a period posterior to the experiment. But this was kept in secret and the process was repeated later in four schools. In three of them the failure was almost complete; in the fourth (whose director died accidentally during the first excavations) the students unearthed – or produced – a gold mask, an archaic sword, two or three clay urns and the mouldy and mutilated torso of a king whose chest bore an inscription which it has not yet been possible to decipher. Thus was discovered the unreliability of witnesses who knew the experimental nature of the search.... Mass investigations produce contradictory objects; now individual and almost improvised jobs are preferred. The methodical fabrication of *hrönir* (says the Eleventh Volume) has performed prodigious services for archaeologists. It has made possible the interrogation and even the modification of the past, which is now no less plastic and docile than the future. Curiously, the *hrönir* of second and third degree – the *hrönir* derived from another *hrön*, those derived from the *hrön* and a *hrön* – exaggerate the aberrations of the initial one; those of fifth degree are almost uniform; those of ninth degree become confused with those of the second; in those of the eleventh there is a purity of line not found in the original. The process is cyclical: the *hrön* of twelfth degree begins to fall off in quality. Stranger and more pure than any *hrön* is, at times, the *ur*: the object produced through suggestion, educed by hope. The great golden mask I have mentioned is an illustrious example.

Things become duplicated in Tlön; they also tend to become effaced and lose their details when they are forgotten. A classic example is the doorway which survived so long as it was visited by a beggar and disappeared at his death. At times some birds, a horse, have saved the ruins of an amphitheatre.

Postscript (1947). I reproduce the preceding article just as it appeared in the *Anthology of Fantastic Literature* (1940), with no omission other than that of a few metaphors and a kind of sarcastic summary which now seems frivolous. So many things have happened since then.... I shall do no more than recall them here.

In March 1941 a letter written by Gunnar Erfjord was discovered in a book by Hinton which had belonged to Herbert Ashe. The envelope bore a cancellation from Ouro Preto; the letter completely elucidated the mystery of Tlön. Its text corroborated the hypotheses of Martínez Estrada. One night in Lucerne or in London, in the early seventeenth century, the splendid history has its beginning. A secret and benevolent society (among whose members were Dalgarno and later George Berkeley) arose to invent a country. Its vague initial programme included 'hermetic studies', philanthropy and the cabala. From the first period dates the curious book of Andreä. After a few years of secret conclaves and premature syntheses it was understood that one generation was not sufficient to give articulate form to a country. They resolved that each of the masters should elect a disciple who would continue his work. This hereditary arrangement prevailed; after an interval of two centuries the persecuted fraternity sprang up again in America. In 1824, in Memphis (Tennessee), one of its affiliates conferred with the ascetic millionaire Ezra Buckley. The latter, somewhat disdainfully, let him speak – and laughed at the plan's modest scope. He told the agent that in America it was absurd to invent a country and proposed the invention of a planet. To this gigantic idea he added another, a product of his nihilism:* that of keeping the enormous enterprise secret. At that time the twenty volumes of the *Encyclopaedia Britannica* were circulating in the United States; Buckley suggested that a methodical encyclopaedia of the imaginary planet be written. He was to leave them his mountains of gold, his navigable rivers, his pasture lands roamed by cattle and buffalo, his Negroes, his brothels and his dollars, on one condition: 'The work will make no pact with the impostor Jesus Christ.' Buckley did not believe in God, but he wanted to demonstrate to this non-existent God that mortal man was capable of conceiving a world. Buckley was poisoned in Baton Rouge in 1828; in 1914 the society delivered to its collaborators, some three hundred in number, the last volume of the First Encyclopaedia of Tlön. The edition was a secret one; its forty volumes (the vastest undertaking ever carried out by man) would be the basis for another more detailed edition, written not in English but in one of the languages of Tlön. This revision of an illusory world, was called, provisionally, *Orbis Tertius* and one of its modest demiurgi was Herbert Ashe, whether as an agent of Gunnar Erfjord or as an affiliate, I do not know. His having received a copy of the Eleventh Volume would seem to favour the latter assumption. But what about the others?

In 1942 events became more intense. I recall one of the first of these with particular clarity and it seems that I perceived then something of its premonitory character. It happened in an apartment on Laprida Street, facing a high and light balcony which looked out towards the sunset. Princess Faucigny Lucinge had received her silverware from Poitiers. From the vast depths of a box embellished with foreign stamps, delicate immobile objects emerged: silver from Utrecht and Paris covered with hard heraldic fauna, and a samovar. Among them – with the perceptible and tenuous tremor of a sleeping bird – a compass vibrated mysteriously. The Princess did not recog-

* Buckley was a freethinker, a fatalist and a defender of slavery.

nize it. Its blue needle longed for magnetic north; its metal case was concave in shape; the letters around its edge corresponded to one of the alphabets of Tlön. Such was the first intrusion of this fantastic world into the world of reality.

I am still troubled by a stroke of chance which made me the witness of the second intrusion as well. It happened some months later, at a country store owned by a Brazilian in Cuchilla Negra. Amorim and I were returning from Sant' Anna. The River Tacuarembó had flooded and we were obliged to sample (and endure) the proprietor's rudimentary hospitality. He provided us with some creaking cots in a large room cluttered with barrels and hides. We went to bed, but were kept from sleeping until dawn by the drunken ravings of an unseen neighbour, who intermingled inextricable insults with snatches of *milongas* – or rather with snatches of the same *milonga*. As might be supposed, we attributed this insistent uproar to the store owner's fiery cane liquor. By daybreak, the man was dead in the hallway. The roughness of his voice had deceived us : he was only a youth. In his delirium a few coins had fallen from his belt, along with a cone of bright metal, the size of a die In vain a boy tried to pick up this cone. A man was scarcely able to raise it from the ground. I held it in my hand for a few minutes; I remember that its weight was intolerable and that after it was removed, the feeling of oppressiveness remained. I also remember the exact circle it pressed into my palm. This sensation of a very small and at the same time extremely heavy object produced a disagreeable impression of repugnance and fear. One of the local men suggested we throw it into the swollen river; Amorim acquired it for a few pesos. No one knew anything about the dead man, except that 'he came from the border'. These small, very heavy cones (made from a metal which is not of this world) are images of the divinity in certain regions of Tlön.

Here I bring the personal part of my narrative to a close. The rest is in the memory (if not in the hopes or fears) of all my readers. Let it suffice for me to recall or mention the following facts, with a mere brevity of words which the reflective recollection of all will enrich or amplify. Around 1944, a person doing research for the newspaper *The American* (of Nashville, Tennessee) brought to light in a Memphis library the forty volumes of the First Encyclopedia of Tlön. Even today there is a controversy over whether this discovery was accidental or whether it was permitted by the directors of the still nebulous *Orbis Tertius*. The latter is most likely. Some of the incredible aspects of the Eleventh Volume (for example, the multiplication of the *hrönir*) have been eliminated or attenuated in the Memphis copies; it is reasonable to imagine that these omissions follow the plan of exhibiting a world which is not too incompatible with the real world. The dissemination of objects from Tlön over different countries would complement this plan . . .* The fact is that the international press infinitely proclaimed the 'find'. Manuals, anthologies, summaries, literal versions, authorized re-editions and pirated editions of the Greatest Work of Man flooded and still flood the earth. Almost immediately reality yielded on more than one account. The truth is that it longed to yield. Ten years ago any symmetry with a semblance of order – dialectial materialism, anti-Semitism, Nazism – was sufficient to entrance the minds of men. How could one do other than submit to Tlön, to the minute and vast evidence of an orderly planet? It is useless to answer that reality is also orderly. Perhaps it is, but in accordance with divine laws – I translate: inhuman laws – which we never quite grasp. Tlön is surely a labyrinth, but it is a labyrinth devised by men, a labyrinth destined to be deciphered by men.

The contact and the habit of Tlön have disintegrated this world. Enchanted by its rigour, humanity forgets over and again that it is a rigour of chess masters, not of angels. Already the schools have been invaded by the (conjectural) 'primitive language' of Tlön; already the teaching of its harmonious history (filled with moving episodes) has wiped out the one which governed in my childhood; already a fictitious past occu-

* There remains, of course, the problem of the *material* of some objects.

pies in our memories the place of another, a past of which we know nothing with certainty– not even that it is false. Numismatology, pharmacology and archaeology have been reformed. I understand that biology and mathematics also await their avatars. . . . A scattered dynasty of solitary men has changed the face of the world. Their task continues. If our forecasts are not in error, a hundred years from now someone will discover the hundred volumes of the Second Encyclopedia of Tlön.

Then English and French and mere Spanish will disappear from the globe. The world will be Tlön. I pay no attention to all this and go on revising, in the still days at the Adrogué hotel, an uncertain Quevedian translation (which I do not intend to publish) of Browne's *Urn Burial*.

Translated by J.E.I.

The Garden
of Forking Paths

ON page 22 of Liddell Hart's *History of World War I* you will read that an attack against the Serre-Montauban line by thirteen British divisions (supported by 1,400 artillery pieces), planned for 24 July 1916, had to be postponed until the morning of the 29th. The torrential rains, Captain Liddell Hart comments, caused this delay, an insignificant one, to be sure.

The following statement, dictated, reread and signed by Dr Yu Tsun, former professor of English at the *Hochschule* at Tsingtao, throws an unsuspected light over the whole affair. The first two pages of the document are missing.

'... and I hung up the receiver. Immediately afterwards, I recognized the voice that had answered in German. It was that of Captain Richard Madden. Madden's presence in Viktor Runeberg's apartment meant the end of our anxieties and – but this seemed, *or should have seemed*, very secondary to me – also the end of our lives. It meant that Runeberg had been arrested or murdered.* Before the sun set on that day, I would encounter the same fate. Madden was implacable. Or rather, he was obliged to be so. An Irishman at the service of England, a man accused of laxity and perhaps of treason, how could he fail to seize and be thankful for such a miraculous opportunity: the discovery, capture, maybe even the death of two agents of the German Reich? I went up to my room; absurdly I locked the door and threw myself on my back on the narrow

* An hypothesis both hateful and odd. The Prussian spy Hans Rabener, alias Viktor Runeberg, attacked with drawn automatic the bearer of the warrent for his arrest, Captain Richard Madden. The latter, in self-defence, inflicted the wound which brought about Runeberg's death. (Editor's note.)

iron cot. Through the window I saw the familiar roofs and the cloud-shaded six o'clock sun. It seemed incredible to me that that day without premonitions or symbols should be the one of my inexorable death. In spite of my dead father, in spite of having been a child in a symmetrical garden of Hai Feng, was I – now – going to die? Then I reflected that everything happens to a man precisely, precisely *now*. Centuries of centuries and only in the present do things happen; countless men in the air, on the face of the earth and the sea, and all that really is happening is happening to me.... The almost intolerable recollection of Madden's horselike face banished these wanderings. In the midst of my hatred and terror (it means nothing to me now to speak of terror, now that I have mocked Richard Madden, now that my throat yearns for the noose) it occurred to me that that tumultuous and doubtless happy warrior did not suspect that I possessed the Secret. The name of the exact location of the new British artillery park on the River Ancre. A bird streaked across the grey sky and blindly I translated it into an aeroplane and that aeroplane into many (against the French sky) annihilating the artillery station with vertical bombs. If only my mouth, before a bullet shattered it, could cry out that secret name so it could be heard in Germany.... My human voice was very weak. How might I make it carry to the ear of the Chief? To the ear of that sick and hateful man who knew nothing of Runeberg and me save that we were in Staffordshire and who was waiting in vain for our report in his arid office in Berlin, endlessly examining newspapers.... I said out loud: *I must flee.* I sat up noiselessly, in a useless perfection of silence, as if Madden were already lying in wait for me. Something – perhaps the mere vain ostentation of proving my resources were nil – made me look through my pockets. I found what I knew I would find. The American watch, the nickel chain and the square coin, the key ring with the incriminating useless keys to Runeberg's apartment, the notebook, a letter which I resolved to destroy immediately (and which I did not destroy), a crown, two shillings and a few pence, the red and blue pencil, the handkerchief, the revolver with one bullet.

Absurdly, I took it in my hand and weighed it in order to inspire courage within myself. Vaguely I thought that a pistol report can be heard at a great distance. In ten minutes my plan was perfected. The telephone book listed the name of the only person capable of transmitting the message; he lived in a suburb of Fenton, less than a half hour's train ride away.

I am a cowardly man. I say it now, now that I have carried to its end a plan whose perilous nature no one can deny. I know its execution was terrible. I didn't do it for Germany, no. I care nothing for a barbarous country which imposed upon me the abjection of being a spy. Besides, I know of a man from England – a modest man – who for me is no less great than Goethe. I talked with him for scarcely an hour, but during that hour he was Goethe . . . I did it because I sensed that the Chief somehow feared people of my race – for the innumerable ancestors who merge within me. I wanted to prove to him that a yellow man could save his armies. Besides, I had to flee from Captain Madden. His hands and his voice could call at my door at any moment. I dressed silently, bade farewell to myself in the mirror, went downstairs, scrutinized the peaceful street and went out. The station was not far from my home, but I judged it wise to take a cab. I argued that in this way I ran less risk of being recognized; the fact is that in the deserted street I felt myself visible and vulnerable, infinitely so. I remember that I told the cab driver to stop a short distance before the main entrance. I got out with voluntary, almost painful slowness; I was going to the village of Ashgrove but I bought a ticket for a more distant station. The train left within a very few minutes, at eight-fifty. I hurried; the next one would leave at nine-thirty. There was hardly a soul on the platform. I went through the coaches; I remember a few farmers, a woman dressed in mourning, a young boy who was reading with fervour the *Annals* of Tacitus, a wounded and happy soldier. The coaches jerked forward at last. A man whom I recognized ran in vain to the end of the platform. It was Captain Richard Madden. Shattered, trembling, I shrank into the far corner of the seat, away from the dreaded window.

From this broken state I passed into an almost abject felicity. I told myself that the duel had already begun and that I had won the first encounter by frustrating, even if for forty minutes, even if by a stroke of fate, the attack of my adversary. I argued that this slightest of victories foreshadowed a total victory. I argued (no less fallaciously) that my cowardly felicity proved that I was a man capable of carrying out the adventure successfully. From this weakness I took strength that did not abandon me. I foresee that man will resign himself each day to more atrocious undertakings; soon there will be no one but warriors and brigands; I give them this counsel : *The author of an atrocious undertaking ought to imagine that he has already accomplished it, ought to impose upon himself a future as irrevocable as the past.* Thus I proceeded as my eyes of a man already dead registered the elapsing of that day, which was perhaps the last, and the diffusion of the night. The train ran gently along, amid ash trees. It stopped, almost in the middle of the fields. No one announced the name of the station. 'Ashgrove?' I asked a few lads on the platform. 'Ashgrove,' they replied. I got off.

A lamp enlightened the platform but the faces of the boys were in shadow. One questioned me, 'Are you going to Dr Stephen Albert's house?' Without waiting for my answer, another said, 'The house is a long way from here, but you won't get lost if you take this road to the left and at every crossroads turn again to your left.' I tossed them a coin (my last), descended a few stone steps and started down the solitary road. It went downhill, slowly. It was of elemental earth; overhead the branches were tangled; the low full moon seemed to accompany me.

For an instant, I thought that Richard Madden in some way had penetrated my desperate plan. Very quickly, I understood that that was impossible. The instructions to turn always to the left reminded me that such was the common procedure for discovering the central point of certain labyrinths. I have some understanding of labyrinths : not for nothing am I the great grandson of that Ts'ui Pên who was governor of Yunnan and who renounced worldly power in order to write a novel that might be even more populous than the *Hung Lu Meng* and to construct a labyrinth in which all men would become lost. Thirteen years he dedicated to these heterogeneous tasks, but the hand of a stranger murdered him – and his novel was incoherent and no one found the labyrinth. Beneath English trees I meditated on that lost maze : I imagined it inviolate and perfect at the secret crest of a mountain; I imagined it erased by rice fields or beneath the water; I imagined it infinite, no longer composed of octagonal kiosks and returning paths, but of rivers and provinces and kingdoms.... I thought of a labyrinth of labyrinths, of one sinuous spreading labyrinth that would encompass the past and the future and in some way involve the stars. Absorbed in these illusory images, I forgot my destiny of one pursued. I felt myself to be, for an unknown period of time, an abstract perceiver of the world. The vague, living countryside, the moon, the remains of the day worked on me, as well as the slope of the road which eliminated any possibility of weariness. The afternoon was intimate, infinite. The road descended and forked among the now confused meadows. A high-pitched, almost syllabic music approached and receded in the shifting of the wind, dimmed by leaves and distance. I thought that a man can be an enemy of other men, of the moments of other men, but not of a country : not of fireflies, words, gardens, streams of water, sunsets. Thus I arrived before a tall, rusty gate. Between the iron bars I made out a poplar grove and a pavilion. I understood suddenly two things, the first trivial, the second almost unbelievable : the music came from the pavilion, and the music was Chinese. For precisely that reason I had openly accepted it without paying it any heed. I do not remember whether there was a bell or whether I knocked with my hand. The sparkling of the music continued.

From the rear of the house within a lantern approached : a lantern that the trees sometimes striped and sometimes eclipsed, a paper lantern that had the form of a drum and the colour of the moon. A tall man bore it. I didn't see his face for the light blinded me. He opened the door and said slowly, in my own language: 'I see that the pious Hsi P'êng persists in correcting my solitude. You no doubt wish to see the garden?'

I recognized the name of one of our consuls and I replied, disconcerted, 'The garden?'

'The garden of forking paths.'

Something stirred in my memory and I uttered with incomprehensible certainty, 'The garden of my ancestor Ts'ui Pên.'

'Your ancestor? Your illustrious ancestor? Come in.'

The damp path zigzagged like those of my childhood. We came to a library of Eastern and Western books. I recognized bound in yellow silk several volumes of the Lost Encyclopaedia, edited by the Third Emperor of the Luminous Dynasty but never printed. The record on the phonograph revolved next to a bronze phoenix. I also recall a *famille rose* vase and another, many centuries older, of that shade of blue which our craftsmen copied from the potters of Persia ...

Stephen Albert observed me with a smile. He was, as I have said, very tall, sharp-featured, with grey eyes and a grey beard. He told me that he had been a missionary in Tientsin 'before aspiring to become a Sinologist'.

We sat down – I on a long, low divan, he with his back to the window and a tall circular clock. I calculated that my pursuer, Richard Madden, could not arrive for at least an hour. My irrevocable determination could wait.

'An astounding fate, that of Ts'ui Pên,' Stephen Albert said. 'Governor of his native province, learned in astronomy, in astrology and in the tireless interpretation of the canonical books, chess player, famous poet and calligrapher – he abandoned all this in order to compose a book and a maze. He renounced the pleasures of both tyranny and justice, of his populous couch, of his banquets and even of erudition – all to close himself up for thirteen years in the Pavilion of the Limpid Solitude. When he died, his heirs found nothing save chaotic manuscripts. His family, as you may be aware, wished to condemn them to the fire, but his executor – a Taoist or Buddhist monk – insisted on their publication.'

'We descendants of Ts'ui Pên,' I replied, 'continue to curse that monk. Their publication was senseless. The book is an indeterminate heap of contradictory drafts. I examined it once: in the third chapter the hero dies, in the fourth he is alive. As for the other undertaking of Ts'ui Pên, his labyrinth...'

'Here is Ts'ui Pên's labyrinth,' he said, indicating a tall lacquered desk.

'An ivory labyrinth!' I exclaimed. 'A minimum labyrinth.'

'A labyrinth of symbols,' he corrected. 'An invisible labyrinth of time. To me, a barbarous Englishman, has been entrusted the revelation of this diaphanous mystery. After more than a hundred years, the details are irretrievable; but it is not hard to conjecture what happened. Ts'ui Pên must have said once: *I am withdrawing to write a book.* And another time: *I am withdrawing to construct a labyrinth.* Every one imagined two works; to no one did it occur that the book and the maze were one and the same thing. The Pavilion of the Limpid Solitude stood in the centre of a garden that was perhaps intricate; that circumstance could have suggested to the heirs a physical labyrinth. Ts'ui Pên died; no one in the vast territories that were his came upon the labyrinth; the confusion of the novel suggested to me that *it* was the maze. Two circumstances gave me the correct solution of the problem. One: the curious legend that Ts'ui Pên had planned to create a labyrinth which would be strictly infinite. The other: a fragment of a letter I discovered.'

Albert rose. He turned his back on me for a moment; he opened a drawer of the black and gold desk. He faced me and in his hands he held a sheet of paper that had once been crimson, but was now pink and tenuous and cross-sectioned. The fame of Ts'ui Pên as a calligrapher had been justly won. I read, uncomprehendingly and with fervour, these words written with a minute brush by a man of my blood: *I leave to the various futures (not to all) my garden of forking paths.* Wordlessly, I returned the sheet. Albert continued:

'Before unearthing this letter, I had questioned myself about

50

the ways in which a book can be infinite. I could think of nothing other than a cyclic volume, a circular one. A book whose last page was identical with the first, a book which had the possibility of continuing indefinitely. I remembered too that night which is at the middle of the Thousand and One Nights when Scheherazade (through a magical oversight of the copyist) begins to relate word for word the story of the Thousand and One Nights, establishing the risk of coming once again to the night when she must repeat it, and thus on to infinity. I imagined as well a Platonic, hereditary work, transmitted from father to son, in which each new individual adds a chapter or corrects with pious care the pages of his elders. These conjectures diverted me; but none seemed to correspond, not even remotely, to the contradictory chapters of Ts'ui Pên. In the midst of this perplexity, I received from Oxford the manuscript you have examined. I lingered, naturally, on the sentence: *I leave to the various futures (not to all) my garden of forking paths*. Almost instantly, I understood: "the garden of forking paths" was the chaotic novel; the phrase "the various futures (not to all)" suggested to me the forking in time, not in space. A broad rereading of the work confirmed the theory. In all fictional works, each time a man is confronted with several alternatives, he chooses one and eliminates the others; in the fiction of Ts'ui Pên, he chooses – simultaneously – all of them. He creates, in this way, diverse futures, diverse times which themselves also proliferate and fork. Here, then, is the explanation of the novel's contradictions. Fang, let us say, has a secret; a stranger calls at his door; Fang resolves to kill him. Naturally, there are several possible outcomes: Fang can kill the intruder, the intruder can kill Fang, they both can escape, they both can die, and so forth. In the work of Ts'ui Pên, all possible outcomes occur; each one is the point of departure for other forkings. Sometimes, the paths of this labyrinth converge: for example, you arrive at this house, but in one of the possible pasts you are my enemy, in another, my friend. If you will resign yourself to my incurable pronunciation, we shall read a few pages.'

His face, within the vivid circle of the lamplight, was unquestionably that of an old man, but with something unalterable about it, even immortal. He read with slow precision two versions of the same epic chapter. In the first, an army marches to a battle across a lonely mountain; the horror of the rocks and shadows makes the men undervalue their lives and they gain an easy victory. In the second, the same army traverses a palace where a great festival is taking place; the resplendent battle seems to them a continuation of the celebration and they win the victory. I listened with proper veneration to these ancient narratives, perhaps less admirable in themselves than the fact that they had been created by my blood and were being restored to me by a man of remote empire, in the course of a desperate adventure, on a Western isle. I remember the last words, repeated in each version like a secret commandment: *Thus fought the heroes, tranquil their admirable hearts, violent their swords, resigned to kill and to die.*

From that moment on, I felt about me and within my dark body an invisible, intangible swarming. Not the swarming of the divergent, parallel and finally coalescent armies, but a more inaccessible, more intimate agitation that they in some manner prefigured. Stephen Albert continued:

'I don't believe that your illustrious ancestor played idly with these variations. I don't consider it credible that he would sacrifice thirteen years to the infinite execution of a rhetorical experiment. In your country, the novel is a subsidiary form of literature; in Ts'ui Pên's time it was a despicable form. Ts'ui Pên was a brilliant novelist, but he was also a man of letters who doubtless did not consider himself a mere novelist. The testimony of his contemporaries proclaims – and his life fully confirms – his metaphysical and mystical interests. Philosophic controversy usurps a good part of the novel. I know that of all problems, none disturbed him so greatly nor worked upon him so much as the abysmal problem of time. Now then, the latter is the only problem that does not figure in the pages of the *Garden*. He does not even use the word that signifies time. How do you explain this voluntary omission?'

I proposed several solutions – all unsatisfactory. We discussed them. Finally, Stephen Albert said to me:

'In a riddle whose answer is chess, what is the only prohibited word?'

I thought a moment and replied, 'The word *chess*.'

'Precisely,' said Albert. '*The Garden of Forking Paths* is an enormous riddle, or parable, whose theme is time; this recondite cause prohibits its mention. To omit a word always, to resort to inept metaphors and obvious periphrases, is perhaps the most emphatic way of stressing it. That is the tortuous method preferred, in each of the meanderings of his indefatigable novel, by the oblique Ts'ui Pên. I have compared hundreds of manuscripts, I have corrected the errors that the negligence of the copyists has introduced, I have guessed the plan of this chaos, I have re-established – I believe I have re-established – the primordial organization, I have translated the entire work: it is clear to me that not once does he employ the word "time". The explanation is obvious: *The Garden of Forking Paths* is an incomplete, but not false, image of the universe as Ts'ui Pên conceived it. In contrast to Newton and Schopenhauer, your ancestor did not believe in a uniform, absolute time. He believed in an infinite series of times, in a growing, dizzying net of divergent, convergent and parallel times. This network of times which approached one another, forked, broke off, or were unaware of one another for centuries, embraces *all* possibilities of time. We do not exist in the majority of these times; in some you exist, and not I; in others I, and not you; in others, both of us. In the present one, which a favourable fate has granted me, you have arrived at my house; in another, while crossing the garden, you found me dead; in still another, I utter these same words, but I am a mistake, a ghost.'

'In every one,' I pronounced, not without a tremble to my voice, 'I am grateful to you and revere you for your re-creation of the garden of Ts'ui Pên.'

'Not in all,' he murmured with a smile. 'Time forks perpetually towards innumerable futures. In one of them I am your enemy.'

Once again I felt the swarming sensation of which I have spoken. It seemed to me that the humid garden that surrounded the house was infinitely saturated with invisible persons. Those persons were Albert and I, secret, busy and multiform in other dimensions of time. I raised my eyes and the tenuous nightmare dissolved. In the yellow and black garden there was only one man; but this man was as strong as a statue ... this man was approaching along the path and he was Captain Richard Madden.

'The future already exists,' I replied, 'but I am your friend. Could I see the letter again?'

Albert rose. Standing tall, he opened the drawer of the tall desk; for the moment his back was to me. I had readied the revolver. I fired with extreme caution. Albert fell uncomplainingly, immediately. I swear his death was instantaneous – a lightning stroke.

The rest is unreal, insignificant. Madden broke in, arrested me. I have been condemned to the gallows. I have won out abominably; I have communicated to Berlin the secret name of the city they must attack. They bombed it yesterday; I read it in the same papers that offered to England the mystery of the learned Sinologist Stephen Albert who was murdered by a stranger, one Yu Tsun. The Chief had deciphered this mystery. He knew my problem was to indicate (through the uproar of the war) the city called Albert, and that I had found no other means to do so than to kill a man of that name. He does not know (no one can know) my innumerable contrition and weariness.

For Victoria Ocampo   *Translated by D.A.Y.*

The Lottery in Babylon

LIKE all men in Babylon, I have been proconsul; like all, a slave. I have also known omnipotence, opprobrium, imprisonment. Look: the index finger on my right hand is missing. Look: through the rip in my cape you can see a vermilion tattoo on my stomach. It is the second symbol, Beth. This letter, on nights when the moon is full, gives me power over men whose mark is Gimmel, but it subordinates me to the men of Aleph, who on moonless nights owe obedience to those marked with Gimmel. In the half light of dawn, in a cellar, I have cut the jugular vein of sacred bulls before a black stone. During a lunar year I have been declared invisible. I shouted and they did not answer me; I stole bread and they did not behead me. I have known what the Greeks do not know, incertitude. In a bronze chamber, before the silent handkerchief of the strangler, hope has been faithful to me, as has panic in the river of pleasure. Heraclides Ponticus tells with amazement that Pythagoras remembered having been Pyrrhus and before that Euphorbus and before that some other mortal. In order to remember similar vicissitudes I do not need to have recourse to death or even to deception.

I owe this almost atrocious variety to an institution which other republics do not know or which operates in them in an imperfect and secret manner: the lottery. I have not looked into its history; I know that the wise men cannot agree. I know of its powerful purposes what a man who is not versed in astrology can know about the moon. I come from a dizzy land where the lottery is the basis of reality. Until today I have thought as little about it as I have about the conduct of indecipherable divinities or about my heart. Now, far from Babylon and its beloved customs, I think with a certain amount of amazement about the lottery and about the blasphemous conjectures which veiled men murmur in the twilight.

My father used to say that formerly – a matter of centuries, of years? – the lottery in Babylon was a game of plebeian character. He recounted (I don't know whether rightly) that barbers sold, in exchange for copper coins, squares of bone or of parchment adorned with symbols. In broad daylight a drawing took place. Those who won received silver coins without any other test of luck. The system was elementary, as you can see.

Naturally these 'lotteries' failed. Their moral virtue was nil. They were not directed at all of man's faculties, but only at hope. In the face of public indifference, the merchants who founded these venal lotteries began to lose money. Someone tried a reform : The interpolation of a few unfavourable tickets in the list of favourable numbers. By means of this reform, the buyers of numbered squares ran the double risk of winning a sum and of paying a fine that could be considerable. This slight danger (for every thirty favourable numbers there was one unlucky one) awoke, as is natural, the interest of the public. The Babylonians threw themselves into the game. Those who did not acquire chances were considered pusillanimous, cowardly. In time, that justified disdain was doubled. Those who did not play were scorned, but also the losers who paid the fine were scorned. The Company (as it came to be known then) had to take care of the winners, who could not cash in their prizes if almost the total amount of the fines was unpaid. It started a lawsuit against the losers. The judge condemned them to pay the original fine and costs or spend several days in jail. All chose jail in order to defraud the Company. The bravado of a few is the source of the omnipotence of the Company and of its metaphysical and ecclesiastical power.

A little while afterwards the lottery lists omitted the amounts of fines and limited themselves to publishing the days of imprisonment that each unfavourable number indicated. That laconic spirit, almost unnoticed at the time, was of capital importance. *It was the first appearance in the lottery of non-monetary elements.* The success was tremendous. Urged by the clientele, the Company was obliged to increase the unfavourable numbers.

Everyone knows that the people of Babylon are fond of logic and even of symmetry. It was illogical for the lucky numbers to be computed in round coins and the unlucky ones in days and nights of imprisonment. Some moralists reasoned that the possession of money does not always determine happiness and that other forms of happiness are perhaps more direct.

Another concern swept the quarters of the poorer classes. The members of the college of priests multiplied their stakes and enjoyed all the vicissitudes of terror and hope; the poor (with reasonable or unavoidable envy) knew that they were excluded from that notoriously delicious rhythm. The just desire that all, rich and poor, should participate equally in the lottery, inspired an indignant agitation, the memory of which the years have not erased. Some obstinate people did not understand (or pretended not to understand) that it was a question of a new order, of a necessary historical stage. A slave stole a crimson ticket, which in the drawing credited him with the burning of his tongue. The legal code fixed that same penalty for the one who stole a ticket. Some Babylonians argued that he deserved the burning irons in his status of a thief; others, generously, that the executioner should apply it to him because chance had determined it that way. There were disturbances, there were lamentable drawings of blood, but the masses of Babylon finally imposed their will against the opposition of the rich. The people achieved amply its generous purposes. In the first place, it caused the Company to accept total power. (That unification was necessary, given the vastness and complexity of the new operations.) In the second place, it made the lottery secret, free and general. The mercenary sale of chances was abolished. Once initiated in the mysteries of Baal, every free man automatically participated in the sacred drawings, which took place in the labyrinths of the god every sixty nights and which determined his destiny until the next drawing. The consequences were incalculable. A fortunate play could bring about his promotion to the council of wise men or the imprisonment of an enemy (public or private) or finding, in the peaceful darkness of his room, the woman who begins to excite him and whom he never expected to see again. A bad play : mutilation, different kinds of infamy, death. At times one single fact – the vulgar murder of C, the mysterious apotheosis of B – was the happy solution of thirty or forty drawings. To combine the plays was difficult, but one must remember that the individuals of the Company were (and are) omnipotent and astute. In many cases the knowledge that certain happinesses were the simple product of chance would have diminished their virtue. To avoid that obstacle, the agents of the Company made use of the power of suggestion and magic. Their steps, their manoeuvrings, were secret. To find out about the intimate hopes and terrors of each individual, they had astrologists and spies. There were certain stone lions, there was a sacred latrine called Qaphqa, there were fissures in a dusty aqueduct which, according to general opinion, *led to the Company;* malignant or benevolent persons deposited information in these places. An alphabetical file collected these items of varying truthfulness.

Incredibly, there were complaints. The Company, with its usual discretion, did not answer directly. It preferred to scrawl in the rubbish of a mask factory a brief statement which now figures in the sacred scriptures. This doctrinal item observed that the lottery is an interpolation of chance in the order of the world and that to accept errors is not to contradict chance : it is to corroborate it. It likewise observed that those lions and that sacred receptacle, although not disavowed by the Company (which did not abandon the right to consult them), functioned without official guarantee.

This declaration pacified the public's restlessness. It also produced other effects, perhaps unforeseen by its writer. It deeply modified the spirit and the operations of the Company. I don't have much time left; they tell us that the ship is about to weigh anchor. But I shall try to explain it.

However unlikely it might seem, no one had tried out before then a general theory of chance. Babylonians are not very speculative. They revere the judgements of fate, they deliver to them their lives, their hopes, their panic, but it does not occur to them to investigate fate's labyrinthine laws nor the gyratory spheres which reveal it. Nevertheless, the *unofficial* declaration that I have mentioned inspired many discussions of judicial-mathematical character. From some one of them the following conjecture was born : If the lottery is an intensification of chance, a periodical infusion of chaos in the cosmos, would it not be right for chance to intervene in all stages of the drawing and not in one alone? Is it not ridiculous for chance to dictate someone's death and have the circumstances of that death — secrecy, publicity, the fixed time of an hour or a century — not subject to chance? These just scruples finally caused a considerable reform, whose complexities (aggravated by centuries' practice) only a few specialists understand, but which I shall try to summarize, at least in a symbolic way.

Let us imagine a first drawing, which decrees the death of a man. For its fulfilment one proceeds to another drawing, which proposes (let us say) nine possible executors. Of these executors, four can initiate a third drawing which will tell the name of the executioner, two can replace the adverse order with a fortunate one (finding a treasure, let us say), another will intensify the death penalty (that is, will make it infamous or enrich it with tortures), others can refuse to fulfil it. This is the symbolic scheme. In reality *the number of drawings is infinite.* No decision is final, all branch into others. Ignorant people suppose that infinite drawings require an infinite time; actually it is sufficient for time to be infinitely subdivisible, as the famous parable of the contest with the tortoise teaches. This infinity harmonizes admirably with the sinuous numbers of Chance and with the Celestial Archetype of the Lottery, which the Platonists adore. Some warped echo of our rites seems to have resounded on the Tiber : Ellus Lampridius, in the *Life of Antoninus Heliogabalus*, tell that this emperor wrote on shells the lots that were destined for his guests, so that one received ten pounds of gold and another ten flies, ten dormice, ten bears. It is permissible to recall the Heliogabalus was brought up in Asia Minor, among the priests of the eponymous god.

There are also impersonal drawings, with an indefinite purpose. One decrees that a sapphire of Taprobana be thrown into the waters of the Euphrates; another, that a bird be released from the roof of a tower; another, that each century there be withdrawn (or added) a grain of sand from the innumerable ones on the beach. The consequences are, at times, terrible.

Under the beneficent influence of the Company, our customs are saturated with chance. The buyer of a dozen amphoras of Damascene wine will not be surprised if one of them contains a talisman or a snake. The scribe who writes a contract almost never fails to introduce some erroneous information. I myself, in this hasty declaration, have falsified some splendour, some atrocity. Perhaps, also, some mysterious monotony ... Our historians, who are the most penetrating on the globe, have invented a method to correct chance. It is well known that the operations of this method are (in general) reliable, although, naturally, they are not divulged without some portion of deceit. Furthermore, there is nothing so contaminated with fiction as the history of the Company. A palaeographic document, exhumed in a temple, can be the result of yesterday's lottery or of an age-old lottery. No book is published without some discrepancy in each one of the copies. Scribes take a secret oath to omit, to interpolate, to change. The indirect lie is also cultivated.

The Company, with divine modesty, avoids all publicity. Its agents, as is natural, are secret. The orders which it issues continually (perhaps incessantly) do not differ from those lavished by impostors. Moreover, who can brag about being a mere impostor? The drunkard who improvises an absurd order, the dreamer who awakens suddenly and strangles the woman who sleeps at his side, do they not execute, perhaps, a secret decision of the Company? That silent functioning, comparable to God's, gives rise to all sorts of conjectures. One abominably insinuates that the Company has not existed for centuries and

that the sacred disorder of our lives is purely hereditary, traditional. Another judges it eternal and teaches that it will last
until the last night, when the last god annihilates the world.
Another declares that the Company is omnipotent, but that it
only has influence in tiny things: in a bird's call, in the shad-
ings of rust and of dust, in the half dreams of dawn. Another,
in the words of masked heresiarchs, *that it has never existed
and will not exist.* Another, no less vile, reasons that it is
indifferent to affirm or deny the reality of the shadowy cor-
poration, because Babylon is nothing else than an infinite game
of chance.

Translated by John M. Fein

Pierre Menard,
Author of the *Quixote*

THE *visible* work left by this novelist is easily and briefly enumerated. Impardonable, therefore, are the omissions and additions perpetrated by Madame Henri Bachelier in a fallacious catalogue which a certain daily, whose *Protestant* tendency is no secret, has had the inconsideration to inflict upon its deplorable readers – though these be few and Calvinist, if not Masonic and circumcized. The true friends of Menard have viewed this catalogue with alarm and even with a certain melancholy. One might say that only yesterday we gathered before his final monument, amidst the lugubrious cypresses, and already Error tries to tarnish his Memory.... Decidedly, a brief rectification is unavoidable.

I am aware that it is quite easy to challenge my slight authority. I hope, however, that I shall not be prohibited from mentioning two eminent testimonies. The Baroness de Bacourt (at whose unforgettable *vendredis* I had the honour of meeting the lamented poet) has seen fit to approve the pages which follow. The Countess de Bagnoregio, one of the most delicate spirits of the Principality of Monaco (and now of Pittsburgh, Pennsylvania, following her recent marriage to the international philanthropist Simon Kautzsch, who has been so inconsiderately slandered, alas! by the victims of his disinterested manoeuvres) has sacrificed 'to veracity and to death' (such were her words) the stately reserve which is her distinction, and, in an open letter published in the magazine *Luxe*, concedes me her approval as well. These authorizations, I think, are not entirely insufficient.

I have said that Menard's visible work can be easily enumerated. Having examined with care his personal files, I find that they contain the following items :

a) A Symbolist sonnet which appeared twice (with variants) in the review *La conque* (issues of March and October 1899).

b) A monograph on the possibility of constructing a poetic vocabulary of concepts which would not be synonyms or periphrases of those which make up our everyday language, 'but rather ideal objects created according to convention and essentially designed to satisfy poetic needs' (Nîmes, 1901).

c) A monograph on 'certain connexions or affinities' between the thought of Descartes, Leibniz and John Wilkins (Nîmes, 1903).

d) A monograph on Leibniz's *Characteristica universalis* (Nîmes, 1904).

e) A technical article on the possibility of improving the game of chess, eliminating one of the rook's pawns. Menard proposes, recommends, discusses and finally rejects this innovation.

f) A monograph on Raymond Lully's *Ars magna generalis* (Nîmes, 1906).

g) A translation, with prologue and notes, of Ruy López de Segura's *Libro de la invención liberal y arte del juego del axedrez* (Paris, 1907).

h) The work sheets of a monograph on George Boole's symbolic logic.

i) An examination of the essential metric laws of French prose, illustrated with examples taken from Saint-Simon (*Revue des langues romanes*, Montpellier, October 1909).

j) A reply to Luc Durtain (who had denied the existence of such laws), illustrated with examples from Luc Durtain (*Revue des langues romanes*, Montpellier, December 1909).

k) A manuscript translation of the *Aguja de navegar cultos* of Quevedo, entitled *La boussole des précieux*.

l) A preface to the Catalogue of an exposition of lithographs by Carolus Hourcade (Nîmes, 1914).

m) The work *Les problèmes d'un problème* (Paris, 1917), which discusses, in chronological order, the different solutions given to the illustrious problem of Achilles and the tortoise. Two editions of this book have appeared so far; the second bears as an epigraph Leibniz's recommendation '*Ne craignez point, monsieur, la tortue*' and revises the chapters dedicated to Russell and Descartes.

n) A determined analysis of the 'syntactical customs' of Toulet (*N. R. F.*, March 1921). Menard – I recall – declared that censure and praise are sentimental operations which have nothing to do with literary criticism.

o) A transposition into alexandrines of Paul Valéry's *Le cimetière marin* (*N. R. F.*, January 1928).

p) An invective against Paul Valéry, in the *Papers for the Suppression of Reality* of Jacques Reboul. (This invective, we might say parenthetically, is the exact opposite of his true opinion of Valéry. The latter understood it as such and their old friendship was not endangered.)

q) A 'definition' of the Countess de Bagnoregio, in the 'victorious volume' – the locution is Gabriele d'Annunzio's, another of its collaborators – published annually by this lady to rectify the inevitable falsifications of journalists and to present 'to the world and to Italy' an authentic image of her person, so often exposed (by very reason of her beauty and her activities) to erroneous or hasty interpretations.

r) A cycle of admirable sonnets for the Baroness de Bacourt (1934).

s) A manuscript list of verses which owe their efficacy to their punctuation.*

* Madame Henri Bachelier also lists a literal translation of Quevedo's literal translation of the *Introduction à la vie dévote* of

This, then, is the *visible* work of Menard, in chronological order (with no omission other than a few vague sonnets of circumstance written for the hospitable, or avid, album of Madame Henri Bachelier). I turn now to his other work: the subterranean, the interminably heroic, the peerless. And – such are the capacities of man! – the unfinished. This work, perhaps the most significant of our time, consists of the ninth and thirty-eighth chapters of the first part of *Don Quixote* and a fragment of chapter twenty-two. I know such an affirmation seems an absurdity; to justify this 'absurdity' is the primordial object of this note.*

Two texts of unequal value inspired this undertaking. One is that philological fragment by Novalis – the one numbered 2005 in the Dresden edition – which outlines the theme of a *total* identification with a given author. The other is one of those parasitic books which situate Christ on a boulevard, Hamlet on La Cannebière or Don Quixote on Wall Street. Like all men of good taste, Menard abhorred these useless carnivals, fit only – as he would say – to produce the plebeian pleasure of anachronism or (what is worse) to enthral us with the elementary idea that all epochs are the same or are different. More interesting, though contradictory and superficial of execution, seemed to him the famous plan of Daudet: to conjoin the Ingenious Gentleman and his squire in *one* figure, which was Tartarin.... Those who have insinuated that Menard dedicated his life to writing a contemporary *Quixote* calumniate his illustrious memory.

He did not want to compose another *Quixote* – which is easy – but *the Quixote itself*. Needless to say, he never contemplated a mechanical transcription of the original; he did not propose

---

St Francis of Sales. There are no traces of such a work in Menard's library. It must have been a jest of our friend, misunderstood by the lady.

*I also had the secondary intention of sketching a personal portrait of Pierre Menard. But how could I dare to compete with the golden pages which, I am told, the Baroness de Bacourt is preparing or with the delicate and punctual pencil of Carolus Hourcade?

to copy it. His admirable intention was to produce a few pages which would coincide – word for word and line for line – with those of Miguel de Cervantes.

'My intent is no more than astonishing,' he wrote me the 30 September 1934, from Bayonne. 'The final term in a theological or metaphysical demonstration – the objective world, God, causality, the forms of the universe – is no less previous and common than my famed novel. The only difference is that the philosophers publish the intermediary stages of their labour in pleasant volumes and I have resolved to do away with those stages.' In truth, not one worksheet remains to bear witness to his years of effort.

The first method he conceived was relatively simple. Know Spanish well, recover the Catholic faith, fight against the Moors or the Turk, forget the history of Europe beteen the years 1602 and 1918, *be* Miguel de Cervantes. Pierre Menard studied this procedure (I know he attained a fairly accurate command of seventeenth-century Spanish) but discarded it as too easy. Rather as impossible! my reader will say. Granted, but the undertaking was impossible from the very beginning and of all the impossible ways of carrying it out, this was the least interesting. To be, in the twentieth century, a popular novelist of the seventeenth seemed to him a diminution. To be, in some way, Cervantes and reach the *Quixote* seemed less arduous to him – and, consequently, less interesting – than to go on being Pierre Menard and reach the *Quixote* through the experiences of Pierre Menard. (This conviction, we might say in passing, made him omit the autobiographical prologue to the second part of *Don Quixote.* To include that prologue would have been to create another character – Cervantes – but it would also have meant presenting the *Quixote* in terms of that character and not of Menard. The latter, naturally, declined that facility.) 'My undertaking is not difficult, essentially,' I read in another part of his letter. 'I should only have to be immortal to carry it out.' Shall I confess that I often imagine he did finish it and that I read the *Quixote* – all of it – as if Menard had conceived it? Some nights past, while leafing through chapter XXVI – never essayed by him – I recognized our friend's style and something of his voice in this exceptional phrase : 'the river nymphs and the dolorous and humid Echo.' This happy conjunction of a spiritual and a physical adjective brought to my mind a verse by Shakespeare which we discussed one afternoon :

> Where a malignant and a turbaned Turk ...

But why precisely the *Quixote*? our reader will ask. Such a preference, in a Spaniard, would not have been inexplicable; but it is, no doubt, in a Symbolist from Nîmes, essentially a devoté of Poe, who engendered Baudelaire, who engendered Mallarmé, who engendered Valéry, who engendered Edmond Teste. The aforementioned letter illuminates this point. 'The *Quixote*,' clarifies Menard, 'interests me deeply, but it does not seem – how shall I say it? – inevitable. I cannot imagine the universe without Edgar Allan Poe's exclamation :

> Ah, bear in mind this garden was enchanted!

or without the *Bateau ivre* or the *Ancient Mariner*, but I am quite capable of imagining it without the *Quixote*. (I speak, naturally, of my personal capacity and not of those works' historical resonance.) The *Quixote* is a contingent book; the *Quixote* is unnecessary. I can premeditate writing it, I can write it, without falling into a tautology. When I was ten or twelve years old, I read it, perhaps in its entirety. Later, I have reread closely certain chapters, those which I shall not attempt for the time being. I have also gone through the interludes, the plays, the *Galatea*, the exemplary novels, the undoubtedly laborious tribulations of Persiles and Segismunda and the *Viaje del Parnaso* ... My general recollection of the *Quixote*, simplified by forgetfulness and indifference, can well equal the imprecise and prior image of a book not yet written. Once that image (which no one can legitimately deny me) is postulated, it is certain that my problem is a good bit more difficult than Cervantes' was. My obliging predecessor did not refuse the collaboration of chance : he composed his immortal work somewhat *à la diable*, carried along by the inertias of language and invention. I have taken on the mysterious duty of reconstructing literally his spontaneous work. My solitary game is governed by two polar laws. The first permits me to essay variations of a formal or psychological type; the second obliges me to sacrifice these variations to the 'original' text and reason out this annihilation in an irrefutable manner.... To these artificial hindrances, another – of a congenital kind – must be added. To compose the *Quixote* at the beginning of the seventeenth century was a reasonable undertaking, necessary and perhaps even unavoidable; at the beginning of the twentieth, it is almost impossible. It is not in vain that three hundred years have gone by, filled with exceedingly complex events. Among them, to mention only one, is the *Quixote* itself.'

In spite of these three obstacles, Menard's fragmentary *Quixote* is more subtle than Cervantes'. The latter, in a clumsy fashion, opposes to the fictions of chivalry the tawdry provincial reality of his country; Menard selects as his 'reality' the land of Carmen during the century of Lepanto and Lope de Vega. What a series of *espagnolades* that selection would have suggested to Maurice Barrès or Dr Rodríguez Larreta! Menard eludes them with complete naturalness In his work there are no gipsy flourishes or conquistadors or mystics or Philip the Seconds or *autos da fé*. He neglects or eliminates local colour. This disdain points to a new conception of the historical novel. This disdain condemns *Salammbô*, with no possibility of appeal.

It is no less astounding to consider isolated chapters. For example, let us examine Chapter XXXVIII of the first part, 'which treats of the curious discourse of Don Quixote on arms and letters'. It is well known that Don Quixote (like Quevedo in an analogous and later passage in *La hora de todos*) decided the debate against letters and in favour of arms. Cervantes was a former soldier : his verdict is understandable. But that Pierre Menard's Don Quixote – a contemporary of *La trahison des clercs* and Bertrand Russell – should fall prey to such nebulous sophistries! Madame Bachelier has seen here an admirable and typical subordination on the part of the author to the hero's psychology; others (not at all perspicaciously), a *transcription* of the *Quixote*; the Baroness de Bacourt, the influence of Nietzsche. To this third interpretation (which I judge to be irrefutable) I am not sure I dare to add a fourth, which concords very well with the almost divine modesty of Pierre Menard: his resigned or ironical habit of propagating ideas which were the strict reverse of those he preferred. (Let us recall once more his diatribe against Paul Valéry in Jacques Reboul's ephemeral Surrealist sheet.) Cervantes's text and Menard's are verbally identical, but the second is almost infinitely richer. (More ambiguous, his detractors will say, but ambiguity is richness.)

It is a revelation to compare Menard's *Don Quixote* with Cervantes's. The latter, for example, wrote (part one, chapter nine):

... truth, whose mother is history, rival of time, depository of deeds, witness of the past, exemplar and adviser to the present, and the future's counsellor.

Written in the seventeenth century, written by the 'lay genius' Cervantes, this enumeration is a mere rhetorical praise of history. Menard, on the other, writes:

... truth, whose mother is history, rival of time, depository of deeds, witness of the past, exemplar and adviser to the present, and the future's counsellor.

History, the *mother* of truth: the idea is astounding. Menard, a contemporary of William James, does not define history as an inquiry into reality but as its origin. Historical truth, for him, is not what has happened; it is what we judge to have happened. The final phrases — *exemplar and adviser to the present, and the future's counsellor* — are brazenly pragmatic.

The contrast in style is also vivid. The archaic style of Menard — quite foreign, after all — suffers from a certain affectation. Not so that of his forerunner, who handles with ease the current Spanish of his time.

There is no exercise of the intellect which is not, in the final analysis, useless. A philosophical doctrine begins as a plausible description of the universe; with the passage of the years it becomes a mere chapter – if not a paragraph or a name – in the history of philosophy. In literature, this eventual caducity is even more notorious. The *Quixote* – Menard told me – was, above all, an entertaining book; now it is the occasion for patriotic toasts, grammatical insolence and obscene de luxe editions. Fame is a form of incomprehension, perhaps the worst.

There is nothing new in these nihilistic verifications; what is singular is the determination Menard derived from them. He decided to anticipate the vanity awaiting all man's efforts; he set himself to an undertaking which was exceedingly complex and, from the very beginning, futile. He dedicated his scruples and his sleepless nights to repeating an already extant book in an alien tongue. He multiplied draft upon draft, revised tenaciously and tore up thousands of manuscript pages.* He did not let anyone examine these drafts and took care they should not survive him. In vain have I tried to reconstruct them.

I have reflected that it is permissible to see in this 'final' *Quixote* a kind of palimpsest, through which the traces – tenuous but not indecipherable – of our friend's 'previous' writing should be translucently visible. Unfortunately, only a second Pierre Menard, inverting the other's work, would be able to exhume and revive those lost Troys . . .

'Thinking, analysing, inventing (he also wrote me) are not anomalous acts; they are the normal respiration of the intelligence. To glorify the occasional performance of that function, to hoard ancient and alien thoughts, to recall with incredulous stupor what the *doctor universalis* thought, is to confess our laziness or our barbarity. Every man should be capable of all ideas and I understand that in the future this will be the case.'

*I remember his quadricular notebooks, his black crossed-out passages, his peculiar typographical symbols and his insect-like handwriting. In the afternoons he liked to go out for a walk around the outskirts of Nîmes; he would take a notebook with him and make a merry bonfire.

Pierre Menard, Author of the Quixote

Menard (perhaps without wanting to) has enriched, by means of a new technique, the halting and rudimentary art of reading: this new technique is that of the deliberate anachronism and the erroneous attribution. This technique, whose applications are infinite, prompts us to go through the *Odyssey* as if it were posterior to the *Aeneid* and the book *Le jardin du Centaure* of Madame Henri Bachelier as if it were by Madame Henri Bachelier. This technique fills the most placid works with adventure. To attribute the *Imitatio Christi* to Louis Ferdinand Céline or to James Joyce, is this not a sufficient renovation of its tenuous spiritual indications?

For Silvina Ocampo   *Translated by J.E.I.*

The Circular Ruins

And if he let off dreaming about you ...
Through the Looking Glass, VI

No one saw him disembark in the unanimous night, no one saw the bamboo canoe sinking into the sacred mud, but within a few days no one was unaware that the silent man came from the South and that his home was one of the infinite villages upstream, on the violent mountainside, where the Zend tongue is not contaminated with Greek and where leprosy is infrequent. The truth is that the obscure man kissed the mud, came up the bank without pushing aside (probably without feeling) the brambles which dilacerated his flesh, and dragged himself, nauseous and bloodstained, to the circular enclosure crowned by a stone tiger or horse, which once was the colour of fire and now was that of ashes. This circle was a temple, long ago devoured by fire, which the malarial jungle had profaned and whose god no longer received the homage of men. The stranger stretched out beneath the pedestal. He was awakened by the sun high above. He evidenced without astonishment that this wounds had closed; he shut his pale eyes and slept, not out of bodily weakness but out of determination of will. He knew that this temple was the place required by his invincible purpose; he knew that, downstream, the incessant trees had not managed to choke the ruins of another propitious temple, whose gods were also burned and dead; he knew that his immediate obligation was to sleep. Towards midnight he was awakened by the disconsolate cry of a bird. Prints of bare feet, some figs and a jug told him that men of the region had respectfully spied upon his sleep and were solicitous of his favour or feared his magic. He felt the chill of fear and sought out a burial niche in the dilapidated wall and covered himself with some unknown leaves

The purpose which guided him was not impossible, though it was supernatural. He wanted to dream a man : he wanted to dream him with minute integrity and insert him into reality. This magical project had exhausted the entire content of his soul; if someone had asked him his own name or any trait of his previous life, he would not have been able to answer. The uninhabited and broken temple suited him, for it was a minimum of visible world; the nearness of the peasants also suited him, for they would see that his frugal necessities were supplied. The rice and fruit of their tribute were sufficient sustenance for his body, consecrated to the sole task of sleeping and dreaming.

At first, his dreams were chaotic; somewhat later, they were of a dialectical nature. The stranger dreamt that he was in the centre of a circular amphitheatre which in some way was the burned temple : clouds of silent students filled the gradins; the faces of the last ones hung many centuries away and at a cosmic height, but were entirely clear and precise. The man was lecturing to them on anatomy, cosmography, magic; the countenances listened with eagerness and strove to respond with understanding, as if they divined the importance of the examination which would redeem one of them from his state of vain appearance and interpolate him into the world of reality. The man, both in dreams and awake, considered his phantoms' replies, was not deceived by impostors, divined a growing intelligence in certain perplexities. He sought a soul which would merit participation in the universe.

After nine or ten nights, he comprehended with some bitterness that he could expect nothing of those students who passively accepted his doctrines, but that he could of those who, at times, would venture a reasonable contradiction. The former, though worthy of love and affection, could not rise to the state of individuals; the latter pre-existed somewhat more. One afternoon (now his afternoons too were tributaries of sleep, now he remained awake only for a couple of hours at dawn) he dismissed the vast illusory college for ever and kept one single student. He was a silent boy, sallow, sometimes obstinate, with sharp features which reproduced those of the dreamer. He was not long disconcerted by his companions' sudden elimination; his progress, after a few special lessons, astounded his teacher. Nevertheless, catastrophe ensued. The man emerged from sleep one day as if from a viscous desert, looked at the vain light of afternoon, which at first he confused with that of dawn, and understood that he had not really dreamt. All that night and all day, the intolerable lucidity of insomnia weighed upon him. He tried to explore the jungle, to exhaust himself; amidst the hemlocks, he was scarcely able to manage a few snatches of feeble sleep, fleetingly mottled with some rudimentary visions which were useless. He tried to convoke the college and had scarcely uttered a few brief words of exhortation, when it became deformed and was extinguished. In his almost perpetual sleeplessness, his old eyes burned with tears of anger.

He comprehended that the effort to mould the incoherent and vertiginous matter dreams are made of was the most arduous task a man could undertake, though he might penetrate all enigmas of the upper and lower orders: much more arduous than weaving a rope of sand or coining the faceless wind. He comprehended that an initial failure was inevitable. He swore he would forget the enormous hallucination which had misled him at first, and he sought another method. Before putting it into effect, he dedicated a month to replenishing the powers his delirium had wasted. He abandoned any premeditation of dreaming and, almost at once, was able to sleep for a considerable part of the day. The few times he dreamt during this period, he did not take notice of the dreams. To take up his task again, he waited until the moon's disk was perfect. Then, in the afternoon, he purified himself in the waters of the river, worshipped the planetary gods, uttered the lawful syllables of a powerful name and slept. Almost immediately, he dreamt of a beating heart.

He dreamt it as active, warm, secret, the size of a closed fist, of garnet colour in the penumbra of a human body as yet without face or sex; with minute love he dreamt it, for fourteen lucid nights. Each night he perceived it with greater clarity. He did not touch it, but limited himself to witnessing it, observing it, perhaps correcting it with his eyes. He perceived it, lived it, from many distances and many angles. On the fourteenth night he touched the pulmonary artery with his finger, and then the whole heart, inside and out. The examination satisfied him. Deliberately, he did not dream for a night; then he took the heart again, invoked the name of a planet and set about to envision another of the principal organs. Within a year he reached the skeleton, the eyelids. The innumerable hair was perhaps the most difficult task. He dreamt a complete man, a youth, but this youth could not rise nor did he speak nor could he open his eyes. Night after night, the man dreamt him as asleep.

In the Gnostic cosmogonies, the demiurgi knead and mould a red Adam who cannot stand alone; as unskilful and crude and elementary as this Adam of dust was the Adam of dreams fabricated by the magician's nights of effort. One afternoon, the man almost destroyed his work, but then repented. (It would have been better for him had he destroyed it.) Once he had completed his supplications to the numina of the earth and the river, he threw himself down at the feet of the effigy which was perhaps a tiger and perhaps a horse, and implored its unknown succour. That twilight, he dreamt of the statue. He dreamt of it as a living, tremulous thing : it was not an atrocious mongrel of tiger and horse, but both these vehement creatures at once and also a bull, a rose, a tempest. This multiple god revealed to him that its earthly name was Fire, that in the circular temple (and in others of its kind) people had rendered it sacrifices and cult and that it would magically give life to the sleeping phantom, in such a way that all creatures except Fire itself and the dreamer would believe him to be a man of flesh and blood. The man was ordered by the divinity to instruct his creature in its rites, and send him to the other broken temple whose pyramids survived downstream, so that in this deserted edifice a voice might give glory to the god. In the dreamer's dream, the dreamed one awoke.

The magician carried out these orders. He devoted a period of time (which finally comprised two years) to revealing the arcana of the universe and of the fire cult to his dream child. Inwardly, it pained him to be separated from the boy. Under the pretext of pedagogical necessity, each day he prolonged the hours he dedicated to his dreams. He also redid the right shoulder, which was perhaps deficient. At times, he was troubled by the impression that all this had happened before.... In general, his days were happy; when he closed his eyes, he would think: *Now I shall be with my son.* Or, less often: *The child I have engendered awaits me and will not exist if I do not go to him.*

Gradually, he accustomed the boy to reality. Once he ordered him to place a banner on a distant peak. The following day, the banner flickered from the mountain top. He tried other analogous experiments, each more daring than the last. He understood with certain bitterness that his son was ready – and perhaps impatient – to be born. That night he kissed him for the first time and sent him to the other temple whose debris showed white downstream, through many leagues of inextricable jungle and swamp. But first (so that he would never know he was a phantom, so that he would be thought a man like others) he instilled into him a complete oblivion of his years of apprenticeship.

The man's victory and peace were dimmed by weariness. At dawn and at twilight, he would prostrate himself before the stone figure, imagining perhaps that his unreal child was practising the same rites, in other circular ruins, downstream; at night, he would not dream, or would dream only as all men do. He perceived the sounds and forms of the universe with a certain colourlessness: his absent son was being nurtured with these diminutions of his soul. His life's purpose was complete; the man persisted in a kind of ecstasy. After a time, which some narrators of his story prefer to compute in years and

others in lustra, he was awakened one midnight by two boat-
men; he could not see their faces, but they told him of a magic
man in a temple of the North who could walk upon fire and
not be burned. The magician suddenly remembered the words
of the god. He recalled that, of all the creatures of the world,
fire was the only one that knew his son was a phantom. This
recollection, at first soothing, finally tormented him. He feared
his son might meditate on his abnormal privilege and discover
in some way that his condition was that of a mere image. Not
to be a man, to be the projection of another man's dream, what
a feeling of humiliation, of vertigo! All fathers are interested
in the children they have procreated (they have permitted to
exist) in mere confusion or pleasure; it was natural that the
magician should fear for the future of that son, created in
thought, limb by limb and feature by feature, in a thousand
and one secret nights.

The end of his meditations was sudden, though it was fore-
told in certain signs. First (after a long drought) a faraway
cloud on a hill, light and rapid as a bird; then, towards the
south, the sky which had the rose colour of the leopard's
mouth; then the smoke which corroded the metallic nights;
finally, the panicky flight of the animals. For what was happening had happened many centuries ago. The ruins of the fire
god's sanctuary were destroyed by fire. In a birdless dawn the
magician saw the concentric blaze close round the walls. For a
moment, he thought of taking refuge in the river, but then he
knew that death was coming to crown his old age and absolve
him of his labours. He walked into the shreds of flame. But
they did not bite into his flesh, they caressed him and engulfed
him without heat or combustion. With relief, with humiliation, with terror, he understood that he too was a mere
appearance, dreamt by another.

Translated by J.E.I.

The Library of Babel

By this art you may contemplate the variation of the 23 letters . . .

The Anatomy of Melancholy,
part 2, sect. II, mem. IV

THE universe (which others call the Library) is composed of an indefinite and perhaps infinite number of hexagonal galleries, with vast air shafts between, surrounded by very low railings. From any of the hexagons one can see, interminably, the upper and lower floors. The distribution of the galleries is invariable. Twenty shelves, five long shelves per side, cover all the sides except two; their height, which is the distance from floor to ceiling, scarcely exceeds that of a normal bookcase. One of the free sides leads to a narrow hallway which opens on to another gallery, identical to the first and to all the rest. To the left and right of the hallway there are two very small closets. In the first, one may sleep standing up; in the other, satisfy one's fecal necessities. Also through here passes a spiral stairway, which sinks abysmally and soars upwards to remote distances. In the hallway there is a mirror which faithfully duplicates all appearances. Men usually infer from this mirror that the Library is not infinite (if it really were, why this illusory duplication?); I prefer to dream that its polished surfaces represent and promise the infinite. . . . Light is provided by some spherical fruit which bear the name of lamps. There are two, transversally placed, in each hexagon. The light they emit is insufficient, incessant.

Like all men of the Library, I have travelled in my youth; I have wandered in search of a book, perhaps the catalogue of catalogues; now that my eyes can hardly decipher what I write, I am preparing to die just a few leagues from the hexagon in which I was born. Once I am dead, there will be no lack of pious hands to throw me over the railing; my grave will be the fathomless air; my body will sink endlessly and decay and dissolve in the wind generated by the fall, which is infinite. I say that the Library is unending. The idealists argue that the hexagonal rooms are a necessary form of absolute space or, at least, of our intuition of space. They reason that a triangular or pentagonal room is inconceivable (The mystics claim that their ecstasy reveals to them a circular chamber containing a great circular book, whose spine is continuous and which follows the complete circle of the walls; but their testimony is suspect; their words, obscure. This cyclical book is God.) Let it suffice now for me to repeat the classic dictum: *The Library is a sphere whose exact centre is any one of its hexagons and whose circumference is inaccessible.*

There are five shelves for each of the hexagon's walls; each shelf contains thirty-five books of uniform format; each book is of four hundred and ten pages; each page, of forty lines, each line, of some eighty letters which are black in colour. There are also letters on the spine of each book; these letters do not indicate or prefigure what the pages will say. I know that this incoherence at one time seemed mysterious. Before summarizing the solution (whose discovery, in spite of its tragic projections, is perhaps the capital fact in history) I wish to recall a few axioms.

First: The Library exists *ab aeterno*. This truth, whose immediate corollary is the future eternity of the world, cannot be placed in doubt by any reasonable mind. Man, the imperfect librarian, may be the product of chance or of malevolent demiurgi; the universe, with its elegant endowment of shelves, of enigmatical volumes, of inexhaustible stairways for the traveller and latrines for the seated librarian, can only be the work of a god. To perceive the distance between the divine and the human, it is enough to compare these crude wavering symbols which my fallible hand scrawls on the cover of a book, with the organic letters inside: punctual, delicate, perfectly black, inimitably symmetrical.

Second: *The orthographical symbols are twenty-five in number.** This finding made it possible, three hundred years ago, to formulate a general theory of the Library and solve satisfactorily the problem which no conjecture had deciphered: the formless and chaotic nature of almost all the books. One which my father saw in a hexagon on circuit fifteen ninety-four was made up of the letters MCV, perversely repeated from the first line to the last. Another (very much consulted in this area) is a mere labyrinth of letters, but the next-to-last page says *Oh time thy pyramids.* This much is already known: for every sensible line of straightforward statement, there are leagues of senseless cacophonies, verbal jumbles and incoherences. (I know of an uncouth region whose librarians repudiate the vain and superstitious custom of finding a meaning in books and equate it with that of finding a meaning in dreams or in the chaotic lines of one's palm. . . . They admit that the inventors of this writing imitated the twenty-five natural symbols, but maintain that this application is accidental and that the books signify nothing in themselves. This dictum, we shall see, is not entirely fallacious.)

For a long time it was believed that these impenetrable books corresponded to past or remote languages. It is true that the most ancient men, the first librarians, used a language quite different from the one we now speak; it is true that a few miles to the right the tongue is dialectal and that ninety floors farther up, it is incomprehensible. All this, I repeat, is true, but four hundred and ten pages of inalterable MCV's cannot correspond to any language, no matter how dialectal or rudimentary it may be. Some insinuated that each letter could influence the following one and that the value of MCV in the third line of

*The original manuscript does not contain digits or capital letters. The punctuation has been limited to the comma and the period. These two signs, the space and the twenty-two letters of the alphabet are the twenty-five symbols considered sufficient by this unknown author (*Editor's note.*)

page 71 was not the one the same series may have in another position on another page, but this vague thesis did not prevail. Others thought of cryptographs; generally, this conjecture has been accepted, though not in the sense in which it was formulated by its originators.

Five hundred years ago, the chief of an upper hexagon* came upon a book as confusing as the others, but which had nearly two pages of homogeneous lines. He showed his find to a wandering decoder who told him the lines were written in Portuguese; others said they were Yiddish. Within a century, the language was established: a Samoyedic Lithuanian dialect of Guarani, with classical Arabian inflections. The content was also deciphered: some notions of combinative analysis, illustrated with examples of variation with unlimited repetition. These examples made it possible for a librarian of genius to discover the fundamental law of the Library. This thinker observed that all the books, no matter how diverse they might be, are made up of the same elements: the space, the period, the comma, the twenty-two letters of the alphabet. He also alleged a fact which travellers have confirmed: *In the vast Library there are no two identical books.* From these two incontrovertible premises he deduced that the Library is total and that its shelves register all the possible combinations of the twenty-odd orthographical symbols (a number which, though extremely vast, is not infinite): in other words, all that it is given to express, in all languages. Everything: the minutely detailed history of the future, the archangels' autobiographies, the faithful catalogue of the Library, thousands and thousands of false catalogues, the demonstration of the fallacy of those catalogues, the demonstration of the fallacy of the true catalogue, the Gnostic gospel of Basilides, the commentary on that gospel, the commentary on the commentary on that

* Before, there was a man for every three hexagons. Suicide and pulmonary diseases have destroyed that proportion. A memory of unspeakable melancholy   at times I have travelled for many nights through corridors and along polished stairways without finding a single librarian.

gospel, the true story of your death, the translation of every book in all languages, the interpolations of every book in all books.

When it was proclaimed that the Library contained all books, the first impression was one of extravagant happiness. All men felt themselves to be the masters of an intact and secret treasure. There was no personal or world problem whose eloquent solution did not exist in some hexagon. The universe was justified, the universe suddenly usurped the unlimited dimensions of hope. At that time a great deal was said about the Vindications: books of apology and prophecy which vindicated for all time the acts of every man in the universe and retained prodigious arcana for his future. Thousands of the greedy abandoned their sweet native hexagons and rushed up the stairways, urged on by the vain intention of finding their Vindication. These pilgrims disputed in the narrow corridors, proffered dark curses, strangled each other on the divine stairways, flung the deceptive books into the air shafts, met their death cast down in a similar fashion by the inhabitants of remote regions. Others went mad ... The Vindications exist (I have seen two which refer to persons of the future, to persons who perhaps are not imaginary) but the searchers did not remember that the possibility of a man's finding his Vindication, or some treacherous variation thereof, can be computed as zero.

At that time it was also hoped that a clarification of humanity's basic mysteries – the origin of the Library and of time – might be found. It is verisimilar that these grave mysteries could be explained in words: if the language of philosophers is not sufficient, the multiform Library will have produced the unprecedented language required, with its vocabularies and grammars. For four centuries now men have exhausted the hexagons ... There are official searchers, *inquisitors*. I have seen them in the performance of their function: they always arrive extremely tired from their journeys; they speak of a broken stairway which almost killed them; they talk with the librarian of galleries and stairs; sometimes they pick up the nearest volume and leaf through it, looking for infamous words. Obviously, no one expects to discover anything.

As was natural, this inordinate hope was followed by an excessive depression. The certitude that some shelf in some hexagon held precious books and that these precious books were inaccessible, seemed almost intolerable. A blasphemous sect suggested that the searchers should cease and that all men should juggle letters and symbols until they constructed, by an improbable gift of chance, these canonical books. The authorities were obliged to issue severe orders. The sect disappeared, but in my childhood I have seen old men who, for long periods of time, would hide in the latrines with some metal disks in a forbidden dice cup and feebly mimic the divine disorder.

Others, inversely, believed that it was fundamental to eliminate useless works. They invaded the hexagons, showed credentials which were not always false, leafed through a volume with displeasure and condemned whole shelves : the hygienic, ascetic furor caused the senseless perdition of millions of books. Their name is execrated, but those who deplore the 'treasures' destroyed by this frenzy neglect two notable facts. One : the Library is so enormous that any reduction of human origin is infinitesimal. The other : every copy is unique, irreplaceable, but (since the Library is total) there are always several hundred thousand imperfect facsimilies : works which differ only in a letter or a comma. Counter to general opinion, I venture to suppose that the consequences of the Purifiers' depredations have been exaggerated by the horror these fanatics produced. They were urged on by the delirium of trying to reach the books in the Crimson Hexagon : books whose format is smaller than usual, all-powerful, illustrated and magical.

We also know of another superstition of that time : that of the Man of the Book. On some shelf in some hexagon (men reasoned) there must exist a book which is the formula and perfect compendium *of all the rest* : some librarian has gone through it and he is analogous to a god. In the language of this zone vestiges of this remote functionary's cult still persist. Many wandered in search of Him. For a century they exhausted

in vain the most varied areas. How could one locate the vener-
ated and secret hexagon which housed Him? Someone proposed a regressive method· To locate book A, consult first a
book B which indicates A's position; to locate book B, consult
first a book C., and so on to infinity. . . . In adventures such as
these, I have squandered and wasted my years. It does not seem
unlikely to me that there is a total book on some shelf of the
universe;* I pray to the unknown gods that a man – just one,
even though it were thousands of years ago! – may have
examined and read it. If honour and wisdom and happiness are
not for me, let them be for others. Let heaven exist, though my
place be in hell. Let me be outraged and annihilated, but for
one instant, in one being, let Your enormous Library be justified. The impious maintain that nonsense is normal in the
Library and that the reasonable (and even humble and pure
coherence) is an almost miraculous exception. They speak (I
know) of the 'feverish Library whose chance volumes are constantly in danger of changing into others and affirm, negate and
confuse everything like a delirious divinity'. These words,
which not only denounce the disorder but exemplify it as well,
notoriously prove their authors' abominable taste and desperate ignorance. In truth, the Library includes all verbal structures, all variations permitted by the twenty-five orthographical symbols, but not a single example of absolute nonsense. It is
useless to observe that the best volume of the many hexagons
under my administration is entitled *The Combed Thunderclap*
and another *The Plaster Cramp* and another *Axaxaxas mlö*.
These phrases, at first glance incoherent, can no doubt be
justified in a cryptographical or allegorical manner; such a
justification is verbal and, *ex hypothesi*, already figures in the
Library. I cannot combine some characters

dhcmrlchtdj

*I repeat: it suffices that a book be possible for it to exist. Only
the impossible is excluded. For example: no book can be a ladder,
although no doubt there are books which discuss and negate and
demonstrate this possibility and others whose structure corresponds
to that of a ladder.

which the divine Library has not foreseen and which in one of its secret tongues do not contain a terrible meaning. No one can articulate a syllable which is not filled with tenderness and fear, which is not, in one of these languages, the powerful name of a god. To speak is to fall into tautology. This wordy and useless epistle already exists in one of the thirty volumes of the five shelves of one of the innumerable hexagons - and its refutation as well. (An *n* number of possible languages use the same vocabulary; in some of them, the symbol *library* allows the correct definition *a ubiquitous and lasting system of hexagonal galleries*, but *library* is *bread* or *pyramid* or anything else, and these seven words which define it have another value. You who read me, are You sure of understanding my language?)

The methodical task of writing distracts me from the present state of men. The certitude that everything has been written negates us or turns us into phantoms. I know of districts in which the young men prostrate themselves before books and kiss their pages in a barbarous manner, but they do not know how to decipher a single letter. Epidemics, heretical conflicts, peregrinations which inevitably degenerate into banditry, have decimated the population. I believe I have mentioned the suicides, more and more frequent with the years. Perhaps my old age and fearfulness deceive me, but I suspect that the human species - the unique species - is about to be extinguished, but the Library will endure : illuminated, solitary, infinite, perfectly motionless, equipped with precious volumes, useless, incorruptible, secret.

I have just written the word 'infinite'. I have not interpolated this adjective out of rhetorical habit; I say that it is not illogical to think that the world is infinite. Those who judge it to be limited postulate that in remote places the corridors and stairways and hexagons can conceivably come to an end - which is absurd. Those who imagine it to be without limit forget that the possible number of books does have such a limit. I venture to suggest this solution to the ancient problem : *The Library is unlimited and cyclical.* If an eternal traveller were to cross it in any direction, after centuries he would see that the same volumes were repeated in the same disorder (which, thus repeated, would be an order: the Order). My solitude is gladdened by this elegant hope.*

*Letizia Álvarez de Toledo has observed that this vast Library is useless: rigorously speaking, *a single volume* would be sufficient, a volume of ordinary format, printed in nine or ten point type, containing an infinite number of infinitely thin leaves. (In the early seventeenth century, Cavalieri said that all solid bodies are the superimposition of an infinite number of planes.) The handling of this silky *vade mecum* would not be convenient: each apparent page would unfold into other analogous ones; the inconceivable middle page would have no reverse.

Translated by J.E.I.

Funes the Memorious

I REMEMBER him (I have no right to utter this sacred verb, only one man on earth had that right and he is dead) with a dark passion flower in his hand, seeing it as no one has ever seen it, though he might look at it from the twilight of dawn till that of evening, a whole lifetime. I remember him, with his face taciturn and Indian-like and singularly *remote*, behind the cigarette. I remember (I think) his angular, leather-braiding hands. I remember near those hands a maté gourd bearing the Uruguayan coat of arms; I remember a yellow screen with a vague lake landscape in the window of his house. I clearly remember his voice: the slow, resentful, nasal voice of the old-time dweller of the suburbs, without the Italian sibilants we have today. I never saw him more than three times; the last was in 1887. . . . I find it very satisfactory that all those who knew him should write about him; my testimony will perhaps be the shortest and no doubt the poorest, but not the most impartial in the volume you will edit. My deplorable status as an Argentine will prevent me from indulging in a dithyramb, an obligatory genre in Uruguay whenever the subject is an Uruguayan. *Highbrow, city slicker, dude:* Funes never spoke these injurious words, but I am sufficiently certain I represented for him those misfortunes. Pedro Leandro Ipuche has written that Funes was a precursor of the supermen, 'a vernacular and rustic Zarathustra'; I shall not debate the point, but one should not forget that he was also a kid from Fray Bentos, with certain incurable limitations.

My first memory of Funes is very perspicuous. I can see him on an afternoon in March or February of the year 1884. My

87

father, that year, had taken me to spend the summer in Fray Bentos. I was returning from the San Francisco ranch with my cousin Bernardo Haedo. We were singing as we rode along and being on horseback was not the only circumstance determining my happiness. After a sultry day, an enormous slate-coloured storm had hidden the sky. It was urged on by a southern wind, the trees were already going wild; I was afraid (I was hopeful) that the elemental rain would take us by surprise in the open. We were running a kind of race with the storm. We entered an alleyway that sank down between two very high brick sidewalks. It had suddenly got dark; I heard some rapid and almost secret footsteps up above; I raised my eyes and saw a boy running along the narrow and broken path as if it were a narrow and broken wall. I remember his baggy gaucho trousers, his rope-soled shoes, I remember the cigarette in his hard face, against the now limitless storm cloud. Bernardo cried to him unexpectedly : 'What time is it, Ireneo?' Without consulting the sky, without stopping, he replied : 'It's four minutes to eight, young Bernardo Juan Francisco.' His voice was shrill, mocking.

I am so unperceptive that the dialogue I have just related would not have attracted my attention had it not been stressed by my cousin, who (I believe) was prompted by a certain local pride and the desire to show that he was indifferent to the other's tripartite reply.

He told me the fellow in the alleyway was one Ireneo Funes, known for certain peculiarities such as avoiding contact with people and always knowing what time it was, like a clock. He added that he was the son of the ironing woman in town, María Clementina Funes, and that some people said his father was a doctor at the meat packers, an Englishman by the name of O'Connor, and others that he was a horse tamer or scout from the Salto district. He lived with his mother, around the corner from the Laureles house.

During the years eighty-five and eighty-six we spent the summer in Montevideo. In eighty-seven I returned to Fray Bentos. I asked, as was natural, about all my acquaintances

and, finally, about the 'chronometrical' Funes. I was told he
had been thrown by a half-tamed horse on the San Francisco
ranch and was left hopelessly paralysed. I remember the sensation of uneasy magic the news produced in me : the only time
I had seen him, we were returning from San Francisco on
horseback and he was running along a high place; this fact,
told me by my cousin Bernardo, had much of the quality of a
dream made up of previous elements. I was told he never
moved from his cot, with his eyes fixed on the fig tree in the
back or on a spider web. In the afternoons, he would let himself be brought out to the window. He carried his pride to the
point of acting as if the blow that had felled him were beneficial ... Twice I saw him behind the iron grating of the window,
which harshly emphasized his condition as a perpetual prisoner :
once, motionless, with his eyes closed; another time, again
motionless, absorbed in the contemplation of a fragrant sprig
of santonica.

Not without a certain vaingloriousness, I had begun at that
time my methodical study of Latin. My valise contained the *De
viris illustribus* of Lhomond, Quicherat's *Thesaurus*, the commentaries of Julius Caesar and an odd volume of Pliny's
Naturalis historia, which then exceeded (and still exceeds) my
moderate virtues as a Latinist. Everything becomes public in a
small town; Ireneo, in his house on the outskirts, did not take
long to learn of the arrival of these anomalous books. He sent
me a flowery and ceremonious letter in which he recalled our
encounter, unfortunately brief, 'on the seventh day of February
of the year 1884', praised the glorious services my uncle Gre-
gorio Haedo, deceased that same year, 'had rendered to our two
nations in the valiant battle of Ituzaingó' and requested the
loan of any one of my volumes, accompanied by a dictionary
'for the proper intelligence of the original text, for I am as yet
ignorant of Latin'. He promised to return them to me in good
condition, almost immediately. His handwriting was perfect,
very sharply outlined; his orthography, of the type favoured
by Andrés Bello : *i* for *y*, *j* for *g*. At first I naturally feared a
joke. My cousins assured me that was not the case, that these

were peculiarities of Ireneo. I did not know whether to attribute to insolence, ignorance or stupidity the idea that the arduous Latin tongue should require no other instrument than a dictionary; to disillusion him fully, I sent him the *Gradus ad Parnassum* of Quicherat and the work by Pliny.

On the fourteenth of February, I received a telegram from Buenos Aires saying I should return immediately, because my father was 'not at all well'. May God forgive me; the prestige of being the recipient of an urgent telegram, the desire to communicate to all Fray Bentos the contradiction between the negative form of the message and the peremptory adverb, the temptation to dramatize my suffering, affecting a virile stoicism, perhaps distracted me from all possibility of real sorrow. When I packed my valise, I noticed the *Gradus* and the first volume of the *Naturalis historia* were missing. The *Saturn* was sailing the next day, in the morning; that night, after supper, I headed towards Funes's house. I was astonished to find the evening no less oppressive than the day had been.

At the respectable little house, Funes's mother opened the door for me.

She told me Ireneo was in the back room and I should not be surprised to find him in the dark, because he knew how to pass the idle hours without lighting the candle. I crossed the tile patio, the little passageway; I reached the second patio. There was a grape arbour; the darkness seemed complete to me. I suddenly heard Ireneo's high-pitched, mocking voice. His voice was speaking in Latin; his voice (which came from the darkness) was articulating with morose delight a speech or prayer or incantation. The Roman syllables resounded in the earthen patio; my fear took them to be indecipherable, interminable; afterwards, in the enormous dialogue of that night, I learned they formed the first paragraph of the twenty-fourth chapter of the seventh book of the *Naturalis historia*. The subject of that chapter is memory; the last words were *ut nihil non iisdem verbis redderetur auditum.*

Without the slightest change of voice, Ireneo told me to come in. He was on his cot, smoking. It seems to me I did not

see his face until dawn; I believe I recall the intermittent glow
of his cigarette. The room smelled vaguely of dampness. I sat
down; I repeated the story about the telegram and my father's
illness.

I now arrive at the most difficult point in my story. This
story (it is well the reader know it by now) has no other plot
than that dialogue which took place half a century ago. I shall
not try to reproduce the words, which are now irrecoverable. I
prefer to summarize with veracity the many things Ireneo told
me. The indirect style is remote and weak; I know I am sacrificing the efficacy of my narrative; my readers should imagine
for themselves the hesitant periods which overwhelmed me
that night.

Ireneo began by enumerating, in Latin and in Spanish, the
cases of prodigious memory recorded in the *Naturalis historia*:
Cyrus, king of the Persians, who could call every soldier in his
armies by name; Mithridates Eupator, who administered the
law in the twenty-two languages of his empire; Simonides,
inventor of the science of mnemonics; Metrodorus, who practised the art of faithfully repeating what he had heard only
once. In obvious good faith, Ireneo was amazed that such cases
be considered amazing. He told me that before that rainy
afternoon when the blue-grey horse threw him, he had been
what all humans are: blind, deaf, addle-brained, absent-minded.
(I tried to remind him of his exact perception of time, his
memory for proper names; he paid no attention to me.) For
nineteen years he had lived as one in a dream: he looked
without seeing, listened without hearing, forgetting everything,
almost everything. When he fell, he became unconscious;
when he came to, the present was almost intolerable in its
richness and sharpness, as were his most distant and trivial
memories. Somewhat later he learned that he was paralysed.
The fact scarcely interested him. He reasoned (he felt) that his
immobility was a minimum price to pay. Now his perception
and his memory were infallible.

We, at one glance, can perceive three glasses on a table;
Funes, all the leaves and tendrils and fruit that make up a grape

vine. He knew by heart the forms of the southern clouds at dawn on 30 April 1882, and could compare them in his memory with the mottled streaks on a book in Spanish binding he had only seen once and with the outlines of the foam raised by an oar in the Río Negro the night before the Quebracho uprising. These memories were not simple ones; each visual image was linked to muscular sensations, thermal sensations, etc. He could reconstruct all his dreams, all his half-dreams. Two or three times he had reconstructed a whole day; he never hesitated, but each reconstruction had required a whole day. He told me: 'I alone have more memories than all mankind has probably had since the world has been the world.' And again: 'My dreams are like you people's waking hours.' And again, towards dawn: 'My memory, sir, is like a garbage heap.' A circle drawn on a blackboard, a right triangle, lozenge – all these are forms we can fully and intuitively grasp; Ireneo could do the same with the stormy mane of a pony, with a herd of cattle on a hill, with the changing fire and its innumerable ashes, with the many faces of a dead man throughout a long wake. I don't know how many stars he could see in the sky.

These things he told me; neither then nor later have I ever placed them in doubt. In those days there were no cinemas or phonographs; nevertheless, it is odd and even incredible that no one ever performed an experiment with Funes. The truth is that we live out our lives putting off all that can be put off; perhaps we all know deep down that we are immortal and that sooner or later all men will do and know all things.

Out of the darkness, Funes's voice went on talking to me.

He told me that in 1886 he had invented an original system of numbering and that in a very few days he had gone beyond the twenty-four-thousand mark. He had not written it down, since anything he thought of once would never be lost to him. His first stimulus was, I think, his discomfort at the fact that the famous thirty-three gauchos of Uruguayan history should require two signs and two words, in place of a single word and a single sign. He then applied this absurd principle to the other numbers. In place of seven thousand thirteen, he would say (for example) *Máximo Pérez*; in place of seven thousand fourteen, *The Railroad*; other numbers were *Luis Melián Lafinur, Olimar, sulphur, the reins, the whale, the gas, the cauldron, Napoleon, Agustín de Vedia*. In place of five hundred, he would say *nine*. Each word had a particular sign, a kind of mark; the last in the series were very complicated ... I tried to explain to him that his rhapsody of incoherent terms was precisely the opposite of a system of numbers. I told him that saying 365 meant saying three hundreds, six tens, five ones, an analysis which is not found in the 'numbers' *The Negro Timoteo* or *meat blanket*. Funes did not understand me or refused to understand me.

Locke, in the seventeenth century, postulated (and rejected) an impossible language in which each individual thing, each stone, each bird and each branch, would have its own name; Funes once projected an analogous language, but discarded it because it seemed too general to him, too ambiguous. In fact, Funes remembered not only every leaf of every tree of every wood, but also every one of the times he had perceived or imagined it. He decided to reduce each of his past days to some seventy thousand memories, which would then be defined by means of ciphers. He was dissuaded from this by two considerations: his awareness that the task was interminable, his awareness that it was useless. He thought that by the hour of his death he would not even have finished classifying all the memories of his childhood.

The two projects I have indicated (an infinite vocabulary for the natural series of numbers, a useless mental catalogue of all the images of his memory) are senseless, but they betray a certain stammering grandeur. They permit us to glimpse or infer the nature of Funes's vertiginous world. He was, let us not forget, almost incapable of ideas of a general, Platonic sort. Not only was it difficult for him to comprehend that the generic symbol *dog* embraces so many unlike individuals of diverse size and form; it bothered him that the dog at three fourteen (seen from the side) should have the same name as the dog at three fifteen (seen from the front). His own face in the mirror, his own hands, surprised him every time he saw them. Swift relates that the emperor of Lilliput could discern the movement of the minute hand; Funes could continuously discern the tranquil advances of corruption, of decay, of fatigue. He could note the progress of death, of dampness. He was the solitary and lucid spectator of a multiform, instantaneous and almost intolerably precise world. Babylon, London and New York have overwhelmed with their ferocious splendour the imaginations of men; no one, in their populous towers or their urgent avenues, has felt the heat and pressure of a reality as indefatigable as that which day and night converged upon the hapless Ireneo, in his poor South American suburb. It was very difficult for him to sleep. To sleep is to turn one's mind from the world; Funes, lying on his back on his cot in the shadows, could imagine every crevice and every moulding in the sharply defined houses surrounding him. (I repeat that the least important of his memories was more minute and more vivid than our perception of physical pleasure or physical torment.) Towards the east, along a stretch not yet divided into blocks, there were new houses, unknown to Funes. He imagined them to be black, compact, made of homogeneous darkness; in that direction he would turn his face in order to sleep. He would also imagine himself at the bottom of the river, rocked and annihilated by the current.

With no effort, he had learned English, French, Portuguese and Latin. I suspect, however, that he was not very capable of thought. To think is to forget differences, generalize, make abstractions. In the teeming world of Funes, there were only details, almost immediate in their presence.

The wary light of dawn entered the earthen patio.

Then I saw the face belonging to the voice that had spoken all night long. Ireneo was nineteen years old; he had been born in 1868; he seemed to me as monumental as bronze, more ancient than Egypt, older than the prophecies and the pyramids. I thought that each of my words (that each of my movements) would persist in his implacable memory; I was benumbed by the fear of multiplying useless gestures.

Ireneo Funes died in 1889, of congestion of the lungs.

Translated by J.E.I.

The Shape of the Sword

A SPITEFUL scar crossed his face: an ash-coloured and nearly perfect arc that creased his temple at one tip and his cheek at the other. His real name is of no importance; everyone in Tacaurembó called him the 'Englishman from La Colorada'. Cardoso, the owner of those fields, refused to sell them: I understand that the Englishman resorted to an unexpected argument: he confided to Cardoso the secret of the scar. The Englishman came from the border, from Río Grande del Sur; there are many who say that in Brazil he had been a smuggler. The fields were overgrown with grass, the waterholes brackish; the Englishman, in order to correct those deficiencies, worked fully as hard as his labourers. They say that he was severe to the point of cruelty, but scrupulously just. They say also that he drank: a few times a year he locked himself into an upper room, not to emerge until two or three days later as if from a battle or from vertigo, pale, trembling, confused and as authoritarian as ever. I remember the glacial eyes, the energetic leanness, the grey moustache. He had no dealings with anyone; it is a fact that his Spanish was rudimentary and cluttered with Brazilian. Aside from a business letter or some pamphlet, he received no mail.

The last time I passed through the northern provinces, a sudden overflowing of the Caraguatá stream compelled me to spend the night at La Colorada. Within a few moments, I seemed to sense that my appearance was inopportune; I tried to ingratiate myself with the Englishman: I resorted to the least discerning of passions: patriotism. I claimed as invincible a country with such spirit as England's. My companion agreed, but added with a smile that he was not English. He was Irish, from Dungarvan. Having said this, he stopped short, as if he had revealed a secret.

After dinner we went outside to look at the sky. It had cleared up, but beyond the low hills the southern sky, streaked and gashed by lightning, was conceiving another storm. Into the cleared-up dining room the boy who had served dinner brought a bottle of rum. We drank for some time, in silence.

I don't know what time it must have been when I observed that I was drunk; I don't know what inspiration or what exultation or tedium made me mention the scar. The Englishman's face changed its expression; for a few seconds I thought he was going to throw me out of the house. At length he said in his normal voice:

'I'll tell you the history of my scar under one condition: that of not mitigating one bit of the opprobrium, of the infamous circumstances.'

I agreed. This is the story that he told me, mixing his English with Spanish, and even with Portuguese:

'Around 1922, in one of the cities of Connaught, I was one of the many who were conspiring for the independence of Ireland. Of my comrades, some are still living, dedicated to peaceful pursuits; others, paradoxically, are fighting on desert and sea under the English flag; another, the most worthy, died in the courtyard of a barracks, at dawn, shot by men filled with sleep; still others (not the most unfortunate) met their destiny in the anonymous and almost secret battles of the civil war. We were Republicans, Catholics; we were, I suspect, Romantics. Ireland was for us not only the utopian future and the intolerable present; it was a bitter and cherished mythology, it was the circular towers and the red marshes, it was the repudiation of Parnell and the enormous epic poems which sang of the robbing of bulls which in another incarnation were heroes and in others fish and mountains.... One afternoon I will never forget, an affiliate from Munster joined us: one John Vincent Moon.

'He was scarcely twenty years old. He was slender and flaccid at the same time; he gave the uncomfortable impression

97

of being invertebrate. He had studied with fervour and with vanity nearly every page of Lord knows what Communist manual; he made use of dialectical materialism to put an end to any discussion whatever. The reasons one can have for hating another man, or for loving him, are infinite : Moon reduced the history of the universe to a sordid economic conflict. He affirmed that the revolution was predestined to succeed. I told him that for a gentleman only lost causes should be attractive ... Night had already fallen; we continued our disagreement in the hall, on the stairs, then along the vague streets. The judgements Moon emitted impressed me less than his irrefutable, apodictic note. The new comrade did not discuss : he dictated opinions with scorn and with a certain anger.

'As we were arriving at the outlying houses, a sudden burst of gunfire stunned us. (Either before or afterwards we skirted the blank wall of a factory or barracks.) We moved into an unpaved street; a soldier, huge in the firelight, came out of a burning hut. Crying out, he ordered us to stop. I quickened my pace; my companion did not follow. I turned around : John Vincent Moon was motionless, fascinated, as if eternized by fear. I then ran back and knocked the soldier to the ground with one blow, shook Vincent Moon, insulted him and ordered him to follow. I had to take him by the arm; the passion of fear had rendered him helpless. We fled, into the night pierced by flames. A rifle volley reached out for us, and a bullet nicked Moon's right shoulder; as we were fleeing amid pines, he broke out in a weak sobbing.

'In that fall of 1923 I had taken shelter in General Berkeley's country house. The general (whom I had never seen) was carrying out some administrative assignment or other in Bengal; the house was less than a century old, but it was decayed and shadowy and flourished in puzzling corridors and in pointless antechambers. The museum and the huge library usurped the first floor : controversial and uncongenial books which in some manner are the history of the nineteenth century; scimitars from Nishapur, along whose captured arcs there seemed to persist still the wind and violence of battle. We entered (I seem to recall) through the rear. Moon, trembling, his mouth parched, murmured that the events of the night were interesting; I dressed his wound and brought him a cup of tea; I was able to determine that his "wound" was superficial. Suddenly he stammered in bewilderment:

' "You know, you ran a terrible risk."

'I told him not to worry about it. (The habit of the civil war had incited me to act as I did; besides, the capture of a single member could endanger our cause.)

'By the following day Moon had recovered his poise. He accepted a cigarette and subjected me to a severe interrogation on the "economic resources of our revolutionary party". His questions were very lucid; I told him (truthfully) that the situation was serious. Deep bursts of rifle fire agitated the south. I told Moon our comrades were waiting for us. My overcoat and my revolver were in my room; when I returned, I found Moon stretched out on the sofa, his eyes closed. He imagined he had a fever; he invoked a painful spasm in his shoulder.

'At that moment I understood that his cowardice was irreparable. I clumsily entreated him to take care of himself and went out. This frightened man mortified me, as if I were the coward, not Vincent Moon. Whatever one man does, it is as if all men did it. For that reason it is not unfair that one disobedience in a garden should contaminate all humanity; for that reason it is not unjust that the crucifixion of a single Jew should be sufficient to save it. Perhaps Schopenhauer was right: I am all other men, any man is all men, Shakespeare is in some manner the miserable John Vincent Moon.

'Nine days we spent in the general's enormous house. Of the agonies and the successes of the war I shall not speak: I propose to relate the history of the scar that insults me. In my memory, those nine days form only a single day, save for the next to the last, when our men broke into a barracks and we were able to avenge precisely the sixteen comrades who had been machine-gunned in Elphin. I slipped out of the house towards dawn, in the confusion of daybreak. At nightfall I was back. My companion was waiting for me upstairs: his wound did not permit him to descend to the ground floor. I recall him having some volume of strategy in his hand, F. N. Maude or Clausewitz. "The weapon I prefer is the artillery," he confessed to me one night. He inquired into our plans; he liked to censure them or revise them. He also was accustomed to denouncing "our deplorable economic basis"; dogmatic and gloomy, he predicted the disastrous end. *"C'est une affaire flambée,"* he murmured. In order to show that he was indifferent to being a physical coward, he magnified his mental arrogance. In this way, for good or for bad, nine days elapsed.

'On the tenth day the city fell definitely to the Black and Tans. Tall, silent horsemen patrolled the roads; ashes and smoke rode on the wind; on the corner I saw a corpse thrown to the ground, an impression less firm in my memory than that of a dummy on which the soldiers endlessly practised their marksmanship, in the middle of the square ... I had left when dawn was in the sky; before noon I returned. Moon, in the library, was speaking with someone; the tone of his voice told me he was talking on the telephone. Then I heard my name; then, that I would return at seven; then, the suggestion that they should arrest me as I was crossing the garden. My reasonable friend was reasonably selling me out. I heard him demand guarantees of personal safety.

'Here my story is confused and becomes lost. I know that I pursued the informer along the black, nightmarish halls and along deep stairways of dizzyness. Moon knew the house very well, much better than I. One or two times I lost him. I cornered him before the soldiers stopped me. From one of the general's collections of arms I tore a cutlass: with that half moon I carved into his face for ever a half moon of blood. Borges, to you, a stranger, I have made this confession. Your contempt does not grieve me so much.'

Here the narrator stopped. I noticed that his hands were shaking.

'And Moon?' I asked him.

'He collected his Judas money and fled to Brazil. That afternoon, in the square, he saw a dummy shot up by some drunken men.'

I waited in vain for the rest of the story. Finally I told him to go on.

Then a sob went through his body; and with a weak gentleness he pointed to the whitish curved scar.

'You don't believe me?' he stammered. 'Don't you see that I carry written on my face the mark of my infamy? I have told you the story thus so that you would hear me to the end. I denounced the man who protected me: I am Vincent Moon. Now despise me.'

To E.H.M.   *Translated by D.A.Y.*

Theme of the
Traitor and the Hero

So the Platonic year
Whirls out new right and wrong,
Whirls in the old istead;
All men are dancers and their tread
Goes to the barbarous clangour of a gong.
                              W. B. Yeats: *The Tower*

UNDER the notable influence of Chesterton (contriver and embellisher of elegant mysteries) and the palace counsellor Leibniz (inventor of the pre-established harmony), in my idle afternoons I have imagined this story plot which I shall perhaps write some day and which already justifies me somehow. Details, rectifications, adjustments are lacking; there are zones of the story not yet revealed to me; today, 3 January 1944, I seem to see it as follows:

The action takes place in an oppressed and tenacious country: Poland, Ireland, the Venetian Republic, some South American or Balkan state.... Or rather it has taken place, since, though the narrator is contemporary, his story occurred towards the middle or the beginning of the nineteenth century. Let us say (for narrative convenience) Ireland; let us say in 1824. The narrator's name is Ryan; he is the great-grandson of the young, the heroic, the beautiful, the assassinated Fergus Kilpatrick, whose grave was mysteriously violated, whose name illustrated the verses of Browning and Hugo, whose statue presides over a grey hill amid red marshes.

Kilpatrick was a conspirator, a secret and glorious captain of conspirators; like Moses, who from the land of Moab glimpsed but could not reach the promised land, Kilpatrick perished on the eve of the victorious revolt which he had premeditated and dreamt of. The first centenary of his death draws near; the circumstances of the crime are enigmatic; Ryan, engaged in writing a biography of the hero, discovers that the enigma exceeds the confines of a simple police investigation. Kilpatrick was murdered in a theatre; the British police never found the killer; the historians maintain that this scarcely soils their good reputation, since it was probably the police themselves who had him killed. Other facets of the enigma disturb Ryan. They are of a cyclic nature: they seem to repeat or combine events of remote regions, of remote ages. For example, no one is unaware that the officers who examined the hero's body found a sealed letter in which he was warned of the risk of attending the theatre that evening; likewise Julius Caesar, on his way to the place where his friends' daggers awaited him, received a note he never read, in which the treachery was declared along with the traitors' names. Caesar's wife, Calpurnia, saw in a dream the destruction of a tower decreed him by the Senate; false and anonymous rumours on the eve of Kilpatrick's death publicized throughout the country that the circular tower of Kilgarvan had burned, which could be taken as a presage, for he had been born in Kilgarvan. These parallelisms (and others) between the story of Caesar and the story of an Irish conspirator lead Ryan to suppose the existence of a secret form of time, a pattern of repeated lines. He thinks of the decimal history conceived by Condorcet, of the morphologies proposed by Hegel, Spengler and Vico, of Hesiod's men, who degenerate from gold to iron. He thinks of the transmigration of souls, a doctrine that lends horror to Celtic literature and that Caesar himself attributed to the British druids; he thinks that, before having been Fergus Kilpatrick, Fergus Kilpatrick was Julius Caesar. He is rescued from these circular labyrinths by a curious finding, a finding which then sinks him into other, more inextricable and heterogeneous labyrinths: certain words uttered by a beggar who spoke with Fergus Kilpatrick the day of his death were prefigured by Shakespeare in the tragedy *Macbeth*. That history should have copied history was already sufficiently astonishing; that history should copy literature was inconceivable.... Ryan finds that, in 1814, James Alexander Nolan, the oldest of the hero's companions, had translated the principal dramas of Shakespeare into Gaelic; among these was *Julius Caesar*. He also discovers in the archives the manuscript of an article by Nolan on the Swiss *Festspiele* : vast and errant theatrical representations which require thousands of actors and repeat historical episodes in the very cities and mountains where they took place. Another unpublished document reveals to him that, a few days before the end, Kilpatrick, presiding over the last meeting, had signed the order for the execution of a traitor whose name has been deleted from the records. This order does not accord with Kilpatrick's merciful nature. Ryan investigates the matter (this investigation is one of the gaps in my plot) and manages to decipher the enigma.

Kilpatrick was killed in a theatre, but the entire city was a theatre as well, and the actors were legion, and the drama crowned by his death extended over many days and many nights. This is what happened :

On 2 August 1824, the conspirators gathered. The country was ripe for revolt; something, however, always failed : there was a traitor in the group. Fergus Kilpatrick had charged James Nolan with the responsibility of discovering the traitor. Nolan carried out his assignment : he announced in the very midst of the meeting that the traitor was Kilpatrick himself. He demonstrated the truth of his accusation with irrefutable proof; the conspirators condemned their president to die. He signed his own sentence, but begged that his punishment not harm his country.

It was then that Nolan conceived his strange scheme. Ireland idolized Kilpatrick; the most tenuous suspicion of his infamy would have jeopardized the revolt; Nolan proposed a plan which made of the traitor's execution an instrument for the country's emancipation. He suggested that the condemned man die at the hands of an unknown assassin in deliberately dramatic circumstances which would remain engraved in the imagination of the people and would hasten the revolt. Kilpatrick swore he would take part in the scheme, which gave him the occasion to redeem himself and for which his death would provide the final flourish.

Nolan, urged on by time, was not able to invent all the circumstances of the multiple execution; he had to plagiarize another dramatist, the English enemy William Shakespeare. He repeated scenes from *Macbeth*, from *Julius Caesar*. The public and secret enactment comprised various days. The condemned man entered Dublin, discussed, acted, prayed, reproved, uttered words of pathos, and each of these gestures, to be reflected in his glory, had been pre-established by Nolan. Hundreds of actors collaborated with the protagonist; the role of some was complex; that of others momentary. The things they did and said endure in the history books, in the impassioned memory of Ireland. Kilpatrick, swept along by this minutely detailed destiny which both redeemed and destroyed him, more than once enriched the text of his judge with improvised acts and words. Thus the populous drama unfolded in time, until 6 August 1824, in a theatre box with funereal curtains prefiguring Lincoln's, a long-desired bullet entered the breast of the traitor and hero, who, amid two effusions of sudden blood, was scarcely able to articulate a few foreseen words.

In Nolan's work, the passages imitated from Shakespeare are the *least* dramatic; Ryan suspects that the author interpolated them so that in the future someone might hit upon the truth. He understands that he too forms part of Nolan's plot.... After a series of tenacious hesitations, he resolves to keep his discovery silent. He publishes a book dedicated to the hero's glory; this too, perhaps, was foreseen.

Translated by J.E.I.

Death and the Compass

OF the many problems which exercised the reckless discernment of Lönnrot, none was so strange – so rigorously strange, shall we say – as the periodic series of bloody events which culminated at the villa of Triste-le-Roy, amid the ceaseless aroma of the eucalypti. It is true that Erik Lönnrot failed to prevent the last murder, but that he foresaw it is indisputable. Neither did he guess the identity of Yarmolinsky's luckless assassin, but he did succeed in divining the secret morphology behind the fiendish series as well as the participation of Red Scharlach, whose other nickname is Scharlach the Dandy. That criminal (as countless others) had sworn on his honour to kill Lönnrot, but the latter could never be intimidated. Lönnrot believed himself a pure reasoner, an Auguste Dupin, but there was something of the adventurer in him, and even a little of the gambler.

The first murder occurred in the Hôtel du Nord – that tall prism which dominates the estuary whose waters are the colour of the desert. To that tower (which quite glaringly unites the hateful whiteness of a hospital, the numbered divisibility of a jail, and the general appearance of a bordello) there came on the third day of December the delegate from Podolsk to the Third Talmudic Congress, Doctor Marcel Yarmolinsky, a grey-bearded man with grey eyes. We shall never know whether the Hôtel du Nord pleased him; he accepted it with the ancient resignation which had allowed him to endure three years of war in the Carpathians and three thousand years of oppression and pogroms. He was given a room on Floor R, across from the suite which was occupied – not without splendour – by The Tetrarch of Galilee. Yarmolinsky supped, postponed until the following day an inspection of the unknown city, arranged in a *placard* his many books and few personal possessions, and before midnight extinguished his light. (Thus declared the Tetrarch's chauffeur who slept in the adjoining room.) On the fourth, at 11:03 a.m., the editor of the *Yidische Zaitung* put in a call to him; Doctor Yarmolinsky did not answer. He was found in his room, his face already a little dark, nearly nude beneath a large, anachronistic cape. He was lying not far from the door which opened on the hall; a deep knife wound had split his breast. A few hours later, in the same room amid journalists, photographers and policemen, Inspector Treviranus and Lönnrot were calmly discussing the problem.

'No need to look for a three-legged cat here,' Treviranus was saying as he brandished an imperious cigar. 'We all know that the Tetrarch of Galilee owns the finest sapphires in the world. Someone, intending to steal them, must have broken in here by mistake. Yarmolinsky got up; the robber had to kill him. How does it sound to you?'

'Possible, but not interesting,' Lönnrot answered. 'You'll reply that reality hasn't the least obligation to be interesting. And I'll answer you that reality may avoid that obligation but that hypotheses may not. In the hypothesis that you propose, chance intervenes copiously. Here we have a dead rabbi; I would prefer a purely rabbinical explanation, not the imaginary mischances of an imaginary robber.'

Treviranus replied ill-humouredly:

'I'm not interested in rabbinical explanations. I am interested in capturing the man who stabbed this unknown person.'

'Not so unknown,' corrected Lönnrot. 'Here are his complete works.' He indicated in the wall-cupboard a row of tall books: a *Vindication of the Cabala*; *An Examination of the Philosophy of Robert Fludd*; a literal translation of the *Sepher Yezirah*; a *Biography of the Baal Shem*; a *History of the Hasidic Sect*; a monograph (in German) on the Tetragrammaton; another, on the divine nomenclature of the Pentateuch. The inspector regarded them with dread, almost with repulsion. Then he began to laugh.

'I'm a poor Christian,' he said. 'Carry off those musty volumes if you want; I don't have any time to waste on Jewish superstitions.'

'Maybe the crime belongs to the history of Jewish superstitions,' murmured Lönnrot.

'Like Christianity,' the editor of the *Yidische Zaitung* ventured to add. He was myopic, an atheist and very shy.

No one answered him. One of the agents had found in the small typewriter a piece of paper on which was written the following unfinished sentence:

The first letter of the Name has been uttered

Lönnrot abstained from smiling. Suddenly become a bibliophile or Hebraist, he ordered a package made of the dead man's books and carried them off to his apartment. Indifferent to the police investigation, he dedicated himself to studying them. One large octavo volume revealed to him the teachings of Israel Baal Shem Tobh, founder of the sect of the Pious; another, the virtues and terrors of the Tetragrammaton, which is the unutterable name of God; another, the thesis that God has a secret name, in which is epitomized (as in the crystal sphere which the Persians ascribe to Alexander of Macedonia) his ninth attribute, eternity – that is to say, the immediate knowledge of all things that will be, which are and which have been in the universe. Tradition numbers ninety-nine names of God; the Hebraists attribute that imperfect number to magical fear of even numbers; the Hasidim reason that that hiatus indicates a hundredth name – the Absolute Name.

From this erudition Lönnrot was distracted, a few days later, by the appearance of the editor of the *Yidische Zaitung*. The latter wanted to talk about the murder; Lönnrot preferred to discuss the diverse names of God; the journalist declared, in three columns, that the investigator, Erik Lönnrot, had dedicated himself to studying the names of God in order to come across the name of the murderer. Lönnrot, accustomed to the simplifications of journalism, did not become indignant. One of those enterprising shopkeepers who have discovered that any given man is resigned to buying any given book published a popular edition of the *History of the Hasidic Sect*.

The second murder occurred on the evening of the third of January, in the most deserted and empty corner of the capital's western suburbs. Towards dawn, one of the gendarmes who patrol those solitudes on horseback saw a man in a poncho, lying prone in the shadow of an old paint shop. The harsh features seemed to be masked in blood; a deep knife wound had split his breast. On the wall, across the yellow and red diamonds, were some words written in chalk. The gendarme spelled them out.... That afternoon, Treviranus and Lönnrot headed for the remote scene of the crime. To the left and right of the automobile the city disintegrated; the firmament grew and houses were of less importance than a brick kiln or a poplar tree. They arrived at their miserable destination: an alley's end, with rose-coloured walls which somehow seemed to reflect the extravagant sunset. The dead man had already been identified. He was Daniel Simon Azevedo, an individual of some fame in the old northern suburbs, who had risen from wagon driver to political tough, then degenerated to a thief and even an informer. (The singular style of his death seemed appropriate to them: Azevedo was the last representative of a generation of bandits who knew how to manipulate a dagger, but not a revolver.) The words in chalk were the following:

The second letter of the Name has been uttered

The third murder occurred on the night of the third of February. A little before one o'clock, the telephone in Inspector Treviranus's office rang. In avid secretiveness, a man with a guttural voice spoke; he said his name was Ginzberg (or Ginsburg) and that he was prepared to communicate, for reasonable remuneration, the events surrounding the two sacrifices of Azevedo and Yarmolinsky. A discordant sound of whistles and horns drowned out the informer's voice. Then, the connexion was broken off. Without yet rejecting the possibility of a hoax (after all, it was carnival time), Treviranus found out that he had been called from the Liverpool House, a tavern on the rue de Toulon, that dingy street where side by side exist the cosmorama and the coffee shop, the bawdy house and the bible sellers. Treviranus spoke with the owner. The latter (Black Finnegan, an old Irish criminal who was immersed in, almost overcome by, respectability) told him that the last person to use the phone was a lodger, a certain Gryphius, who had just left with some friends. Treviranus went immediately to Liverpool House. The owner related the following. Eight days ago Gryphius had rented a room above the tavern. He was a sharp-featured man with a nebulous grey beard, and was shabbily dressed in black; Finnegan (who used the room for a purpose which Treviranus guessed) demanded a rent which was undoubtedly excessive; Gryphius paid the stipulated sum without hesitation. He almost never went out; he dined and lunched in his room; his face was scarcely known in the bar. On the night in question, he came downstairs to make a phone call from Finnegan's office. A closed cab stopped in front of the tavern. The driver didn't move from his seat; several patrons recalled that he was wearing a bear's mask. Two harlequins got out of the cab; they were of short stature and no one failed to observe that they were very drunk. With a tooting of horns, they burst into Finnegan's office; they embraced Gryphius, who appeared to recognize them but responded coldly; they exchanged a few words in Yiddish – he in a low, guttural voice, they in high-pitched, false voices – and then went up to the room. Within a quarter hour the three descended, very happy. Gryphius, staggering, seemed as drunk as the others. He walked – tall and dizzy – in the middle, between the masked harlequins. (One of the women at the bar remembered the yellow, red and green diamonds.) Twice he stumbled; twice he was caught and held by the harlequins. Moving off towards the inner harbour which enclosed a rectangular body of water, the three got into the cab and disappeared. From the footboard of the cab, the last of the harlequins scrawled an obscene figure and a sentence on one of the slates of the pier shed.

Treviranus saw the sentence. It was virtually predictable. It said:

The last of the letters of the Name has been uttered

Afterwards, he examined the small room of Gryphius-Ginzberg. On the floor there was a brusque star of blood, in the corners, traces of cigarettes of a Hungarian brand; in a cabinet, a book in Latin – the *Philologus Hebraeo-Graecus* (1739) of Leusden – with several manuscript notes. Treviranus looked it over with indignation and had Lönnrot located. The latter, without removing his hat, began to read while the inspector was interrogating the contradictory witnesses to the possible kidnapping. At four o'clock they left. Out on the twisted rue de Toulon, as they were treading on the dead serpentines of the dawn, Treviranus said:

'And what if all this business tonight were just a mock rehearsal?'

Erik Lönnrot smiled and, with all gravity, read a passage (which was underlined) from the thirty-third dissertation of the *Philologus*: *Dies Judacorum incipit ad solis occasu usque ad solis occasum diei sequentis.*

'This means,' he added, '"The Hebrew day begins at sundown and lasts until the following sundown."'

The inspector attempted an irony.

'Is that fact the most valuable one you've come across tonight?'

'No. Even more valuable was a word that Ginzberg used.'

The afternoon papers did not overlook the periodic disappearances. *La Cruz de la Espada* contrasted them with the admirable discipline and order of the last Hermetical Congress; Ernst Palast, in *El Mártir*, criticized 'the intolerable delays in this clandestine and frugal pogrom, which has taken three months to murder three Jews'; the *Yidische Zaitung* rejected the horrible hypothesis of an anti-Semitic plot, 'even though many penetrating intellects admit no other solution to the triple mystery'; the most illustrious gunman of the south, Dandy Red Scharlach, swore that in his district similar crimes could never occur, and he accused Inspector Franz Treviranus of culpable negligence.

On the night of March first, the inspector received an im-
pressive-looking sealed envelope. He opened it; the envelope
contained a letter signed 'Baruch Spinoza' and a detailed plan
of the city, obviously torn from a Baedeker. The letter prophesied that on the third of March there would not be a fourth
murder, since the paint shop in the west, the tavern on the rue
de Toulon and the Hôtel du Nord were 'the perfect vertices of a
mystic equilateral triangle'; the map demonstrated in red ink
the regularity of the triangle. Treviranus read the *more geo-
metrico* argument with resignation, and sent the letter and the
map to Lönnrot – who, unquestionably, was deserving of such
madnesses.

Erik Lönnrot studied them. The three locations were in fact
equidistant. Symmetry in time (the third of December, the
third of January, the third of February); symmetry in space as
well.... Suddenly, he felt as if he were on the point of solving
the mystery. A set of calipers and a compass completed his
quick intuition. He smiled, pronounced the word Tetragrammaton (of recent acquisition) and phoned the inspector. He said :

'Thank you for the equilateral triangle you sent me last night.
It has enabled me to solve the problem. This Friday the crimi-
nals will be in jail, we may rest assured.'

'Then they're not planning a fourth murder?'

'Precisely because they *are* planning a fourth murder we can
rest assured.'

Lönnrot hung up. One hour later he was travelling on one of
the Southern Railway's trains, in the direction of the abandoned villa of Triste-le-Roy. To the south of the city of our
story flows a blind little river of muddy water, defamed by
refuse and garbage. On the far side is an industrial suburb
where, under the protection of a political boss from Barcelona,
gunmen thrive. Lönnrot smiled at the thought that the most
celebrated gunman of all – Red Scharlach – would have given a
great deal to know of his clandestine visit. Azevedo had been
an associate of Scharlach; Lönnrot considered the remote possibility that the fourth victim might be Scharlach himself. Then
he rejected the idea.... He had very nearly deciphered the

problem; mere circumstances, reality (names, prison records, faces, judicial and penal proceedings) hardly interested him now. He wanted to travel a bit, he wanted to rest from three months of sedentary investigation. He reflected that the explanation of the murders was in an anonymous triangle and a dusty Greek word. The mystery appeared almost crystalline to him now; he was mortified to have dedicated a hundred days to it.

The train stopped at a silent loading station. Lönnrot got off. It was one of those deserted afternoons that seem like dawns. The air of the turbid, puddled plain was damp and cold. Lönnrot began walking along the countryside. He saw dogs, he saw a car on a siding, he saw the horizon, he saw a silver-coloured horse drinking the crapulous water of a puddle. It was growing dark when he saw the rectangular belvedere of the villa of Triste-le-Roy, almost as tall as the black eucalypti which surrounded it. He thought that scarcely one dawning and one nightfall (an ancient splendour in the east and another in the west) separated him from the moment long desired by the seekers of the Name.

A rusty wrought-iron fence defined the irregular perimeter of the villa. The main gate was closed. Lönnrot, without much hope of getting in, circled the area. Once again before the insurmountable gate, he placed his hand between the bars almost mechanically and encountered the bolt. The creaking of the iron surprised him. With a laborious passivity the whole gate swung back.

Lönnrot advanced among the eucalypti treading on confused generations of rigid, broken leaves. Viewed from anear, the house of the villa of Triste-le-Roy abounded in pointless symmetries and in maniacal repetitions : to one Diana in a murky niche corresponded a second Diana in another niche; one balcony was reflected in another balcony; double stairways led to double balustrades. A two-faced Hermes projected a monstrous shadow. Lönnrot circled the house as he had the villa. He examined everything; beneath the level of the terrace he saw a narrow Venetian blind.

He pushed it; a few marble steps descended to a vault. Lönn-rot, who had now perceived the architect's preferences, guessed that at the opposite wall there would be another stair-way. He found it, ascended, raised his hands and opened the trap door.

A brilliant light led him to a window. He opened it: a yellow, rounded moon defined two silent fountains in the melancholy garden. Lönnrot explored the house. Through ante-rooms and galleries he passed to duplicate patios, and time after time to the same patio. He ascended the dusty stairs to circular antechambers; he was multiplied infinitely in opposing mirrors; he grew tired of opening or half-opening windows which revealed outside the same desolate garden from various heights and various angles; inside, only pieces of furniture wrapped in yellow dust sheets and chandeliers bound up in tarlatan. A bedroom detained him; in that bedroom, one single flower in a porcelain vase; at the first touch the ancient petals fell apart. On the second floor, on the top floor, the house seemed infinite and expanding. *The house is not this large,* he thought. *Other things are making it seem larger: the dim light, the symmetry, the mirrors, so many years, my unfamiliarity, the loneliness.*

By way of a spiral staircase he arrived at the oriel. The early evening moon shone through the diamonds of the window; they were yellow, red and green. An astonishing, dizzying recollection struck him.

Two men of short stature, robust and ferocious, threw them-selves on him and disarmed him; another, very tall, saluted him gravely and said:

'You are very kind. You have saved us a night and a day.'

It was Red Scharlach. The men handcuffed Lönnrot. The latter at length recovered his voice.

'Scharlach, are you looking for the Secret Name?'

Scharlach remained standing, indifferent. He had not partici-pated in the brief struggle, and he scarcely extended his hand to receive Lönnrot's revolver. He spoke; Lönnrot noted in his voice a fatigued triumph, a hatred the size of the universe, a sadness not less than that hatred.

'No,' said Scharlach. 'I am seeking something more ephemeral and perishable, I am seeking Erik Lönnrot. Three years ago, in a gambling house on the rue de Toulon, you arrested my brother and had him sent to jail. My men slipped me away in a coupé from the gun battle with a policeman's bullet in my stomach. Nine days and nine nights I lay in agony in this desolate, symmetrical villa; fever was demolishing me, and the odious two-faced Janus who watches the twilights and the dawns lent horror to my dreams and to my waking. I came to abominate my body, I came to sense that two eyes, two hands, two lungs are as monstrous as two faces. An Irishman tried to convert me to the faith of Jesus; he repeated to me the phrase of the *goyim*: All roads lead to Rome. At night my delirium nurtured itself on that metaphor; I felt that the world was a labyrinth, from which it was impossible to flee, for all roads, though they pretend to lead to the north or south, actually lead to Rome, which was also the quadrilateral jail where my brother was dying and the villa of Triste-le-Roy. On those nights I swore by the God who sees with two faces and by all the gods of fever and of the mirrors to weave a labyrinth around the man who had imprisoned my brother. I have woven it and it is firm: the ingredients are a dead heresiologist, a compass, an eighteenth-century sect, a Greek word, a dagger, the diamonds of a paint shop.

'The first term of the sequence was given to me by chance. I had planned with a few colleagues – among them Daniel Azevedo – the robbery of the Tetrarch's sapphires. Azevedo betrayed us: he got drunk with the money that we had advanced him and he undertook the job a day early. He got lost in the vastness of the hotel; around two in the morning he stumbled into Yarmolinsky's room. The latter, harassed by insomnia, had started to write. He was working on some notes, apparently, for an article on the Name of God; he had already written the words: *The first letter of the Name has been uttered*. Azevedo warned him to be silent; Yarmolinsky reached out his hand for the bell which would awaken the hotel's forces; Azevedo countered with a single stab in the chest. It was almost a reflex action; half a century of violence had taught him that the easiest and surest thing is to kill. ... Ten days later I learned through the *Yidische Zaitung* that you were seeking in Yarmolinsky's writings the key to his death. I read the *History of the Hasidic Sect*; I learned that the reverent fear of uttering the Name of God had given rise to the doctrine that that Name is all powerful and recondite. I discovered that some Hasidim, in search of that secret Name, had gone so far as to perform human sacrifices. ... I knew that you would make the conjecture that the Hasidim had sacrificed the rabbi; I set myself the task of justifying that conjecture.

'Marcel Yarmolinsky died on the night of December third; for the second "sacrifice" I selected the night of January third. He died in the north; for the second "sacrifice" a place in the west was suitable. Daniel Azevedo was the necessary victim. He deserved death; he was impulsive, a traitor; his apprehension could destroy the entire plan. One of us stabbed him; in order to link his corpse to the other one I wrote on the paint shop diamonds: *The second letter of the Name has been uttered.*

'The third murder was produced on the third of February. It was, as Treviranus guessed, a mere sham. I am Gryphius-Ginzberg-Ginsburg; I endured an interminable week (supplemented by a tenuous fake beard) in the perverse cubicle on the rue de Toulon, until my friends abducted me. From the footboard of the cab, one of them wrote on a post: *The last of the letters of the Name has been uttered.* That sentence revealed that the series of murders was *triple*. Thus the public understood it; I, nevertheless, interspersed repeated signs that would allow you, Erik Lönnrot, the reasoner, to understand that the series was quadruple. A portent in the north, others in the east and west, demand a fouth portent in the south; the Tetragrammaton – the name of God, JHVH – is made up of *four* letters; the harlequins and the paint shop sign suggested *four* points. In the manual of Leusden I underlined a certain passage: that passage manifests that Hebrews compute the day from sunset to sunset; that passage makes known that the deaths occurred on the *fourth* of each month. I sent the equilateral triangle to Treviranus. I foresaw that you would add the missing point. The point which would form a perfect rhomb, the point which fixes in advance where a punctual death awaits you. I have premeditated everything, Erik Lönnrot, in order to attract you to the solitudes of Triste-le-Roy.'

Lönnrot avoided Scharlach's eyes. He looked at the trees and the sky subdivided into diamonds of turbid yellow, green and red. He felt faintly cold, and he felt, too, an impersonal – almost anonymous – sadness. It was already night; from the dusty garden came the futile cry of a bird. For the last time, Lönnrot considered the problem of the symmetrical and periodic deaths.

'In your labyrinth there are three lines too many,' he said at last. 'I know of one Greek labyrinth which is a single straight line. Along that line so many philosophers have lost themselves that a mere detective might well do so, too. Scharlach, when in some other incarnation you hunt me, pretend to commit (or do commit) a crime at A, then a second crime at B, eight kilometres from A, then a third crime at C, four kilometres from A and B, half-way between the two. Wait for me afterwards at D, two kilometres from A and C, again halfway between both. Kill me at D, as you are now going to kill me at Triste-le-Roy.'

'The next time I kill you,' replied Scharlach, 'I promise you that labyrinth, consisting of a single line which is invisible and unceasing.'

He moved back a few steps. Then, very carefully, he fired.

For Mandie Molina Vedia   *Translated by D.A.Y.*

The Secret Miracle

And God had him die for a hundred years and then revived him
and said:
   'How long have you been here?'
   'A day or a part of a day,' he answered.

Koran, II, 261

THE night of 14 March 1943, in an apartment in the Zeltnergasse
of Prague, Jaromir Hladik, the author of the unfinished drama
entitled *The Enemies*, or *Vindication of Eternity*, and of a study
of the indirect Jewish sources of Jakob Böhme, had a dream of
a long game of chess. The players were not two persons, but
two illustrious families; the game had been going on for centuries. Nobody could remember what the stakes were, but it
was rumoured that they were enormous, perhaps infinite; the
chessmen and the board were in a secret tower. Jaromir (in his
dream) was the first-born of one of the contending families.
The clock struck the hour for the game, which could not be
postponed. The dreamer raced over the sands of a rainy desert,
and was unable to recall either the pieces or the rules of chess.
At that moment he awoke. The clangour of the rain and of the
terrible clocks ceased. A rhythmic, unanimous noise, punctu-
ated by shouts of command, arose from the Zeltnergasse. It was
dawn, and the armoured vanguard of the Third Reich was
entering Prague.
On the nineteenth the authorities received a denunciation;
that same nineteenth, towards evening, Jaromir Hladik was
arrested. He was taken to an aseptic, white barracks on the
opposite bank of the Moldau. He was unable to refute a single
one of the Gestapo's charges; his mother's family name was

Jaroslavski, he was of Jewish blood, his study on Böhme had a marked Jewish emphasis, his signature had been one more on the protest against the *Anschluss*. In 1928 he had translated the *Sepher Yezirah* for the publishing house of Hermann Barsdorf. The fulsome catalogue of the firm had exaggerated, for publicity purposes, the translator's reputation, and the catalogue had been examined by Julius Rothe, one of the officials who held Hladik's fate in his hands. There is not a person who, except in the field of his own specialization, is not credulous; two or three adjectives in Gothic type were enough to persuade Julius Rothe of Hladik's importance, and he ordered him sentenced to death *pour encourager les autres*. The execution was set for 29 March, at 9 a.m. This delay (whose importance the reader will grasp later) was owing to the desire on the authorities' part to proceed impersonally and slowly, after the manner of vegetables and plants.

Hladik's first reaction was mere terror. He felt he would not have shrunk from the gallows, the block, or the knife, but that death by a firing squad was unbearable. In vain he tried to convince himself that the plain, unvarnished fact of dying was the fearsome thing, not the attendant circumstances. He never wearied of conjuring up these circumstances, senselessly trying to exhaust all their possible variations. He infinitely anticipated the process of his dying, from the sleepless dawn to the mysterious volley. Before the day set by Julius Rothe he died hundreds of deaths in courtyards whose forms and angles strained geometrical probabilities, machine-gunned by variable soldiers in changing numbers, who at times killed him from a distance, at others from close by. He faced these imaginary executions with real terror (perhaps with real bravery); each simulacrum lasted a few seconds. When the circle was closed, Jaromir returned once more and interminably to the tremulous vespers of his death. Then he reflected that reality does not usually coincide with our anticipation of it; with a logic of his own he inferred that to foresee a circumstantial detail is to prevent its happening. Trusting in this weak magic, he invented, *so that they would not happen*, the most gruesome details. Finally, as was natural, he came to fear that they were prophetic. Miserable in the night, he endeavoured to find some way to hold fast to the fleeting substance of time. He knew that it was rushing headlong towards the dawn of the twenty-ninth. He reasoned aloud : 'I am now in the night of the twenty-second; while this night lasts (and for six nights more), I am invulnerable, immortal.' The nights of sleep seemed to him deep, dark pools in which he could submerge himself. There were moments when he longed impatiently for the final burst of fire that would free him, for better or for worse, from the vain compulsion of his imaginings. On the twenty-eighth, as the last sunset was reverberating from the high barred windows, the thought of his drama, *The Enemies*, deflected him from these abject considerations.

Hladik had rounded forty. Aside from a few friendships and many habits, the problematic exercise of literature constituted his life. Like all writers, he measured the achievements of others by what they had accomplished, asking of them that they measure him by what he envisaged or planned. All the books he had published had left him with a complex feeling of repentance. His studies of the work of Böhme, of Ibn Ezra, and of Fludd had been characterized essentially by mere application; his translation of the *Sepher Yezirah*, by carelessness, fatigue and conjecture. *Vindication of Eternity* perhaps had fewer shortcomings. The first volume gave a history of man's various concepts of eternity, from the immutable Being of Parmenides to the modifiable Past of Hinton. The second denied (with Francis Bradley) that all the events of the universe make up a temporal series, arguing that the number of man's possible experiences is not infinite, and that a single 'repetition' suffices to prove that time is a fallacy ... Unfortunately, the arguments that demonstrate this fallacy are equally fallacious. Hladik was in the habit of going over them with a kind of contemptuous perplexity. He had also composed a series of Expressionist poems; to the poet's chagrin they had been included in an anthology published in 1924, and no subsequent anthology but inherited them. From all this equivocal, uninspired past Hladik had hoped to redeem himself with his drama in verse, *The Enemies*. (Hladik felt the verse form to be essential because it makes it impossible for the spectators to lose sight of irreality, one of art's requisites.)

The drama observed the unities of time, place and action. The scene was laid in Hradcany, in the library of Baron von Roemerstadt, on one of the last afternoons of the nineteenth century. In the first scene of the first act a strange man visits Roemerstadt. (A clock was striking seven, the vehemence of the setting sun's rays glorified the windows, a passionate, familiar Hungarian music floated in the air.) This visit is followed by others; Roemerstadt does not know the people who are importuning him, but he has the uncomfortable feeling that he has seen them somewhere, perhaps in a dream. They all fawn upon him, but it is apparent — first to the audience and then to the Baron — that they are secret enemies, in league to ruin him. Roemerstadt succeeds in checking or evading their involved schemings. In the dialogue mention is made of his sweetheart, Julia von Weidenau, and a certain Jaroslav Kubin, who at one time pressed his attentions on her. Kubin has now lost his mind, and believes himself to be Roemerstadt. The dangers increase; Roemerstadt, at the end of the second act, is forced to kill one of the conspirators. The third and final act opens. The incoherencies gradually increase; actors who had seemed out of the play reappear; the man Roemerstadt killed returns for a moment. Someone points out that evening has not fallen; the clock strikes seven, the high windows reverberate in the western sun, the air carries an impassioned Hungarian melody. The first actor comes on and repeats the lines he had spoken in the first scene of the first act. Roemerstadt speaks to him without surprise; the audience understands that Roemerstadt is the miserable Jaroslav Kubin. The drama has never taken place; it is the circular delirium that Kubin lives and relives endlessly.

Hladik had never asked himself whether this tragicomedy of errors was preposterous or admirable, well thought out or slipshod. He felt that the plot I have just sketched was best contrived to cover up his defects and point up his abilities and held the possibility of allowing him to redeem (symbolically) the meaning of his life. He had finished the first act and one or two scenes of the third; the metrical nature of the work made it possible for him to keep working it over, changing the hexa-meters, without the manuscript in front of him. He thought how he still had two acts to do, and that he was going to die very soon. He spoke with God in the darkness: 'If in some fashion I exist, if I am not one of Your repetitions and mis-takes, I exist as the author of *The Enemies*. To finish this drama, which can justify me and justify You, I need another year. Grant me these days, You to whom the centuries and time belong.' This was the last night, the most dreadful of all, but ten minutes later sleep flooded over him like a dark water.

Towards dawn he dreamed that he had concealed himself in one of the naves of the Clementine Library. A librarian wearing dark glasses asked him: 'What are you looking for?' Hladik answered: 'I am looking for God.' The librarian said to him: 'God is in one of the letters on one of the pages of one of the four hundred thousand volumes of the Clementine. My fathers and the fathers of my fathers have searched for this letter; I have grown blind seeking it.' He removed his glasses, and Hladik saw his eyes, which were dead. A reader came in to return an atlas. 'This atlas is worthless,' he said, and handed it to Hladik, who opened it at random. He saw a map of India as in a daze. Suddenly sure of himself, he touched one of the tiniest letters. A ubiquitous voice said to him: 'The time of your labour has been granted.' At this point Hladik awoke.

He remembered that men's dreams belong to God, and that Maimonides had written that the words heard in a dream are divine when they are distinct and clear and the person uttering them cannot be seen. He dressed: two soldiers came into the cell and ordered him to follow them.

From behind the door, Hladik had envisaged a labyrinth of passageways, stairs and separate buildings. The reality was less spectacular: they descended to an inner court by a narrow iron stairway. Several soldiers – some with uniform unbuttoned

– were examining a motorcycle and discussing it. The sergeant looked at the clock; it was 8.44. They had to wait until it struck nine. Hladik, more insignificant than pitiable, sat down on a pile of wood. He noticed that the soldiers' eyes avoided his. To ease his wait, the sergeant handed him a cigarette. Hladik did not smoke; he accepted it out of politeness or humility. As he lighted it, he noticed that his hands were shaking. The day was clouding over; the soldiers spoke in a low voice as though he were already dead. Vainly he tried to recall the woman of whom Julia von Weidenau was the symbol.

The squad formed and stood at attention. Hladik, standing against the barracks wall, waited for the volley. Someone pointed out that the wall was going to be stained with blood; the victim was ordered to step forward a few paces. Incongruously, this reminded Hladik of the fumbling preparations of photographers. A big drop of rain struck one of Hladik's temples and rolled slowly down his cheek; the sergeant shouted the final order.

The physical universe came to a halt.

The guns converged on Hladik, but the men who were to kill him stood motionless. The sergeant's arm eternized an unfinished gesture. On a paving stone of the courtyard a bee cast an unchanging shadow. The wind had ceased, as in a picture. Hladik attempted a cry, a word, a movement of the hand. He realized that he was paralysed. Not a sound reached him from the halted world. He thought: 'I am in hell, I am dead.' He thought: 'I am mad.' He thought: 'Time has stopped.' Then he reflected that if that was the case, his mind would have stopped too. He wanted to test this; he repeated (without moving his lips) Vergil's mysterious fourth Eclogue. He imagined that the now remote soldiers must be sharing his anxiety; he longed to be able to communicate with them. It astonished him not to feel the least fatigue, not even the numbness of his protracted immobility. After an indeterminate time he fell asleep. When he awoke the world continued motionless and mute. The drop of water still clung to his cheek, the shadow of the bee to the stone. The smoke from the cigarette he had thrown away had not dispersed. Another 'day' went by before Hladik understood.

He had asked God for a whole year to finish his work; His omnipotence had granted it. God had worked a secret miracle for him; German lead would kill him at the set hour, but in his mind a year would go by between the order and its execution. From perplexity he passed to stupor, from stupor to resignation, from resignation to sudden gratitude.

He had no document but his memory; the training he had acquired with each added hexameter gave him a discipline unsuspected by those who set down and forget temporary, incomplete paragraphs. He was not working for posterity or even for God, whose literary tastes were unknown to him. Meticulously, motionlessly, secretly, he wrought in time his lofty, invisible labyrinth. He worked the third act over twice. He eliminated certain symbols as over-obvious, such as the repeated striking of the clock, the music. Nothing hurried him. He omitted, he condensed, he amplified. In certain instances he came back to the original version. He came to feel an affection for the courtyard, the barracks; one of the faces before him modified his conception of Roemerstadt's character. He discovered that the wearying cacophonies that bothered Flaubert so much are mere visual superstitions, weakness and limitation of the written word, not the spoken.... He concluded his drama. He had only the problem of a single phrase. He found it. The drop of water slid down his cheek. He opened his mouth in a maddened cry, moved his face, dropped under the quadruple blast.

Jaromir Hladik died on 29 March at 9.02 a.m.

Translated by Harriet de Onís

Three Versions of Judas

There seemed a certainty in degradation.
T. E. Lawrence:
Seven Pillars of Wisdom, CIII

IN Asia Minor or in Alexandria, in the second century of our faith, when Basilides disseminated the idea that the cosmos was the reckless or evil improvisation of deficient angels, Nils Runeberg would have directed, with singular intellectual passion, one of the Gnostic conventicles. Dante would have assigned him, perhaps, a fiery grave; his name would extend the list of lesser heresiarchs, along with Satornilus and Carpocrates; some fragment of his preachings, embellished with invective, would survive in the apocryphal *Liber adversus omnes haereses* or would have perished when the burning of a monastery library devoured the last copy of the *Syntagma*. Instead, God afforded Runeberg the twentieth century and the university town of Lund. There, in 1904, he published the first edition of *Kristus och Judas* and, in 1909, his major book, *Den hemlige Frälsaren*. (Of the latter there is a German translation, made in 1912 by Emil Schering; it is called *Der heimliche Heiland*.)

Before essaying an examination of the aforementioned works, it is necessary to repeat that Nils Runeberg, a member of the National Evangelical Union, was deeply religious. In the intellectual circles of Paris or even of Buenos Aires, a man of letters might well rediscover Runeberg's theses; these theses, set forth in such circles, would be frivolous and useless exercises in negligence or blasphemy. For Runeberg, they were the key to one of the central mysteries of theology; they were the subject of meditation and analysis, of historical and philological controversy, of pride, of jubilation and of terror. They justified and wrecked his life. Those who read this article should also consider that it registers only Runeberg's conclusions, not his dialectic or his proof. Someone may observe that the conclusion no doubt preceded the 'proof'. Who would resign himself to seeking proof of something he did not believe or whose preachment did not matter to him?

The first edition of *Kristus och Judas* bears the following categorical epigraph, whose meaning, years later, Nils Runeberg himself would monstrously expand: 'Not one, but all of the things attributed by tradition to Judas Iscariot are false' (De Quincey, 1857). Preceded by a German, De Quincey speculated that Judas reported Jesus to the authorities in order to force him to reveal his divinity and thus ignite a vast rebellion against the tyranny of Rome; Runeberg suggests a vindication of a metaphysical sort. Skilfully, he begins by stressing the superfluity of Judas's act. He observes (as does Robertson) that in order to identify a teacher who preached daily in the synagogue and worked miracles before gatherings of thousands of men, betrayal by an apostle is unnecessary. This, nevertheless, occurred. To suppose an error in the Scriptures is intolerable; no less intolerable is to admit an accidental happening in the most precious event in world history. *Ergo*, Judas's betrayal was not accidental; it was a preordained fact which has its mysterious place in the economy of redemption. Runeberg continues: The Word, when it was made flesh, passed from ubiquity to space, from eternity to history, from limitless satisfaction to change and death; in order to correspond to such a sacrifice, it was necessary that one man, in representation of all men, make a sacrifice of condign nature. Judas Iscariot was that man. Judas, alone among the apostles, sensed the secret divinity and terrible intent of Jesus. The Word had been lowered to mortal condition; Judas, a disciple of the Word, could lower himself to become an informer (the worst crime in all infamy) and reside amidst the perpetual fires of Hell. The lower order is a mirror of the higher; the forms of earth correspond to the forms of Heaven; the spots on one's skin are a chart of the incorruptible constellations; Judas in some way reflects Jesus. Hence the thirty pieces of silver and the kiss; hence the suicide, in order to merit Reprobation even more. Thus Nils Runeberg elucidated the enigma of Judas.

Theologians of all confessions refuted him. Lars Peter Engström accused him of being unaware of, or omitting, the hypostatic union; Axel Borelius, of renewing the heresy of the Docetists, who denied that Jesus was human; the rigid Bishop of Lund, of contradicting the third verse of the twenty-second chapter of the gospel of St Luke.

These varied anathemas had their influence on Runeberg, who partially rewrote the rejected book and modified its doctrine. He left the theological ground to his adversaries and set forth oblique arguments of a moral order. He admitted that Jesus, 'who had at his disposal all the considerable resources which Omnipotence may offer', did not need a man to redeem all men. He then refuted those who maintain we know nothing of the inexplicable traitor; we know, he said, that he was one of the aspostles, one of those chosen to announce the kingdom of heaven, to cure the sick, to clean lepers, to raise the dead and cast out demons (Matthew 10 : 7–8; Luke 9 : 1). A man whom the Redeemer has thus distinguished merits the best interpretation we can give of his acts. To attribute his crime to greed (as some have done, citing John 12 : 6) is to resign oneself to the basest motive. Nils Runeberg proposes the opposite motive: a hyperbolic and even unlimited asceticism. The ascetic, for the greater glory of God, vilifies and mortifies his flesh; Judas did the same with his spirit. He renounced honour, morality, peace and the kingdom of heaven, just as others, less heroically, renounce pleasure.* With terrible lucidity he premeditated his sins. In adultery there is usually tenderness and abnegation; in homicide, courage; in profanity and blasphemy, a certain satanic lustre. Judas chose those sins untouched by any virtue: violation of trust (John 12 : 6) and betrayal. He

* Borelius inquires mockingly: 'Why didn't he renounce his renunciation? Or renounce the idea of renouncing his renunciation?'

acted with enormous humility, he believed himself unworthy of being good. Paul has written : 'He that glorieth, let him glory in the Lord' (I Corinthians 1 : 31); Judas sought Hell, because the happiness of the Lord was enough for him. He thought that happiness, like morality, is a divine attribute and should not be usurped by humans.*

Many have discovered, *post factum*, that in Runeberg's justifiable beginning lies his extravagant end and that *Den hemlige Frälsaren* is a mere perversion or exasperation of *Kristus och Judas*. Towards the end of 1907, Runeberg completed and corrected the manuscript text; almost two years went by without his sending it to the printer. In October 1909, the book appeared with a prologue (tepid to the point of being enigmatic) by the Danish Hebraist Erik Erfjord and with this perfidious epigraph : 'He was in the world, and the world was made by him, and the world knew him not' (John 1 : 10). The general argument is not complex, though the conclusion is monstrous. God, argues Nils Runeberg, lowered Himself to become a man for the redemption of mankind; we may conjecture that His sacrifice was perfect, not invalidated or attenuated by any omission. To limit what He underwent to the agony of one afternoon on the cross is blasphemous.† To main-

---

* Euclides da Cunha, in a book unknown to Runeberg, notes that for the heresiarch of Canudos, Antonio Conselheiro, virtue 'was almost an impiety'. The Argentine reader will recall analogous passages in the work of Almafuerte. In the symbolist sheet *Sju insegel*, Runeberg published an assiduous descriptive poem, *The Secret Waters*; the first stanzas narrate the events of a tumultuous day; the last, the discovery of a glacial pond; the poet suggests that the permanence of those silent waters corrects our useless violence and in some ways allows and absolves it. The poem ends as follows : 'The waters of the forest are good; we can be evil and suffer.'

† Maurice Abramowicz observes : '*Jésus, d'après ce scandinave, a toujours le beau rôle; ses déboires, grâce à la science des typographes, jouissent d'une réputation polyglotte; sa résidence de trente-trois ans parmi les humains ne fut, en somme, qu'une villégiature.*' Erfjord, in the third appendix to the *Christelige Dogmatik*, refutes this passage. He notes that the crucifixion of God has not

tain he was a man and incapable of sin involves a contradiction; the attributes of *impeccabilitas* and of *humanitas* are not compatible. Kemnitz admits that the Redeemer could feel fatigue, cold, embarrassment, hunger and thirst; we may also admit that he could sin and go astray. The famous text 'For he shall grow up before him as a tender plant, and as a root out of a dry ground; he hath no form nor comeliness; and when we shall see him, there is no beauty that we should desire him. He is despised and rejected of men; a man of sorrows, and acquainted with grief' (Isaah 53 : 2–3) is, for many, a future vision of the Saviour at the moment of his death; for others (for example, for Hans Lassen Martensen), a refutation of the beauty which vulgar opinion attributes to Christ; for Runeberg, the punctual prophecy not of a moment but of the whole atrocious future, in time and in eternity, of the Word made flesh. God made Himself totally a man but a man to the point of infamy, a man to the point of reprobation and the abyss. To save us, He could have chosen *any* of the destinies which make up the complex web of history; He could have been Alexander of Pythagoras or Rurik or Jesus; He chose the vilest destiny of all : He was Judas.

In vain the bookshops of Stockholm and Lund proposed this revelation to the public. The incredulous considered it, *a priori*, an insipid and laborious theological game, the theologians scorned it. Runeberg sensed in this ecumenical indifference an almost miraculous confirmation. God had ordained this indifference; God did not want His terrible secret divulged on earth. Runeberg understood that the hour had not yet arrived. He felt that ancient and divine maledictions were converging upon him; he remembered Elijah and Moses, who on the mountain top covered their faces in order not to see God;

ceased, for what has happened once in time is repeated ceaselessly in eternity. Judas, *now*, goes on receiving his pieces of silver, goes on kissing Christ, goes on throwing the coins into the temple, goes on making a noose in the rope on the field of blood. (Erfjord, in order to justify this affirmation, invokes the last chapter of the first volume of Jaromir Hladík's *Vindication of Eternity*.)

Isaiah, who was terrified when he saw the One whose glory fills the earth; Saul, whose eyes were struck blind on the road to Damascus; the rabbi Simeon ben Azai, who saw Paradise and died; the famous sorcerer John of Viterbo, who became mad when he saw the Trinity; the Midrashim, who abhor the impious who utter the *Shem Hamephorash*, the Secret Name of God. Was he not perhaps guilty of that dark crime? Would this not be the blasphemy against the Spirit, the one never to be forgiven (Matthew 12 : 31)? Valerius Soranus died for having divulged the hidden name of Rome; what infinite punishment would be his for having discovered and divulged the horrible name of God?

Drunk with insomnia and vertiginous dialectic, Nils Runeberg wandered through the streets of Malmö, begging at the top of his voice that he be granted the grace of joining his Redeemer in Hell.

He died of a ruptured aneurysm on the first of March, 1912. The heresiologists will perhaps remember him; to the concept of the Son, which seemed exhausted, he added the complexities of evil and misfortune.

Translated by J.E.I.

The Sect of the Phoenix

THOSE who write that the sect of the Phoenix had its origin in Heliopolis and derive it from the religious restoration following upon the death of the reformer Amenophis IV, cite texts from Herodotus, Tacitus and the monuments of Egypt, but they ignore, or prefer to ignore, that the designation 'Phoenix' does not date before Hrabanus Maurus and that the oldest sources (the *Saturnales* of Flavius Josephus, let us say) speak only of the People of the Custom or of the People of the Secret. Gregorovius has already observed, in the conventicles of Ferrara, that mention of the Phoenix was very rare in oral speech; in Geneva I have known artisans who did not understand me when I inquired if they were men of the Phoenix, but who immediately admitted being men of the Secret. If I am not deceived, the same is true of the Buddhists; the name by which the world knows them is not the one they themselves utter.

Miklosich, in a page much too famous, has compared the sectarians of the Phoenix with the gipsies. In Chile and in Hungary there are gipsies and there are also sectarians; aside from this sort of ubiquity, one and the other have very little in common. The gipsies are traders, coppersmiths, blacksmiths and fortune-tellers; the sectarians usually practise the liberal professions with success. The gipsies constitute a certain physical type and speak, or used to speak, a secret language; the sectarians are confused with the rest of men and the proof lies in that they have not suffered persecutions. The gipsies are picturesque and inspire bad poets; ballads, cheap illustrations and foxtrots omit the sectarians.... Martin Buber declares that the Jews are essentially pathetic; not all sectarians are and some deplore the pathetic; this public and notorious truth is

131

sufficient to refute the common error (absurdly defended by Urmann) which sees the Phoenix as a derivation of Israel. People more or less reason in this manner: Urmann was a sensitive man; Urmann was a Jew; Urmann came in frequent contact with the sectarians in the ghetto of Prague; the affinity Urmann sensed proves the reality of the fact. In all sincerity, I cannot concur with this dictum. That sectarians in a Jewish environment should resemble the Jews proves nothing; the undeniable fact is that, like Hazlitt's infinite Shakespeare, they resemble all the men in the world. They are everything for everyone, like the Apostle; several days ago, Dr Juan Francisco Amaro, of Paysandú, admired the facility with which they assimilated Creole ways.

I have said that the history of the sect records no persecutions. This is true, but since there is no human group in which members of the sect do not figure, it is also true that there is no persecution or rigour they have not suffered and perpetrated. In the Occidental wars and in the remote wars of Asia they have shed their blood secularly, under opposing banners; it avails them very little to identify themselves with all the nations of the world.

Without a sacred book to join them as the scriptures do for Israel, without a common memory, without that other memory which is a language, scattered over the face of the earth, diverse in colour and features, one thing alone – the Secret – unites them and will unite them until the end of time. Once, in addition to the Secret, there was a legend (and perhaps a cosmogonic myth), but the shallow men of the Phoenix have forgotten it and now only retain the obscure tradition of a punishment. Of a punishment, of a pact or of a privilege, for the versions differ and scarcely allow us to glimpse the verdict of a God who granted eternity to a lineage if its members, generation after generation, would perform a rite. I have collated accounts by travellers, I have conversed with patriarchs and theologians; I can testify that fulfilment of the rite is the only religious practice observed by the sectarians. The rite constitutes the Secret. This Secret, as I have already indicated, is transmitted from generation to generation, but good usage prefers that mothers should not teach it to their children, nor that priests should; initiation into the mystery is the task of the lowest individuals. A slave, a leper or a beggar serve as mystagogues. Also one child may indoctrinate another. The act in itself is trivial, momentary and requires no description. The materials are cork, wax or gum arabic. (In the liturgy, mud is mentioned; this is often used as well.) There are no temples especially dedicated to the celebration of this cult, but certain ruins, a cellar or an entrance hall are considered propitious places. The Secret is sacred but is always somewhat ridiculous; its performance is furtive and even clandestine and the adept do not speak of it. There are no decent words to name it, but it is understood that all words name it or, rather, inevitably allude to it, and thus, in a conversation I say something or other and the adept smile or become uncomfortable, for they realize I have touched upon the Secret. In Germanic literatures there are poems written by sectarians whose nominal subject is the sea or the twilight of evening; they are, in some way, symbols of the Secret, I hear it said repeatedly. *Orbis terrarum est speculum Ludi* reads an apocryphal adage recorded by Du Cange in his Glossary. A kind of sacred horror prevents some faithful believers from performing this very simple rite; the others despise them, but they despise themselves even more. Considerable credit is enjoyed, however, by those who deliberately renounce the custom and attain direct contact with the divinity; these sectarians, in order to express this contact, do so with figures taken from the liturgy and thus John of the Rood wrote:

> *May the Seven Firmaments know that God*
> *Is as delectable as the Cork and the Slime.*

I have attained on three continents the friendship of many devotés of the Phoenix; I know that the Secret, at first, seemed to them banal, embarrassing, vulgar and (what is even stranger) incredible. They could not bring themselves to admit their parents had stooped to such manipulations. What is odd is that the Secret was not lost long ago; in spite of the vicissitudes of the Universe, in spite of wars and exoduses, it reaches, awesomely, all the faithful. Someone had not hesitated to affirm that it is now instinctive.

Translated by J.E.I.

The Immortal

Salomon saith, *There is no new thing upon the earth.* So that as Plato had an imagination, *that all knowledge was but remembrance;* so Salomon giveth his sentence, *that all novelty is but oblivion.*

Francis Bacon: Essays, LVIII

IN London, in the first part of June 1929, the antique dealer Joseph Cartaphilus of Smyrna offered the Princess of Lucinge the six volumes in small quarto (1715–20) of Pope's *Iliad.* The Princess acquired them; on receiving the books, she exchanged a few words with the dealer. He was, she tells us, a wasted and earthen man, with grey eyes and grey beard, of singularly vague features. He could express himself with fluency and ignorance in several languages; in a very few minutes, he went from French to English and from English to an enigmatic conjunction of Salonika Spanish and Macao Portuguese. In October the Princess heard from a passenger of the *Zeus* that Cartaphilus had died at sea while returning to Smyrna, and that he had been buried on the island of Ios. In the last volume of the *Iliad* she found this manuscript.

The original is written in English and abounds in Latinisms. The version we offer is literal.

I

As far as I can recall, my labours began in a garden in Thebes Hekatompylos, when Diocletian was emperor. I had served (without glory) in the recent Egyptian wars, I was tribune of a legion quartered in Berenice, facing the Red Sea: fever and magic consumed many men who had magnanimously coveted the steel. The Mauretanians were vanquished; the land previously occupied by the rebel cities was eternally dedicated to the Plutonic gods; Alexandria, once subdued, vainly implored Caesar's mercy; within a year the legions reported victory, but I scarcely managed a glimpse of Mars's countenance. This privation pained me and perhaps caused me precipitously to undertake the discovery, through fearful and diffuse deserts, of the secret City of the Immortals.

My labours began, I have related, in a garden in Thebes. All that night I was unable to sleep, for something was struggling within my heart. I arose shortly before dawn; my slaves were sleeping, the moon was of the same colour as the infinite sand. An exhausted and bloody horseman came from the east. A few steps from me, he tumbled from his mount. In a faint, insatiable voice he asked me in Latin the name of the river bathing the city's walls. I answered that it was the Egypt, fed by the rains. 'Another is the river I seek,' he replied sadly, 'the secret river which cleanses men of death.' Dark blood surged from his breast. He told me that his homeland was a mountain on the other side of the Ganges and that on this mountain it was said that if one travelled to the west, where the world ends, he would reach the river whose waters grant immortality. He added that on its far bank the City of the Immortals rises, rich in bastions and amphitheatres and temples. Before dawn he died, but I had determined to discover the city and its river. Interrogated by the executioner, some Mauretanian prisoners confirmed the traveller's tale; someone recalled the Elysian plain, at the end of the earth, where men's lives are perdurable; someone else, the peaks where the Pactolus rises, whose inhabitants live for a century. In Rome, I conversed with philosophers who felt that to extend man's life is to extend his agony and multiply his deaths. I do not know if I ever believed in the City of the Immortals: I think that then the task of finding it was sufficient. Flavius, proconsul of Getulia, gave me two hundred soldiers for the undertaking. I also recruited mercenaries, who said they knew the roads and were the first to desert.

Later events have deformed inextricably the memory of the

first days of our journey. We departed from Arsinoe and entered the burning desert. We crossed the land of the troglodytes, who devour serpents and are ignorant of verbal commerce; that of the garamants, who keep their women in common and feed on lions; that of the augyls, who worship only Tartarus. We exhausted other deserts where the sand is black, where the traveller must usurp the hours of night, for the fervour of day is intolerable. From afar, I glimpsed the mountain which gave its name to the Ocean : on its sides grows the spurge plant, which counteracts poisons; on its peak live the satyrs, a nation of fell and savage men, given to lewdness. That these barbarous regions, where the earth is mother of monsters, could shelter in their interior a famous city seemed inconceivable to all of us. We continued our march, for it would have been dishonour to turn back. A few foolhardy men slept with their faces exposed to the moon; they burned with fever; in the corrupted water of the cisterns others drank madness and death. Then the desertions began; very shortly thereafter, mutinies. To repress them, I did not hesitate to exercise severity. I proceeded justly, but a centurion warned me that the seditious (eager to avenge the crucifixion of one of their number) were plotting my death. I fled from the camp with the few soldiers loyal to me. I lost them in the desert, amid the sandstorms and the vast night. I was lacerated by a Cretan arrow. I wandered several days without finding water, or one enormous day multiplied by the sun, my thirst or my fear of thirst. I left the route to the judgement of my horse. In the dawn, the distance bristled up into pyramids and towers. Intolerably, I dreamt of an exiguous and nitid labyrinth : in the centre was a water jar; my hands almost touched it, my eyes could see it, but so intricate and perplexed were the curves that I knew I would die before reaching it.

2

When finally I became untangled from this nightmare, I found myself lying with my hands tied, in an oblong stone niche no larger than a common grave, shallowly excavated into the sharp slope of a mountain. Its sides were damp, polished by time rather than by human effort. I felt a painful throbbing in my chest, I felt that I was burning with thirst. I looked out and shouted feebly. At the foot of the mountain, an impure stream spread noiselessly, clogged with débris and sand; on the opposite bank (beneath the last sun or beneath the first) shone the evident City of the Immortals. I saw walls, arches, façades and fora: the base was a stone plateau. A hundred or so irregular niches, analogous to mine, furrowed the mountain and the valley. In the sand there were shallow pits; from these miserable holes (and from the niches) naked, grey-skinned, scraggly bearded men emerged. I thought I recognized them: they belonged to the bestial breed of the troglodytes, who infest the shores of the Arabian Gulf and the caverns of Ethiopia; I was not amazed that they could not speak and that they devoured serpents.

The urgency of my thirst made me reckless. I calculated that I was some thirty feet from the sand; I threw myself headlong down the slope, my eyes closed, my hands behind my back. I sank my bloody face into the dark water. I drank just as animals water themselves. Before losing myself again in sleep and delirium, I repeated, inexplicably, some words in Greek: 'the rich Trojans from Zelea who drink the black water of the Aisepos.'

I do not know how many days and nights turned above me. Aching, unable to regain the shelter of the caverns, naked on the unknown sand, I let the moon and the sun gamble with my unfortunate destiny. The troglodytes, infantile in their barbarity, did not aid me to survive or to die. In vain I begged them to put me to death. One day, I broke my bindings on an edge of flint. Another day, I got up and managed to beg or steal – I, Marcus Flaminius Rufus, military tribute of one of Rome's legions – my first detested portion of serpent flesh.

My covetousness to see the Immortals, to touch the superhuman city, almost kept me from sleep. As if they penetrated my purpose, neither did the troglodytes sleep: at first I inferred that they were watching me; later, that they had become contaminated by my uneasiness, much as dogs may do. To leave the barbarous village, I chose the most public of hours, the coming of evening, when almost all the men emerge from their crevices and pits and look at the setting sun, without seeing it. I prayed out loud, less as a supplication to divine favour than as an intimidation of the tribe with articulate words. I crossed the stream clogged by the dunes and headed towards the City. Confusedly, two or three men followed me. They were (like the others of that breed) of slight stature; they did not inspire fear but rather repulsion. I had to skirt several irregular ravines which seemed to me like quarries; obfuscated by the City's grandeur, I had thought it nearby. Towards midnight, I set foot upon the black shadow of its walls, bristling out in idolatrous forms on the yellow sand. I was halted by a kind of sacred horror. Novelty and the desert are so abhorred by man that I was glad one of the troglodytes had followed me to the last. I closed my eyes and awaited (without sleeping) the light of day.

I have said that the City was founded on a stone plateau. This plateau, comparable to a high cliff, was no less arduous than the walls. In vain I fatigued myself: the black base did not disclose the slightest irregularity, the invariable walls seemed not to admit a single door. The force of the sun obliged me to seek refuge in a cave; in the rear was a pit, in the pit a stairway which sank down abysmally into the darkness below. I went down; through a chaos of sordid galleries I reached a vast circular chamber, scarcely visible. There were nine doors in this cellar; eight led to a labyrinth that treacherously returned to the same chamber; the ninth (through another labyrinth) led to a second circular chamber equal to the first. I do not know the total number of these chambers; my misfortune and anxiety multiplied them. The silence was hostile and almost perfect; there was no sound in this deep stone network save that of a subterranean wind, whose cause I did not discover; noiselessly, tiny streams of rusty water disappeared between the crevices. Horribly, I became habituated to this doubtful world; I found it incredible that there could be anything but cellars with nine doors and long branched-out cellars; I do not know how long I must have walked beneath the ground; I know that I once confused, in the same nostalgia, the atrocious village of the barbarians and my native city, amid the clusters.

In the depths of a corridor, an unforeseen wall halted me; a remote light fell from above. I raised my confused eyes : in the vertiginous, extreme heights I saw a circle of sky so blue that it seemed purple. Some metal rungs scaled the wall. I was limp with fatigue, but I climbed up, stopping only at times to sob clumsily with joy. I began to glimpse capitals and astragals, triangular pediments and vaults, confused pageants of granite and marble. Thus I was afforded this ascension from the blind region of dark interwoven labyrinths into the resplendent City.

I emerged into a kind of little square or, rather, a kind of courtyard. It was surrounded by a single building of irregular form and variable height; to this heterogeneous building belonged the different cupolas and columns. Rather than by any other trait of this incredible monument, I was held by the extreme age of its fabrication. I felt that it was older than mankind, than the earth. This manifest antiquity (though in some way terrible to the eyes) seemed to me in keeping with the work of immortal builders. At first cautiously, later indifferently, at last desperately, I wandered up the stairs and along the pavements of the inextricable palace. (Afterwards I learned that the width and height of the steps were not constant, a fact which made me understand the singular fatigue they produced). 'This palace is a fabrication of the gods,' I thought at the beginning. I explored the uninhabited interiors and corrected myself : 'The gods who built it have died.' I noted its peculiarities and said : 'The gods who built it were mad.' I said it, I know, with an incomprehensible reprobation which was almost remorse, with more intellectual horror than palpable fear. To the impression of enormous antiquity others were added : that of the interminable, that of the atrocious, that of the complexly senseless. I had crossed a labyrinth, but the nitid City of the Immortals filled me with fright and repugnance. A labyrinth is a structure compounded to confuse men; its architecture, rich in symmetries, is subordinated to that end. In the palace I imperfectly explored, the architecture lacked any such finality. It abounded in dead-end corridors, high unattainable windows, portentous doors which led to a cell or pit, incredible inverted stairways whose steps and balustrades hung downwards. Other stairways, clinging airily to the side of the monumental wall, would die without leading anywhere, after making two or three turns in the lofty darkness of the cupolas. I do not know if all the examples I have enumerated are literal; I know that for many years they infested my nightmares; I am no longer able to know if such and such a detail is a transcription of reality or of the forms which unhinged my nights. 'This City' (I thought) 'is so horrible that its mere existence and perdurance, though in the midst of a secret desert, contaminates the past and the future and in some way even jeopardizes the stars. As long as it lasts, no one in the world can be strong or happy.' I do not want to describe it; a chaos of heterogeneous words, the body of a tiger or a bull in which teeth, organs and heads monstrously pullulate in mutual conjunction and hatred can (perhaps) be approximate images.

I do not remember the stages of my return, amid the dusty and damp hypogea. I only know I was not abandoned by the fear that, when I left the last labyrinth, I would again be surrounded by the nefarious City of the Immortals. I can remember nothing else. This oblivion, now insuperable, was perhaps voluntary; perhaps the circumstances of my escape were so unpleasant that, on some day no less forgotten as well, I swore to forget them.

3

Those who have read the account of my labours with attention will recall that a man from the tribe followed me as a dog might up to the irregular shadow of the walls. When I came

out of the last cellar, I found him at the mouth of the cave. He
was stretched out on the sand, where he was tracing clumsily
and erasing a string of signs that, like the letters in our dreams,
seem on the verge of being understood and then dissolve. At
first, I thought it was some kind of primitive writing; then I
saw it was absurd to imagine that men who have not attained
to the spoken word could attain to writing. Besides, none of the
forms was equal to another, which excluded or lessened the
possibility that they were symbolic. The man would trace
them, look at them and correct them. Suddenly, as if he were
annoyed by this game, he erased them with his palm and
forearm. He looked at me, seemed not to recognize me. However, so great was the relief which engulfed me (or so great and
fearful was my loneliness) that I supposed this rudimentary
troglodyte looking up at me from the floor of the cave had
been waiting for me. The sun heated the plain; when we began
the return to the village, beneath the first stars, the sand burned
under our feet. The troglodyte went ahead; that night I conceived the plan of teaching him to recognize and perhaps to
repeat a few words. The dog and the horse (I reflected) are
capable of the former; many birds, like the Caesars' nightingales, of the latter. No matter how crude a man's mind may be,
it will always be superior to that of irrational creatures.

The humility and wretchedness of the troglodyte brought to
my memory the image of Argos, the moribund old dog in the
Odyssey, and so I gave him the name Argos and tried to teach
it to him. I failed over and again. Conciliation, rigour and
obstinacy were completely in vain. Motionless, with lifeless
eyes, he seemed not to perceive the sounds I tried to press upon
him. A few steps from me, he seemed to be very distant. Lying
on the sand like a small ruinous lava sphinx, he let the heavens
turn above him from the twilight of dawn till that of evening. I
judged it impossible that he not be aware of my purpose. I
recalled that among the Ethiopians it is well known that
monkeys deliberately do not speak so they will not be obliged
to work, and I attributed Argos's silence to suspicion or fear.
From that imagination I went on to others, even more ex-

travagant. I thought that Argos and I participated in different universes; I thought that our perceptions were the same, but that he combined them in another way and made other objects of them; I thought that perhaps there were no objects for him, only a vertiginous and continuous play of extremely brief impressions. I thought of a world without memory, without time; I considered the possibility of a language without nouns, a language of impersonal verbs or indeclinable epithets. Thus the days went on dying and with them the years, but something akin to happiness happened one morning. It rained, with powerful deliberation.

Desert nights can be cold, but that night had been fire. I dreamt that a river in Thessaly (to whose waters I had returned a goldfish) came to rescue me; over the red sand and black rock I heard it approach; the coolness of the air and the busy murmur of the rain awoke me. I ran naked to meet it. Night was fading; beneath the yellow clouds, the tribe, no less joyful than I, offered themselves to the vivid downpour in a kind of ecstasy. They seemed like Corybantes possessed by the divinity. Argos, his eyes turned towards the sky, groaned; torrents ran down his face, not only of water but (I later learned) of tears. Argos, I cried, Argos.

Then, with gentle admiration, as if he were discovering something lost and forgotten a long time ago, Argos stammered these words: 'Argos, Ulysses's dog.' And then, also without looking at me: 'This dog lying in the manure.'

We accept reality easily, perhaps because we intuit that nothing is real. I asked him what he knew of the *Odyssey*. The exercise of Greek was painful for him; I had to repeat the question.

'Very little,' he said. 'Less than the poorest rhapsodist. It must be a thousand and one hundred years since I invented it.'

4

Everything was elucidated for me that day. The troglodytes were the Immortals; the rivulet of sandy water, the River sought by the horseman. As for the city whose renown had spread as far as the Ganges, it was some nine centuries since the Immortals had razed it. With the relics of its ruins they erected, in the same place, the mad city I had traversed : a kind of parody or inversion and also temple of the irrational gods who govern the world and of whom we know nothing, save that they do not resemble man. This establishment was the last symbol to which the Immortals condescended; it marks a stage at which, judging that all undertakings are in vain, they determined to live in thought, in pure speculation. They erected their structure, forgot it and went to dwell in the caves. Absorbed in thought, they hardly perceived the physical world.

These things were told me by Homer, as one would speak to a child. He also related to me his old age and the last voyage he undertook, moved, as was Ulysses, by the purpose of reaching the men who do not know what the sea is nor eat meat seasoned with salt nor suspect what an oar is. He lived for a century in the City of the Immortals. When it was razed, he advised that the other be founded. This should not surprise us; it is famous that after singing of the war of Ilion, he sang of the war of the frogs and mice. He was like a god who might create the cosmos and then create a chaos.

To be immortal is commonplace; except for man, all creatures are immortal, for they are ignorant of death; what is divine, terrible, incomprehensible, is to know that one is immortal. I have noted that, in spite of religions, this conviction is very rare. Israelites, Christians and Moslems profess immortality, but the veneration they render this world proves they believe only in it, since they destine all other worlds, in infinite number, to be its reward or punishment. The wheel of certain Hindustani religions seems more reasonable to me; on this wheel, which has neither beginning nor end, each life is the effect of the preceding and engenders the following, but none determines the totality.... Indoctrinated by a practice of centuries, the republic of immortal men had attained the perfection of tolerance and almost that of indifference. They knew that in an infinite period of time, all things happen to all men.

Because of his past or future virtues, every man is worthy of all goodness, but also of all perversity, because of his infamy in the past or future. Thus, just as in games of chance the odd and even numbers tend towards equilibrium, so also wit and stolidity cancel out and correct each other and perhaps the rustic *Poem of the Cid* is the counter-balance demanded by one single epithet from the *Eclogues* or by an epigram of Heraclitus. The most fleeting thought obeys an invisible design and can crown, or inaugurate, a secret form. I know of those who have done evil so that in future centuries good would result, or would have resulted in those already past.... Seen in this manner, all our acts are just, but they are also indifferent. There are no moral or intellectual merits. Homer composed the *Odyssey*; if we postulate an infinite period of time, with infinite circumstances and changes, the impossible thing is not to compose the *Odyssey*, at least once. No one is anyone, one single immortal man is all men. Like Cornelius Agrippa, I am god, I am hero, I am philosopher, I am demon and I am world, which is a tedious way of saying that I do not exist.

The concept of the world as a system of precise compensations influenced the Immortals vastly. In the first place, it made them invulnerable to pity. I have mentioned the ancient quarries which broke the fields on the other bank; a man once fell headlong into the deepest of them; he could not hurt himself or die but he was burning with thirst; before they threw him a rope, seventy years went by. Neither were they interested in their own fate. The body, for them, was a submissive domestic animal and it sufficed to give it, every month, the pittance of a few hours of sleep, a bit of water and a scrap of meat. Let no one reduce us to the status of ascetics. There is no pleasure more complex than that of thought and we surrendered ourselves to it. At times, an extraordinary stimulus would restore us to the physical world. For example, that morning, the old elemental joy of the rain. Those lapses were quite rare; all the Immortals were capable of perfect quietude; I remember one whom I never saw stand up: a bird had nested on his breast.

Among the corollaries of the doctrine that there is nothing lacking compensation in something else, there is one whose theoretical importance is very small, but which induced us, towards the end or the beginning of the tenth century, to disperse ourselves over the face of the earth. It can be stated in these words: 'There exists a river whose waters grant immortality; in some region there must be another river whose waters remove it.' The number of rivers is not infinite; an immortal traveller who traverses the world will finally, some day, have drunk from all of them. We proposed to discover that river.

Death (or its allusion) makes men precious and pathetic. They are moving because of their phantom condition; every act they execute may be their last; there is not a face that is not on the verge of dissolving like a face in a dream. Everything among the mortals has the value of the irretrievable and the perilous. Among the Immortals, on the other hand, every act (and every thought) is the echo of others that preceded it in the past, with no visible beginning, or the faithful presage of others that in the future will repeat it to a vertiginous degree. There is nothing that is not as if lost in a maze of indefatigable mirrors. Nothing can happen only once, nothing is preciously precarious. The elegiacal, the serious, the ceremonial, do not hold for the Immortals. Homer and I separated at the gates of Tangier; I think we did not even say goodbye.

5

I travelled over new kingdoms, new empires. In the fall of 1066, I fought at Stamford Bridge, I do not recall whether in the forces of Harold, who was not long in finding his destiny, or in those of the hapless Harald Hardrada, who conquered six feet of English soil, or a bit more. In the seventh century of the Hegira, in the suburb of Bulaq, I transcribed with measured calligraphy, in a language I have forgotten, in an alphabet I do not know, the seven adventures of Sinbad and the history of the City of Bronze. In the courtyard of a jail in Samarkand I

played a great deal of chess. In Bikaner I professed the science
of astrology and also in Bohemia. In 1638 I was at Kolozsvár
and later in Leipzig. In Aberdeen, in 1714, I subscribed to the
six volumes of Pope's *Iliad*; I know that I frequented its pages
with delight. About 1729 I discussed the origin of that poem
with a professor of rhetoric named, I think, Giambattista; his
arguments seemed to me irrefutable. On the fourth of October,
1921, the *Patna*, which was taking me to Bombay, had to cast
anchor in a port on the Eritrean coast.* I went ashore; I recalled other very ancient mornings, also facing the Red Sea,
when I was a tribune of Rome and fever and magic and idle-
ness consumed the soldiers. On the outskirts of the city I saw a
spring of clear water; I tasted it, prompted by habit. When I
came up the bank, a spiny bush lacerated the back of my hand.
The unusual pain seemed very acute to me. Incredulous, speech-
less and happy, I contemplated the precious formation of a
slow drop of blood. Once again I am mortal, I repeated to
myself, once again I am like all men. That night, I slept until
dawn ...

After a year's time, I have inspected these pages. I am certain they reflect the truth, but in the first chapters, and even in
certain paragraphs of the others, I seem to perceive something
false. This is perhaps produced by the abuse of circumstantial
details, a procedure I learned from the poet and which contaminates everything with falsity, since those details can
abound in the realities but not in their recollection.... I believe, however, that I have discovered a more intimate reason. I
shall write it; no matter if I am judged fantastic.

*The story I have narrated seems unreal because in it are
mixed the events of two different men.* In the first chapter, the
horseman wants to know the name of the river bathing the
walls of Thebes; Flaminius Rufus, who before has applied to
the city the epithet of Hekatompylos, says that the river is the
Egypt; none of these locutions is proper to him but rather to
Homer, who makes express mention in the *Iliad* of Thebes

---

*There is an erasure in the manuscript; perhaps the name of the
port has been removed.

Hekatompylos and who in the *Odyssey*, by way of Proteus and Ulysses, invariably says Egypt for Nile. In the second chapter, the Roman, upon drinking the immortal water, utters some words in Greek; these words are Homeric and may be sought at the end of the famous catalogue of the ships. Later, in the vertiginous palace, he speaks of 'a reprobation which was almost remorse'; these words belong to Homer, who had projected that horror. Such anomalies disquieted me; others, of an aesthetic order, permitted me to discover the truth. They are contained in the last chapter; there it is written that I fought at Stamford Bridge, that I transcribed in Bulaq the travels of Sinbad the Sailor and that I subscribed in Aberdeen to the English *Iliad* of Pope. One reads, *inter alia* : 'In Bikaner I professed the science of astrology and also in Bohemia.' None of these testimonies is false; what is significant is that they were stressed. The first of them seems proper to a warrior, but later one notes that the narrator does not linger over warlike deeds, but does over the fates of men. Those which follow are even more curious. A dark elemental reason obliged me to record them; I did it because I knew they were pathetic. Spoken by the Roman Flaminius Rufus, they are not. They are, spoken by Homer; it is strange that the latter should copy in the thirteenth century the adventures of Sinbad, another Ulysses, and should discover after many centuries, in a northern kingdom and a barbarous tongue, the forms of his *Iliad*. As for the sentence containing the name of Bikaner, one can see that it was fabricated by a man of letters, desirous (as was the author of the ship catalogue) of exhibiting splendid words.*

When the end draws near, there no longer remain any remembered images; only words remain. It is not strange that time should have confused the words that once represented me with those that were symbols of the fate of he who accompanied me for so many centuries. I have been Homer; shortly, I

---

*Ernesto Sábato suggests that the 'Giambattista' who discussed the formation of the *Iliad* with the antique dealer Cartaphilus is Giambattista Vico; this Italian defended the idea that Homer is a symbolic character, after the manner of Pluto or Achilles.

shall be No One, like Ulysses; shortly, I shall be all men; I shall be dead.

Postcript (*1950*). – Among the commentaries elicited by the preceding publication, the most curious, if not the most urbane, is biblically entitled *A Coat of Many Colours* (Manchester, 1948) and is the work of the most tenacious pen of Doctor Nahum Cordovero. It comprises some one hundred pages. The author speaks of the Greek centos, of the centos of late Latinity, of Ben Jonson, who defined his contemporaries with bits of Seneca, of the *Virgilius evangelizans* of Alexander Ross, of the artifices of George Moore and of Eliot and, finally, of 'the narrative attributed to the antique dealer Joseph Cartaphilus.' He denounces, in the first chapter, brief interpolations from Pliny (*Historia naturalis*, V, 8); in the second, from Thomas de Quincey (*Writings*, III, 439); in the third, from an epistle of Descartes to the ambassador Pierre Chanut; in the fourth, from Bernard Shaw (*Back to Methuselah*, V). He infers from these intrusions or thefts that the whole document is apocryphal.

In my opinion, such a conclusion is inadmissible. 'When the end draws near,' wrote Cartaphilus, 'there no longer remain any remembered images; only words remain.' Words, displaced and mutilated words, words of others, were the poor pittance left him by the hours and the centuries.

To Cecilia Ingenieros   *Translated by J.E.I.*

The Theologians

AFTER having razed the garden and profaned the chalices and altars, the Huns entered the monastery library on horseback and trampled the incomprehensible books and vituperated and burned them, perhaps fearful that the letters concealed blasphemies against their god, which was an iron scimitar. Palimpsests and codices were consumed, but in the heart of the fire, amid the ashes, there remained almost intact the twelfth book of the *Civitas Dei*, which relates how in Athens Plato taught that, at the centuries' end, all things will recover their previous state and he in Athens, before the same audience, will teach this same doctrine anew. The text pardoned by the flames enjoyed special veneration and those who read and reread it in that remote province came to forget that the author had only stated this doctrine in order better to refute it. A century later, Aurelian, coadjutor of Aquileia, learned that on the shores of the Danube the very recent sect of the Monotones (called also the Annulars) professed that history is a circle and that there is nothing which has been and will not be. In the mountains, the Wheel and the Serpent had displaced the Cross. All were afraid, but all were comforted by the rumour that John of Pannonia, who had distinguished himself with a treatise on the seventh attribute of God, was going to impugn such an abominable heresy.

Aurelian deplored this news, particularly the latter part. He knew that in questions of theology there is no novelty without risk; then he reflected that the thesis of a circular time was too different, too astounding, for the risk to be serious. (The heresies we should fear are those which can be confused with orthodoxy.) John of Pannonia's intervention – his intrusion –

pained him more. Two years before, with his verbose *De septima affectione Dei sive de aeternitate*, he had usurped a topic in Aurelian's speciality; now, as if the problem of time belonged to him, he was going to rectify the Annulars, perhaps with Procrustean arguments, with theriacas more fearful than the Serpent ... That night, Aurelian turned the pages of Plutarch's ancient dialogue on the cessation of the oracles; in the twenty-ninth paragraph he read a satire against the Stoics, who defend an infinite cycle of worlds, with infinite suns, moons, Apollos, Dianas and Poseidons. The discovery seemed to him a favourable omen; he resolved to anticipate John of Pannonia and refute the heretics of the Wheel.

There are those who seek a woman's love in order to forget her, to think no more of her; Aurelian, in a similar fashion, wanted to surpass John of Pannonia in order to be rid of the resentment he inspired in him, not in order to harm him. Tempered by mere diligence, by the fabrication of syllogisms and the invention of insults, by the *negos* and *autems* and *nequaquams*, he managed to forget that rancour. He erected vast and almost inextricable periods encumbered with parentheses, in which negligence and solecism seemed as forms of scorn. He made an instrument of cacophony. He foresaw that John would fulminate the Annulars with prophetic gravity; so as not to coincide with him, he chose mockery as his weapon. Augustine had written that Jesus is the straight path that saves us from the circular labyrinth followed by the impious; these Aurelian, laboriously trivial, compared with Ixion, with the liver of Prometheus, with Sisyphus, with the king of Thebes who saw two suns, with stuttering, with parrots, with mirrors, with echoes, with the mules of a noria and with two-horned syllogisms. (Here the heathen fables survived, relegated to the status of adornments.) Like all those possessing a library, Aurelian was aware that he was guilty of not knowing his in its entirety; this controversy enabled him to fulfil his obligations with many books which seemed to reproach him for his neglect. Thus he was able to insert a passage from Origen's work *De principiis*, where it is denied that Judas Iscariot will again betray the Lord and that Paul will again witness Stephen's martyrdom in Jerusalem, and another from Cicero's *Academica priora*, where the author scoffs at those who imagine that, while he converses with Lucullus, other Luculluses and Ciceros in infinite number say precisely the same thing in an infinite number of equal worlds. In addition, he wielded against the Monotones the text from Plutarch and denounced the scandalousness of an idolator's valuing the *lumen naturae* more than they did the word of God. The writing took him nine days; on the tenth, he was sent a transcript of John of Pannonia's refutation.

It was almost derisively brief; Aurelian looked at it with disdain and then with fear. The first part was a gloss on the end verses of the ninth chapter of the Epistle to the Hebrews, where it is said that Jesus was not sacrificed many times since the beginning of the world, but now, once, in the consummation of the centuries. The second part adduced the biblical precept concerning the vain repetitions of the pagans (Matthew 6 : 7) and the passage from the seventh book of Pliny which ponders that in the wide universe there are no two faces alike. John of Pannonia declared that neither are there two like souls and that the vilest sinner is as precious as the blood Jesus shed for him. One man's act (he affirmed) is worth more than the nine concentric heavens and imagining that this act can be lost and return again is a pompous frivolity. Time does not remake what we lose; eternity saves it for heaven and also for hell. The treatise was limpid, universal; it seemed not to have been written by a concrete person, but by any man or, perhaps, by all men.

Aurelian felt an almost physical humiliation. He thought of destroying or reforming his own work; then, with resentful integrity, he sent it to Rome without modifying a letter. Months later, when the council of Pergamum convened, the theologian entrusted with impugning the Monotones' errors was (predictably) John of Pannonia; his learned and measured refutation was sufficient to have Euphorbus the heresiarch condemned to the stake. 'This has happened and will happen again,' said Euphorbus. 'You are not lighting a pyre, you are lighting a labyrinth of flames. If all the fires I have seen were gathered together here, they would not fit on earth and the angels would be blinded. I have said this many times.' Then he cried out, because the flames had reached him.

The Wheel fell before the Cross,* but Aurelian and John of Pannonia continued their secret battle. Both served in the same army, coveted the same guerdon, warred against the same Enemy, but Aurelian did not write a word which secretly did not strive to surpass John. Their duel was an invisible one; if the copious indices do not deceive me, the name of the *other* does not figure once in the many volumes by Aurelian preserved in Migne's *Patrology*. (Of John's works only twenty words have survived.) Both condemned the anathemas of the second council of Constantinople; both persecuted the Arrianists, who denied the eternal generation of the Son; both testified to the orthodoxy of Cosmas's *Topographia christiana*, which teaches that the earth is quadrangular, like the Hebrew tabernacle. Unfortunately, to the four corners of the earth another tempestuous heresy spread. Originating in Egypt or in Asia (for the testimonies differ and Bousset will not admit Harnack's reasoning), it infested the eastern provinces and erected sanctuaries in Macedonia, in Carthage and in Treves. It seemed to be everywhere; it was said that in the diocese of Britannia the crucifixes had been inverted and that in Caesarea the image of the Lord had been replaced by a mirror. The mirror and the obolus were the new schismatics' emblems.

History knows them by many names (Speculars, Abysmals, Cainites), but the most common of all is Histriones, a name Aurelian gave them and which they insolently adopted. In Frigia they were called Simulacra, and also in Dardania. John of Damascus called them Forms; it is well to note that the passage has been rejected by Erfjord. There is no heresiologist who does not relate with stupor their wild customs. Many Histriones professed asceticism; some mutilated themselves, as

*In the Runic crosses the two contrary emblems coexist entwined.

did Origen; others lived underground in the sewers; others tore out their eyes; others (the Nabucodonosors of Nitria) 'grazed like oxen and their hair grew like an eagle's'. They often went from mortification and severity to crime; some communities tolerated thievery; others, homicide; others, sodomy, incest and bestiality. All were blasphemous; they cursed not only the Christian God but also the arcane divinities of their own pantheon. They contrived sacred books whose disappearance is lamented by scholars. In the year 1658, Sir Thomas Browne wrote: 'Time has annihilated the ambitious Histrionic gospels, not the Insults with which their Impiety was fustigated' : Erfjord has suggested that these 'insults' (preserved in a Greek codex) are the lost gospels. This is incomprehensible if we do not know the Histriones' cosmology.

In the hermetic books it is written that what is down below is equal to what is on high, and what is on high is equal to what is down below; in the *Zohar*, that the higher world is a reflection of the lower. The Histriones founded their doctrine on a perversion of this idea. They invoked Matthew 6 : 12 ('and forgive us our debts, as we forgive our debtors') and 11 : 12 ('the kingdom of heaven suffereth violence') to demonstrate that the earth influences heaven, and I Corinthians 13 : 12 ('for now we see through a glass, darkly') to demonstrate that every-thing we see is false. Perhaps contaminated by the Monotones, they imagined that all men are two men and that the real one is the other, the one in heaven. They also imagined that our acts project an inverted reflection, in such a way that if we are awake, the other sleeps, if we fornicate, the other is chaste, if we steal, the other is generous. When we die, we shall join this other and be him. (Some echo of these doctrines persisted in Léon Bloy.) Other Histriones reasoned that the world would end when the number of its possibilities was exhausted; since there can be no repetitions, the righteous should eliminate (commit) the most infamous acts, so that these will not soil the future and will hasten the coming of the kingdom of Jesus. This article was negated by other sects, who held that the history of the world should be fulfilled in every man. Most, like

Pythagoras, will have to transmigrate through many bodies
before attaining their liberation; some, the Proteans, 'in the
period of one lifetime are lions, dragons, boars, water and a
tree'. Demosthenes tells how the initiates into the Orphic
mysteries were submitted to purification with mud; the Proteans, analogously, sought purification through evil. They
knew, as did Carpocrates, that no one will be released from
prison until he has paid the last obolus (Luke 12 : 59) and used
to deceive penitents with this other verse: 'I am come that
they might have life, and that they might have it more
abundantly' (John 10 : 10). They also said that not to be evil is
a satanic arrogance ... Many and divergent mythologies were
devised by the Histriones; some preached asceticism, others
licentiousness. All preached confusion. Theopompus, a His-
trione of Berenice, denied all fables; he said that every man is
an organ put forth by the divinity in order to perceive the
world.

The heretics of Aurelian's diocese were of those who
affirmed that time does not tolerate repetitions, not of those
who affirmed that every act is reflected in heaven. This circumstance was strange; in a report to the authorities in Rome,
Aurelian mentioned it. The prelate who was to receive the
report was the empress's confessor; everyone knew that this
demanding post kept him from the intimate delights of speculative theology. His secretary – a former collaborator of John
of Pannonia, now hostile to him – enjoyed fame as a punctual
inquisitor of heterodoxies; Aurelian added an exposition of the
Histrionic heresy, just as it was found in the conventicles of
Genua and of Aquileia. He composed a few paragraphs; when
he tried to write the atrocious thesis that there are no two
moments alike, his pen halted. He could not find the necessary
formula; the admonitions of this new doctrine ('Do you want
to see what human eyes have never seen? Look at the moon.
Do you want to hear what ears have never heard? Listen to the
bird's cry. Do you want to touch what hands have never
touched? Touch the earth. Verily I say that God is about to
create the world.') were much too affected and metaphorical to

be transcribed. Suddenly, a sentence of twenty words came to his mind. He wrote it down, joyfully; immediately afterwards, he was troubled by the suspicion that it was the work of another. The following day, he remembered that he had read it many years before in the *Adversus annulares* composed by John of Pannonia. He verified the quotation; there it was. He was tormented by incertitude. If he changed or suppressed those words he would weaken the expression; if he left them he would be plagiarizing a man he abhorred; if he indicated their source, he would be denouncing him. He implored divine assistance. Towards the beginning of the second twilight, his guardian angel dictated to him an intermediate solution. Aurelian kept the words, but preceded them with this notice: 'What the heresiarchs now bark in confusion of the faith was said in our realm by a most learned man, with more frivolity than guilt.' Then the dreaded, hoped for, inevitable thing happened. Aurelian had to declare who the man was; John of Pannonia was accused of professing heretical opinions.

Four months later, a blacksmith of Aventinus, deluded by the Histriones' deceptions, placed a huge iron sphere on the shoulders of his small son, so that his double might fly. The boy died; the horror engendered by this crime obliged John's judges to assume an unexceptionable severity. He would not retract; he repeated that if he negated his proposition he would fall into the pestilential heresy of the Monotones. He did not understand (did not want to understand) that to speak of the Monotones was to speak of the already forgotten. With somewhat senile insistence, he abundantly gave forth with the most brilliant periods of his former polemics; the judges did not even hear what had once enraptured them. Instead of trying to cleanse himself of the slightest blemish of Histrionism, he strove to demonstrate that the proposition of which he was accused was rigorously orthodox. He argued with the men on whose judgement his fate depended and committed the extreme ineptitude of doing so with wit and irony. On 26 October, after a discussion lasting three days and three nights, he was sentenced to die at the stake.

The Theologians

Aurelian witnessed the execution, for refusing to do so meant confessing his own guilt. The place for the ceremony was a hill, on whose green top there was a pole driven deep into the ground, surrounded by many bundles of wood. A bailiff read the tribunal's sentence. Under the noonday sun, John of Pannonia lay with his face in the dust, howling like an animal. He clawed the ground but the executioners pulled him away, stripped him naked and finally tied him to the stake. On his head they placed a straw crown dipped in sulphur; at his side, a copy of the pestilential *Adversus annulares*. It had rained the night before and the wood burned badly. John of Pannonia prayed in Greek and then in an unknown language. The fire was about to engulf him when Aurelian finally dared to raise his eyes. The bursts of flame halted; Aurelian saw for the first and last time the face of the hated heretic. It reminded him of someone, but he could not remember who. Then he was lost in the flames; then he cried out and it was as if a fire had cried out.

Plutarch has related that Julius Caesar wept for the death of Pompey; Aurelian did not weep for the death of John, but he felt what a man would feel when rid of an incurable disease that had become a part of his life. In Aquileia, in Ephesus, in Macedonia, he let the years pass over him. He sought the arduous limits of the Empire, the torpid swamps and contemplative deserts, so that solitude might help him understand his destiny. In a cell in Mauretania, in a night laden with lions, he reconsidered the complex accusation brought against John of Pannonia and justified, for the nth time, the sentence. It was much more difficult to justify his own tortuous denunciation. In Rusaddir he preached the anachronistic sermon 'Light of lights burning in the flesh of a reprobate.' In Hibernia, in one of the hovels of a monastery surrounded by the forest, he was startled one night towards dawn by the sound of rain. He remembered a night in Rome when that minute noise had also startled him. At midday, a lightning bolt set fire to the trees and Aurelian died just as John had.

The end of this story can only be related in metaphors since it takes place in the kingdom of heaven, where there is no time. Perhaps it would be correct to say that Aurelian spoke with God and that He was so little interested in religious differences that He took him for John of Pannonia. This, however, would imply a confusion in the divine mind. It is more correct to say that in Paradise, Aurelian learned that, for the unfathomable divinity, he and John of Pannonia (the orthodox believer and the heretic, the abhorrer and the abhorred, the accuser and the accused) formed one single person.

Translated by J.E.I.

Story of the Warrior
and the Captive

ON page 278 of his book *La poesia* (Bari, 1942), Croce, abbreviating a Latin text of the historian Peter the Deacon, narrates the destiny and cites the epitaph of Droctulft; both these moved me singularly; later I understood why. Droctulft was a Lombard warrior who, during the siege of Ravenna, left his companions and died defending the city he had previously attacked. The Ravennese gave him burial in a temple and composed an epitaph in which they manifested their gratitude (*contempsit caros, dum nos amat ille, parentes*) and observed the peculiar contrast evident between the barbarian's fierce countenance and his simplicity and goodness:

> *Terribilis visu facies, sed mente benignus,*
> *Longaque robusto pectore barba fuit!**

Such is the story of the destiny of Droctulft, a barbarian who died defending Rome, or such is the fragment of his story Peter the Deacon was able to salvage. I do not even know in what period it took place: whether towards the middle of the sixth century, when the Longobardi desolated the plains of Italy, or in the eighth, before the surrender of Ravenna. Let us imagine (this is not a historical work) the former.

Let us imagine Droctulft *sub specie aeternitatis*, not the individual Droctulft, who no doubt was unique and unfathomable (all individuals are), but the generic type formed from him and many others by tradition, which is the effect of oblivion and of memory. Through an obscure geography of forests and marshes, the wars brought him to Italy from the banks of the Danube and the Elbe, and perhaps he did not know he was

* Also Gibbon (*Decline and Fall*, XLV) transcribes these verses.

going south and perhaps he did not know he was fighting
against the name of Rome. Perhaps he professed the Arrianist
faith, which holds that the Son's glory is a reflection of the
Holy Father's, but it is more congruous to imagine him a
worshipper of the Earth, of Hertha, whose covered idol went
from hut to hut in a cow-drawn cart, or of the gods of war and
thunder, which were crude wooden figures wrapped in home-
spun clothing and hung with coins and bracelets. He came
from the inextricable forests of the boar and the bison; he was
light-skinned, spirited, innocent, cruel, loyal to his captain and
his tribe, but not to the universe. The wars bring him to
Ravenna and there he sees something he has never seen before,
or has not seen fully. He sees the day and the cypresses and the
marble. He sees a whole whose multiplicity is not that of disorder; he sees a city, an organism composed of statues, temples,
gardens, rooms, amphitheatres, vases, columns, regular and
open spaces. None of these fabrications (I know) impresses him
as beautiful; he is touched by them as we now would be by a
complex mechanism whose purpose we could not fathom but
in whose design an immortal intelligence might be divined.
Perhaps it is enough for him to see a single arch, with an
incomprehensible inscription in eternal Roman letters. Suddenly he is blinded and renewed by this revelation, the City. He
knows that in it he will be a dog, or a child, and that he will
not even begin to understand it, but he also knows that it is
worth more than his gods and his sworn faith and all the
marshes of Germany. Droctulft abandons his own and fights
for Ravenna. He dies and on his grave they inscribe these
words which he would not have understood :

> *Contempsit caros, dum nos amat ille, parentes,*
> *Hanc patriam reputans esse, Ravenna, suam.*

He was not a traitor (traitors seldom inspire pious epitaphs);
he was a man enlightened, a convert. Within a few generations, the Longobardi who had condemned this turncoat proceeded just as he had; they became Italians, Lombards, and
perhaps one of their blood – Aldiger – could have engendered

those who engendered the Alighieri. . . . Many conjectures may be applied to Droctulft's act; mine is the most economical; if it is not true as fact it will be so as symbol.

When I read the story of this warrior in Croce's book, it moved me in an unusual way and I had the impression of having recovered, in a different form, something that had been my own. Fleetingly I thought of the Mongolian horsemen who tried to make of China an infinite pasture ground and then grew old in the cities they had longed to destroy; this was not the memory I sought. At last I found it: it was a tale I had once heard from my English grandmother, who is now dead.

In 1872, my grandfather Borges was commander of the northern and western frontiers of Buenos Aires and the southern frontier of Santa Fe. His headquarters was in Junín; beyond that, four or five leagues distant from each other, the chain of outposts; beyond that, what was then termed the *pampa* and also the 'hinterland'. Once – half out of wonder, half out of sarcasm – my grandmother commented upon her fate as a lone Englishwoman exiled to that far corner of the earth; people told her that she was not the only one there and, months later, pointed out to her an Indian girl who was slowly crossing the plaza. She wore two brightly coloured blankets and went barefoot; her hair was blonde. A soldier told her another Englishwoman wanted to speak to her. The girl agreed; she entered the headquarters without fear but not without suspicion. In her copper-coloured face, which was daubed in ferocious colours, her eyes were of that reluctant blue the English call grey. Her body was lithe, like a deer's; her hands, strong and bony. She came from the desert, from the hinterland, and everything seemed too small for her: doors, walls, furniture.

Perhaps the two women felt for an instant as sisters; they were far from their beloved island and in an incredible country. My grandmother uttered some kind of question; the other woman replied with difficulty, searching for words and repeating them, as if astonished by their ancient flavour. For some fifteen years she had not spoken her native language and it was not easy for her to recover it. She said that she was from Yorkshire, that her parents had emigrated to Buenos Aires, that she had lost them in an Indian raid, that she had been carried off by the Indians and was now the wife of a chieftain, to whom she had already given two sons, and that he was very brave. All this she said in a rustic English, interwoven with Araucanian or Pampan, and behind her story one could glimpse a savage life: the horsehide shelters, the fires made of dry manure, the feasts of scorched meat or raw entrails, the stealthy departures at dawn, the attacks on corrals, the yelling and the pillaging, the wars, the sweeping charges on the haciendas by naked horsemen, the polygamy, the stench and the superstition. An Englishwoman had lowered herself to this barbarism. Moved by pity and shock, my grandmother urged her not to return. She swore to protect her, to retrieve her children. The woman answered that she was happy and returned that night to the desert. Francisco Borges was to die a short time later, in the revolution of seventy-four; perhaps then my grandmother was able to perceive in this other woman, also held captive and transformed by the implacable continent, a monstrous mirror of her own destiny . . .

Every year, the blonde Indian woman used to come to the country stores at Junín or at Fort Lavalle to obtain trinkets or makings for maté; she did not appear after the conversation with my grandmother. However, they saw each other once again. My grandmother had gone hunting one day; on a ranch, near the sheep dip, a man was slaughtering one of the animals. As if in a dream, the Indian woman passed by on horseback. She threw herself to the ground and drank the warm blood. I do not know whether she did it because she could no longer act any other way, or as a challenge and a sign.

A thousand three hundred years and the ocean lie between the destiny of the captive and the destiny of Droctulft. Both these, now, are equally irrecoverable. The figure of the barbarian who embraced the cause of Ravenna, the figure of the European woman who chose the wasteland, may seem antagonistic. And yet, both were swept away by a secret impulse, an impulse more profound than reason, and both heeded this impulse, which they would not have known how to justify. Perhaps the stories I have related are one single story. The obverse and the reverse of this coin are, for God, the same.

For Ulrike von Kühlmann   *Translated by J.E.I.*

Emma Zunz

RETURNING home from the Tarbuch and Loewenthal textile mills on 14 January 1922, Emma Zunz discovered in the rear of the entrance hall a letter, posted in Brazil, which informed her that her father had died. The stamp and the envelope deceived her at first; then the unfamiliar handwriting made her uneasy. Nine or ten lines tried to fill up the page; Emma read that Mr Maier had taken by mistake a large dose of veronal and had died on the third of the month in the hospital of Bagé. A boarding-house friend of her father had signed the letter, some Fein or Fain from Río Grande, with no way of knowing that he was addressing the deceased's daughter.

Emma dropped the paper. Her first impression was of a weak feeling in her stomach and in her knees; then of blind guilt, of unreality, of coldness, of fear; then she wished that it were already the next day. Immediately afterwards she realized that that wish was futile because the death of her father was the only thing that had happened in the world, and it would go on happening endlessly. She picked up the piece of paper and went to her room. Furtively, she hid it in a drawer, as if somehow she already knew the ulterior facts. She had already begun to suspect them, perhaps; she had already become the person she would be.

In the growing darkness, Emma wept until the end of that day for the suicide of Manuel Maier, who in the old happy days was Emmanuel Zunz. She remembered summer vacations at a little farm near Gualeguay, she remembered (tried to remember) her mother, she remembered the little house at Lanús which had been auctioned off, she remembered the yellow lozenges of a window, she remembered the warrant for arrest, the ignominy, she remembered the poison-pen letters with the newspaper's account of 'the cashier's embezzlement', she remembered (but this she never forgot) that her father, on the last night, had sworn to her that the thief was Loewenthal. Loewenthal, Aaron Loewenthal, formerly the manager of the factory and now one of the owners. Since 1916 Emma had guarded the secret. She had revealed it to no one, not even to her best friend, Elsa Urstein. Perhaps she was shunning profane incredulity; perhaps she believed that the secret was a link between herself and the absent parent. Loewenthal did not know that she knew; Emma Zunz derived from this slight fact a feeling of power.

She did not sleep that night and when the first light of dawn defined the rectangle of the window, her plan was already perfected. She tried to make the day, which seemed interminable to her, like any other. At the factory there were rumours of a strike. Emma declared herself, as usual, against all violence. At six o'clock, with work over, she went with Elsa to a women's club that had a gymnasium and a swimming pool. They signed their names; she had to repeat and spell out her first and her last name, she had to respond to the vulgar jokes that accompanied the medical examination. With Elsa and with the youngest of the Kronfuss girls she discussed what movie they would go to Sunday afternoon. Then they talked about boyfriends and no one expected Emma to speak. In April she would be nineteen years old, but men inspired in her, still, an almost pathological fear.... Having returned home, she prepared a tapioca soup and a few vegetables, ate early, went to bed and forced herself to sleep. In this way, laborious and trivial, Friday the fifteenth, the day before, elapsed.

Impatience awoke her on Saturday. Impatience it was, not uneasiness, and the special relief of it being that day at last. No longer did she have to plan and imagine; within a few hours the simplicity of the facts would suffice. She read in *La Prensa* that the *Nordstjärnan*, out of Malmö, would sail that evening from Pier 3. She phoned Loewenthal, insinuated that she wanted to confide in him, without the other girls knowing, something pertaining to the strike; and she promised to stop by at his office at nightfall. Her voice trembled; the tremor was suitable to an informer. Nothing else of note happened that morning. Emma worked until twelve o'clock and then settled with Elsa and Perla Kronfuss the details of their Sunday stroll. She lay down after lunch and reviewed, with her eyes closed, the plan she had devised. She thought that the final step would be less horrible than the first and that it would doubtlessly afford her the taste of victory and justice. Suddenly, alarmed, she got up and ran to the dresser drawer. She opened it; beneath the picture of Milton Sills, where she had left it the night before, was Fain's letter. No one could have seen it; she began to read it and tore it up.

To relate with some reality the events of that afternoon would be difficult and perhaps unrighteous. One attribute of a hellish experience is unreality, an attribute that seems to allay its terrors and which aggravates them perhaps. How could one make credible an action which was scarcely believed in by the person who executed it, how to recover that brief chaos which today the memory of Emma Zunz repudiates and confuses? Emma lived in Almagro, on Liniers Street: we are certain that in the afternoon she went down to the waterfront. Perhaps on the infamous Paseo de Julio she saw herself multiplied in mirrors, revealed by lights and denuded by hungry eyes, but it is more reasonable to suppose that at first she wandered, unnoticed, through the indifferent portico. . . . She entered two or three bars, noted the routine or technique of the other women. Finally she came across men from the *Nordstjärnan*. One of them, very young, she feared might inspire some tenderness in her and she chose instead another, perhaps shorter than she and coarse, in order that the purity of the horror might not be mitigated. The man led her to a door, then to a murky entrance hall and afterwards to a narrow stairway and then a vestibule (in which there was a window with lozenges identical to those in the house at Lanús) and then to a passageway and then to a door which was closed behind her. The arduous events are outside of time, either because the immediate past is as if disconnected from the future, or because the parts which form these events do not seem to be consecutive.

During that time outside of time, in that perplexing disorder of disconnected and atrocious sensations, did Emma Zunz think *once* about the dead man who motivated the sacrifice? It is my belief that she did think once, and in that moment she endangered her desperate undertaking. She thought (she was unable not to think) that her father had done to her mother the hideous thing that was being done to her now. She thought of it with weak amazement and took refuge, quickly, in vertigo. The man, a Swede or Finn, did not speak Spanish. He was a tool for Emma, as she was for him, but she served him for pleasure whereas he served her for justice.

When she was alone, Emma did not open her eyes immediately. On the little night table was the money that the man had left: Emma sat up and tore it to pieces as before she had torn the letter. Tearing money is an impiety, like throwing away bread; Emma repented the moment after she did it. An act of pride and on that day.... Her fear was lost in the grief of her body, in her disgust. The grief and the nausea were chaining her, but Emma got up slowly and proceeded to dress herself. In the room there were no longer any bright colours; the last light of dusk was weakening. Emma was able to leave without anyone seeing her; at the corner she got on a Lacroze streetcar heading west. She selected, in keeping with her plan, the seat farthest towards the front, so that her face would not be seen. Perhaps it comforted her to verify in the insipid movement along the streets that what had happened had not contaminated things. She rode through the diminishing opaque suburbs, seeing them and forgetting them at the same instant, and got off on one of the side streets of Warnes. Paradoxically her fatigue was turning out to be a strength, since it obligated her to concentrate on the details of the adventure and concealed from her the background and the objective.

Aaron Loewenthal was to all persons a serious man, to his intimate friends a miser. He lived above the factory, alone. Situated in the barren outskirts of the town, he feared thieves;

in the patio of the factory there was a large dog and in the drawer of his desk, everyone knew, a revolver. He had mourned with gravity, the year before, the unexpected death of his wife – a Gauss who had brought him a fine dowry – but money was his real passion. With intimate embarrassment, he knew himself to be less apt at earning it than at saving it. He was very religious; he believed he had a secret pact with God which exempted him from doing good in exchange for prayers and piety. Bald, fat, wearing the band of mourning, with smoked glasses and blond beard, he was standing next to the window awaiting the confidential report of worker Zunz.

He saw her push the iron gate (which he had left open for her) and cross the gloomy patio. He saw her make a little detour when the chained dog barked. Emma's lips were moving rapidly, like those of someone praying in a low voice; weary, they were repeating the sentence which Mr Loewenthal would hear before dying.

Things did not happen as Emma Zunz had anticipated. Ever since the morning before she had imagined herself wielding the firm revolver, forcing the wretched creature to confess his wretched guilt and exposing the daring strategem which would permit the Justice of God to triumph over human justice. (Not out of fear but because of being an instrument of Justice she did not want to be punished.) Then, one single shot in the centre of his chest would seal Loewenthal's fate. But things did not happen that way.

In Aaron Loewenthal's presence, more than the urgency of avenging her father, Emma felt the need of inflicting punishment for the outrage she had suffered. She was unable not to kill him after that thorough dishonour. Nor did she have time for theatrics. Seated, timid, she made excuses to Loewenthal, she invoked (as a privilege of the informer) the obligation of loyalty, uttered a few names, inferred others and broke off as if fear had conquered her. She managed to have Loewenthal leave to get a glass of water for her. When the former, unconvinced by such a fuss but indulgent, returned from the dining room, Emma had already taken the heavy revolver out of the drawer.

Emma Zunz

She squeezed the trigger twice. The large body collapsed as if
the reports and the smoke had shattered it, the glass of water
smashed, the face looked at her with amazement and anger, the
mouth of the face swore at her in Spanish and Yiddish. The evil
words did not slacken; Emma had to fire again. In the patio the
chained dog broke out barking, and a gush of rude blood
flowed from the obscene lips and soiled the beard and the
clothing. Emma began the accusation she had prepared ('I have
avenged my father and they will not be able to punish me . . .'),
but she did not finish it, because Mr Loewenthal had already
died. She never knew if he managed to understand.

The straining barks reminded her that she could not, yet, rest.
She disarranged the divan, unbuttoned the dead man's jacket,
took off the bespattered glasses and left them on the filing
cabinet. Then she picked up the telephone and repeated what
she would repeat so many times again with these and with
other words: *Something incredible has happened. . . . Mr Loewenthal had me come over on the pretext of the strike. . . . He
abused me, I killed him . . .*

Actually, the story *was* incredible, but it impressed everyone because substantially it was true. True was Emma Zunz's
tone, true was her shame, true was her hate. True also was the
outrage she had suffered: only the circumstances were false,
the time and one or two proper names.

Translated by D.A.Y.

The House of Asterion

And the queen gave birth to a child who was called Asterion.

Apollodorus: *Bibliotheca*, III, I

I KNOW they accuse me of arrogance, and perhaps of misanthropy, and perhaps of madness. Such accusations (for which I shall extract punishment in due time) are derisory. It is true that I never leave my house, but it is also true that its doors (whose number is infinite)* are open day and night to men and to animals as well. Anyone may enter. He will find here no female pomp nor gallant court formality, but he will find quiet and solitude. And he will also find a house like no other on the face of the earth. (There are those who declare there is a similar one in Egypt, but they lie.) Even my detractors admit there is not *one single piece of furniture* in the house. Another ridiculous falsehood has it that I, Asterion, am a prisoner. Shall I repeat that there are no locked doors, shall I add that there are no locks? Besides, one afternoon I did step into the street; if I returned before night, I did so because of the fear that the faces of the common people inspired in me, faces as discoloured and flat as the palm of one's hand. The sun had already set, but the helpless crying of a child and the rude supplications of the faithful told me I had been recognized. The people prayed, fled, prostrated themselves; some climbed on to the stylobate of the temple of the Axes, others gathered stones. One of them, I believe, hid himself beneath the sea. Not for nothing was my mother a queen; I cannot be confused with the populace, though my modesty might so desire.

*The original says *fourteen*, but there is ample reason to infer that, as used by Asterion, this numeral stands for *infinite*.

The House of Asterion

The fact is that I am unique. I am not interested in what one man may transmit to other men; like the philosopher, I think that nothing is communicable by the art of writing. Bothersome and trivial details have no place in my spirit, which is prepared for all that is vast and grand; I have never retained the difference between one letter and another. A certain generous impatience has not permitted that I learn to read. Sometimes I deplore this, for the nights and days are long.

Of course, I am not without distractions. Like the ram about to charge, I run through the stone galleries until I fall dizzy to the floor. I crouch in the shadow of a pool or around a corner and pretend I am being followed. There are roofs from which I let myself fall until I am bloody. At any time I can pretend to be asleep, with my eyes closed and my breathing heavy. (Sometimes I really sleep, sometimes the colour of the day has changed when I open my eyes.) But of all the games, I prefer the one about the other Asterion. I pretend that he comes to visit me and that I show him my house. With great obeisance I say to him: *Now we shall return to the first intersection* or *Now we shall come out into another courtyard* or *I knew you would like the drain* or *Now you will see a pool that was filled with sand* or *You will soon see how the cellar branches out.* Sometimes I make a mistake and the two of us laugh heartily.

Not only have I imagined these games, I have also meditated on the house. All the parts of the house are repeated many times, any place is another place. There is no one pool, courtyard, drinking trough, manger; the mangers, drinking troughs, courtyards, pools are fourteen (infinite) in number. The house is the same size as the world; or rather, it is the world. However, by dint of exhausting the courtyards with pools and dusty grey stone galleries I have reached the street and seen the temple of the Axes and the sea. I did not understand this until a night vision revealed to me that the seas and temples are also fourteen (infinite) in number. Everything is repeated many times, fourteen times, but two things in the world seem to be only once: above, the intricate sun; below, Asterion. Perhaps I have created the stars and the sun and this enormous house, but I no longer remember.

Every nine years nine men enter the house so that I may deliver them from all evil. I hear their steps or their voices in the depths of the stone galleries and I run joyfully to find them. The ceremony lasts a few minutes. They fall one after another without my having to bloody my hands. They remain where they fell and their bodies help distinguish one gallery from another. I do not know who they are, but I know that one of them prophesied, at the moment of his death, that some day my redeemer would come. Since then my loneliness does not pain me, because I know my redeemer lives and he will finally rise above the dust. If my ear could capture all the sounds of the world, I should hear his steps. I hope he will take me to a place with fewer galleries and fewer doors. What will my redeemer be like?, I ask myself. Will he be a bull or a man? Will he perhaps be a bull with the face of a man? Or will he be like me?

The morning sun reverberated from the bronze sword. There was no longer even a vestige of blood.

'Would you believe it, Ariadne?' said Theseus 'The Minotaur scarcely defended himself.'

For Marta Mosquera Eastman   *Translated by J.E.I.*

Deutsches Requiem

Though he slay me, yet will I trust in him.
Job 13:15

MY name is Otto Dietrich zur Linde. One of my ancestors,
Christoph zur Linde, died in the cavalry charge which decided
the victory of Zorndorf. My maternal great-grandfather, Ulrich
Forkel, was shot in the forest of Marchenoir by franc-tireurs,
late in the year 1870; my father, Captain Dietrich zur Linde,
distinguished himself in the siege of Namur in 1914, and, two
years later, in the crossing of the Danube.* As for me, I will be
executed as a torturer and murderer. The tribunal acted justly;
from the start I declared myself guilty. Tomorrow, when the
prison clock strikes nine, I will have entered into death's realm;
it is natural that I think now of my forebears, since I am so
close to their shadow, since, after a fashion, I am already my
ancestors.

I kept silent during the trial, which fortunately was brief; to
try to justify myself at that time would have obstructed the
verdict and would have seemed an act of cowardice. Now
things have changed; on the eve of the execution I can speak
without fear. I do not seek pardon, because I feel no guilt; but I
would like to be understood. Those who care to listen to me
will understand the history of Germany and the future history

*It is significant that the narrator has omitted the name of his
most illustrious ancestor, the theologian and Hebraist Johannes
Forkel (1799–1846), who applied the Hegelian dialectic to Christ-
ology, and whose literal version of several books of the Apocrypha
merited the censure of Hengstenberg and the approval of Thilo and
Gesenius. (Editor's note.)

of the world. I know that cases like mine, which are now exceptional and astonishing, will shortly be commonplace. Tomorrow I will die, but I am a symbol of future generations.

I was born in Marienburg in 1908. Two passions, which now are almost forgotten, allowed me to bear with valour and even happiness the weight of many unhappy years: music and metaphysics. I cannot mention all my benefactors, but there are two names which I may not omit, those of Brahms and Schopenhauer. I also studied poetry; to these last I would add another immense Germanic name, William Shakespeare. Formerly I was interested in theology, but from this fantastic discipline (and from the Christian faith) I was led away by Schopenhauer, with his direct arguments; and by Shakespeare and Brahms, with the infinite variety of their worlds. He who pauses in wonder, moved with tenderness and gratitude, before any facet of the work of these auspicious creators, let him know that I also paused there, I, the abominable.

Nietzsche and Spengler entered my life about 1927. An eighteenth-century author has observed that no one wants to owe anything to his contemporaries. I, in order to free myself from an influence which I felt to be oppressive, wrote an article titled *Abrechnung mit Spengler*, in which I noted that the most unequivocal monument to those traits which the author calls Faust-like is not the miscellaneous drama of Goethe* but a poem written twenty centuries ago, the *De rerum natura*. I paid homage, however, to the sincerity of the philosopher of history, to his essentially German (*kerndeutsch*) and military spirit. In 1929 I entered the Party.

I will say little of my years of apprenticeship. They were more difficult for me than for others, since, although I do not lack courage, I am repelled by violence. I understood, however,

---

*Other nations live innocently, in themselves and for themselves, like minerals or meteors; Germany is the universal mirror which receives all, the consciousness of the world (*das Weltbewusstsein*). Goethe is the prototype of that ecumenic comprehension. I do not censure him, but I do not see in him the Faust-like man of Spengler's thesis.

that we were on the verge of a new era, and that this era, comparable to the initial epochs of Islam and Christianity, demanded a new kind of man. Individually my comrades were disgusting to me; in vain did I try to reason that we had to suppress our individuality for the lofty purpose which brought us together.

The theologians maintain that if God's attention were to wander for a single second from the right hand which traces these words, that hand would plunge into nothingness, as if fulminated by a lightless fire. No one, I say, can exist, no one can taste a glass of water or break a piece of bread, without justification. For each man that justification must be different; I awaited the inexorable war that would prove our faith. It was enough for me to know that I would be a soldier in its battles. At times I feared that English and Russian cowardice would betray us. But chance, or destiny, decided my future differently. On 1 March 1939, at nightfall, there was a disturbance in Tilsit which was not mentioned in the newspapers; in the street behind the synagogue, my leg was pierced by two bullets and it was necessary to amputate.* A few days later our armies entered Bohemia. As the sirens announced their entry, I was in a quiet hospital, trying to lose and forget myself in Schopenhauer. An enormous and flaccid cat, symbol of my vain destiny, was sleeping on the window sill.

In the first volume of *Parerga und Paralipomena* I read again that everything which can happen to a man, from the instant of his birth until his death, has been preordained by him. Thus, every negligence is deliberate, every chance encounter an appointment, every humiliation a penitence, every failure a mysterious victory, every death a suicide. There is no more skilful consolation than the idea that we have chosen our own misfortunes; this individual teleology reveals a secret order and prodigiously confounds us with the divinity. What unknown intention (I questioned vainly) made me seek, that afternoon, those bullets and that mutilation? Surely not fear of war, I

*It has been rumoured that the consequences of this wound were very serious. (Editor's note.)

knew; something more profound. Finally I hit upon it. To die for a religion is easier than to live it absolutely; to battle in Ephesus against the wild beasts is not so trying (thousands of obscure martyrs did it) as to be Paul, servant of Jesus; one act is less than a man's entire life. War and glory are *facilities*; more arduous than the undertaking of Napoleon was that of Raskolnikov. On 7 February 1941, I was named subdirector of the concentration camp at Tarnowitz.

The carrying out of this task was not pleasant, but I was never negligent. The coward proves his mettle under fire; the merciful, the pious, seeks his trial in jails and in the suffering of others. Essentially, Nazism is an act of morality, a purging of corrupted humanity, to dress him anew. This transformation is common in battle, amidst the clamour of the captains and the shouting; such is not the case in a wretched cell, where insidious deceitful mercy tempts us with ancient tenderness. Not in vain do I pen this word: for this superior man of Zarathustra, mercy is the greatest of sins. I almost committed it (I confess) when they sent us the eminent poet David Jerusalem from Breslau.

He was about fifty years old. Poor in the goods of this world, persecuted, denied, vituperated, he had dedicated his genius to the praise of Happiness. I recall that Albert Soergel, in his work *Dichtung der Zeit*, compared him with Whitman. The comparison is not exact. Whitman celebrates the universe in a preliminary, abstract, almost indifferent manner; Jerusalem takes joy in each thing, with a scrupulous and exact love. He never falls into the error of enumerations and catalogues. I can still repeat from memory many hexameters from that superb poem, *Tse Yang, Painter of Tigers*, which is, as it were, streaked with tigers, over-burdened and criss-crossed with transversal and silent tigers. Nor will I ever forget the soliloquy called *Rosencrantz Speaks with the Angel*, in which a sixteenth-century London moneylender vainly tries on his deathbed to vindicate his crimes, without suspecting that the secret justification of his life is that of having inspired in one of his clients (whom he has seen but once and does not remember) the character of Shylock. A man of memorable eyes, jaundiced complexion, with an almost black beard, David Jerusalem was the prototype of the Sephardic Jew, although, in fact, he belonged to the depraved and hated Ashkenazim. I was severe with him; I permitted neither my compassion nor his glory to make me relent. I had come to understand many years before that there is nothing on earth that does not contain the seed of a possible Hell; a face, a word, a compass, a cigarette advertisement, are capable of driving a person mad if he is unable to forget them. Would not a man who continually imagined the map of Hungary be mad? I decided to apply this principle to the disciplinary regimen of our camp, and ...* By the end of 1942, Jerusalem had lost his reason; on 1 March 1943, he managed to kill himself.†

I do not know whether Jerusalem understood that, if I destroyed him, it was to destroy my compassion. In my eyes he was not a man, not even a Jew; he had been transformed into a detested zone of my soul. I agonized with him, I died with him and somehow I was lost with him; therefore, I was implacable.

Meanwhile we revelled in the great days and nights of a successful war. In the very air we breathed there was a feeling not unlike love. Our hearts beat with amazement and exaltation, as if we sensed the sea nearby. Everything was new and different then, even the flavour of our dreams. (I, perhaps, was never entirely happy. But it is known that misery requires lost paradises.) Every man aspires to the fullness of life, that is, to the sum of experiences which he is capable of enjoying; nor is there a man unafraid of being cheated out of some part of his

*It has been necessary to omit a few lines here. (Editor's note.)

†We have been unable to find any reference to the name of Jerusalem, even in Soergel's work. Nor is he mentioned in the histories of German literature. Nevertheless, I do not believe that he is fictitious. Many Jewish intellectuals were tortured at Tarnowitz under orders of Otto Dietrich zur Linde; among them, the pianist Emma Rosenzweig. 'David Jerusalem' is perhaps a symbol of several individuals. It is said that he died 1 March 1943; on 1 March 1939, the narrator was wounded in Tilsit. (Editor's note.)

infinite patrimony. But it can be said that my generation enjoyed the extremes of experience, because first we were granted victory and later defeat.

In October or November of 1942 my brother Friedrich perished in the second battle of El Alamein, on the Egyptian sands. Months later an aerial bombardment destroyed our family's home; another, at the end of 1943, destroyed my laboratory. The Third Reich was dying, harassed by vast continents; it struggled alone against innumerable enemies. Then a singular event occurred, which only now do I believe I understand. I thought I was emptying the cup of anger, but in the dregs I encountered an unexpected flavour, the mysterious and almost terrible flavour of happiness. I essayed several explanations, but none seemed adequate. I thought: *I am pleased with defeat, because secretly I know I am guilty, and only punishment can redeem me.* I thought: *I am pleased with the defeat because it is an end and I am very tired.* I thought: *I am pleased with defeat because it has occurred, because it is irrevocably united to all those events which are, which were, and which will be, because to censure or to deplore a single real occurrence is to blaspheme the universe.* I played with these explanations, until I found the true one.

It has been said that every man is born an Aristotelian or a Platonist. This is the same as saying that every abstract contention has its counterpart in the polemics of Aristotle or Plato; across the centuries and latitudes, the names, faces and dialects change but not the eternal antagonists. The history of nations also registers a secret continuity. Arminius, when he cut down the legions of Varus in a marsh, did not realize that he was a precursor of the German Empire; Luther, translator of the Bible, could not suspect that his goal was to forge a people destined to destroy the Bible for all time; Christoph zur Linde, killed by a Russian bullet in 1758, was in some way preparing the victories of 1914; Hitler believed he was fighting for *a* nation but he fought for all, even for those which he detested and attacked. It matters not that his *I* was ignorant of this fact; his blood and his will were aware of it. The world was dying of

Judaism and from that sickness of Judaism, the faith of Jesus; we taught it violence and the faith of the sword. That sword is slaying us, and we are comparable to the wizard who fashioned a labyrinth and was then doomed to wander in it to the end of his days; or to David, who, judging an unknown man, condemns him to death, only to hear the revelation : *You are that man*. Many things will have to be destroyed in order to construct the New Order; now we know that Germany also was one of those things. We have given more than our lives, we have sacrificed the destiny of our beloved Fatherland. Let others curse and weep; I rejoice in the fact that our destiny completes its circle and is perfect.

An inexorable epoch is spreading over the world. We forged it, we who are already its victim. What matters if England is the hammer and we the anvil, so long as violence reigns and not servile Christian timidity? If victory and injustice and happiness are not for Germany, let them be for other nations. Let Heaven exist, even though our dwelling place is Hell.

I look at myself in the mirror to discover who I am, to discern how I will act in a few hours, when I am face to face with death. My flesh may be afraid; I am not.

Translated by Julian Palley

Averroes's Search

S'imaginant que la tragédie n'est autre chose que l'art de louer...

Ernest Renan: *Averroès*, 48 (1861)

ABULGUALID Muhammad Ibn-Ahmad ibn-Muhammad ibn-Rushd (a century this long name would take to become Averroes, first becoming Benraist and Avenryz and even Aben-Rassad and Filius Rosadis) was writing the eleventh chapter of his work *Tahafut-ul-Tahafut* (Destruction of Destruction), in which it is maintained, contrary to the Persian ascetic Ghazali, author of the *Tahafut-ul-falasifa* (Destruction of Philosophers), that the divinity knows only the general laws of the universe, those pertaining to the species, not to the individual. He wrote with slow sureness, from right to left; the effort of forming syllogisms and linking vast paragraphs did not keep him from feeling, like a state of well-being, the cool and deep house surrounding him. In the depths of the siesta amorous doves called huskily; from some unseen patio arose the murmur of a fountain; something in Averroes, whose ancestors came from the Arabian deserts, was thankful for the constancy of the water. Down below were the gardens, the orchard; down below, the busy Guadalquivir and then the beloved city of Cordova, no less eminent than Baghdad or Cairo, like a complex and delicate instrument, and all around (this Averroes felt also) stretched out to the limits of the earth the Spanish land, where there are few things, but where each seems to exist in a substantive and eternal way.

His pen moved across the page, the arguments entwined irrefutably, but a slight preoccupation darkened Averroes's felicity. It was not caused by the *Tahafut*, a fortuitous piece of work, but rather by a problem of philological nature related to the monumental work which would justify him in the eyes of men: his commentary on Aristotle. This Greek, fountainhead of all philosophy, had been bestowed upon men to teach them all that could be known; to interpret his works as the ulema interpret the Koran was Averroes's arduous purpose. Few things more beautiful and more pathetic are recorded in history than this Arab physician's dedication to the thoughts of a man separated from him by fourteen centuries; to the intrinsic difficulties we should add that Averroes, ignorant of Syriac and of Greek, was working with the translation of a translation. The night before, two doubtful words had halted him at the beginning of the *Poetics*. These words were *tragedy* and *comedy*. He had encountered them years before in the third book of the *Rhetoric*; no one in the whole world of Islam could conjecture what they meant. In vain he had exhausted the pages of Alexander of Aphrodisia, in vain he had compared the versions of the Nestorian Hunain ibn-Ishaq and of Abu-Bashar Mata. These two arcane words pullulated throughout the text of the *Poetics*; it was impossible to elude them.

Averroes put down his pen. He told himself (without excessive faith) that what we seek is often nearby, put away the manuscript of the *Tahafut* and went over to the shelf where the many volumes of the blind Abensida's *Mohkam*, copied by Persian calligraphers, were aligned. It was derisory to imagine he had not consulted them, but he was tempted by the idle pleasure of turning their pages. From this studious distraction, he was distracted by a kind of melody. He looked through the lattice-work balcony; below, in the narrow earthen patio, some half-naked children were playing. One, standing on another's shoulders, was obviously playing the part of a muezzin; with his eyes tightly closed, he chanted 'There is no god but the God'. The one who held him motionlessly played the part of the minaret; another, abject in the dust and on his knees, the part of the faithful worshippers. The game did not last long; all wanted to be the muezzin, none the congregation or the tower. Averroes heard them dispute in the *vulgar* dialect, that is, in the incipient Spanish of the peninsula's Moslem populace. He opened the *Quitab ul ain* of Jalil and thought proudly that in all Cordova (perhaps in all Al-Andalus) there was no other copy of that perfect work than this one the emir Yacub Almansur had sent him from Tangier. The name of this port reminded him that the traveller Abulcasim Al-Ashari, who had returned from Morocco, would dine with him that evening in the home of the Koran scholar Farach. Abulcasim claimed to have reached the dominions of the empire of Sin (China); his detractors, with that peculiar logic of hatred, swore he had never set foot in China and that in the temples of that land he had blasphemed the name of Allah. Inevitably the gathering would last several hours; Averroes quickly resumed his writing of the *Tahafut*. He worked until the twilight of evening.

The conversation, at Farach's home, passed from the incomparable virtues of the governor to those of his brother the emir; later, in the garden, they spoke of roses. Abulcasim, who had not looked at them, swore there were no roses like those adorning the Andalusian country villas. Farach would not be bought with flattery; he observed that the learned Ibn Qutaiba describes an excellent variety of the perpetual rose, which is found in the gardens of Hindustan and whose petals, of a blood red, exhibit characters which read: 'There is no god but the God, Mohammed is the Apostle of God.' He added that surely Abulcasim would know of those roses. Abulcasim looked at him with alarm. If he answered yes, all would judge him, justifiably, the readiest and most gratuitous of impostors; if he answered no, he would be judged an infidel. He elected to muse that the Lord possesses the key to all hidden things and that there is not a green or withered thing on earth which is not recorded in His Book. These words belong to one of the first chapters of the Koran; they were received with a great murmur. Swelled with vanity by this dialectical victory, Abulcasim was about to announce that the Lord is perfect in His works and inscrutable. Then Averroes, prefiguring the remote arguments of an as yet problematical Hume, declared:

'It is less difficult for me to admit an error in the learned Ibn

Qutaiba, or in the copyists, than to admit that the earth has roses with the profession of the faith.'

'So it is. Great and truthful words,' said Abulcasim.

'One traveller,' recalled Abdalmalik the poet, 'speaks of a tree whose fruit are green birds. It is less painful for me to believe in it than in roses with letters.'

'The colour of the birds,' said Averroes, 'seems to facilitate the portent. Besides, fruit and birds belong to the world of nature, but writing is an art. Going from leaves to birds is easier than from roses to letters.'

Another guest denied indignantly that writing is an art, since the original of the Koran – *the mother of the Book* – is prior to Creation and is kept in heaven. Another spoke of Chahiz of Basra, who said that the Koran is a substance which may take the form of a man or animal, an opinion seeming to concord with the opinion of those who attribute two faces to the sacred book. Farach expounded at length the orthodox doctrine. The Koran (he said) is one of the attributes of God, as is His piety; it is copied in a book, uttered by the tongue, remembered in the heart, and the language and the signs and the writing are the work of man, but the Koran is irrevocable and eternal. Averroes, who had written a commentary on the *Republic*, could have said that the mother of the Book is something like its Platonic model, but he noted that theology was a subject totally inaccessible to Abulcasim.

Others who had also noticed this urged Abulcasim to relate some marvel. Then as now, the world was an atrocious place; the daring could travel it as well as the despicable, those who stooped to anything. Abulcasim's memory was a mirror of intimate cowardices. What could he tell? Besides, they demanded marvels of him and marvels are perhaps incommunicable; the moon of Bengal is not the same as the moon of Yemen, but it may be described in the same words. Abulcasim hesitated; then he spoke.

'He who travels the climates and cities,' he proclaimed with unction, 'sees many things worthy of credit. This one, for example, which I have told only once, to the king of the Turks.

It happened in Sin Kalan (Canton), where the river of the Water of Life spills into the sea.'

Farach asked if the city stood many leagues from the wall Iskandar Zul Qarnain (Alexander the Great of Macedonia) raised to halt Gog and Magog.

'Deserts separate them,' said Abulcasim, with involuntary arrogance. 'Forty days a *cafila* (caravan) would take to glimpse its towers and they say another forty to reach it. In Sin Kalan I know of no one who has seen it or has seen anyone who has seen it.'

The fear of the crassly infinite, of mere space, of mere matter, touched Averroes for an instant. He looked at the symmetrical garden; he felt aged, useless, unreal. Abulcasim continued:

'One afternoon, the Moslem merchants of Sin Kalan took me to a house of painted wood where many people lived. It is impossible to describe the house, which was rather a single room, with rows of cabinets or balconies on top of each other. In these cavities there were people who were eating and drinking, and also on the floor, and also on a terrace. The persons on this terrace were playing the drum and the lute, save for some fifteen or twenty (with crimson-coloured masks) who were praying, singing and conversing. They suffered prison, but no one could see the jail; they travelled on horseback, but no one could see the horse; they fought, but the swords were of reed; they died and then stood up again.'

'The acts of madmen,' said Farach, 'exceed the previsions of the sane.'

'These were no madmen,' Abulcasim had to explain. 'They were representing a story, a merchant told me.'

No one understood, no one seemed to want to understand. Abulcasim, confused, now went from his narration to his inept explanation. With the aid of his hands, he said:

'Let us imagine that someone performs a story instead of telling it. Let that story be the one about the sleepers of Ephesus. We see them retire into the cavern, we see them pray and sleep, we see them sleep with their eyes open, we see them grow as they sleep, we see them awaken after three hundred and nine years, we see them give the merchant an ancient coin, we see them awaken in Paradise, we see them awaken with the dog. Something like this was shown to us that afternoon by the people of the terrace.'

'Did those people speak?' asked Farach.

'Of course they spoke,' said Abulcasim, now become the apologist of a performance he scarcely remembered and which had annoyed him quite a bit. 'They spoke and sang and perorated.'

'In that case,' said Farach, 'twenty persons are unnecessary. One single speaker can tell anything, no matter how complicated it might be.'

Everyone approved this dictum. The virtues of Arabic were extolled, which is the language God uses to direct the angels; then, those of Arabic poetry. Abdalmalik, after giving this poetry due praise and consideration, labelled as antiquated the poets who in Damascus or in Cordova adhered to pastoral images and a Bedouin vocabulary. He said it was absurd for a man having the Guadalquivir before his eyes to exalt the water of a well. He urged the convenience of renewing the old metaphors; he said that at the time Zuhair compared destiny to a blind camel, such a figure could move people, but that five centuries of admiration had rendered it valueless. All approved this dictum, which they had already heard many times, from many tongues. Averroes was silent. Finally he spoke, less to the others than to himself.

'With less eloquence,' Averroes said, 'but with related arguments, I once defended the proposition Abdalmalik maintains. In Alexandria, it has been said that the only persons incapable of a sin are those who have already committed it and repented; to be free of an error, let us add, it is well to have professed it. Zuhair in his *mohalaca* says that in the course of eighty years of suffering and glory many times he has seen destiny suddenly trample men into the dust, like a blind camel; Abdalmalik finds that this figure can no longer marvel us. Many things could be offered in response to this objection. The first, that if the purpose of the poem is to surprise us, its life span would not be measured in centuries, but in days and hours and perhaps minutes. The second, that a famous poet is less of an inventor than he is a discoverer. In praise of Ibn-Sharaf of Berja it has been repeated that only he could imagine that the stars at dawn fall slowly, like leaves from a tree; if this were so, it would be evidence that the image is banal. The image one man can form is an image that touches no one. There are infinite things on earth; any one of them may be likened to any other. Likening stars to leaves is no less arbitrary than likening them to fish or birds. However, there is no one who has not felt at some time that destiny is clumsy and powerful, that it is innocent and also inhuman. For that conviction, which may be passing or continuous, but which no one may elude, Zuhair's verse was written. What was said there will not be said better. Besides (and this is perhaps the essential part of my reflections), time, which despoils castles, enriches verses. Zuhair's verse, when he composed it in Arabia, served to confront two images, the old camel and destiny; when we repeat it now, it serves to evoke the memory of Zuhair and to fuse our misfortune with that dead Arab's. The figure had two terms then and now it has four. Time broadens the scope of verses and I know of some which, like music, are everything for all men. Thus, when I was tormented years ago in Marrakesh by memories of Cordova, I took pleasure in repeating the apostrophe Abdurrahman addressed in the gardens of Ruzafa to an African palm:

> You too, oh palm!, are
> Foreign to this soil . . .

The singular benefit of poetry: words composed by a king who longed for the Orient served me, exiled in Africa, to express my nostalgia for Spain.'

Averroes then spoke of the first poets, of those who in the Time of Ignorance, before Islam, had already said all things in the infinite language of the deserts. Alarmed, and not without reason, by Ibn-Sharaf's trivialities, he said that in the ancients and in the Koran all poetry is contained and he condemned as illiterate and vain the desire for innovation. The others listened with pleasure, for he was vindicating the traditional.

The muezzins were calling the faithful to their early morning prayers when Averroes entered his library again. (In the harem, the dark-haired slave girls had tortured a red-haired slave girl, but he would not know it until the afternoon.) Something had revealed to him the meaning of the two obscure words. With firm and careful calligraphy he added these lines to the manuscript: 'Aristu (Aristotle) gives the name of tragedy to panegyrics and that of comedy to satires and anathemas. Admirable tragedies and comedies abound in the pages of the Koran and in the *mohalacas* of the sanctuary.'

He felt sleepy, he felt somewhat cold. Having unwound his turban, he looked at himself in a metal mirror. I do not know what his eyes saw, because no historian has ever described the forms of his face. I do know that he disappeared suddenly, as if fulminated by an invisible fire, and with him disappeared the houses and the unseen fountain and the books and the manuscript and the doves and the many dark-haired slave girls and the tremulous red-haired slave girl and Farach and Abulcasim and the rose bushes and perhaps the Guadalquivir.

In the foregoing story, I tried to narrate the process of a defeat. I first thought of that archbishop of Canterbury who took it upon himself to prove there is a God; then, of the alchemists who sought the philosopher's stone; then, of the vain trisectors of the angle and squarers of the circle. Later I reflected that it would be more poetic to tell the case of a man who sets himself a goal which is not forbidden to others, but is to him. I remembered Averroes who, closed within the orb of Islam, could never know the meaning of the terms *tragedy* and *comedy*. I related his case; as I went along, I felt what that god mentioned by Burton must have felt when he tried to create a bull and created a buffalo instead. I felt that the work was mocking me. I felt that Averroes, wanting to imagine what a drama is without ever having suspected what a theatre is, was no more absurd than I, wanting to imagine Averroes with no other sources than a few fragments from Renan, Lane and Asín Palacios. I felt, on the last page, that my narration was a symbol of the man I was as I wrote it and that, in order to compose that narration, I had to be that man and, in order to be that man, I had to compose that narration, and so on to infinity. (The moment I cease to believe in him, 'Averroes' disappears.)

Translated by J.E.I.

The Zahir

In Buenos Aires the Zahir is an ordinary coin worth twenty centavos. The letters N T and the number 2 are scratched as if with a razor-blade or penknife; 1929 is the date on the obverse. (In Guzerat, towards the end of the eighteenth century, the Zahir was a tiger; in Java, a blind man from the Mosque of Surakarta whom the Faithful pelted with stones; in Persia, an astrolabe which Nadir Shah caused to be sunk to the bottom of the sea; in the Mahdi's prisons, along about 1892, it was a little compass which Rudolf Carl von Slatin touched, tucked into the fold of a turban; in the Mosque of Cordova, according to Zotenberg, it was a vein in the marble of one of the twelve-hundred pillars; in the Tetuán ghetto, it was the bottom of a well.) Today is the thirteenth of November; the Zahir came into my possession at dawn on June seventh. I am no longer the 'I' of that episode; but it is still possible for me to remember what happened, perhaps even to tell it. I am still, however incompletely, Borges.

Clementina Villar died on the sixth of June. Around 1930, her pictures were clogging the society magazines: perhaps it was this ubiquity that contributed to the legend that she was extremely pretty, although not every portrait bore out this hypothesis unconditionally. At any rate, Clementina Villar was interested less in beauty than in perfection. The Hebrews and the Chinese codified every conceivable human eventuality; it is written in the *Mishnah* that a tailor is not to go out into the street carrying a needle once the Sabbath twilight has set in, and we read in the *Book of Rites* that a guest should assume a grave air when offered the first cup, and a respectfully contented air upon receiving the second. Something of this sort, though in much greater detail, was to be discerned in the uncompromising strictness which Clementina Villar demanded of herself. Like any Confucian adept or Talmudist, she strove for irreproachable correctness in every action; but her zeal was more admirable and more exigent than theirs because the tenets of her creed were not eternal, but submitted to the shifting caprices of Paris or Hollywood. Clementina Villar appeared at the correct places, at the correct hour, with the correct appurtenances and the correct boredom; but the boredom, the appurtenances, the hour and the places would almost immediately become *passé* and would provide Clementina Villar with the material for a definition of cheap taste. She was in search of the Absolute, like Flaubert; only hers was an Absolute of a moment's duration. Her life was exemplary, yet she was ravaged unremittingly by an inner despair. She was for ever experimenting with new metamorphoses, as though trying to get away from herself; the colour of her hair and the shape of her coiffure were celebratedly unstable. She was always changing her smile, her complexion, the slant of her eyes. After thirty-two she was scrupulously slender ... The war gave her much to think about: with Paris occupied by the Germans, how could one follow the fashions? A foreigner whom she had always distrusted presumed so far upon her good faith as to sell her a number of cylindrical hats; a year later it was divulged that those absurd creations *had never been worn in Paris at all*! – consequently they were not hats, but arbitrary, unauthorized eccentricities. And troubles never come singly: Dr Villar had to move to Aráoz Street, and his daughter's portrait was now adorning advertisements for cold cream and automobiles. (The cold cream that she abundantly applied, the automobiles she *no longer* possessed.) She knew that the successful exercise of her art demanded a large fortune, and she preferred retirement from the scene to halfway effects. Moreover, it pained her to have to compete with giddy little nobodies. The gloomy Aráoz apartment was too much to bear: on the sixth of June Clementina Villar committed the solecism of dying in the very middle of the Southern district. Shall I confess that I – moved by that

most sincere of Argentinian passions, snobbery – was en-
amoured of her, and that her death moved me to tears? Probably the reader has already suspected as much.

At a wake, the progress of corruption brings it about that the
corpse reassumes its earlier faces. At some stage of that confused night of the sixth, Clementina Villar was magically what
she had been twenty years before: her features recovered that
authority which is conferred by pride, by money, by youth, by
the awareness of rounding off a hierarchy, by lack of imagination, by limitations, by stolidity. Somehow, I thought, no
version of that face which has disturbed me so will stay in my
memory as long as this one; it is right that it should be the last,
since it might have been the first. I left her rigid among the
flowers, her disdain perfected by death. It must have been
about two in the morning when I went away. Outside, the
predictable rows of one- and two-storey houses had taken on
the abstract appearance that is theirs at night, when darkness
and silence simplify them. Drunk with an almost impersonal
piety, I walked through the streets. At the corner of Chile and
Tacuarí I saw an open shop. And in that shop, unhappily for
me, three men were playing cards.

In the figure of speech called oxymoron a word is modified
by an epithet which seems to contradict it: thus, the Gnostics
spoke of dark light, and the alchemists of a black sun. For me it
was a kind of oxymoron to go straight from my last visit with
Clementina Villar to buy a drink at a bar; I was intrigued by the
coarseness of the act, by its ease. (The contrast was heightened
by the circumstance that there was a card game in progress.) I
asked for a brandy. They gave me the Zahir in my change. I
stared at it for a moment and went out into the street, perhaps
with the beginnings of a fever. I reflected that every coin in the
world is a symbol of those famous coins which glitter in
history and fable. I thought of Charon's obol; of the obol for
which Belisarius begged; of Judas's thirty coins; of the drach-
mas of Laïs, the famous courtesan; of the ancient coin which
one of the Seven Sleepers proffered; of the shining coins of the
wizard in the 1001 Nights, that turned out to be bits of paper;

of the inexhaustible penny of Isaac Laquedem; of the sixty thousand pieces of silver, one for each line of an epic, which Firdusi sent back to a king because they were not of gold; of the doubloon which Ahab nailed to the mast; of Leopold Bloom's irreversible florin; of a louis whose pictured face betrayed the fugitive Louis XVI near Varennes. As if in a dream, the thought that every piece of money entails such illustrious connotations as these, seemed to me of huge, though inexplicable, importance. My speed increased as I passed through the empty squares and along the empty streets. At length, weariness deposited me at a corner. I saw a patient iron grating and, beyond, the black and white flagstones of the Concepción. I had wandered in a circle and was now a block away from the store where they had given me the Zahir.

I turned back. The dark window told me from a distance that the shop was now closed. In Belgrano Street I took a cab. Sleepless, obsessed, almost happy, I reflected that there is nothing less material than money, since any coin whatsoever (let us say a coin worth twenty centavos) is, strictly speaking, a repertory of possible futures. Money is abstract, I repeated; money is the future tense. It can be an evening in the suburbs, or music by Brahms; it can be maps, or chess, or coffee; it can be the words of Epictetus teaching us to despise gold; it is a Proteus more versatile than the one on the isle of Pharos. It is unforeseeable time, Bergsonian time, not the rigid time of Islam or the Porch. The determinists deny that there is such a thing in the world as a single possible act, *id est* an act that could or could not happen; a coin symbolizes man's free will. (I did not suspect that these 'thoughts' were an artifice opposed to the Zahir and an initial form of its demoniacal influence.) I fell asleep after much brooding, but I dreamed that I was the coins guarded by a griffon.

The next day I decided that I had been drunk. I also made up my mind to get rid of the coin that had caused me so much worry. I looked at it: there was nothing out of the ordinary about it except for some scratches. The best thing to do would be to bury it in the garden or hide it in some corner of the library, but I wanted to remove myself from its orbit. I preferred to lose it. I did not go to the Pilar that morning, or to the cemetery; I took the underground to Constitución and from Constitución to the corner of San Juan and Boedo. I got off, on an impulse, at Urquiza and walked west and south. With scrupulous lack of plan I rounded a number of corners, and in a street which looked to me like all the others I went into a wretched little tavern, asked for a drink of brandy, and paid for it with the Zahir. I half closed my eyes behind my dark spectacles, managing not to see the house-numbers or the name of the street. That night I took a veronal tablet and slept peacefully.

Up till the end of June I was busy writing a tale of fantasy. This contained two or three enigmatic circumlocutions, or 'kennings' : for example, instead of *blood* it says *sword-water*, and *gold* is the *serpent's bed*; the story is told in the first person. The narrator is an ascetic who has abjured the society of men and who lives in a kind of wilderness. (The name of this place is Gnitaheidr.) Because of the simplicity and candour of his life there are those who consider him an angel; but this is a pious exaggeration, for there is no man who is free of sin. As a matter of fact, he has cut his own father's throat, the old man having been a notorious wizard who by magic arts had got possession of a limitless treasure. To guard this treasure from the insane covetousness of human beings is the purpose to which our ascetic has dedicated his life : day and night he keeps watch over the hoard. Soon, perhaps too soon, his vigil will come to an end : the stars have told him that the sword had already been forged which will cut it short for ever. (Gram is the name of that sword.) In a rhetoric increasingly more complex he contemplates the brilliance and the flexibility of his body : in one paragraph he speaks distractedly of his scales; in another he says that the treasure which he guards is flashing gold and rings of red. In the end we understand that the ascetic is the serpent Fafnir, that the treasure upon which he lies is the treasure of the Nibelungs. The appearance of Sigurd brings the story to an abrupt end.

I have said that the composition of this trifle (into which I inserted, in a pseudo-erudite fashion, a verse or two from the *Fáfnismál*) gave me a chance to forget the coin. There were nights when I felt so sure of being able to forget it that I deliberately recalled it to mind. What is certain is that I over-did these occasions: it was easier to start the thing than to have done with it. It was in vain that I told myself that that abominable nickel disk was no different from others that pass from one hand to another, alike, countless, innocuous. Attracted by this idea, I tried to think of other coins; but I could not. I remember, too, a frustrated experiment I made with Chilean five- and ten-centavo pieces and an Uruguayan *vintén*. On the sixteenth of July I acquired a pound sterling. I did not look at it during the day, but that night (and other nights) I put it under a magnifying glass and studied it by the light of a powerful electric lamp. Afterwards I traced it on paper with a pencil. But the brilliance and the dragon and Saint George were of no help to me: I could not manage to change obsessions.

In August I decided to consult a psychiatrist. I did not tell him the whole of my ridiculous story; I said I was bothered by insomnia, that I was being haunted by the image of something or other ... let us say a poker-chip or a coin. A little later, in a bookshop in Sarmiento Street, I dug up a copy of Julius Barlach's *Urkunden zur Geschichte der Zahirsage* (Breslau, 1899).

In this book my disease was clearly revealed. According to the preface, the author proposed 'to gather together in one handy octavo volume all the documents having to do with the Zahir superstition, including four papers from the Habicht collection and the original manuscript of the study by Philip Meadows Taylor.' Belief in the Zahir is of Islamic origin, and seems to date from the eighteenth century. (Barlach rejects the passages which Zotenberg attributes to Abulfeda.) *Zahir* in Arabic means 'notorious', 'visible'; in this sense it is one of the ninety-nine names of God, and the people (in Muslim territories) use it to signify 'beings or things which possess the terrible property of being unforgettable, and whose image

finally drive one mad'. The first irrefutable testimony is that of
the Persian Lutf Ali Azur. In the precise pages of the biographical encyclopaedia entitled *Temple of Fire* this polygraph
dervish writes that in a school at Shiraz there was a copper
astrolabe 'fashioned in such a way that whoever looked once
upon it could thereafter think of nothing else; whence the King
ordered that it should be sunk in the deepest part of the sea,
lest men forget the universe'. The study of Meadows Taylor is
more detailed (he was in the service of the Nizam of Hyder-
abad, and wrote the famous novel, *Confessions of a Thug*). In
about 1832, in the outskirts of Bhuj, Taylor heard the unusual
expression 'Verily he has looked on the Tiger', to signify madness or saintliness. He was informed that the reference was to a
magic tiger which was the ruin of whoever beheld it, even
from far away, since the beholder continued to think about it
to the end of his days. Someone said that one of these unfor-
tunates had fled to Mysore, where he had painted the figure of
the tiger on the walls of some palace. Years later, Taylor was
inspecting the jails of the kingdom; and in the one at Nittur the
governor showed him a cell where the floor, the walls and the
ceiling had been covered, in barbaric colours, which time was
subtilizing before erasing them, by a Muslim fakir's elaboration
of a kind of infinite Tiger. This Tiger was composed of many
tigers in the most vertiginous fashion : it was traversed by
tigers, scored by tigers and it contained seas and Himalayas
and armies which seemed to reveal still other tigers. The
painter had died many years ago in this very cell; he had come
from Sind, or maybe Guzerat, and his original purpose had
been to design a map of the world. Indeed, some traces of
this were yet to be discerned in the monstrous image.... Taylor
told the story to Mohammed Al-Yemeni, of Fort William;
Mohammed informed him that there was no created thing in this
world which could not take on the properties of *Zaheer*,* but
that the All-merciful does not allow two things to be it at the
same time, since one alone is able to fascinate multitudes. He
said that there is always a Zahir; that in the Age of Innocence

* Such is Taylor's spelling of the word.

it was an idol named Yaúq; and later, a prophet of Jorasán who used to wear a veil embroidered with stones, or a golden mask.* He also said that God is inscrutable.

I read Barlach's monograph – read it and reread it. I hardly need describe my feelings. I remember my despair when I realized that nothing could save me; the sheer relief of knowing that I was not to blame for my predicament; the envy I felt for those whose Zahir was not a coin, but a piece of marble, or a tiger. How easy it would be not to think of a tiger! And I also remember the odd anxiety with which I studied this paragraph: 'A commentator on the *Gulshan i Raz* says that he who has seen the Zahir will soon see the Rose; and he cites a verse interpolated in the *Asrar Nama* (Book of Things Unknown) of Attar: "The Zahir is the shadow of the Rose, and the Rending of the Veil." '

That night at Clementina's house I had been surprised not to see her younger sister, Mrs Abascal. In October one of her friends told me about it: 'Poor Julie! She got awfully *queer*, and they had to shut her up in the Bosch. She's just going to be the *death* of the nurses who have to *spoon*-feed her! Why, she keeps on talking about a *coin*, just like Morena Sackmann's *chauffeur*.'

Time, which generally attenuates memories, only aggravates that of the Zahir. There was a time when I could visualize the obverse, and then the reverse. Now I see them simultaneously. This is not as though the Zahir were crystal, because it is not a matter of one face being superimposed upon another; rather, it is as though my eyesight were spherical, with the Zahir in the centre. Whatever is not the Zahir comes to me fragmentarily, as if from a great distance: the arrogant image of Clementina; physical pain. Tennyson once said that if we could understand a single flower, we should know what we are and what the world is. Perhaps he meant that there is no fact, however

* Barlach observes that Yaúq, is mentioned in the Koran (71, 23) and that the Prophet is Al-Mokanna (the Veiled One), and that no one except Philip Meadows Taylor's surprising informant has identified them with the Zahir.

insignificant, that does not involve universal history and the infinite concatenation of cause and effect. Perhaps he meant that the visible world is implicit in every phenomenon, just as the will, according to Schopenhauer, is implicit in every subject. The Cabalists pretend that man is a microcosm, a symbolic mirror of the universe; according to Tennyson, everything would be. Everything, even the intolerable Zahir.

Before 1948 Julie's destiny will have caught up with me. They will have to feed me and dress me, I shall not know whether it is afternoon or morning, I shall not know who Borges was. To call this prospect terrible is a fallacy, for none of its circumstances will exist for me. One might as well say that an anaesthetized man feels terrible pain when they open his cranium. I shall no longer perceive the universe: I shall perceive the Zahir. According to the teaching of the Idealists, the words 'live' and 'dream' are rigorously synonymous. From thousands of images I shall pass to one; from a highly complex dream to a dream of utter simplicity. Others will dream that I am mad; I shall dream of the Zahir. When all the men on earth think, day and night, of the Zahir, which will be a dream and which a reality – the earth or the Zahir?

In the empty night hours I can still walk through the streets. Dawn may surprise me on a bench in Garay Park, thinking (trying to think) of the passage in the *Asrar Nama* where it says that the Zahir is the shadow of the Rose and the Rending of the Veil. I associate that saying with this bit of information: In order to lose themselves in God, the Sufis recite their own names, or the ninety-nine divine names, until they become meaningless. I long to travel that path. Perhaps I shall conclude by wearing away the Zahir simply through thinking of it again and again. Perhaps behind the coin I shall find God.

To Wally Zenner   *Translated by Dudley Fitts*

The Waiting

THE cab left him at number four thousand and four on that street in the northwest part of Buenos Aires. It was not yet nine in the morning; the man noted with approval the spotted plane trees, the square plot of earth at the foot of each, the respectable houses with their little balconies, the pharmacy alongside, the dull lozenges of the paint and hardware store. A long windowless hospital wall backed the sidewalk on the other side of the street; the sun reverberated, farther down, from some greenhouses. The man thought that these things (now arbitrary and accidental and in no special order, like the things one sees in dreams) would in time, if God willed, become invariable, necessary and familiar. In the pharmacy window porcelain letters spelled out the name 'Breslauer'; the Jews were displacing the Italians, who had displaced the Creoles. It was better that way; the man preferred not to mingle with people of his kind.

The cabman helped him take down his trunk; a woman with a distracted or tired air finally opened the door. From his seat, the cabman returned one of the coins to him, a Uruguayan twenty-centavo piece which had been in his pocket since that night in the hotel at Melo. The man gave him forty centavos and immediately felt: 'I must act so that everyone will forgive me. I have made two errors: I have used a foreign coin and I have shown that the mistake matters to me.'

Led by the woman, he crossed the entrance hall and the first patio. The room they had reserved for him opened, happily, on to the second patio. The bed was of iron, deformed by the craftsmen into fantastic curves representing branches and tendrils; there was also a tall pine wardrobe, a bedside table, a shelf with books at floor level, two odd chairs and a washstand with its basin, jar, soap dish and bottle of turbid glass. A map of the province of Buenos Aires and a crucifix adorned the walls; the wallpaper was crimson, with a pattern of huge spread-tailed peacocks. The only door opened on to the patio. It was necessary to change the placement of the chairs in order to get the trunk in. The roomer approved of everything; when the woman asked him his name, he said Villari, not as a secret challenge, not to mitigate the humiliation which actually he did not feel, but because that name troubled him, because it was impossible for him to think of any other. Certainly he was not seduced by the literary error of thinking that assumption of the enemy's name might be an astute manoeuvre.

Mr Villari, at first, did not leave the house; after a few weeks, he took to going out for a while at sundown. One night he went into the movie theatre three blocks away. He never went beyond the last row of seats, he always got up a little before the end of the feature. He would see tragic stories of the underworld; these stories, no doubt, contained errors; these stories, no doubt, contained images which were also those of his former life; Villari took no notice of them because the idea of a coincidence between art and reality was alien to him. He would submissively try to like the things; he wanted to anticipate the intention with which they were shown. Unlike people who read novels, he never saw himself as a character in a work of art.

No letters nor even a circular ever arrived for him, but with vague hope he would always read one of the sections of the newspaper. In the afternoons, he would put one of the chairs by the door and gravely make and drink his maté, his eyes fixed on the vine covering the wall of the several-storied building next door. Years of solitude had taught him that, in one's memory, all days tend to be the same, but that there is not a day, not even in jail or in the hospital, which does not bring surprises, which is not a translucent network of minimal surprises. In other confinements, he had given in to the temptation of counting the days and the hours, but this confinement was different, for it had no end – unless one morning the newspaper brought news of Alejandro Villari's death. It was also possible that Villari *had already died* and in that case this life was a dream. This possibility disturbed him, because he could never quite understand whether it seemed a relief or a misfortune; he told himself it was absurd and discounted it. In distant days, less distant because of the passage of time than because of two or three irrevocable acts, he had desired many things with an unscrupulous passion; this powerful will, which had moved the hatred of men and the love of some women, no longer wanted any particular thing: it only wanted to endure, not to come to an end. The taste of the maté, the taste of black tobacco, the growing line of shadows gradually covering the patio – these were sufficient incentives.

In the house there was a wolf-dog, now old. Villari made friends with him. He spoke to him in Spanish, in Italian, in the few words he still retained of the rustic dialect of his childhood. Villari tried to live in the simple present, with no memories or anticipation; the former mattered less to him than the latter. In an obscure way, he thought he could see that the past is the stuff time is made of; for that reason, time immediately turns into the past. His weariness, one day, was like a feeling of contentment; in moments like this, he was not much more complex than the dog.

One night he was left astonished and trembling by an intimate discharge of pain in the back of his mouth. This horrible miracle recurred in a few minutes and again towards dawn. Villari, the next day, sent for a cab which left him at a dentist's office in the Once section. There he had the tooth pulled. In this ordeal he was neither more cowardly nor more tranquil than other people.

Another night, returning from the movies, he felt that he was being pushed. With anger, with indignation, with secret relief, he faced the insolent person. He spat out a coarse insult; the other man, astonished, stammered an excuse. He was tall, young, with dark hair, accompanied by a German-looking woman; that night, Villari repeated to himself that he did not know them. Nevertheless, four or five days went by before he went out into the street.

Among the books on the shelf there was a copy of the *Divine Comedy*, with the old commentary by Andreoli. Prompted less by curiosity than by a feeling of duty, Villari undertook the reading of this capital work; before dinner, he would read a canto and then, in rigorous order, the notes. He did not judge the punishments of hell to be unbelievable or excessive and did not think Dante would have condemned him to the last circle, where Ugolino's teeth endlessly gnaw Ruggieri's neck.

The peacocks on the crimson wallpaper seemed destined to be food for tenacious nightmares, but Mr Villari never dreamed of a monstrous arbour inextricably woven of living birds. At dawn he would dream a dream whose substance was the same, with varying circumstances. Two men and Villari would enter the room with revolvers or they would attack him as he left the movie house or all three of them at once would be the stranger who had pushed him or they would sadly wait for him in the patio and seem not to recognize him. At the end of the dream, he would take his revolver from the drawer of the bedside table (and it was true he kept a revolver in that drawer) and open fire on the men. The noise of the weapon would wake him, but it was always a dream and in another dream the attack would be repeated and in another dream he would have to kill them again.

One murky morning in the month of July, the presence of strange people (not the noise of the door when they opened it) woke him. Tall in the shadows of the room, curiously simplified by those shadows (in the fearful dreams they had always been clearer), vigilant, motionless and patient, their eyes lowered as if weighted down by the heaviness of their weapons, Alejandro Villari and a stranger had overtaken him at last. With a gesture, he asked them to wait and turned his face to the wall, as if to resume his sleep. Did he do it to arouse the pity of those who killed him, or because it is less difficult to endure a frightful happening than to imagine it and endlessly await it, or – and this is perhaps most likely – so that the murderers would be a dream, as they had already been so many times, in the same place, at the same hour?

He was in this act of magic when the blast obliterated him.

Translated by J.E.I.

The God's Script

THE prison is deep and of stone; its form, that of a nearly perfect hemisphere, though the floor (also of stone) is somewhat less than a great circle, a fact which in some way aggravates the feelings of oppression and of vastness. A dividing wall cuts it at the centre; this wall, although very high, does not reach the upper part of the vault; in one cell am I, Tzinacán, magician of the pyramid of Qaholom, which Pedro de Alvarado devastated by fire; in the other there is a jaguar measuring with secret and even paces the time and space of captivity. A long window with bars, flush with the floor, cuts the central wall. At the shadowless hour [midday], a trap in the high ceiling opens and a jailer whom the years have gradually been effacing manoeuvres an iron sheave and lowers for us, at the end of a rope, jugs of water and chunks of flesh. The light breaks into the vault; at that instant I can see the jaguar.

I have lost count of the years I have lain in the darkness; I, who was young once and could move about this prison, am incapable of more than waiting, in the posture of my death, the end destined to me by the gods. With the deep obsidian knife I have cut open the breasts of victims and now I could not, without magic, lift myself from the dust.

On the eve of the burning of the pyramid, the men who got down from the towering horses tortured me with fiery metals to force me to reveal the location of a hidden treasure. They struck down the idol of the god before my very eyes, but he did not abandon me and I endured the torments in silence. They scourged me, they broke and deformed me, and then I awoke in this prison from which I shall not emerge in mortal life.

Impelled by the fatality of having something to do, of

populating time in some way, I tried, in my darkness, to recall all I knew. Endless nights I devoted to recalling the order and the number of stone-carved serpents or the precise form of a medicinal tree. Gradually, in this way, I subdued the passing years; gradually, in this way, I came into possession of that which was already mine. One night I felt I was approaching the threshold of an intimate recollection; before he sights the sea, the traveller feels a quickening in the blood. Hours later I began to perceive the outline of the recollection. It was a tradition of the god. The god, foreseeing that at the end of time there would be devastation and ruin, wrote on the first day of Creation a magical sentence with the power to ward off those evils. He wrote it in such a way that it would reach the most distant generations and not be subject to chance. No one knows where it was written nor with what characters, but it is certain that it exists, secretly, and that a chosen one shall read it. I considered that we were now, as always, at the end of time and that my destiny as the last priest of the god would give me access to the privilege of intuiting the script. The fact that a prison confined me did not forbid my hope; perhaps I had seen the script of Qaholom a thousand times and needed only to fathom it.

This reflection encouraged me, and then instilled in me a kind of vertigo. Throughout the earth there are ancient forms, forms incorruptible and eternal; any one of them could be the symbol I sought. A mountain could be the speech of the god, or a river or the empire or the configuration of the stars. But in the process of the centuries the mountain is levelled and the river will change its course, empires experience mutation and havoc and the configuration of the stars varies. There is change in the firmament. The mountain and the star are individuals and individuals perish. I sought something more tenacious, more invulnerable. I thought of the generations of cereals, of grasses, of birds, of men. Perhaps the magic would be written on my face, perhaps I myself was the end of my search. That anxiety was consuming me when I remembered the jaguar was one of the attributes of the god.

Then my soul filled with pity. I imagined the first morning of time; I imagined my god confiding his message to the living skin of the jaguars, who would love and reproduce without end, in caverns, in cane fields, on islands, in order that the last men might receive it. I imagined that net of tigers, that teeming labyrinth of tigers, inflicting horror upon pastures and flocks in order to perpetuate a design. In the next cell there was a jaguar; in his vicinity I perceived a confirmation of my conjecture and a secret favour.

I devoted long years to learning the order and the configuration of the spots. Each period of darkness conceded an instant of light, and I was able thus to fix in my mind the black forms running through the yellow fur. Some of them included points, others formed cross lines on the inner side of the legs; others, ring-shaped, were repeated. Perhaps they were a single sound or a single word. Many of them had red edges.

I shall not recite the hardships of my toil. More than once I cried out to the vault that it was impossible to decipher that text. Gradually, the concrete enigma I laboured at disturbed me less than the generic enigma of a sentence written by a god. What type of sentence (I asked myself) will an absolute mind construct? I considered that even in the human languages there is no proposition that does not imply the entire universe; to say *the tiger* is to say the tigers that begot it, the deer and turtles devoured by it, the grass on which the deer fed, the earth that was mother to the grass, the heaven that gave birth to the earth. I considered that in the language of a god every word would enunciate that infinite concatenation of facts, and not in an implicit but in an explicit manner, and not progressively but instantaneously. In time, the notion of a divine sentence seemed puerile or blasphemous. A god, I reflected, ought to utter only a single word and in that word absolute fullness. No word uttered by him can be inferior to the universe or less than the sum total of time. Shadows or simulacra of that single word equivalent to a language and to all a language can embrace are the poor and ambitious human words, *all, world, universe.*

One day or one night – what difference between my days and nights can there be? – I dreamt there was a grain of sand on the floor of the prison. Indifferent, I slept again; I dreamt I awoke and that on the floor there were two grains of sand. I slept again; I dreamt that the grains of sand were three. They went on multiplying in this way until they filled the prison and I lay dying beneath that hemisphere of sand. I realized that I was dreaming; with a vast effort I roused myself and awoke. It was useless to awake; the innumerable sand was suffocating me. Someone said to me: *You have not awakened to wakefulness, but to a previous dream. This dream is enclosed within another, and so on to infinity, which is the number of grains of sand. The path you must retrace is interminable and you will die before you ever really awake.*

I felt lost. The sand burst my mouth, but I shouted: *A sand of dreams cannot kill me nor are there dreams within dreams.* A blaze of light awoke me. In the darkness above there grew a circle of light. I saw the face and hands of the jailer, the sheave, the rope, the flesh and the water jugs.

A man becomes confused, gradually, with the form of his destiny; a man is, by and large, his circumstances. More than a decipherer or an avenger, more than a priest of the god, I was one imprisoned. From the tireless labyrinth of dreams I returned as if to my home to the harsh prison. I blessed its dampness, I blessed its tiger, I blessed the crevice of light, I blessed my old, suffering body, I blessed the darkness and the stone.

Then there occurred what I cannot forget nor communicate. There occurred the union with the divinity, with the universe (I do not know whether these words differ in meaning). Ecstasy does not repeat its symbols; God has been seen in a blazing light, in a sword or in the circles of a rose. I saw an exceedingly high Wheel, which was not before my eyes, nor behind me, nor to the sides, but every place at one time. That Wheel was made of water, but also of fire, and it was (although the edge could be seen) infinite. Interlinked, all things that are, were and shall be formed it, and I was one of the fibres of that total fabric and Pedro de Alvarado who tortured me was

another. There lay revealed the causes and the effects and it
sufficed me to see that Wheel in order to understand it all,
without end. O bliss of understanding, greater than the bliss of
imagining or feeling. I saw the universe and I saw the intimate
designs of the universe. I saw the origins narrated in the Book
of the Common. I saw the mountains that rose out of the
water, I saw the first men of wood, the cisterns that turned
against the men, the dogs that ravaged their face. I saw the
faceless god concealed behind the other gods. I saw infinite
processes that formed one single felicity and, understanding all,
I was able also to understand the script of the tiger.

It is a formula of fourteen random words (they appear
random) and to utter it in a loud voice would suffice to make
me all powerful. To say it would suffice to abolish this stone
prison, to have daylight break into my night, to be young, to be
immortal, to have the tiger's jaws crush Alvarado, to sink the
sacred knife into the breasts of Spaniards, to reconstruct the
pyramid, to reconstruct the empire. Forty syllables, fourteen
words, and I, Tzinacán, would rule the lands Moctezuma ruled.
But I know I shall never say those words, because I no longer
remember Tzinacán.

May the mystery lettered on the tigers die with me. Whoever has seen the universe, whoever has beheld the fiery designs of the universe, cannot think in terms of one man, of that
man's trivial fortunes or misfortunes, though he be that very
man. That man *has been he* and now matters no more to him.
What is the life of that other to him, the nation of that other
to him, if he, now, is no one? This is why I do not pronounce
the formula, why, lying here in the darkness, I let the days
obliterate me.

Translated by L. A. Murillo

Essays

The Argentine
Writer and Tradition

I WISH to formulate and justify here some sceptical proposals concerning the problem of the Argentine writer and tradition. My scepticism does not relate to the difficulty or impossibility of solving this problem, but rather to its very existence. I believe we are faced with a mere rhetorical topic which lends itself to pathetic elaborations; rather than with a true mental difficulty, I take it we are dealing with an appearance, a simulacrum, a pseudo problem.

Before examining it, I want to consider the most commonly offered statements and solutions. I shall begin with a solution which has become almost instinctive, which appears without the aid of logical reasoning; it maintains that the Argentine literary tradition already exists in the gauchesque poetry. According to this solution, the vocabulary, devices and themes of gauchesque poetry should guide the contemporary writer, and are a point of departure and perhaps an archetype. This is the usual solution and for that reason I intend to examine it at some length.

This same solution was set forth by Lugones in *El payador*; there one may read that we Argentines possess a classic poem, *Martín Fierro*, and that this poem should be for us what the Homeric poems were for the Greeks. It seems difficult to contradict this opinion without slighting *Martín Fierro*. I believe that *Martín Fierro* is the most lasting work we Argentines have written; and I believe with the same intensity that we cannot suppose *Martín Fierro* is, as it has sometimes been said, our Bible, our canonical book.

Ricardo Rojas, who has also recommended the canonization of *Martín Fierro*, has a page in his *Historia de la literatura argentina* that almost seems to be commonplace and is really quite astute.

Rojas studies the poetry of the gauchesque writers – in other words, the poetry of Hidalgo, Ascasubi, Estanislao del Campo and José Hernández – and sees it as being derived from the poetry of the *payadores*, from the spontaneous poetry of the gauchos. He points out that the metre of popular poetry is the octosyllable and that the authors of gauchesque poetry employ this metre and ends up by considering the poetry of the gauchesque writers as a continuation or enlargement of the poetry of the *payadores*.

I suspect there is a grave error in this affirmation; we might even say a skilful error, for it is evident that Rojas, in order to give the gauchesque poetry a popular basis beginning with Hidalgo and culminating with Hernández, presents this poetry as a continuation or derivation of that of the gauchos. Thus Bartolomé Hidalgo is, not the Homer of this poetry as Mitre said, but simply a link in its development.

Ricardo Rojas makes of Hidalgo a *payador*; however, according to his own *Historia de la literatura argentina*, this supposed *payador* began by composing hendecasyllabic verses, a metre by nature unavailable to the *payadores*, who could not perceive its harmony, just as Spanish readers could not perceive the harmony of the hendecasyllable when Garcilaso imported it from Italy.

I take it there is a fundamental difference between the poetry of the gauchos and the poetry of the gauchesque writers. It is enough to compare any collection of popular poetry with *Martín Fierro*, with *Paulino Lucero*, with *Fausto*, to perceive this difference, which lies no less in the vocabulary than in the intent of the poets. The popular poets of the country and the suburbs compose their verses on general themes: the pangs of love and loneliness, the unhappiness of love, and do so in a vocabulary which is also very general; on the other hand, the gauchesque poets cultivate a deliberately popular language never essayed by the popular poets themselves. I do not mean that the idiom of the popular poets is a correct Spanish, I mean that if there are errors they are the result of ignorance. On the other hand, in the gauchesque poets there is a seeking out of native words, a profusion of local colour. The proof is this: a Colombian, Mexican or Spaniard can immediately understand the poetry of the *payadores*, of the gauchos, and yet they need a glossary in order to understand, even approximately, Estanislao del Campo or Ascasubi.

All this can be summed up as follows: gauchesque poetry, which has produced – I hasten to repeat – admirable works, is a literary genre as artificial as any other. In the first gauchesque compositions, in Bartolomé Hidalgo's *trovas*, we already see the intention of presenting the work in terms of the gaucho, as uttered by the gaucho, so that the reader will read it in a gaucho intonation. Nothing could be further removed from popular poetry. The people, while versifying, – and I have observed this not only in the country *payadores*, but also in those from the outskirts of Buenos Aires – have the conviction that they are executing something important and instinctively avoid popular words and seek high-sounding terms and expressions. It is probable that gauchesque poetry has now influenced the *payadores* and that they too now abound in *criollismos*, but in the beginning it was not so, and we have proof of this (which no one has ever pointed out) in *Martín Fierro*.

Martín Fierro is cast in a Spanish of gauchesque intonation, and for a long while never lets us forget that it is a gaucho who is singing; it abounds in comparisons taken from country life; however, there is a famous passage in which the author forgets this preoccupation with local colour and writes in a general Spanish, and does not speak of vernacular themes, but of great abstract themes, of time, of space, of the sea, of the night. I refer to the *payada* between Martín Fierro and the Negro, which comes at the end of the second part. It is as if Hernández himself had wanted to show the difference between his gauchesque poetry and the genuine poetry of the gauchos. When these two gauchos, Fierro and the Negro, begin to sing, they leave behind all gauchesque affectation and address themselves to philosophical themes. I have observed the same while listening to the *payadores* of the suburbs; they avoid using the dialect of that area and try to express themselves correctly. Of course they fail, but their intention is to make their poetry something elevated; something distinguished, we might say with a smile.

The idea that Argentine poetry should abound in differential Argentine traits and Argentine local colour seems to me a mistake. If we are asked which book is more Argentine, *Martín Fierro* or the sonnets in Enrique Banchs's *La urna*, there is no reason to say that it is the first. It will be said that in *La urna* of Banchs we do not find the Argentine countryside, Argentine topography, Argentine botany, Argentine zoology: however, there are other Argentine conditions in *La urna*.

I recall now some lines from *La urna* which seem to have been written so that no one could say it was an Argentine book, the lines which read: '. . . The sun shines on the slanting roofs / and on the windows. Nightingales / try to say they are in love.'

Here it seems we cannot avoid condemning the phrase 'the sun shines on the slanting roofs and on the windows'. Enrique Banchs wrote these lines in a suburb of Buenos Aires, and in the suburbs of Buenos Aires there are no slanting roofs, but rather flat roofs. 'Nightingales try to say they are in love': the nightingale is less a bird of reality than of literature, of Greek and Germanic tradition. However, I would say that in the use of these conventional images, in these anomalous roofs and nightingales, Argentine architecture and ornithology are of course absent, but we do find in them the Argentine's reticence, his constraint; the fact that Banchs, when speaking of this great suffering which overwhelms him, when speaking of this woman who has left him and has left the world empty for him, should have recourse to foreign and conventional images like slanted roofs and nightingales, is significant: significant of Argentine reserve, distrust and reticence, of the difficulty we have in making confessions, in revealing our intimate nature.

Besides, I do not know if it is necessary to say that the idea that a literature must define itself in terms of its national traits is a relatively new concept; also new and arbitrary is the idea that writers must seek themes from their own countries. Without going any further, I think Racine would not even have understood a person who denied him his right to the title of poet of France because he cultivated Greek and Roman themes. I think Shakespeare would have been amazed if people had tried to limit him to English themes, and if they had told him that, as an Englishman, he had no right to compose *Hamlet*, whose theme is Scandinavian, or *Macbeth*, whose theme is Scottish. The Argentine cult of local colour is a recent European cult which the nationalists ought to reject as foreign.

Some days past I have found a curious confirmation of the fact that what is truly native can and often does dispense with local colour; I found this confirmation in Gibbon's *Decline and Fall of the Roman Empire*. Gibbon observes that in the Arabian book *par excellence*, in the Koran, there are no camels; I believe if there were any doubt as to the authenticity of the Koran, this absence of camels would be sufficient to prove it is an Arabian work. It was written by Mohammed, and Mohammed, as an Arab, had no reason to know that camels were especially Arabian; for him they were a part of reality, he had no reason to emphasize them; on the other hand, the first thing a falsifier, a tourist, an Arab nationalist would do is have a surfeit of camels, caravans of camels, on every page; but Mohammed, as an Arab, was unconcerned: he knew he could be an Arab without camels. I think we Argentines can emulate Mohammed, can believe in the possibility of being Argentine without abounding in local colour.

Perhaps I may be permitted to make a confession here, a very small confession. For many years, in books now happily forgotten, I tried to copy down the flavour, the essence of the outlying suburbs of Buenos Aires. Of course, I abounded in local words; I did not omit such words as *cuchilleros*, *milonga*, *tapia* and others, and thus I wrote those forgettable and forgotten books. Then, about a year ago, I wrote a story called *La muerte y la brújula* ('Death and the Compass'), which is a kind of nightmare, a nightmare in which there are elements of Buenos Aires, deformed by the horror of the nightmare. There I think of the Paseo Colón and call it rue de Toulon; I think of the country houses of Adrogué and call them Triste-le-Roy; when this story was published, my friends told me that at last they had found in what I wrote the flavour of the outskirts of Buenos Aires. Precisely because I had not set out to find that flavour, because I had abandoned myself to a dream, I was able to accomplish, after so many years, what I had previously sought in vain.

Now I want to speak of a justly illustrious work which the nationalists often invoke. I refer to Güiraldes's *Don Segundo Sombra*. The nationalists tell us that *Don Segundo Sombra* is the model of a national book; but if we compare it with the works of the gauchesque tradition, the first thing we note are differences. *Don Segundo Sombra* abounds in metaphors of a kind having nothing to do with country speech but a great deal to do with the metaphors of the then current literary circles of Montmartre. As for the fable, the story, it is easy to find in it the influence of Kipling's *Kim*, whose action is set in India and which was, in turn, written under the influence of Mark Twain's *Huckleberry Finn*, the epic of the Mississippi. When I make this observation, I do not wish to lessen the value of *Don Segundo Sombra*; on the contrary, I want to emphasize the fact that, in order that we might have this book, it was necessary for Güiraldes to recall the poetic technique of the French circles of his time and the work of Kipling which he had read many years before; in other words, Kipling and Mark Twain and the metaphors of French poets were necessary for this Argentine book, for this book which, I repeat, is no less Argentine for having accepted such influences.

I want to point out another contradiction: the nationalists pretend to venerate the capacities of the Argentine mind but want to limit the poetic exercises of that mind to a few impoverished local themes, as if we Argentines could only speak of *orillas* and *estancias* and not of the universe.

Let us move on to another solution. It is said that there is a tradition to which Argentine writers should adhere and that that tradition is Spanish literature. This second recommendation is of course somewhat less limited than the first, but it also tends to restrict us; many objections could be raised against it, but it is sufficient to mention two. The first is this: Argentine history can be unmistakably defined as a desire to become separated from Spain, as a voluntary withdrawal from Spain. The second objection is this: among us, the enjoyment of Spanish literature – an enjoyment which I personally happen to share – is usually an acquired taste; many times I have loaned French and English works to persons without special literary preparations, and these works have been enjoyed immediately, with no effort. However, when I have proposed to my friends the reading of Spanish works, I have evidenced that it was difficult for them to find pleasure in these books without special apprenticeship; for that reason, I believe the fact that certain illustrious Argentines write like Spaniards is less the testimony of an inherited capacity than it is a proof of Argentine versatility.

I now arrive at a third opinion on Argentine writers and tradition which I have read recently and which has surprised me very much. It says in essence that in Argentina we are cut off from the past, that there has been something like a dissolution of continuity between us and Europe. According to this singular observation, we Argentines find ourselves in a situation like that of the first days of Creation; the search for European themes and devices is an illusion, an error; we should understand that we are essentially alone and cannot play at being Europeans.

This opinion seems unfounded to me. I find it understandable that many people should accept it, because this declaration of our solitude, of our loss, of our primeval character, has, like existentialism, the charm of the pathetic. Many people can accept this opinion because, once they have done so, they feel alone, disconsolate and, in some way or another, interesting. However, I have observed that in our country, precisely because it is a new country, we have a great sense of time. Everything that has taken place in Europe, the dramatic happenings of the last few years in Europe, have had profound resonance here. The fact that a person was a sympathizer of Franco or of the Republic during the Spanish Civil War, or a sympathizer of the Nazis or of the Allies, has in many cases caused very grave quarrels and animosity. This would not occur if we were cut off from Europe. As far as Argentine history is concerned, I believe we all feel it profoundly; and it is natural that we should feel it in this way, because it is, in terms of chronology and in terms of our own inner being, quite close to us; the names, the battles of the civil war, the War of Independence, all of these are, both in time and in tradition, very close to us.

What is our Argentine tradition? I believe we can answer this question easily and that there is no problem here. I believe our tradition is all of Western culture, and I also believe we have a right to this tradition, greater than that which the inhabitants of one or another Western nation might have. I recall here an essay of Thorstein Veblen, the North American sociologist, on the pre-eminence of Jews in Western culture. He asks if this pre-eminence allows us to conjecture about the innate superiority of the Jews, and answers in the negative; he says that they are outstanding in Western culture because they act within that culture and, at the same time, do not feel tied to it by any special devotion; 'for that reason,' he says, 'a Jew will always find it easier than a non-Jew to make innovations in Western culture'; and we can say the same of the Irish in English culture. In the case of the Irish, we have no reason to suppose that the profusion of Irish names in British literature and philosophy is due to any racial pre-eminence, for many of those illustrious Irishmen (Shaw, Berkeley, Swift) were the descendants of Englishmen, were people who had no Celtic blood; however, it was sufficient for them to feel Irish, to feel different, in order to be innovators in English culture. I believe that we Argentines, we South Americans in general, are in an analogous situation; we can handle all European themes, handle them without superstition, with an irreverence which can have, and already does have, fortunate consequences.

This does not mean that all Argentine experiments are equally successful; I believe that this problem of tradition and Argentina is simply a contemporary and passing form of the eternal problem of determination. If I am going to touch the table with one of my hands and I ask myself whether I should touch it with my left or my right, as soon as I touch it with my right, the determinists will say that I could not act in any other way and that the entire previous history of the universe obliged me to touch it with my right hand and that touching it with the left would have been a miracle. However, if I had touched it with my left hand, they would have said the same : that I was obliged to do so. The same thing happens with literary themes and devices. Anything we Argentine writers can do successfully will become part of our Argentine tradition, in the same way that the treatment of Italian themes belongs to the tradition of England through the efforts of Chaucer and Shakespeare.

I believe, in addition, that all these *a priori* discussions concerning the intent of literary execution are based on the error of supposing that intentions and plans matter a great deal. Let us take the case of Kipling: Kipling dedicated his life to writing in terms of certain political ideals, he tried to make his work an instrument of propaganda and yet, at the end of his life, he was obliged to confess that the true essence of a writer's work is usually unknown to him. He recalled the case of Swift, who, when he wrote *Gulliver's Travels*, tried to bring an indictment against all humanity but actually left a book for children. Plato said that poets are the scribes of a god who moves them against their own will, against their intentions, just as a magnet moves a series of iron rings.

For that reason I repeat that we should not be alarmed and that we should feel that our patrimony is the universe; we should essay all themes, and we cannot limit ourselves to purely Argentine subjects in order to be Argentine; for either being Argentine is an inescapable act of fate – and in that case we shall be so in all events – or being Argentine is a mere affectation, a mask.

I believe that if we surrender ourselves to that voluntary dream which is artistic creation, we shall be Argentine and we shall be good or tolerable writers.

Translated by J.E.I.

The Wall and the Books

He, whose long wall the wand'ring Tartar bounds ...

Dunciad, II, 76

I READ, some days past, that the man who ordered the erection of the almost infinite wall of China was that first Emperor, Shih Huang Ti, who also decreed that all books prior to him be burned. That these two vast operations – the five to six hundred leagues of stone opposing the barbarians, the rigorous abolition of history, that is, of the past – should originate in one person and be in some way his attributes inexplicably satisfied and, at the same time, disturbed me. To investigate the reasons for that emotion is the purpose of this note.

Historically speaking, there is no mystery in the two measures. A contemporary of the wars of Hannibal, Shih Huang Ti, king of Tsin, brought the Six Kingdoms under his rule and abolished the feudal system; he erected the wall, because walls were defences; he burned the books, because his opposition invoked them to praise the emperors of olden times. Burning books and erecting fortifications is a common task of princes; the only thing singular in Shih Huang Ti was the scale on which he operated. Such is suggested by certain Sinologists, but I feel that the facts I have related are something more than an exaggeration or hyperbole of trivial dispositions. Walling in an orchard or a garden is ordinary, but not walling in an empire. Nor is it banal to pretend that the most traditional of races renounce the memory of its past, mythical or real. The Chinese had three thousand years of chronology (and during those years, the Yellow Emperor and Chuang Tsu and Confucius and Lao Tzu) when Shih Huang Ti ordered that history begin with him.

Shih Huang Ti had banished his mother for being a libertine; in his stern justice the orthodox saw nothing but an impiety; Shih Huang Ti, perhaps, wanted to obliterate the canonical books because they accused him; Shih Huang Ti, perhaps, tried to abolish the entire past in order to abolish one single memory : his mother's infamy. (Not in an unlike manner did a king of Judea have all male children killed in order to kill one.) This conjecture is worthy of attention, but tells us nothing about the wall, the second part of the myth. Shih Huang Ti, according to the historians, forbade that death be mentioned and sought the elixir of immortality and secluded himself in a figurative palace containing as many rooms as there are days in the year; these facts suggest that the wall in space and the fire in time were magic barriers designed to halt death. All things long to persist in their being, Baruch Spinoza has written; perhaps the Emperor and his sorcerers believed that immortality is intrinsic and that decay cannot enter a closed orb. Perhaps the Emperor tried to recreate the beginning of time and called himself The First, so as to be really first, and called himself Huang Ti, so as to be in some way Huang Ti, the legendary emperor who invented writing and the compass. The latter, according to the *Book of Rites*, gave things their true name; in a parallel fashion, Shih Huang Ti boasted, in inscriptions which endure, that all things in his reign would have the name which was proper to them. He dreamt of founding an immortal dynasty; he ordered that his heirs be called Second Emperor, Third Emperor, Fourth Emperor, and so on to infinity.... I have spoken of a magical purpose; it would also be fitting to suppose that erecting the wall and burning the books were not simultaneous acts. This (depending on the order we select) would give us the image of a king who began by destroying and then resigned himself to preserving, or that of a disillusioned king who destroyed what he had previously defended. Both conjectures are dramatic, but they lack, as far as I know, any basis in history. Herbert Allen Giles tells that those who hid books were branded with a red-hot iron and sentenced to labour until the day of their death on the construction of the outrageous wall. This information favours or tolerates another interpretation. Perhaps the wall was a metaphor, perhaps Shih Huang Ti sentenced those who worshipped the past to a task as immense, as gross and as useless as the past itself. Perhaps the wall was a challenge and Shih Huang Ti thought: 'Men love the past and neither I nor my executioners can do anything against that love, but someday there will be a man who feels as I do and he will efface my memory and be my mirror and not know it.' Perhaps Shih Huang Ti walled in his empire because he knew that it was perishable and destroyed the books because he understood that they were sacred books, in other words, books that teach what the entire universe or the mind of every man teaches. Perhaps the burning of the libraries and the erection of the wall are operations which in some secret way cancel each other.

The tenacious wall which at this moment, and at all moments, casts its system of shadows over lands I shall never see, is the shadow of a Caesar who ordered the most reverent of nations to burn its past; it is plausible that this idea moves us in itself, aside from the conjectures it allows. (Its virtue may lie in the opposition of constructing and destroying on an enormous scale.) Generalizing from the preceding case, we could infer that *all* forms have their virtue in themselves and not in any conjectural 'content'. This would concord with the thesis of Benedetto Croce; already Pater in 1877 had affirmed that all arts aspire to the state of music, which is pure form. Music, states of happiness, mythology, faces belaboured by time, certain twilights and certain places try to tell us something, or have said something we should have missed, or are about to say something; this imminence of a revelation which does not occur is, perhaps, the aesthetic phenomenon.

Translated by J.E.I.

The Fearful
Sphere of Pascal

IT may be that universal history is the history of a handful of metaphors. The purpose of this note will be to sketch a chapter of this history.

Six centuries before the Christian era, the rhapsodist Xenophanes of Colophon, wearied of the Homeric verses he recited from city to city, lashed out at the poets who attributed anthropomorphic traits to the gods, and offered the Greeks a single God, a god who was an eternal sphere. In the *Timaeus* of Plato we read that the sphere is the most perfect and most uniform figure, for all points of its surface are equidistant from its centre; Olof Gigon (*Ursprung der griechischen Philosophie*, 183) understands Xenophanes to speak analogically: God is spherical because that form is best – or least inadequate – to represent the Divinity. Parmenides, forty years later, rephrased the image: 'The Divine Being is like the mass of a well-rounded sphere, whose force is constant from the centre in any direction.' Calogero and Mondolfo reasoned that Parmenides intuited an infinite, or infinitely expanding sphere, and that the words just transcribed possess a dynamic meaning (Albertelli: *Gli Eleati*, 148). Parmenides taught in Italy; a few years after his death, the Sicilian Empedocles of Agrigentum constructed a laborious cosmogony: a stage exists in which the particles of earth, water, air and fire make up a sphere without end, 'the rounded *Sphairos*, which exults in its circular solitude'.

Universal history continued to unroll, the all-too-human gods whom Xenophanes had denounced were demoted to figures of poetic fiction, or to demons – although it was reported that one of them, Hermes Trismegistus, had dictated a

224

variable number of books (42 according to Clement of Alexandria; 20,000 according to Hamblicus; 36,525 according to the priests of Thoth – who is also Hermes) in the pages of which are written all things. Fragments of this illusory library, compiled or concocted beginning in the third century, go to form what is called the *Corpus Hermeticum*; in one of these fragments, or in the *Asclepius*, which was also attributed to Trismegistus, the French theologian Alain de Lille (Alanus de Insulis) discovered, at the end of the twelfth century, the following formula, which future ages would not forget: 'God is an intelligible sphere, whose centre is everywhere and whose circumference is nowhere.' The Pre-Socratics spoke of a sphere without end; Albertelli (as Aristotle before him) thinks that to speak in this wise is to commit a *contradictio in adjecto*, because the subject and predicate cancel each other; this may very well be true, but still, the formula of the Hermetic books allows us, almost, to intuit this sphere. In the thirteenth century, the image reappeared in the symbolic *Roman de la Rose*, where it is given as a citation from Plato, and in the encyclopaedia *Speculum Triplex*; in the sixteenth century, the last chapter of the last book of *Pantagruel* referred to 'that intellectual sphere, whose centre is everywhere and whose circumference is nowhere and which we call God'. For the medieval mind the sense was clear: God is in each one of His creatures, but none of them limits Him. 'The heaven and heaven of heavens cannot contain thee,' said Solomon (I Kings 8 : 27); the geometric metaphor of the sphere seemed a gloss on these words.

Dante's poem preserved the Ptolemaic astronomy which for 1,400 years reigned in the imagination of mankind. The earth occupies the centre of the universe. It is an impossible sphere; around it circle nine concentric spheres. The first seven are 'planetary' skies (the firmaments of the Moon, Mercury, Venus, the Sun, Mars, Jupiter, Saturn); the eighth, the firmament of the fixed stars; the ninth, the crystal firmament which is also called the *Primum mobile*. This in turn is surrounded by the Empyrean, which is composed of light. All this elaborate apparatus of hollow, transparent and gyrating spheres (one system required 55 of them) had come to be an intellectual necessity; *De hypothesibus motuum coelestium commentariolus* is the timid title which Copernicus, denier of Aristotle, placed at the head of the manuscript that transformed our vision of the cosmos.

For one man, for Giordano Bruno, the rupture of the stellar vaults was a liberation. He proclaimed, in the *Cena de la ceneri*, that the world is the infinite effect of an infinite cause, and that divinity is close by, 'for it is within us even more than we ourselves are within ourselves'. He searched for words to tell men of Copernican space, and on one famous page he inscribed: 'We can assert with certitude that the universe is all centre, or that the centre of the universe is everywhere and the circumference nowhere' (*Della causa, principio ed uno, V*).

This phrase was written with exultation, in 1584, still in the light of the Renaissance; seventy years later there was no reflection of that fervour left and men felt lost in time and space. In time, because if the future and the past are infinite, there cannot really be a *when*; in space, because if every being is equidistant from the infinite and the infinitesimal, neither can there be a *where*. No one exists on a certain day, in a certain place; no one knows the size of his own countenance. In the Renaissance, humanity thought to have reached the age of virility, and it declares as much through the lips of Bruno, of Campanella, and of Bacon. In the seventeenth century, humanity was cowed by a feeling of senescence; in order to justify itself it exhumed the belief in the slow and fatal degeneration of all creatures consequent on Adam's sin. (We know – from the fifth chapter of Genesis – that 'all the days of Methuselah were nine hundred sixty and nine years'; from the sixth chapter, that 'there were giants in the earth in those days'.) The First Anniversary of John Donne's elegy, *Anatomy of the World*, lamented the very brief life and limited stature of contemporary men, who are like pigmies and fairies; Milton, according to Johnson's biography, feared that the appearance on earth of a heroic species was no longer possible; Glanvill was of the opinion that Adam, 'the medal of God', enjoyed both telescopic and microscopic vision; Robert South conspicuously wrote: 'An Aristotle was but the fragment of an Adam, and Athens the rudiments of Paradise.' In that dispirited century, the absolute space which had inspired the hexametres of Lucretius, the absolute space which had meant liberation to Bruno, became a labyrinth and an abyss for Pascal. He abhorred the universe and would have liked to adore God; but God, for him, was less real than the abhorred universe. He deplored the fact that the firmament did not speak, and he compared our life with that of castaways on a desert island. He felt the incessant weight of the physical world, he experienced vertigo, fright and solitude, and he put his feelings into these words: 'Nature is an infinite sphere, whose centre is everywhere and whose circumference is nowhere.' Thus do the words appear in the Brunschvicg text; but the critical edition published by Torneur (Paris, 1941), which reproduces the crossed-out words and variations of the manuscript, reveals that Pascal started to write the word *effroyable*: 'a fearful sphere, whose centre is everywhere and whose circumference is nowhere.'

It may be that universal history is the history of the different intonations given a handful of metaphors.

Translated by Anthony Kerrigan

Partial Magic in
the *Quixote*

It is plausible that these observations may have been set forth at some time and, perhaps, many times; a discussion of their novelty interests me less than one of their possible truth.

Compared with other classic books (the *Iliad*, the *Aeneid*, the *Pharsalia*, Dante's *Commedia*, Shakespeare's tragedies and comedies), the *Quixote* is a realistic work; its realism, however, differs essentially from that practised by the nineteenth century. Joseph Conrad could write that he excluded the supernatural from his work because to include it would seem a denial that the everyday was marvellous; I do not know if Miguel de Cervantes shared that intuition, but I do know that the form of the *Quixote* made him counterpose a real prosaic world to an imaginary poetic world. Conrad and Henry James wrote novels of reality because they judged reality to be poetic; for Cervantes the real and the poetic were antinomies. To the vast and vague geographies of the *Amadís*, he opposes the dusty roads and sordid wayside inns of Castille; imagine a novelist of our time centring attention for purposes of parody on some filling stations. Cervantes has created for us the poetry of seventeenth-century Spain, but neither that century nor that Spain were poetic for him; men like Unamuno or Azorín or Antonio Machado, who were deeply moved by any evocation of La Mancha, would have been incomprehensible to him. The plan of his book precluded the marvellous; the latter, however, had to figure in the novel, at least indirectly, just as crimes and a mystery in a parody of a detective story. Cervantes could not resort to talismans or enchantments, but he insinuated the supernatural in a subtle – and therefore more effective – manner. In his intimate being, Cervantes loved the supernatural. Paul Groussac observed in 1924: 'With a delible colouring of Latin and Italian, Cervantes's literary production derived mostly from the pastoral novel and the novel of chivalry, soothing fables of captivity.' The *Quixote* is less an antidote for those fictions than it is a secret, nostalgic farewell.

Every novel is an ideal plane inserted into the realm of reality; Cervantes takes pleasure in confusing the objective and the subjective, the world of the reader and the world of the book. In those chapters which argue whether the barber's basin is a helmet and the donkey's packsaddle a steed's fancy regalia, the problem is dealt with explicitly; other passages, as I have noted, insinuate this. In the sixth chapter of the first part, the priest and the barber inspect Don Quixote's library; astoundingly, one of the books examined is Cervantes's own *Galatea* and it turns out that the barber is a friend of the author and does not admire him very much, and says that he is more versed in misfortunes than in verses and that the book possesses some inventiveness, proposes a few ideas and concludes nothing. The barber, a dream or the form of a dream of Cervantes, passes judgement on Cervantes.... It is also surprising to learn, at the beginning of the ninth chapter, that the entire novel has been transplanted from the Arabic and that Cervantes acquired the manuscript in the market-place of Toledo and had it translated by a *morisco* whom he lodged in his house for more than a month and a half while the job was being finished. We think of Carlyle, who pretended that the *Sartor Resartus* was the fragmentary version of a work published in Germany by Doctor Diogenes Teufelsdroeckh; we think of the Spanish rabbi Moses of Léon, who composed the *Zohar* or *Book of Splendour* and divulged it as the work of a Palestinian rabbi of the second century.

This play of strange ambiguities culminates in the second part; the protagonists have read the first part, the protagonists of the *Quixote* are, at the same time, readers of the *Quixote*. Here it is inevitable to recall the case of Shakespeare, who includes on the stage of *Hamlet* another stage where a tragedy more or less like that of *Hamlet* is presented; the imperfect correspondence of the principal and secondary works lessens the efficacy of this inclusion. An artifice analogous to Cervantes's, and even more astounding, figures in the *Ramayana*, the poem of Valmiki, which narrates the deeds of Rama and his war with the demons. In the last book, the sons of Rama, who do not know who their father is, seek shelter in a forest, where an ascetic teaches them to read. This teacher is, strangely enough, Valmiki; the book they study, the *Ramayana*. Rama orders a sacrifice of horses; Valmiki and his pupils attend this feast. The latter, accompanied by their lute, sing the *Ramayana*. Rama hears his own story, recognizes his own sons and then rewards the poet.... Something similar is created by accident in the *Thousand and One Nights*. This collection of fantastic tales duplicates and reduplicates to the point of vertigo the ramifications of a central story in later and subordinate stories, but does not attempt to gradate its realities, and the effect (which should have been profound) is superficial, like a Persian carpet. The opening story of the series is well known : the terrible pledge of the king who every night marries a virgin who is then decapitated at dawn, and the resolution of Scheherazade, who distracts the king with her fables until a thousand and one nights have gone by and she shows him their son. The necessity of completing a thousand and one sections obliged the copyists of the work to make all manner of interpolations. None is more perturbing than that of the six hundred and second night, magical among all the nights. On that night, the king hears from the queen his own story. He hears the beginning of the story, which comprises all the others and also – monstrously – itself. Does the reader clearly grasp the vast possibility of this interpolation, the curious danger? That the queen may persist and the motionless king hear for ever the truncated story of the *Thousand and One Nights*, now infinite and circular.... The inventions of philosophy are no less fantastic than those of art : Josiah Royce, in the first volume of his work *The World and the Individual* (1899), has formulated the following : 'Let us imagine that a portion of the soil of England has been levelled off perfectly and that on it a cartographer traces a map of England. The job is perfect; there is no detail of the soil of England, no matter how minute, that is not registered on the map; everything has there its correspondence. This map, in such a case, should contain a map of the map, which should contain a map of the map of the map, and so on to infinity.'

Why does it disturb us that the map be included in the map and the thousand and one nights in the book of the *Thousand and One Nights*? Why does it disturb us that Don Quixote be a reader of the *Quixote* and Hamlet a spectator of *Hamlet*? I believe I have found the reason: these inversions suggest that if the characters of a fictional work can be readers or spectators, we, its readers or spectators, can be fictitious. In 1833, Carlyle observed that the history of the universe is an infinite sacred book that all men write and read and try to understand, and in which they are also written.

Translated by J.E.I.

Valéry as Symbol

BRINGING together the names of Whitman and Paul Valéry is, at first glance, an arbitrary and (what is worse) inept operation. Valéry is a symbol of infinite dexterities but, at the same time, of infinite scruples; Whitman, of an almost incoherent but titanic vocation of felicity; Valéry illustriously personifies the labyrinths of the mind; Whitman, the interjections of the body. Valéry is a symbol of Europe and of its delicate twilight; Whitman, of the morning in America. The whole realm of literature would not seem to admit two more antagonistic applications of the word 'poet'. One act, however, links them : the work of both is less valuable as poetry than it is as the sign of an exemplary poet created by that work. Thus, the English poet Lascelles Abercrombie could praise Whitman for having created 'from the richness of his noble experience that vivid and personal figure which is one of the few really great things of the poetry of our time : the figure of himself'. The dictum is vague and superlative, but it has the singular virtue of not identifying Whitman, the man of letters and devoté of Tennyson, with Whitman, the semi-divine hero of *Leaves of Grass*. The distinction is valid; Whitman wrote his rhapsodies in terms of an imaginary identity, formed partly of himself, partly of each of his readers. Hence the discrepancies that have exasperated the critics; hence the custom of dating his poems in places where he had never been; hence the fact that, on one page of his work, he was born in the Southern states, and on another (and also in reality) on Long Island.

One of the purposes of Whitman's compositions is to define a possible man – Walt Whitman – of unlimited and negligent felicity; no less hyperbolic, no less illusory, is the man defined by Valéry's compositions. The latter does not magnify, as does the former, the human faculties of philanthropy, fervour and joy; he magnifies the virtues of the mind. Valéry created Edmond Teste; this character would be one of the myths of our time if intimately we did not all judge him to be a mere *Doppelgänger* of Valéry. For us, Valéry is Edmond Teste. In other words, Valéry is a derivation of Poe's Chevalier Dupin and the inconceivable God of the theologians. Which fact, plausibly enough, is not true.

Yeats, Rilke and Eliot have written verses more memorable than those of Valéry; Joyce and Stefan George have effected more profound modifications in their instrument (perhaps French is less modifiable than English and German); but behind the work of these eminent artificers there is no personality comparable to Valéry's. The circumstance that that personality is, in some way, a projection of the work does not diminish this fact. To propose lucidity to men in a lowly romantic era, in the melancholy era of Nazism and dialectical materialism, of the augurs of Freudianism and the merchants of *surréalisme*, such is the noble mission Valéry fulfilled (and continues to fulfil).

Paul Valéry leaves us at his death the symbol of a man infinitely sensitive to every phenomenon and for whom every phenomenon is a stimulus capable of provoking an infinite series of thoughts. Of a man who transcends the differential traits of the self and of whom we can say, as William Hazlitt did of Shakespeare, 'he is nothing in himself'. Of a man whose admirable texts do not exhaust, do not even define, their all-embracing possibilities. Of a man who, in an age that worships the chaotic idols of blood, earth and passion, preferred always the lucid pleasures of thought and the secret adventures of order.

Translated by J.E.I.

Kafka
and His Precursors

I ONCE premeditated making a study of Kafka's precursors. At first I had considered him to be as singular as the phoenix of rhetorical praise; after frequenting his pages a bit, I came to think I could recognize his voice, or his practices, in texts from diverse literatures and periods. I shall record a few of these here, in chronological order.

The first is Zeno's paradox against movement. A moving object at A (declares Aristotle) cannot reach point B, because it must first cover half the distance between the two points, and before that, half of the half, and before that, half of the half of the half, and so on to infinity; the form of this illustrious problem is, exactly, that of *The Castle*, and the moving object and the arrow and Achilles are the first Kafkian characters in literature. In the second text which chance laid before me, the affinity is not one of form but one of tone. It is an apologue of Han Yu, a prose writer of the ninth century, and is reproduced in Margouliès's admirable *Anthologie raisonnée de a littérature chinoise* (1948). This is the paragraph, mysterious and calm, which I marked: 'It is universally admitted that the unicorn is a supernatural being of good omen; such is declared in all the odes, annals, biographies of illustrious men and other texts whose authority is unquestionable. Even children and village women know that the unicorn constitutes a favourable presage. But this animal does not figure among the domestic beasts, it is not always easy to find, it does not lend itself to classification. It is not like the horse or the bull, the wolf or the deer. In such conditions, we could be face to face with a unicorn and not know for certain what it was. We know that such and such an animal with a mane is a horse and that such and such an animal with horns is a bull. But we do not know what the unicorn is like.'*

The third text derives from a more easily predictable source: the writings of Kierkegaard. The spiritual affinity of both writers is something of which no one is ignorant; what has not yet been brought out, as far as I know, is the fact that Kierkegaard, like Kafka, wrote many religious parables on contemporary and bourgeois themes. Lowrie, in his *Kierkegaard* (Oxford University Press, 1938), transcribes two of these. One is the story of a counterfeiter who, under constant surveillance, counts banknotes in the Bank of England; in the same way, God would distrust Kierkegaard and have given him a task to perform, precisely because He knew that he was familiar with evil. The subject of the other parable is the North Pole expeditions. Danish ministers had declared from their pulpits that participation in these expeditions was beneficial to the soul's eternal well-being. They admitted, however, that it was difficult, and perhaps impossible to reach the Pole and that not all men could undertake the adventure. Finally, they would announce that any trip – from Denmark to London, let us say, on the regularly scheduled steamer – was, properly considered, an expedition to the North Pole. The fourth of these prefigurations I have found is Browning's poem 'Fears and Scruples', published in 1876. A man has, or believes he has, a famous friend. He has never seen this friend and the fact is that the friend has so far never helped him, although tales are told of his most noble traits and authentic letters of his circulate about. Then someone places these traits in doubt and the handwriting experts declare that the letters are apocryphal. The man asks, in the last line: 'And if this friend were ... God?'

My notes also register two stories. One is from Léon Bloy's *Histoires désobligeantes* and relates the case of some people who possess all manner of globes, atlases, railroad guides and

---

*Non-recognition of the sacred animal and its opprobious or accidental death at the hands of the people are traditional themes in Chinese literature. See the last chapter of Jung's *Psychologie und Alchemie* (Zürich, 1944), which contains two curious illustrations.

trunks, but who die without ever having managed to leave their home town. The other is entitled 'Carcassonne' and is the work of Lord Dunsany. An invincible army of warriors leaves an infinite castle, conquers kingdoms and sees monsters and exhausts the deserts and the mountains, but they never reach Carcassonne, though once they glimpse it from afar. (This story is, as one can easily see, the strict reverse of the previous one; in the first, the city is never left; in the second, it is never reached.)

If I am not mistaken, the heterogeneous pieces I have enumerated resemble Kafka; if I am not mistaken, not all of them resemble each other. This second fact is the more significant. In each of these texts we find Kafka's idiosyncrasy to a greater or lesser degree, but if Kafka had never written a line, we would not perceive this quality; in other words, it would not exist. The poem 'Fears and Scruples' by Browning foretells Kafka's work, but our reading of Kakfa perceptibly sharpens and deflects our reading of the poem. Browning did not read it as we do now. In the critics' vocabulary, the word 'precursor' is indispensable, but it should be cleansed of all connotation of polemics or rivalry. The fact is that every writer *creates* his own precursors. His work modifies our conception of the past, as it will modify the future.* In this correlation the identity or plurality of the men involved is unimportant. The early Kafka of *Betrachtung* is less a precursor of the Kafka of sombre myths and atrocious institutions than is Browning or Lord Dunsany.

Translated by J.E.I.

* See T. S. Eliot: *Points of View* (1941), pp. 25–26.

Avatars
of the Tortoise

THERE is a concept which corrupts and upsets all others. I refer not to Evil, whose limited realm is that of ethics; I refer to the infinite. I once longed to compile its mobile history. The numerous Hydra (the swamp monster which amounts to a prefiguration or emblem of geometric progressions) would lend convenient horror to its portico; it would be crowned by the sordid nightmares of Kafka and its central chapters would not ignore the conjectures of that remote German cardinal – Nicholas of Krebs, Nicholas of Cusa – who saw in the circumference of the circle a polygon with an infinite number of sides and wrote that an infinite line would be a straight line, a triangle, a circle and a sphere (*De docta ignorantia*, I, 13). Five or seven years of metaphysical, theological and mathematical apprenticeship would allow me (perhaps) to plan decorously such a book. It is useless to add that life forbids me that hope and even that adverb.

The following pages in some way belong to that illusory *Biography of the Infinite*. Their purpose is to register certain avatars of the second paradox of Zeno.

Let us recall, now, that paradox.

Achilles runs ten times faster than the tortoise and gives the animal a headstart of ten metres. Achilles runs those ten metres, the tortoise one; Achilles runs that metre, the tortoise runs a decimetre; Achilles runs that decimetre, the tortoise runs a centimetre; Achilles runs that centimetre, the tortoise, a millimetre; Fleet-footed Achilles, the millimetre, the tortoise, a tenth of a millimetre, and so on to infinity, without the tortoise ever being overtaken.... Such is the customary version. Wilhelm Capelle (*Die Vorsokratiker*, 1935, page 178) translates the original text by Aristotle: 'The second argument of Zeno is the one known by the name of Achilles. He reasons that the slowest will never be overtaken by the swiftest, since the pursuer has to pass through the place the pursued has just left, so that the slowest will always have a certain advantage.' The problem does not change, as you can see; but I would like to know the name of the poet who provided it with a hero and a tortoise. To those magical competitors and to the series

$$10 + 1 + \frac{1}{10} + \frac{1}{100} + \frac{1}{1,000} + \frac{1}{10,000} + : : :$$

the argument owes its fame. Almost no one recalls the one preceding it – the one about the track – though its mechanism is identical. Movement is impossible (argues Zeno) for the moving object must cover half of the distance in order to reach its destination, and before reaching the half, half of the half, and before half of the half, half of the half of the half, and before . . .*

We owe to the pen of Aristotle the communication and first refutation of these arguments. He refutes them with a perhaps disdainful brevity, but their recollection served as an inspiration for his famous *argument of the third man* against the Platonic doctrine. This doctrine tries to demonstrate that two individuals who have common attributes (for example, two men) are mere temporal appearances of an eternal archetype. Aristotle asks if the many men and the Man – the temporal individuals and the archetype – have attributes in common. It is obvious that they do: the general attributes of humanity. In that case, maintains Aristotle, one would have to postulate *another* archetype to include them all, and then a fourth. . . . Patricio de Azcárate, in a note to his translation of the *Metaphysics*, attributes this presentation of the problem to one of Aristotle's disciples: 'If what is affirmed of many things is at the same time a separate being, different from the things about

*A century later, the Chinese sophist Hui Tzu reasoned that a staff cut in two every day is interminable (H. A. Giles: *Chuang Tzu*, 1889, page 453).

which the affirmation is made (and this is what the Platonists pretend), it is necessary that there be a third man. *Man* is a denomination applicable to individuals and the idea. There is, then, a third man separate and different from individual men and the idea. There is at the same time a fourth man who stands in the same relationship to the third and to the idea and individual men; then a fifth and so on to infinity.' Let us postulate two individuals, *a* and *b*, who make up the generic type *c*. We would then have:

$$a + b = c$$

But also, according to Aristotle:

$$a + b + c = d$$
$$a + b + c + d = e$$
$$a + b + c + d + e = f \ldots$$

Rigorously speaking, two individuals are not necessary: it is enough to have one individual and the generic type in order to determine the *third man* denounced by Aristotle. Zeno of Elea resorts to the idea of infinite regression against movement and number; his refuter, against the idea of universal forms.*

* In the *Parmenides* – whose Zenonian character is irrefutable – Plato expounds a very similar argument to demonstrate that the one is really many. If the one exists, it participates in being; therefore, there are two parts in it, which are being and the one, but each of these parts is one and exists, so that they enclose two more parts, which in turn enclose two more, infinitely. Russell (*Introduction to Mathematical Philosophy*, 1919, page 138) substitutes for Plato's geometrical progression an arithmetical one. If one exists, it participates in being: but since being and the one are different, duality exists; but since being and two are different, trinity exists, etc. Chuang Tzu (Waley: *Three Ways of Thought in Ancient China*, page 25) resorts to the same interminable *regressus* against the monists who declared that the Ten Thousand Things (the Universe) are one. In the first place – he argues – cosmic unity and the declaration of that unity are already two things; these two and the declaration of their duality are already three; those three and the declaration of their trinity are already four.... Russell believes that

The next avator of Zeno my disorderly notes register is Agrippa the sceptic. He denies that anything can be proven, since every proof requires a previous proof (*Hypotyposes*, I, 166). Sextus Empiricus argues in a parallel manner that definitions are in vain, since one will have to define each of the words used and then define the definition (*Hypotyposes*, II, 207). One thousand six hundred years later, Byron, in the dedication to *Don Juan*, will write of Coleridge: 'I wish he would explain his Explanation.'

So far, the *regressus in infinitum* has served to negate; Saint Thomas Aquinas resorts to it (*Summa theologica*, I, 2, 3) in order to affirm that God exists. He points out that there is nothing in the universe without an effective cause and that this cause, of course, is the effect of another prior cause. The world is an interminable chain of causes and each cause is also an effect. Each state derives from a previous one and determines the following, but the whole series could have not existed, since its terms are conditional, i.e. fortuitous. However, the world *does* exist: from this we may infer a non-contingent first cause, which would be the Divinity. Such is the cosmological proof; it is prefigured by Aristotle and Plato; later Leibniz rediscovers it.*

Hermann Lotze has recourse to the *regressus* in order not to understand that an alteration of object A can produce an alteration of object B. He reasons that if A and B are independent, to postulate an influence of A and B is to postulate a third element C, an element which in order to affect B will require a fourth element D, which cannot work its effect without E, which cannot work its effect without F.... In order to elude this multiplication of chimeras, he resolves that in the

---

the vagueness of the term *being* is sufficient to invalidate this reasoning. He adds that numbers do not exist, that they are mere logical fictions.

* An echo of this proof, now defunct, resounds in the first verse of the *Paradiso*:

La gloria di Colui che tutto move.

world there is one sole object: an infinite and absolute substance, comparable to the God of Spinoza. Transitive causes are
reduced to immanent causes; phenomena, to manifestations or
modalities of the cosmic substance.*

Analogous, but even more alarming, is the case of F. H.
Bradley. This thinker (*Appearance and Reality*, 1897, pages
19–34) does not limit himself to combatting the relation of
cause; he denies all relations. He asks if a relation is related to
its terms. The answer is yes and he infers that this amounts to
admitting the existence of two other relations, and then of two
more. In the axiom 'the part is less than the whole' he does not
perceive two terms and the relation 'less than'; he perceives
three ('part', 'less than', 'whole') whose linking implies two
more relations, and so on to infinity. In the statement 'John is
mortal', he perceives three invariable concepts (the third is the
copula) which we can never bring together. He transforms all
concepts into incommunicable, solidified objects. To refute him
is to become contaminated with unreality.

Lotze inserts Zeno's periodic chasms between the cause and
the effect; Bradley, between the subject and the predicate, if
not between the subject and its attributes; Lewis Carroll (*Mind*,
volume four, page 278), between the second premise of the
syllogism and the conclusion. He relates an endless dialogue,
whose interlocutors are Achilles and the tortoise. Having now
reached the end of their interminable race, the two athletes
calmly converse about geometry. They study this lucid reasoning:

a) Two things equal to a third are equal to one another.
b) The two sides of this triangle are equal to MN.
c) The two sides of this triangle are equal to one another.

The tortoise accepts the premises *a* and *b*, but denies that
they justify the conclusion. He has Achilles interpolate a
hypothetical proposition:

*I follow the exposition by James (*A Pluralistic Universe*, 1909,
pages 55–60). Cf. Wentscher: *Fechner und Lotze*, 1924, pages 166–
71.

a) Two things equal to a third are equal to one another.
b) The two sides of this triangle are equal to MN.
c) If *a* and *b* are valid, *z* is valid.
z) The two sides of this triangle are equal to one another.

Having made this brief clarification, the tortoise accepts the validity of *a*, *b* and *c*, but not of *z*. Achilles, indignant, interpolates :

d) If *a*, *b* and *c* are valid, *z* is valid.

And then, now with a certain resignation :

e) If *a*, *b*, *c* and *d* are valid, *z* is valid.

Carroll observes that the Greek's paradox involves an infinite series of distances which diminish, whereas in his, the distances grow.

One final example, perhaps the most elegant of all, but also the one differing least from Zeno. William James (*Some Problems of Philosophy*, 1911, page 182) denies that fourteen minutes can pass, because first it is necessary for seven to pass, and before the seven, three and a half, and before the three and a half, a minute and three quarters, and so on until the end, the invisible end, through tenuous labyrinths of time.

Descartes, Hobbes, Leibniz, Mill, Renouvier, Georg Cantor, Gomperz, Russell and Bergson have formulated explanations – not always inexplicable and vain in nature – of the paradox of the tortoise. (I have registered some of them in my book *Discusión*, 1932, pages 151–61.) Applications abound as well, as the reader has seen. The historical applications do not exhaust its possibilities : the vertiginous *regressus in infinitum* is perhaps applicable to all subjects. To aesthetics : such and such a verse moves us for such and such a reason, such and such a reason for such and such a reason.... To the problem of knowledge : cognition is recognition, but it is necessary to have known in order to recognize, but cognition is recognition.... How can we evaluate this dialectic? Is it a legitimate instrument of investigation or only a bad habit?

It is venturesome to think that a co-ordination of words (philosophies are nothing more than that) can resemble the universe very much. It is also venturesome to think that of all these illustrious co-ordinations, one of them – at least in an infinitesimal way – does not resemble the universe a bit more than the others. I have examined those which enjoy certain prestige; I venture to affirm that only in the one formulated by Schopenhauer have I recognized some trait of the universe. According to this doctrine, the world is a fabrication of the will. Art – always – requires visible unrealities. Let it suffice for me to mention one : the metaphorical or numerous or carefully accidental diction of the interlocutors in a drama ... Let us admit what all idealists admit : the hallucinatory nature of the world. Let us do what no idealist has done : seek unrealities which confirm that nature. We shall find them, I believe, in the antinomies of Kant and in the dialectic of Zeno.

'The greatest magician (Novalis has memorably written) would be the one who would cast over himself a spell so complete that he would take his own phantasmagorias as autonomous appearances. Would not this be our case?' I conjecture that this is so. We (the undivided divinity operating within us) have dreamt the world. We have dreamt it as firm, mysterious, visible, ubiquitous in space and durable in time; but in its architecture we have allowed tenuous and eternal crevices of unreason which tell us it is false.

Translated by J.E.I.

The Mirror of Enigmas

THE idea that the Sacred Scriptures have (aside from their literal value) a symbolic value is ancient and not irrational: it is found in Philo of Alexandria, in the Cabalists, in Swedenborg. Since the events related in the Scriptures are true (God is Truth, Truth cannot lie, etc.), we should admit that men, in acting out those events, blindly represent a secret drama determined and premeditated by God. Going from this to the thought that the history of the universe – and in it our lives and the most tenuous detail of our lives – has an incalculable, symbolical value, is a reasonable step. Many have taken that step; no one so astonishingly as Léon Bloy. (In the psychological fragments by Novalis and in that volume of Machen's autobiography called *The London Adventure* there is a similar hypothesis: that the outer world – forms, temperatures, the moon – is a language we humans have forgotten or which we can scarcely distinguish.... It is also declared by De Quincey:* 'Even the articulate or brutal sounds of the globe must be all so many languages and ciphers that somewhere have their corresponding keys – have their own grammar and syntax; and thus the least things in the universe must be secret mirrors to the greatest.')

A verse from St Paul (1 Corinthians, 13 : 12) inspired Léon Bloy. *Videmus nunc per speculum in aenigmate: tunc autem facie ad faciem. Nunc cognosco ex parte: tunc autem cognoscam sicut et cognitus sum.* Torres Amat has miserably translated: 'At present we do not see God except as in a mirror and beneath dark images; but later we shall see him face to face. I only know him now imperfectly; but later I shall know

* *Writings*, 1896, Vol. I, page 129.

him in a clear vision, in the same way that I know myself.' 49 words do the work of 22; it is impossible to be more languid and verbose. Cipriano de Valera is more faithful: 'Now we see in a mirror, in darkness; but later we shall see face to face. Now I know in part; but later I shall know as I am known.' Torres Amat opines that the verse refers to our vision of the divinity; Cipriano de Valera (and Léon Bloy), to our general vision of things.

So far as I know, Bloy never gave his conjecture a definitive form. Throughout this fragmentary work (in which there abound, as everyone knows, lamentations and insults) there are different versions and facets. Here are a few that I have rescued from the clamorous pages of *Le mendiant ingrat*, *Le Vieux de la Montagne* and *L'invendable*. I do not believe I have exhausted them: I hope that some specialist in Léon Bloy (I am not one) may complete and rectify them.

The first is from June 1894. I translate it as follows: 'The statement by St Paul: *Videmus nunc per speculum in aenigmate* would be a skylight through which one might submerge himself in the true Abyss, which is the soul of man. The terrifying immensity of the firmament's abysses is an illusion, an external reflection of *our own* abysses, perceived "in a mirror". We should invert our eyes and practice a sublime astronomy in the infinitude of our hearts, for which God was willing to die.... If we see the Milky Way, it is because it *actually exists in our souls*.'

The second is from November of the same year. 'I recall one of my oldest ideas. The Czar is the leader and spiritual father of a hundred and fifty million men. An atrocious responsibility which is only apparent. Perhaps he is not responsible to God, but rather to a few human beings. If the poor of his empire are oppressed during his reign, if immense catastrophies result from that reign, who knows if the servant charged with shining his boots is not the real and sole person guilty? In the mysterious dispositions of the Profundity, who is really Czar, who is king, who can boast of being a mere servant?'

The third is from a letter written in December. 'Everything is a symbol, even the most piercing pain. We are dreamers who shout in our sleep. We do not know whether the things afflicting us are the secret beginning of our ulterior happiness or not. We now see, St Paul maintains, *per speculum in aenigmate*, literally: "in an enigma by means of a mirror" and we shall not see in any other way until the coming of the One who is all in flames and who must teach us all things.'

The fourth is from May 1904. '*Per speculum in aenigmate*, says St Paul. We see everything backwards. When we believe we give, we receive, etc. Then (a beloved, anguished soul tells me) we are in Heaven and God suffers on earth.'

The fifth is from May 1908. 'A terrifying idea of Jeanne's, about the text *Per speculum*. The pleasures of this world would be the torments of Hell, seen backwards, in a mirror.'

The sixth is from 1912. It is each of the pages of *L'Âme de Napoléon*, a book whose purpose is to decipher the symbol Napoleon, considered as the precursor of another hero – man and symbol as well – who is hidden in the future. It is sufficient for me to cite two passages. One: 'Every man is on earth to symbolize something he is ignorant of and to realize a particle or a mountain of the invisible materials that will serve to build the City of God.' The other: 'There is no human being on earth capable of declaring with certitude who he is. No one knows what he has come into this world to do, what his acts correspond to, his sentiments, his ideas, or what his real name is, his enduring Name in the register of Light.... History is an immense liturgical text where the iotas and the dots are worth no less than the entire verses or chapters, but the importance of one and the other is indeterminable and profoundly hidden.'

The foregoing paragraphs will perhaps seem to the reader mere gratuities by Bloy. So far as I know, he never took care to reason them out. I venture to judge them verisimilar and perhaps inevitable within the Christian doctrine. Bloy (I repeat) did no more than apply to the whole of Creation the method which the Jewish Cabalists applied to the Scriptures. They thought that a work dictated by the Holy Spirit was an absolute text: in other words, a text in which the collaboration of chance was calculable as zero. This portentous premise of a book impenetrable to contingency, of a book which is a mechanism of infinite purposes, moved them to permute the scriptural words, add up the numerical value of the letters, consider their form, observe the small letters and capitals, seek acrostics and anagrams and perform other exegetical rigours which it is not difficult to ridicule. Their excuse is that nothing can be contingent in the work of an infinite mind.* Léon Bloy postulates this hieroglyphical character – this character of a divine writing, of an angelic cryptography – at all moments and in all beings on earth. The superstitious person believes he can decipher this organic writing: thirteen guests form the symbol of death; a yellow opal, that of misfortune.

It is doubtful that the world has a meaning; it is even more doubtful that it has a double or triple meaning, the unbeliever will observe. I understand that this is so; but I understand that the hieroglyphical world postulated by Bloy is the one which best befits the dignity of the theologian's intellectual God.

No man knows who he is, affirmed Léon Bloy. No one could illustrate that intimate ignorance better than he. He believed himself a rigorous Catholic and he was a continuer of the Cabalists, a secret brother of Swedenborg and Blake: heresiarchs.

Translated by J.E.I.

* What is a divine mind? the reader will perhaps inquire. There is not a theologian who does not define it; I prefer an example. The steps a man takes from the day of his birth until that of his death trace in time an inconceivable figure. The Divine Mind intuitively grasps that form immediately, as men do a triangle. This figure (perhaps) has its given function in the economy of the universe.

A Note on (towards)
Bernard Shaw

AT the end of the thirteenth century, Raymond Lully (Rai-
mundo Lulio) was prepared to solve all arcana by means of an
apparatus of concentric, revolving disks of different sizes, subdivided into sectors with Latin words; John Stuart Mill, at the
beginning of the nineteenth, feared that some day the number
of musical combinations would be exhausted and there would
be no place in the future for indefinite Webers and Mozarts;
Kurd Lasswitz, at the end of the nineteenth, toyed with the
staggering fantasy of a universal library which would register
all the variations of the twenty-odd orthographical symbols, in
other words, all that it is given to express in all languages.
Lully's machine, Mill's fear and Lasswitz's chaotic library can
be the subject of jokes, but they exaggerate a propension
which is common: making metaphysics and the arts into a
kind of play with combinations. Those who practise this game
forget that a book is more than a verbal structure or series of
verbal structures; it is the dialogue it establishes with its reader
and the intonation it imposes upon his voice and the changing
and durable images it leaves in his memory. This dialogue is
infinite; the words *amica silentia lunae* now mean the intimate,
silent and shining moon, and in the *Aeneid* they meant the
interlunar period, the darkness which allowed the Greeks to
enter the stronghold of Troy....* Literature is not exhaustible,

*Thus Milton and Dante interpreted them, to judge by certain
passages which seem to be imitative. In the *Commedia* (*Inferno*, I,
60; V, 28) we have: *d'ogni luce muto* and *dove il sol tace* to signify
dark places; in the *Samson Agonistes* (86–89):

> The Sun to me is dark
> And silent as the Moon

for the sufficient and simple reason that no single book is. A book is not an isolated being: it is a relationship, an axis of innumerable relationships. One literature differs from another, prior or posterior, less because of the text than because of the way in which it is read: if I were granted the possibility of reading any present-day page – this one, for example – as it will be read in the year two thousand, I would know what the literature of the year two thousand will be like. The conception of literature as a formalistic game leads, in the best of cases, to the fine chiseling of a period or a stanza, to an artful decorum (Johnson, Renan, Flaubert), and in the worst, to the discomforts of a work made of surprises dictated by vanity and chance (Gracián, Herrera y Reissig).

If literature were nothing more than verbal algebra, anyone could produce any book by essaying variations. The lapidary formula 'Everything flows' abbreviates in two words the philsosophy of Heraclitus: Raymond Lully would say that, with the first word given, it would be sufficient to essay the intransitive verbs to discover the second and obtain, thanks to methodical chance, that philosophy and many others. Here it is fitting to reply that the formula obtained by this process of elimination would lack all value and even meaning; for it to have some virtue we must conceive it in terms of Heraclitus, in terms of an experience of Heraclitus, even though 'Heraclitus' is nothing more than the presumed subject of that experience. I have said that a book is a dialogue, a form of relationship; in a dialogue, an interlocutor is not the sum or average of what he says: he may not speak and still reveal that he is intelligent, he may omit intelligent observations and reveal his stupidity. The same happens with literature; d'Artagnan executes innumerable feats and Don Quixote is beaten and ridiculed, but one feels the valour of Don Quixote more. The foregoing leads us to an aesthetic problem never before posed: Can an author create

---

When she deserts the night
Hid in her vacant interlunar cave.

Cf. E. M. W. Tillyard: *The Miltonic Setting*, 101.

characters superior to himself? I would say no and in that negation include both the intellectual and the moral. I believe that from us cannot emerge creatures more lucid or more noble than our best moments. It is on this opinion that I base my conviction of Shaw's pre-eminence. The collective and civic problems of his early works will lose their interest, or have lost it already; the jokes in the *Pleasant Plays* run the risk of becoming, some day, no less uncomfortable than those of Shakespeare (humour, I suspect, is an oral genre, a sudden flavour of conversation, not something written); the ideas declared in his prologues and his eloquent tirades will be found in Schopenhauer and Samuel Butler;* but Lavinia, Blanco Posnet, Keegan, Shotover, Richard Dudgeon and, above all, Julius Caesar, surpass any character imagined by the art of our time. If we think of Monsieur Teste alongside them or Nietzsche's histrionic Zarathustra, we can perceive with astonishment and even outrage the primacy of Shaw. In 1911, Albert Soergel could write, repeating a commonplace of the time, 'Bernard Shaw is an annihilator of the heroic concept, a killer of heroes' (*Dichtung und Dichter der Zeit*, 214); he did not understand that the heroic might dispense with the romantic and be incarnated in Captain Bluntschli of *Arms and the Man*, not in Sergius Saranoff.

The biography of Bernard Shaw by Frank Harris contains an admirable letter by the former, from which I copy the following words: 'I understand everything and everyone and I am nothing and no one.' From this nothingness (so comparable to that of God before creating the world, so comparable to that primordial divinity which another Irishman, Johannes Scotus Erigena, called *Nihil*), Bernard Shaw educed almost innumerable persons or dramatis personae: the most ephemeral of these is, I suspect, that G. B. S. who represented him in public

* And in Swedenborg. In *Man and Superman* we read that Hell is not a penal establishment but rather a state dead sinners elect for reasons of intimate affinity, just as the blessed do with Heaven; the treatise *De Coelo et Inferno* by Swedenborg, published in 1758, expounds the same doctrine.

and who lavished in the newspaper columns so many facile witticisms.

Shaw's fundamental themes are philosophy and ethics : it is natural and inevitable that he should not be valued in this country, or that he be so only in terms of a few epigrams. The Argentine feels that the universe is nothing but a manifestation of chance, the fortuitous concourse of Democritus's atoms; philosophy does not interest him. Nor does ethics : the social realm, for him, is reduced to a conflict of individuals or classes or nations, in which everything is licit, save being ridiculed or defeated.

Man's character and its variations are the essential theme of the novel of our time; lyric poetry is the complacent magnification of amorous fortunes or misfortunes; the philosophies of Heidegger and Jaspers make each of us the interesting interlocutor in a secret and continuous dialogue with nothingness or the divinity; these disciplines, which in the formal sense can be admirable, foment that illusion of the ego which the Vedanta censures as a capital error. They usually make a game of desperation and anguish, but at bottom they flatter our vanity; they are, in this sense, immoral. The work of Shaw, however, leaves one with a flavour of liberation. The flavour of the stoic doctrines and the flavour of the sagas.

Translated by J.E.I.

A New
Refutation of Time

Vor mir war keine Zeit, nach mir wird keine seyn,
Mit mir gebiert sie sich, mit mir geht sie auch ein.

Daniel von Czepko:
Sexcenta monodisticha sapientum, III, 11 (1655)

PROLOGUE

If published towards the middle of the eighteenth century, this refutation (or its name) would persist in Hume's bibliographies and perhaps would have merited a line by Huxley or Kemp Smith. Published in 1947 – after Bergson – it is the anachronistic reductio ad absurdum of a preterite system or, what is worse, the feeble artifice of an Argentine lost in the maze of metaphysics. Both conjectures are verisimilar and perhaps true; in order to correct them, I cannot promise a novel conclusion in exchange for my rudimentary dialectic. The thesis I shall divulge is as ancient as Zeno's arrow or the Greek king's carriage in the Milinda Panha; the novelty, if any, consists in applying to my purpose the classic instrument of Berkeley. Both he and his continuer David Hume abound in paragraphs which contradict or exclude my thesis; nevertheless, I believe I have deduced the inevitable consequences of their doctrine.

The first article (A) was written in 1944 and appeared in number 115 of the review Sur; *the second, of 1946, is a reworking of the first. Deliberately I did not make the two into one, understanding that the reading of two analogous texts might facilitate the comprehension of an indocile subject.*

A word about the title. I am not unaware that it is an example of the monster termed by the logicians contradictio in adjecto, *because stating that a refutation of time is new (or old) attributes to it a predicate of temporal nature which establishes the very notion the subject would destroy. I leave it as it is, however, so that its slight mockery may prove that I do not exaggerate the importance of these verbal games. Besides, our language is so saturated and animated by time that it is quite possible there is not one statement in these pages which in some way does not demand or invoke the idea of time.*

I dedicate these exercises to my forebear Juan Crisóstomo Lafinur (1797–1824), who left some memorable endecasyllables to Argentine letters and who tried to reform the teaching of philosophy, purifying it of theological shadows and expounding in his course the principles of Locke and Condillac. He died in exile; like all men, he was given bad times in which to live.

Buenos Aires, 23 December 1946   J.L.B.

A

I

In the course of a life dedicated to letters and (at times) to metaphysical perplexity, I have glimpsed or foreseen a refutation of time, in which I myself do not believe, but which regularly visits me at night and in the weary twilight with the illusory force of an axiom. This refutation is found in some way or another in all my books: it is prefigured by the poems 'Inscription on Any Grave' and 'The Trick' from my *Fervor of Buenos Aires* (1923); it is declared by two articles in *Inquisitions* (1925), page 46 of *Evaristo Carriego* (1930), the narration 'Feeling in Death' from my *History of Eternity* (1936) and the note on page 24 of *The Garden of Forking Paths* (1941). None of the texts I have enumerated satisfies me, not even the penultimate one, less demonstrative and well-reasoned than it is divinatory and pathetic. I shall try to establish a basis for all of them in this essay.

Two arguments led me to this refutation: the idealism of Berkeley and Leibniz's principle of indiscernibles.

253

Berkeley (*Principles of Human Knowledge*, 3) observed:
'That neither our thoughts, nor passions, nor ideas formed by
the imagination, exist without the mind, is what everybody
will allow. And it seems no less evident that the various sensations or ideas imprinted on the sense, however blended or
combined together (that is, whatever objects they compose)
cannot exist otherwise than in a mind perceiving them.... The
table I write on, I say, exists, that is, I see and feel it; and if I
were out of my study I should say it existed, meaning thereby
that if I was in my study I might perceive it, or that some
other spirit actually does perceive it.... For as to what is said
of the absolute existence of unthinking things without any
relation to their being perceived, that seems perfectly unintelligible. Their *esse* is *percipi*, nor is it possible they should have
any existence out of the minds or thinking things which perceive them.' In paragraph twenty-three he added, forestalling
objections: 'But say you, surely there is nothing easier than to
imagine trees, for instance, in a park or books existing in a
closet, and nobody by to perceive them. I answer, you may so,
there is no difficulty in it: but what is all this, I beseech you,
more than framing in your mind certain ideas which you call
books and *trees*, and at the same time omitting to frame the
idea of any one that may perceive them? But do not you yourself perceive or think of them all the while? This therefore is
nothing to the purpose: it only shows you have the power of
imagining or forming ideas in your mind; but it doth not shew
that you can conceive it possible, the objects of your thought
may exist without the mind...' In another paragraph, number
six, he had already declared: 'Some truths there are so near
and obvious to the mind, that a man need only open his eyes to
see them. Such I take this important one to be, to wit, that all
the choir of heaven and furniture of the earth, in a word all
those bodies which compose the mighty frame of the world,
have not any substance without a mind, that their being is to
be perceived or known; that consequently so long as they are
not actually perceived by me, or do not exist in any mind or
that of any other created spirit, they must either have no exis-

tence at all, or else subsist in the mind of some eternal spirit ...'

Such is, in the words of its inventor, the idealist doctrine. To understand it is easy; what is difficult is to think within its limits. Schopenhauer himself, when expounding it, committed culpable negligences. In the first lines of the first volume of his *Welt als Wille und Vorstellung* – from the year 1819 – he formulated this declaration which makes him worthy of the enduring perplexity of all men : 'The world is my idea : this is a truth which holds good for everything that lives and knows, though man alone can bring it into reflective and abstract consciousness. If he really does this, he has attained to philosophical wisdom. It then becomes clear and certain to him what he knows is not a sun and an earth, but only an eye that sees a sun, a hand that feels an earth ...' In other words, for the idealist Schopenhauer, man's eyes and hands are less illusory or apparent than the earth and the sun. In 1844 he published a complementary volume. In its first chapter he rediscovers and aggravates the previous error : he defines the universe as a phenomenon of the brain and distinguishes the 'world in the head' from 'the world outside the head'. Berkeley, however, had his Philonous say in 1713 : 'The brain therefore you speak of, being a sensible thing, exists only in the mind. Now, I would fain know whether you think it reasonable to suppose, that one idea or thing existing in the mind, occasions all other ideas. And if you think so, pray how do you account for the origin of the primary idea or brain itself?' Schopenhauer's dualism or cerebralism may also be licitly opposed by Spiller's monism. Spiller (*The Mind of Man*, chapter VIII, 1902) argues that the retina and the cutaneous surface invoked in order to explain visual and tactile phenomena are, in turn, two tactile and visual systems and that the room we see (the 'objective' one) is no greater than the one imagined (the 'cerebral' one) and does not contain it, since what we have here are two independent visual systems. Berkeley (*Principles of Human Knowledge*, 10 and 116) likewise denied the existence of primary qualities – the solidity and extension of things – and of absolute space.

Berkeley affirmed the continuous existence of objects, since when no individual sees them, God does; Hume, with greater logic, denies such an existence (*Treatise of Human Nature*, I, 4, 2). Berkeley affirmed the existence of personal identity, 'I myself am not my ideas, but somewhat else, a thinking active principle that perceives ...' (*Dialogues*, 3); Hume, the sceptic, refutes this identity and makes of every man 'a bundle or collection of different perceptions, which succeed each other with an inconceivable rapidity' (op. cit., I, 4, 6). Both affirm the existence of time : for Berkeley, it is 'the succession of ideas in my mind, which flows uniformly, and is participated by all beings' (*Principles of Human Knowledge*, 98); for Hume, 'a succession of indivisible moments' (op. cit., I, 2, 2).

I have accumulated transcriptions from the apologists of idealism, I have abounded in their canonical passages, I have been reiterative and explicit, I have censured Schopenhauer (not without ingratitude), so that my reader may begin to penetrate into this unstable world of the mind. A world of evanescent impressions; a world without matter or spirit, neither objective nor subjective; a world without the ideal architecture of space; a world made of time, of the absolute uniform time of the *Principia*; a tireless labyrinth, a chaos, a dream. This almost perfect dissolution was reached by David Hume.

Once the idealist argument is admitted, I see that it is possible – perhaps inevitable – to go further. For Hume it is not licit to speak of the form of the moon or of its colour; the form and colour *are* the moon; neither can one speak of the perceptions of the mind, since the mind is nothing other than a series of perceptions. The Cartesian 'I think, therefore I am' is thus invalidated; to say 'I think' postulates the self, is a begging of the question; Lichtenberg in the eighteenth century, proposed that in place of 'I think' we should say impersonally, 'it thinks', just as one would say 'it thunders' or 'it rains'. I repeat : behind our faces there is no secret self which governs our acts and receives our impressions; we are, solely, the series of these imaginary acts and these errant impressions. The series? Once matter and spirit, which are continuities, are negated, once space too has been negated, I do not know what right we have to that continuity which is time. Let us imagine a present moment of any kind. During one of his nights on the Mississippi, Huckleberry Finn awakens; the raft, lost in partial darkness, continues downstream; it is perhaps a bit cold. Huckleberry Finn recognizes the soft indefatigable sound of the water; he negligently opens his eyes; he sees a vague number of stars, an indistinct line of trees; then, he sinks back into his immemorable sleep as into the dark waters.* Idealist metaphysics declares that to add a material substance (the object) and a spiritual substance (the subject) to those perceptions is venturesome and useless; I maintain that it is no less illogical to think that such perceptions are terms in a series whose beginning is as inconceivable as its end. To add to the river and the bank, Huck perceives the notion of another substantive river and another bank, to add another perception to that immediate network of perceptions, is, for idealism, unjustifiable; for myself, it is no less unjustifiable to add a chronological precision : the fact, for example, that the foregoing event took place on the night of the seventh of June, 1849, between ten and eleven minutes past four. In other words : I deny, with the arguments of idealism, the vast temporal series which idealism admits. Hume denied the existence of an absolute space, in which all things have their place; I deny the existence of one single time, in which all things are linked as in a chain. The denial of coexistence is no less arduous than the denial of succession.

I deny, in an elevated number of instances, the successive; I deny, in an elevated number of instances, the contemporary as well. The lover who thinks 'While I was so happy, thinking of the fidelity of my love, she was deceiving me' deceives himself : if every state we experience is absolute, such happiness was not contemporary to the betrayal; the discovery of that

---

*For the convenience of the reader I have selected a moment between two periods of sleep, a literary moment, not a historical one. If anyone suspects a fallacy, he may substitute another example, one from his own life if he so chooses.

betrayal is another state, which cannot modify the 'previous' ones, though it can modify their recollection. The misfortune of today is no more real than the happiness of the past. I shall seek a more concrete example. In the first part of August 1824, Captain Isidoro Suárez, at the head of a squadron of Peruvian hussars, decided the victory of Junín; in the first part of August 1824, De Quincey published a diatribe against *Wilhelm Meisters Lehrjahre*; these events were not contemporary (they are now), since the two men died – one in the city of Montevideo, the other in Edinburgh – without knowing anything about each other.... Each moment is autonomous. Neither vengeance nor pardon nor prisons nor even oblivion can modify the invulnerable past. To me, hope and fear seem no less vain, for they always refer to future events: that is, to events that will not happen to us, who are the minutely detailed present. I am told that the present, the specious present of the psychologists, lasts from a few seconds to a minute fraction of a second; that can be the duration of the history of the universe. In other words, there is no such history, just as a man has no life: not even one of his rights exists; each moment we live exists, but not their imaginary combination. The universe, the sum of all things, is a collection no less ideal than that of all the horses Shakespeare dreamt of – one, many, none? – between 1592 and 1594. I add: if time is a mental process, how can thousands of men – or even two different men – share it?

The argument of the preceding paragraphs, interrupted and encumbered with illustrations, may seem intricate. I shall seek a more direct method. Let us consider a life in whose course there is an abundance of repetitions: mine, for example. I never pass in front of the Recoleta without remembering that my father, my grandparents and great-grandparents are buried there, just as I shall be some day; then I remember that I have remembered the same thing an untold number of times already; I cannot walk through the suburbs in the solitude of the night without thinking that the night pleases us because it suppresses idle details, just as our memory does; I cannot lament the loss of a love or a friendship without meditating that one loses only what one really never had; every time I cross one of the street corners of the southern part of the city, I think of you, Helen; every time the wind brings me the smell of eucalyptus, I think of Adrogué in my childhood; every time I remember the ninety-first fragment of Heraclitus 'You shall not go down twice to the same river', I admire its dialectical dexterity, because the ease with which we accept the first meaning ('The river is different') clandestinely imposes upon us the second ('I am different') and grants us the illusion of having invented it; every time I hear a Germanophile vituperate the Yiddish language, I reflect that Yiddish is, after all, a German dialect, scarcely coloured by the language of the Holy Spirit. These tautologies (and others I leave in silence) make up my entire life. Of course, they are repeated imprecisely; there are differences of emphasis, temperature, light and general physiological condition. I suspect, however, that the number of circumstantial variants is not infinite: we can postulate, in the mind of an individual (or of two individuals who do not know of each other but in whom the same process works), two identical moments. Once this identity is postulated, one may ask: Are not these identical moments the same? Is not one single repeated term sufficient to break down and confuse the series of time? Do not the fervent readers who surrender themselves to Shakespeare become, literally, Shakespeare?

As yet I am ignorant of the ethics of the system I have outlined. I do not know if it even exists. The fifth paragraph of the fourth chapter of the treatise *Sanhedrin* of the Mishnah declares that, for God's Justice, he who kills one man destroys the world; if there is no plurality, he who annihilates all men would be no more guilty than the primitive and solitary Cain, which fact is orthodox, nor more universal in his destruction, which fact may be magical. I understand that this is so. The vociferous catastrophes of a general order – fires, wars, epidemics – are one single pain, illusorily multiplied in many mirrors. Thus Bernard Shaw sees it (*Guide to Socialism*, 86): 'What you can suffer is the maximum that can be suffered on earth. If you die of starvation, you will suffer all the starvation there has been or will be. If ten thousand people die with you, their participation in your lot will not make you be ten thousand times more hungry nor multiply the time of your agony ten thousand times. Do not let yourself be overcome by the horrible sum of human sufferings; such a sum does not exist. Neither poverty nor pain are cumulative.' Cf. also *The Problem of Pain*, VII, by C. S. Lewis.

Lucretius (*De rerum natura*, I, 830) attributes to Anaxagoras the doctrine that gold consists of particles of gold, fire of sparks, bone of tiny imperceptible bones; Josiah Royce, perhaps influenced by St Augustine, judges that time is made of time and that 'every *now* within which something happens is therefore *also* a succession' (*The World and the Individual*, II, 139). This proposition is compatible with that of this essay.

2

All language is of a successive nature; it does not lend itself to a reasoning of the eternal, the intemporal. Those who have followed the foregoing argumentation with displeasure will perhaps prefer this page from the year 1928. I have already mentioned it; it is the narrative entitled 'Feeling in Death':

'I want to set down here an experience which I had some nights ago: a trifle too evanescent and ecstatic to be called an adventure, too irrational and sentimental to be called a thought. It consists of a scene and its word: a word already stated by me, but not lived with complete dedication until then. I shall now proceed to give its history, with the accidents of time and place which were its declaration.

'I remember it as follows. The afternoon preceding that night, I was in Barracas: a locality not visited by my habit and whose distance from those I later traversed had already lent a strange flavour to that day. The evening had no destiny at all; since it was clear, I went out to take a walk and to recollect after dinner. I did not want to determine a route for my stroll; I tried to attain a maximum latitude of probabilities in order not to fatigue my expectation with the necessary foresight of

any one of them. I managed, to the imperfect degree of possibility, to do what is called walking at random; I accepted,
with no other conscious prejudice than that of avoiding the
wider avenues or streets, the most obscure invitations of
chance. However, a kind of familiar gravitation led me farther
on, in the direction of certain neighbourhoods, the names of
which I have every desire to recall and which dictate reverence
to my heart. I do not mean by this my own neighbourhood, the
precise surroundings of my childhood, but rather its still mysterious environs: an area I have possessed often in words but
seldom in reality, immediate and at the same time mythical.
The reverse of the familiar, its far side, are for me those
penultimate streets, almost as effectively unknown as the hidden foundations of our house or our invisible skeleton. My
progress brought me to a corner. I breathed in the night, in a
most serene holiday from thought. The view, not at all complex, seemed simplified by my tiredness. It was made unreal by
its very typicality. The street was one of low houses and
though its first meaning was one of poverty, its second was
certainly one of contentment. It was as humble and enchanting
as anything could be. None of the houses dared open itself to
the street; the fig tree darkened over the corner; the little
arched doorways – higher than the taut outlines of the walls -
seemed wrought from the same infinite substance of the night.
The sidewalk formed an escarpment over the street; the street
was of elemental earth, the earth of an as yet unconquered
America. Farther down, the alleyway, already open to the
pampa, crumbled into the Maldonado. Above the turbid and
chaotic earth, a rose-coloured wall seemed not to house the
moonlight, but rather to effuse an intimate light of its own.
There can be no better way of naming tenderness than that
soft rose colour.

'I kept looking at this simplicity. I thought, surely out loud:
This is the same as thirty years ago ... I conjectured the date:
a recent time in other countries but now quite remote in this
changeable part of the world. Perhaps a bird was singing and
for it I felt a tiny affection, the same size as the bird; but the

most certain thing was that in this now vertiginous silence there was no other sound than the intemporal one of the crickets. The easy thought "I am in the eighteen-nineties" ceased to be a few approximate words and was deepened into a reality. I felt dead, I felt as an abstract spectator of the world; an indefinite fear imbued with science, which is the best clarity of metaphysics. I did not think that I had returned upstream on the supposed waters of Time; rather I suspected that I was the possessor of a reticent or absent sense of the inconceivable word *eternity*. Only later was I able to define that imagination.

'I write it now as follows: That pure representation of homogeneous objects – the night in serenity, a limpid little wall, the provincial scent of the honeysuckle, the elemental earth – is not merely identical to the one present on that corner so many years ago; it is, without resemblances or repetitions, the very same. Time, if we can intuitively grasp such an identity, is a delusion: the difference and inseparability of one moment belonging to its apparent past from another belonging to its apparent present is sufficient to disintegrate it.

'It is evident that the number of such human moments is not infinite. The elemental ones – those of physical suffering and physical pleasure, those of the coming of sleep, those of the hearing of a piece of music, those of great intensity or great lassitude – are even more impersonal. Aforehand I derive this conclusion: life is too poor not to be immortal as well. But we do not even have the certainty of our poverty, since time, which is easily refutable in sense experience, is not so in the intellectual, from whose essence the concept of succession seems inseparable. Thus shall remain as an emotional anecdote the half-glimpsed idea and as the confessed irresolution of this page the true moment of ecstasy and possible suggestion of eternity with which that night was not parsimonious for me.'

B

Of the many doctrines registered by the history of philosophy, perhaps idealism is the oldest and most widespread. This observation was made by Carlyle (*Novalis*, 1829); to the philosophers he alleges it is fitting to add, with no hope of completing the infinite census, the Platonists, for whom the only reality is that of the archetype (Norris, Judas Abrabanel, Gemistus, Plotinus), the theologians, for whom all that is not the divinity is contingent (Malebranche, Johannes Eckhart), the monists, who make the universe an idle adjective of the Absolute (Bradley, Hegel, Parmenides).... Idealism is as ancient as metaphysical restlessness itself; its most acute apologist, George Berkeley, flourished in the eighteenth century; contrary to what Schopenhauer declares (*Welt als Wille und Vorstellung*, II, i), his merit cannot be the intuition of that doctrine but rather the arguments he conceived in order to reason it; Hume applied them to the mind; my purpose is to apply them to time. But first I shall recapitulate the diverse states of this dialectic.

Berkeley denied the existence of matter. This does not mean, one should note, that he denied the existence of colours, odours, tastes, sounds and tactile sensations; what he denied was that, aside from these perceptions, which make up the external world, there was anything invisible, intangible, called matter. He denied that there were pains that no one feels, colours that no one sees, forms that no one touches. He reasoned that to add a matter to our perceptions is to add an inconceivable, superfluous world to the world. He believed in the world of appearances woven by our senses, but understood that the material world (that of Toland, say) is an illusory duplication. He observed (*Principles of Human Knowledge*, 3): 'That neither our thoughts, nor passions, nor ideas formed by the imagination, exist without the mind, is what everybody will allow. And it seems no less evident that the various sensations or ideas imprinted on the sense, however blended or combined together (that is, whatever objects they compose) cannot exist otherwise than in a mind perceiving them.... The table I write on, I say, exists, that is, I see and feel it; and if I were out of my study I should say it existed, meaning thereby that if I was in my study I might perceive it, or that some other spirit actually does perceive it.... For as to what is said of the absolute existence of unthinking things without any relation to their being perceived, that seems perfectly unintelligible. Their *esse* is *percipi*, nor is it possible they should have any existence, out of the minds or thinking things which perceive them.' In paragraph twenty-three he added, forestalling objections: 'But say you, surely there is nothing easier than to imagine trees, for instance, in a park or books existing in a closet, and nobody by to perceive them. I answer, you may so, there is no difficulty in it: but what is all this, I beseech you, more than framing in your mind certain ideas which you call *books* and *trees* and at the same time omitting to frame the idea of anyone that may perceive them? But do not you your self perceive or think of them all the while? This therefore is nothing to the purpose: it only shows you have the power of imagining or forming ideas in your mind; but it doth not shew that you can conceive it possible, the objects of your thought may exist without the mind...' In another paragraph, number six, he had already declared: 'Some truths there are so near and obvious to the mind, that a man need only open his eyes to see them. Such I take this important one to be, to wit, that all the choir of heaven and furniture of the earth, in a word all those bodies which compose the mighty frame of the world, have not any substance without a mind, that their being is to be perceived or known; that consequently so long as they are not actually perceived by me, or do not exist in any mind or that of any other created spirit, they must either have no existence at all, or else subsist in the mind of some eternal spirit...' (The God of Berkeley is a ubiquitous spectator whose function is that of lending coherence to the world.)

The doctrine I have just expounded has been interpreted in perverse ways. Herbert Spencer thought he had refuted it (*Principles of Psychology*, VIII, 6), reasoning that if there is nothing outside consciousness, consciousness must be infinite in time and space. The first is certain if we understand that all time is time perceived by someone, but erroneous if we infer that this time must necessarily embrace an infinite number of centuries; the second is illicit, since Berkeley (*Principles of Human Knowledge*, 116; *Siris*, 266) repeatedly denied the existence of an absolute space. Even more indecipherable is the error into which Scopenhauer falls (*Welt als Wille und Vorstellung*, II, i) when he shows that for the idealists the world is a phenomenon of the brain; Berkeley, however, had written (*Dialogues between Hylas and Philonous*, II): 'The brain therefore you speak of, being a sensible thing, exists only in the mind. Now, I would fain know whether you think it reasonable to suppose, that one idea or thing existing in the mind, occasions all other ideas. And if you think so, pray how do you account for the origin of this primary idea or brain itself?' The brain, in fact, is no less a part of the external world than is the constellation of the Centaur.

Berkeley denied that there was an object behind our sense impressions; David Hume, that there was a subject behind the perception of changes. The former had denied the existence of matter, the latter denied the existence of spirit; the former had not wanted us to add to the succession of impressions the metaphysical notion of matter, the latter did not want us to add to the succession of mental states the metaphysical notion of self. So logical is this extension of Berkeley's arguments that Berkeley himself had already foreseen it, as Alexander Campbell Fraser notes, and even tried to reject it by means of the Cartesian *ergo sum*. 'If your principles are valid, you your self are nothing more than a system of fluctuating ideas, unsustained by any substance, since it is as absurd to speak of a spiritual substance as it is of a material substance,' reasons Hylas, anticipating David Hume in the third and last of the *Dialogues*. Hume corroborates (*Treatise of Human Nature*, I, 4, 6): 'We are a bundle or collection of different perceptions, which succeed each other with an inconceivable rapidity.... The mind is a kind of theatre, where several perceptions successively make their appearance; pass, re-pass, glide away, and mingle in an infinite variety of postures and situations.... The comparison of the theatre must not mislead us. They are the successive perceptions only, that constitute the mind; nor have we the most distant notion of the place, where these scenes are represented, or of the materials, of which it is compos'd.'

Once the idealist argument is admitted, I see that it is possible – perhaps inevitable – to go further. For Berkeley, time is 'the succession of ideas in my mind, which flows uniformly, and is participated by all beings' (*Principles of Human Knowledge*, 98); for Hume, 'a succession of indivisible moments' (*Treatise of Human Nature*, I, 2, 2). However, once matter and spirit – which are continuities – are negated, once space too is negated, I do not know with what right we retain that continuity which is time. Outside each perception (real or conjectural) matter does not exist; outside each mental state spirit does not exist; neither does time exist outside each present moment. Let us take a moment of maximum simplicity: for example, that of Chuang Tzu's dream (Herbert Allen Giles: *Chuang Tzu*, 1889). Chuang Tzu, some twenty-four centuries ago, dreamt he was a butterfly and did not know, when he awoke, if he was a man who had dreamt he was a butterfly or a butterfly who now dreamt he was a man. Let us not consider the awakening; let us consider the moment of the dream itself, or one of its moments. 'I dreamt I was a butterfly flying through the air and knowing nothing of Chuang Tzu,' reads the ancient text. We shall never know if Chuang Tzu saw a garden over which he seemed to fly or a moving yellow triangle which no doubt was he, but we do know that the image was subjective, though furnished by his memory. The doctrine of psychophysical parallelism would judge that the image must have been accompanied by some change in the dreamer's nervous system; according to Berkeley, the body of Chuang Tzu did not exist at that moment, save as a perception in the mind of God. Hume simplifies even more what happened. According to him, the spirit of Chuang Tzu did not exist at that moment; only the colours of the dream and the certainty of being a butterfly existed. They existed as a momentary term in the 'bundle or collection of perceptions' which, some four centuries before Christ, was the mind of Chuang Tzu; they existed as a term n in an infinite temporal series, between $n-1$ and $n+1$. There is no other reality, for idealism, than that of mental processes; adding an objective butterfly to the butterfly which is perceived seems a vain duplication; adding a self to these processes seems no less exorbitant. Idealism judges that there was a dreaming, a perceiving, but not a dreamer or even a dream; it judges that speaking of objects and subjects is pure mythology. Now if each psychic state is self-sufficient, if linking it to a circumstance or to a self is an illicit and idle addition, with what right shall we then ascribe to it a place in time? Chuang Tzu dreamt that he was a butterfly and during that dream he was not Chuang Tzu, but a butterfly. How, with space and self abolished, shall we link those moments to his waking moments and to the feudal period of Chinese history? This does not mean that we shall never know, even in an approximate fashion, the date of that dream; it means that the chronological fixing of an event, of an event in the universe, is alien and external to it. In China the dream of Chuang Tzu is proverbial; let us imagine that of its almost infinite readers, one dreams that he is a butterfly and then dreams that he is Chuang Tzu. Let us imagine that, by a not impossible stroke of chance, this dream reproduces point for point the master's. Once this identity is postulated, it is fitting to ask: Are not these moments which coincide one and the same? Is not one repeated term sufficient to break down and confuse the history of the world, to denounce that there is no such history?

The denial of time involves two negations: the negation of the succession of the terms of a series, negation of the synchronism of the terms in two different series. In fact, if each term is absolute, its relations are reduced to the consciousness that those relations exist. A state precedes another if it is known to be prior; a state of G is contemporary to a state of H if it is known to be contemporary. Contrary to what was declared by Schopenhauer* in his table of fundamental truths (*Welt als Wille und Vorstellung*, II, 4), each fraction of time

---

* And, earlier, by Newton, who maintained: 'Each particle of space is eternal, each indivisible moment of duration is everywhere' (*Principia*, III, 42).

does not simultaneously fill the whole of space; time is not ubiquitous. (Of course, at this stage in the argument, space no longer exists.)

Meinong, in his theory of apprehension, admits the apprehension of imaginary objects: the fourth dimension, let us say, or the sensitive statue of Condillac or the hypothetical animal of Lotze or the square root of minus one. If the reasons I have indicated are valid, then matter, self, the external world, world history and our lives also belong to this same nebulous orb.

Besides, the phrase 'negation of time' is ambiguous. It can mean the eternity of Plato or Boethius and also the dilemmas of Sextus Empiricus. The latter (*Adversus mathematicos*, XI, 197) denies the existence of the past, that which already was, and the future, that which is not yet, and argues that the present is divisible or indivisible. It is not indivisible, for in such a case it would have no beginning to link it to the past nor end to link it to the future, nor even a middle, since what has no beginning or end can have no middle; neither is it divisible, for in such a case it would consist of a part that was and another that is not. *Ergo*, it does not exist, but since the past and the future do not exist either, time does not exist. F. H. Bradley rediscovers and improves this perplexity. He observes (*Appearance and Reality*, IV) that if the present is divisible in other presents, it is no less complicated than time itself, and if it is indivisible, time is a mere relation between intemporal things. Such reasoning, as can be seen, negates the parts in order then to negate the whole; I reject the whole in order to exalt each of the parts. Via the dialectics of Berkeley and Hume I have arrived at Schopenhauer's dictum: 'The form of the phenomenon of will . . . is really only the *present*, not the future nor the past. The latter are only in the conception, exist only in the connexion of knowledge, so far as it follows the principle of sufficient reason. No man has ever lived in the past, and none will live in the future; the *present* alone is the form of all life, and is its sure possession which can never be taken from it. . . . We might compare time to a constantly revolving sphere; the half that was always sinking would be the past, that which was always rising would be the future; but the indivisible point at the top, where the tangent touches, would be the extensionless present. As the tangent does not revolve with the sphere, neither does the present, the point of contact of the object, the form of which is time, with the subject, which has no form, because it does not belong to the knowable, but is the condition of all that is knowable' (*Welt als Wille und Vorstellung*, I, 54). A Buddhist treatise of the fifth century, the *Visuddhimagga* (Road to Purity), illustrates the same doctrine with the same figure: 'Strictly speaking, the duration of the life of a living being is exceedingly brief, lasting only while a thought lasts. Just as a chariot wheel in rolling rolls only at one point of the tyre, and in resting rests only at one point; in exactly the same way the life of a living being lasts only for the period of one thought' (Radhakrishnan: *Indian Philosophy*, I, 373). Other Buddhist texts say that the world annihilates itself and reappears six thousand five hundred million times a day and that all men are an illusion, vertiginously produced by a series of momentaneous and solitary men. 'The being of a past moment of thought – the *Road to Purity* tells us – has lived, but does not live nor will it live. The being of a future moment will live, but has not lived nor does it live. The being of the present moment of thought does live, but has not lived nor will it live' (op. cit., I, 407), a dictum which we may compare with the following of Plutarch (*De E apud Delphos*, 18): 'The man of yesterday has died in that of today, that of today dies in that of tomorrow.'

And yet, and yet.... Denying temporal succession, denying the self, denying the astronomical universe, are apparent desperations and secret consolations. Our destiny (as contrasted with the hell of Swedenborg and the hell of Tibetan mythology) is not frightful by being unreal; it is frightful because it is irreversible and iron-clad. Time is the substance I am made of. Time is a river which sweeps me along, but I am the river; it is a tiger which destroys me, but I am the tiger; it is a fire which consumes me, but I am the fire. The world, unfortunately, is real; I, unfortunately, am Borges.

FOOTNOTE TO THE PROLOGUE

There is no exposition of Buddhism that does not mention the *Milinda Panha*, an apologetic work of the second century, which relates a debate whose interlocutors are the king of Bactriana, Menader, and the monk Nagasena. The latter reasons that just as the king's carriage is neither its wheels nor its body nor its axle nor its pole nor its yoke, neither is man his matter, form, impressions, ideas, instincts or consciousness. He is not the combination of these parts nor does he exist outside of them.... After a controversy of many days, Menander (Milinda) is converted to the Buddhist faith.

The *Milinda Panha* has been translated into English by Rhys Davids (Oxford, 1890–4).

Translated by J.E.I.

Parables

Inferno, I, 32

FROM the twilight of day till the twilight of evening, a leopard, in the last years of the thirteenth century, would see some wooden planks, some vertical iron bars, men and women who changed, a wall and perhaps a stone gutter filled with dry leaves. He did not know, could not know, that he longed for love and cruelty and the hot pleasure of tearing things to pieces and the wind carrying the scent of a deer, but something suffocated and rebelled within him and God spoke to him in a dream: 'You live and will die in this prison so that a man I know of may see you a certain number of times and not forget you and place your figure and symbol in a poem which has its precise place in the scheme of the universe. You suffer captivity, but you will have given a word to the poem.' God, in the dream, illumined the animal's brutishness and the animal understood these reasons and accepted his destiny, but, when he awoke, there was in him only an obscure resignation, a valorous ignorance, for the machinery of the world is much too complex for the simplicity of a beast.

Years later, Dante was dying in Ravenna, as unjustified and as lonely as any other man. In a dream, God declared to him the secret purpose of his life and work; Dante, in wonderment, knew at last who and what he was and blessed the bitterness of his life. Tradition relates that, upon waking, he felt that he had received and lost an infinite thing, something he would not be able to recuperate or even glimpse, for the machinery of the world is much too complex for the simplicity of men.

Translated by J.E.I

273

Paradiso, XXXI, 108

DIODORUS SICULUS relates the story of a broken and scattered god; who of us has never felt, while walking through the twilight or writing a date from his past, that something infinite had been lost?

Men have lost a face, an irrecoverable face, and all long to be that pilgrim (envisioned in the Empyrean, beneath the Rose) who in Rome sees the Veronica and faithfully murmurs: 'My Lord, Jesus Christ, true God, and was this, then, the fashion of thy semblance?'

There is a stone face beside a road with an inscription saying 'The True Portrait of the Holy Face of the God of Jaén'; if we really knew what it was like, the key to all parables would be ours and we would know if the carpenter's son was also the Son of God.

Paul saw it as a light which hurled him to the ground; John saw it as the sun when it blazes in all its force: Teresa of Léon saw it many times, bathed in a tranquil light, and could never determine the colour of its eyes.

We have lost these features, just as one may lose a magic number made up of customary digits, just as one loses for ever an image in a kaleidoscope. We may see them and be unaware of it. A Jew's profile in the subway is perhaps that of Christ; the hands giving us our change at a ticket window perhaps repeat those that one day were nailed to the cross by some soldiers.

Perhaps some feature of that crucified countenance lurks in every mirror; perhaps the face died, was obliterated, so that God could be all of us.

Paradiso, XXXI, 108

Who knows whether tonight we shall not see it in the labyrinths of our dreams and not even know it tomorrow.

Translated by J.E.I.

Ragnarök

IN our dreams (writes Coleridge) images represent the sensations we think they cause; we do not feel horror because we are threatened by a sphinx; we dream of a sphinx in order to explain the horror we feel. If this is so, how could a mere chronicle of its forms transmit the stupor, the exaltation, the alarm, the menace and jubilance which made up the fabric of that dream that night? I shall attempt such a chronicle, however; perhaps the fact that the dream was composed of one single scene may remove or mitigate this essential difficulty.

The place was the School of Philosophy and Letters; the time, towards sundown. Everything (as usually happens in dreams) was somewhat different; a slight magnification altered things. We were electing officials: I was talking with Pedro Henríquez Ureña, who in the world of waking reality died many years ago. Suddenly we were stunned by the clamour of a demonstration or disturbance. Human and animal cries came from the Bajo. A voice shouted 'Here they come!' and then 'The Gods! The Gods!' Four or five individuals emerged from the mob and occupied the platform of the main lecture hall. We all applauded, tearfully; these were the Gods returning after a centuries-long exile. Made larger by the platform, their heads thrown back and their chests thrust forward, they arrogantly received our homage. One held a branch which no doubt conformed to the simple botany of dreams; another, in a broad gesture, extended his hand which was a claw; one of the faces of Janus looked with distrust at the curved beak of Thoth. Perhaps aroused by our applause, one of them – I no longer know which – erupted in a victorious clatter, unbelievably harsh, with something of a gargle and of a whistle. From that moment, things changed.

It all began with a suspicion (perhaps exaggerated) that the Gods did not know how to talk. Centuries of fell and fugitive life had atrophied the human element in them; the moon of Islam and the cross of Rome had been implacable with these outlaws. Very low foreheads, yellow teeth, stringy mulatto or Chinese moustaches and thick bestial lips showed the degeneracy of the Olympian lineage. Their clothing corresponded not to a decorous poverty but rather to the sinister luxury of the gambling houses and brothels of the Bajo. A carnation bled crimson in a lapel and the bulge of a knife was outlined beneath a close-fitting jacket. Suddenly we sensed that they were playing their last card, that they were cunning, ignorant and cruel like old beasts of prey and that, if we let ourselves be overcome by fear or piety, they would finally destroy us.

We took out our heavy revolvers (all of a sudden there were revolvers in the dream) and joyfully killed the Gods.

Translated by J.E.I.

Parable of
Cervantes and the *Quixote*

TIRED of his Spanish land, an old soldier of the king sought solace in the vast geographies of Ariosto, in that valley of the moon where the time wasted by dreams is contained and in the golden idol of Mohammed stolen by Montalbán.

In gentle mockery of himself, he imagined a credulous man who, perturbed by his reading of marvels, decided to seek prowess and enchantment in prosaic places called El Toboso or Montiel.

Vanquished by reality, by Spain, Don Quixote died in his native village in the year 1614. He was survived but a short time by Miguel de Cervantes.

For both of them, for the dreamer and the dreamed one, the whole scheme of the work consisted in the opposition of two worlds: the unreal world of the books of chivalry, the ordinary everyday world of the seventeenth century.

They did not suspect that the years would finally smooth away that discord, they did not suspect that La Mancha and Montiel and the knight's lean figure would be, for posterity, no less poetic than the episodes of Sinbad or the vast geographies of Ariosto.

For in the beginning of literature is the myth, and in the end as well.

Translated by J.E.I.

The Witness

In a stable which is almost in the shadow of the new stone church, a man with grey eyes and grey beard, lying amidst the odour of the animals, humbly seeks death as one would seek sleep. The day, faithful to vast and secret laws, is shifting and confusing the shadows inside the poor shelter; outside are the ploughed fields and a ditch clogged with dead leaves and the tracks of a wolf in the black mud where the forests begin. The man sleeps and dreams, forgotten. He is awakened by the bells tolling the Angelus. In the kingdoms of England the ringing of bells is now one of the customs of the evening, but this man, as a child, has seen the face of Woden, the divine horror and exultation, the crude wooden idol hung with Roman coins and heavy clothing, the sacrificing of horses, dogs and prisoners. Before dawn he will die and with him will die, and never return, the last immediate images of these pagan rites; the world will be a little poorer when this Saxon has died.

Deeds which populate the dimensions of space and which reach their end when someone dies may cause us wonderment, but one thing, or an infinite number of things, dies in every final agony, unless there is a universal memory as the theosophists have conjectured. In time there was a day that extinguished the last eyes to see Christ; the battle of Junín and the love of Helen died with the death of a man. What will die with me when I die, what pathetic or fragile form will the world lose? The voice of Macedonio Fernández, the image of a red horse in the vacant lot at Serrano and Charcas, a bar of sulphur in the drawer of a mahogany desk?

Translated by J.E.I.

279

A Problem

LET us imagine that in Toledo a paper is discovered containing a text in Arabic which the paleographers declare to be in the handwriting of the Cide Hamete Benengeli from whom Cervantes derived the *Quixote*. In this text we read that the hero (who, as is famous, wandered over the roads of Spain, armed with sword and lance, and challenged anyone for any reason at all) discovers, after one of his many combats, that he has killed a man. At that point the fragment ends; the problem is to guess or conjecture how Don Quixote would react.

As far as I know, there are three possible answers. The first is of a negative nature: nothing particular happens, because in the hallucinatory world of Don Quixote death is no less common than magic and having killed a man should not perturb a person who fights, or believes he fights, with fabulous monsters and sorcerers. The second answer is of a pathetic nature.

Don Quixote never managed to forget that he was a projection of Alonso Quijano, a reader of fabulous tales; seeing death, understanding that a dream has led him to the sin of Cain, awakens him from his pampered madness, perhaps for ever. The third answer is perhaps the most plausible. Once the man is dead, Don Quixote cannot admit that this tremendous act is a product of delirium; the reality of the effect makes him presuppose a parallel reality of the cause and Don Quixote will never emerge from his madness.

There is another conjecture, which is alien to the Spanish orb and even to the orb of the Western world and requires a more ancient, more complex and more weary atmosphere. Don Quixote – who is no longer Don Quixote but a king of the

A Problem

cycles of Hindustan – senses, standing before the dead body of his enemy, that killing and engendering are divine or magical acts which notably transcend the human condition. He knows that the dead man is illusory, the same as the bloody sword weighing in his hand and himself and all his past life and the vast gods and the universe.

Translated by J.E.I.

Borges and I

THE other one, the one called Borges, is the one things happen to. I walk through the streets of Buenos Aires and stop for a moment, perhaps mechanically now, to look at the arch of an entrance hall and the grillwork on the gate; I know of Borges from the mail and see his name on a list of professors or in a biographical dictionary. I like hourglasses, maps, eighteenth-century typography, the taste of coffee and the prose of Stevenson; he shares these preferences, but in a vain way that turns them into the attributes of an actor. It would be an exaggeration to say that ours is a hostile relationship; I live, let myself go on living, so that Borges may contrive his literature, and this literature justifies me. It is no effort for me to confess that he has achieved some valid pages, but those pages cannot save me, perhaps because what is good belongs to no one, not even to him, but rather to the language and to tradition. Besides, I am destined to perish, definitively, and only some instant of myself can survive in him. Little by little, I am giving over everything to him, though I am quite aware of his perverse custom of falsifying and magnifying things. Spinoza knew that all things long to persist in their being; the stone eternally wants to be a stone and the tiger a tiger. I shall remain in Borges, not in myself (if it is true that I am someone), but I recognize myself less in his books than in many others or in the laborious strumming of a guitar. Years ago I tried to free myself from him and went from the mythologies of the suburbs to the games with time and infinity, but those games belong to Borges now and I shall have to imagine other things. Thus my life is a flight and I lose everything and everything belongs to oblivion, or to him.

I do not know which of us has written this page.

Translated by J.E.I.

Everything and Nothing

THERE was no one in him; behind his face (which even through the bad paintings of those times resembles no other) and his words, which were copious, fantastic and stormy, there was only a bit of coldness, a dream dreamt by no one. At first he thought that all people were like him, but the astonishment of a friend to whom he had begun to speak of this emptiness showed him his error and made him feel always that an individual should not differ in outward appearance. Once he thought that in books he would find a cure for his ill and thus he learned the small Latin and less Greek a contemporary would speak of; later he considered that what he sought might well be found in an elemental rite of humanity, and let himself be initiated by Anne Hathaway one long June afternoon. At the age of twenty-odd years he went to London. Instinctively he had already become proficient in the habit of simulating that he was someone, so that others would not discover his condition as no one; in London he found the profession to which he was predestined, that of the actor, who on a stage plays at being another before a gathering of people who play at taking him for that other person. His histrionic tasks brought him a singular satisfaction, perhaps the first he had ever known; but once the last verse had been acclaimed and the last dead man withdrawn from the stage, the hated flavour of unreality returned to him. He ceased to be Ferrex or Tamberlane and became no one again. Thus hounded, he took to imagining other heroes and other tragic fables. And so, while his flesh fulfilled its destiny as flesh in the taverns and brothels of London, the soul that inhabited him was Caesar, who disregards the augur's admonition, and Juliet, who abhors the lark, and

Macbeth, who converses on the plain with the witches who are also Fates. No one has ever been so many men as this man who like the Egyptian Proteus could exhaust all the guises of reality. At times he would leave a confession hidden away in some corner of his work, certain that it would not be deciphered; Richard affirms that in his person he plays the part of many and Iago claims with curious words 'I am not what I am'. The fundamental identity of existing, dreaming and acting inspired famous passages of his.

For twenty years he persisted in that controlled hallucination, but one morning he was suddenly gripped by the tedium and the terror of being so many kings who die by the sword and so many suffering lovers who converge, diverge and melodiously expire. That very day he arranged to sell his theatre. Within a week he had returned to his native village, where he recovered the trees and rivers of his childhood and did not relate them to the others his muse had celebrated, illustrious with mythological allusions and Latin terms. He had to be someone; he was a retired impresario who had made his fortune and concerned himself with loans, lawsuits and petty usury. It was in this character that he dictated the arid will and testament known to us, from which he deliberately excluded all traces of pathos or literature. His friends from London would visit his retreat and for them he would take up again his role as poet.

History adds that before or after dying he found himself in the presence of God and told Him: 'I who have been so many men in vain want to be one and myself.' The voice of the Lord answered from a whirlwind: 'Neither am I anyone; I have dreamt the world as you dreamt your work, my Shakespeare, and among the forms in my dream are you, who like myself are many and no one.'

Translated by J.E.I.

Elegy

Oh destiny of Borges
to have sailed across the diverse seas of the world
or across that single and solitary sea of diverse names,
to have been a part of Edinburgh, of Zürich, of the two
    Cordobas,
of Columbia and of Texas,
to have returned at the end of changing generations
to the ancient lands of his forbears,
to Andalucia, to Portugal and to those countries
where the Saxon warred with the Dane and they mixed their
    blood,
to have wandered through the red and tranquil labyrinth of
    London,
to have grown old in so many mirrors,
to have sought in vain the marble gaze of the statues,
to have questioned lithographs, encyclopedias, atlases,
to have seen the things that men see,
death, the sluggish dawn, the plains,
and the delicate stars,
and to have seen nothing, or almost nothing
except the face of a girl from Buenos Aires
a face that does not want you to remember it.
Oh destiny of Borges,
perhaps no stranger than your own.

(1964)   *Translated by D.A.Y.*

After Darwin: It is not God
that is absent from the universe
after Darwin - but Man's concept
of God. A finite concept - projected
on and put in place of
an infinite concept.
Or rather - Victorian Man's
religious concept of God

Few people understand
the implications of Christianity
+ Christ - let alone having
their fixed concept redefined.

If God is infinite - then anything
which gives access to infinity
must give access to God.